For Stafford, for giving me the push to get started and for Mum, Dad and Red, my support and stalwart proof-readers.

Halcyon Rebirth

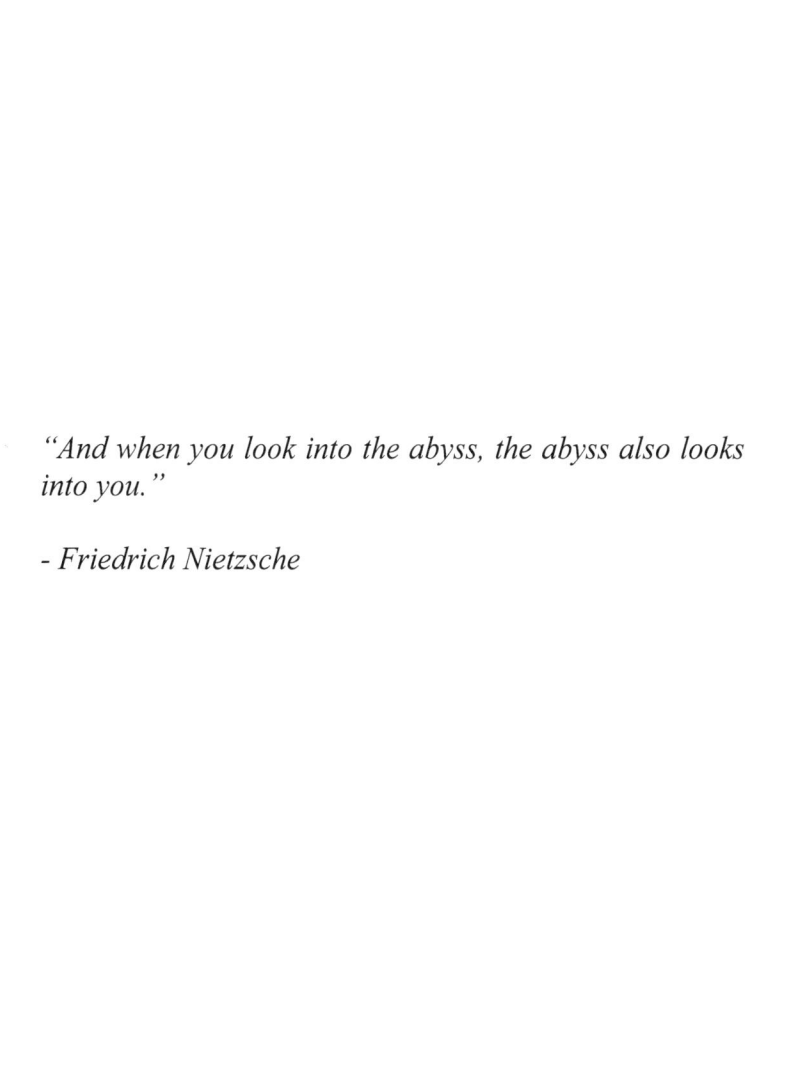

"And when you look into the abyss, the abyss also looks into you."

- Friedrich Nietzsche

Chapter 1

The door creaked as Gabriel strolled into the pub, greeted by the familiar smell of beer and cigarette smoke. Ordinarily, he hated the smell of cigarette smoke. However, he'd always felt that it added something to the atmosphere of a pub. It seemed to smell different when it mixed with the collective aroma of the multitude of drinks sold by the average waterhole.

It had to be said that this pub, The Hunter's Moon, had seen better days; the varnish on the bar was worn on the edges and the carpet was threadbare in places. That didn't really matter; it had character, so the locals said. Gabriel held the belief that character, along with attractive bar maids, are key selling points, especially in a small village like Hoggersbrook. The Hunter's Moon was a reasonably small establishment; the walls were adorned with paintings, alongside old photographs of village landmarks and historically important local people. There were five stools regimented along the bar, each with mahogany legs and a synthetic red leather seat.

An old man sat on the furthest stool, a half empty pint glass of bitter sitting idly in front of him. He wore a tatty brown coat that came to his waist, with a pair of grey trousers that were slightly too short for him, and a brown shirt. Despite his advanced years he had maintained a full head of straggly silver hair. The still bright sparkle in his eyes and the pronounced lines on his face reflected the events they had witnessed in his long years. When the man moved, he moved with a lethargy that resulted from a lifetime of hard work. Gabriel pulled out the stool next to the old man.

"Good afternoon, Mr Jones," the gentleman croaked as he turned his leathery face to acknowledge Gabriel. "How are we today?" He clasped his hand on Gabriel's shoulder as Gabriel sat beside him.

"Can't complain, Mr Conway. How are you?" Gabriel replied, awkwardly shifting the stool towards the bar with one hand, his other hand grasping the edge of the counter.

"Can't complain myself lad, how's the writing coming along? You famous yet?"

"Not that I know of, but it might be that I'm just not paying enough attention to the news. As for the novel, it's coming along very slowly. I've sent a couple of articles off to a couple of magazines. Hopefully they'll get published. I'm not holding my breath though."

"Sounds like you could use a drink. Miss Moordomus, get our Mr Jones a pint of the usual please."

Elizabeth Moordomus picked up a pint glass and started to pull a Guinness from the pump.

"Thanks, boss," Gabriel said smiling. Gabriel and Eric Conway had known each other for years, since Gabriel was a boy. Gabriel had grown up in the village; both his parents were killed in a car crash when he was too young to even remember. He had been raised by his mother's sister, 'Aunty Gladys' (she had never allowed him to call her Mum, out of respect, she always said). However Gabriel had always thought of her as his mother. She was a deeply kind woman who could be stern, but it was always tempered with fairness. As he got older he often regarded her as a female Atticus Finch. Unfortunately, Aunty Gladys suffered a stroke and passed away while Gabriel was at university. He inherited her cottage in the village which was poor consolation for the loss of the only parent he'd ever known.

The village was a true community. When Gladys passed, many of her friends started to look upon Gabriel as one of their own family. Eric and Martha Conway were two of these people. Eric called everyone by their title - even his late wife. People generally felt compelled to reply to him in kind, or at least in some affectionate and respectful term.

Elizabeth brought Gabriel a Guinness over and placed it on the beer mat in front of him, a little of the head running down the side.

"Cheers, Liz," said Gabriel, lifting the glass and taking his first sip.

"You're welcome, our kid," she replied with a sly smile on her face. Gabriel and Elizabeth had been friends for a few years. She was in her mid-twenties, a year younger than him. Elizabeth was the type of woman most men found attractive; thin, with strong features, fair skin, and blonde shoulder length hair. Her eyes were deep blue but often showed the sadness of a soul that had seen too much for its years. She was generally outgoing with a lively sense of humour. The young woman had moved to Hoggersbrook with her mother when she was seventeen, and promptly left for university. She moved back after graduation. The village may not have had any night life and only a few shops, one church and a couple of pubs, but it had incredibly nice scenery. Elizabeth was in the middle of her PhD, some history related subject that Gabriel forgot on a weekly basis. She generally came back to the village at weekends and non-term time, working the bar for a bit of added income.

"What you doing here anyway?" she enquired. "Shouldn't you be slaving over a hot keyboard right now?"

"I'm meeting Jim for a drink. He reckons he's got a contact at Future Publishing who might be able to throw some work my way."

"And this needs to be done with alcohol… because?" Elizabeth asked, slowing drawing out her last word as she raised an eyebrow.

"Because we're a couple of piss-heads, and it's any excuse," Gabriel said with a shrug of his shoulders.

"Oh yes, I was forgetting that," she replied with a laugh in her voice, then turned and disappeared into the back of the pub. Eric looked at Gabriel.

"Are you two courting yet?" he asked, also smiling.

"Are you kidding? I need her to complain to when other women drive me nuts." Eric was still smiling.

"Mrs Conway always told me that women were put on this earth to drive men nuts."

"Mrs Conway knew what she was talking about," Gabriel replied with an earnest look on his face as he raised his glass.

"That she did, lad." Eric raised his own glass in reply and downed the rest of his drink. Anyway it's time for me to make a move, tell Jim I said hello."

"See yah later Mr Conway, thanks again for the drink."

"Any time lad, any time." Gabriel continued to drink his Guinness as he watched Eric walk out of the pub. Elizabeth emerged from the back.

"He teasing you again kid?" She asked.

"Only slightly, we both know these old folks need some fun in their lives. Anyway haven't you got some bloke on the go in Sheffield?"

"The hot undergraduate with the nice bum who's working part time in the records office?" Elizabeth replied, grinning as her eyes rolled upwards.

"I didn't ask for details," Gabriel said, frowning.

"Jealous?"

"No, just feeling a sudden lack of testosterone in this conversation. Speaking of which, Jim's late." Gabriel's attention shifted to the window, looking for any sign of him. Jim and Gabriel had been friends since they were kids; they'd gone to school together, they'd grown up together. The first time they'd got drunk, it had been together. Aunty Gladys liked to comment that Jim was the Butch to Gabriel's Sundance. There was no sign of him yet though, he'd never been a good timekeeper. Gabriel surveyed the pub as he finished his drink. There wasn't much custom in there that day, mostly just empty seats. Of course, it was only quarter to twelve in the morning. "Liz, give us another Guinness and whatever poof lager Jim's drinking these days."

"That's your second," Elizabeth commented with a disapproving look on her face. "It's not even twelve o'clock yet."

"With observational skills like that, I can see why you're PhD material. Get yourself a drink as well."

"Well, it's nearly twelve... I could have one, couldn't I?" The disapproving look melted into a smile and a wink.

"I thought that might change your tune." They both smiled. Elizabeth handed over the drinks, took the money and thanked him. Gabriel promptly picked up the filled glasses and took them outside into the sun. He walked over and sat on one of the old pub benches, the kind you see outside most pubs with a table in the middle with a plank on each side forming two seats. The bench matched the rest of the pub in that it had seen better days. The wood was a pale brown, almost grey in parts, and was rough to the touch with sharp splinters at the edges. As he sat down the entire bench complained with a predictable creaking sound.

Gabriel looked up and down the street, then at the front of the pub. A few fresh hanging baskets had been placed out but the plants were starting to wilt a little; it hadn't rained in the past week. The pub had a swinging sign with an image of a moon and a blunderbuss in front of it. Atop the sign sat a crow, quietly preening its feathers and giving Gabriel the occasional glance. Gabriel looked up and down the road again. Hoggersbrook was a small village in the Peak District, very picturesque, but as Elizabeth was fond of saying: "It's just far enough off the beaten track to keep most of the god damn tourists out of our hair."

"Sorry I'm late mate, got a bit caught up in things." The voice came from behind Gabriel. This was a stock greeting for Jim. Most people would say: "Hello, how are you?" Jim would normally say: "Sorry I'm late."

"That I know of, you've been on time twice in twenty years, and one of those occasions was your wedding. I'd probably get distraught if you were on time, thinking it was one of the signs of the apocalypse. I'd spend the rest of the day looking over my shoulder for four horsemen." Jim sat down on the bench across from Gabriel. The bench creaked again, mimicking the sound it had made earlier. "Here, I got you a pint in - if the horsemen do turn up at least we'll both have a drink inside us."

"Thanks mate, is Liz working?" Jim had a big smile on his face.

"You're married," Gabriel replied dryly.

"I can still look," Jim responded, giving a cheeky wink that made Gabriel snigger.

The two friends sat in the sun, drank and caught up on what they'd missed in the past few days. They sank a few more beers, then conversation turned to Jim's contact.

"So what's this job then?"

"Eddie reckons that his editor is after a few articles about the occult in rural England." Gabriel winced a little.

"The occult?" he asked, turning his head a little and speaking mostly out of one side of his mouth. Much the same as a plumber would when informing someone that they need a new boiler.

"Yeah, witchcraft and all that," Jim clarified needlessly.

"In rural England?" The writer was still wincing slightly.

"Yeah," Jim repeated, before taking a good sip of lager.

Gabriel leaned in close to Jim and whispered: "Jim, it's old wives' tales, it's sensationalised pap. We both know that there's no real occultism, in rural England or anywhere else for that matter. The most you get is some teenagers playing at devil worship or some mental Yanks over in America who never grew up."

"*I* know that," Jim said slowly pointing at himself, "*you* know that," pointing at Gabriel, "but your average pleb on the street. . ." this time waving his fingertips from left to right, ''has no real clue."

"You have a point. Thanks for bringing this to me, but it's not really my style. I don't believe in it, as you know. And I'd rather not start fabricating stuff until I get really desperate for money."

"You mean when you can't afford to drink anymore?"

"Precisely," Gabriel replied, raising his glass.

Gabriel took a steady walk home, strolling down the quiet streets enjoying the sun and chewing over what Jim had said. He reached his home, a small stone cottage with sash windows and unreliable central heating. It was a modest cottage containing a medium sized kitchen and lounge on the ground floor, with two bedrooms and a bathroom upstairs. On the way in he picked up his post off the floor, a few bills and two rejections for the articles he'd submitted.

"No surprise there," Gabriel exclaimed while exhaling heavily and tossing his keys onto the kitchen counter. The kitchen was a square room, with worktops down three sides and a double sink. It contained the usual paraphernalia that you would expect to find in a kitchen along with far too much clutter. Gabriel switched on the kettle, walked into the living room and slumped down in front of his computer, tapping the power button with his foot as he did so. The machine wearily started up, wheezing and chugging along like an asthmatic steam engine. Gabriel forced himself out of the chair and returned a few minutes later, cup of tea in hand. He checked his emails; nothing came through beyond the normal spam.

"Still no surprise." He took a sip of his tea. The milk was close to being off. Gabriel paused, considering whether it tasted bad enough to leave. He shrugged his shoulders and continued to drink it. Loading the word processor he decided to do a little work on his novel, which was basically Gabriel's way of postponing doing actual work that might pay the odd bill. As Liz put it more than once: "You'd procrastinate until your dying breath if you could get away with it, Jones."

The words were flowing well that day. Gabriel was deep in thought, words flowing from his fingertips, into the keyboard and onto the screen. The real world became muted as he constructed his own narrative on screen. After about three hours, Gabriel was snapped back to reality by the noise of the back door opening.

"Hiya sugar, it's only me," the friendly voice resonated from the kitchen. Gabriel was a little peeved to be interrupted; however, he couldn't help but grin.

"Hello Anj, want a cup of tea?" He shouted back.

"Is your milk in date?"

Gabriel regarded the now cold cup in front of him and frowned before walking into the kitchen to greet his guest.

"Probably not."

Anji's red curly hair bounced a little as she walked over to the bottle of milk that had been left out. She raised it to her nose and cautiously gave it a sniff before screwing her nose up for a second. She turned to look at Gabriel, her pale blue eyes levelling a cold stare at him.

"There's a surprise," she scolded, then broke into a giggle and headed for the door. "I'll nip to the shops. I need some fag papers anyway, see you soon babes."

Anji was an unusual person. She rolled her own cigarettes, normally containing a fair amount of marijuana. She was a rampant environmentalist, at least when it suited her. She talked to her car, laptop, mp3 player, and most likely a few other things that Gabriel wasn't even aware of. On top of this she had a habit of dressing like a hippie, her red curls adding to the effect. She liked to play Jazz on the guitar in her spare time, and had recently trained as a car mechanic. Gabriel liked her immensely; they'd only met eighteen months ago, but became close friends very quickly. He often joked that she had the ability of relaxing him just by talking to him, although he was never sure about the calming effects of the second hand dope smoke. Gabriel filled the kettle and switched it on for the second time, then returned to his novel.

The back door opened again. "Come on you lazy bastard, here's some milk. Make us both a cup of tea while I roll a joint, then we're going outside so I can smoke it."

It was still bright sunshine outside, and the cottage garden was a tranquil place. It had tall trees across the north edge where they wouldn't block the sun, and shrubs on the other sides. At the bottom of the garden flowed a small stream giving the relaxing sound of running water. The grass was getting a little long and some of the borders were ready for weeding. Anji was wandering around and looking through the intertwined branches of the trees. Gabriel placed both cups of tea on a grey cast-iron garden table, then sat on one of the four matching chairs. Anji joined him, sitting to his left and stretching her legs out resting them on his knee. She took a drag of her cigarette and looked at him. "So then, you got any work lined up?"

Gabriel gave her a 'You must be joking' expression.

"Have I 'eck. Jim said that he could throw some work my way, but it's writing about the occult. Occultism in rural England to be precise." He took a sip of tea; it tasted better than his last cup.

"What's wrong with that?" Anji asked, mirroring his own actions.

"The fact that there is no occultism in rural England, for a start."

"Bollocks, you don't know that," She mumbled as forcefully as she could with a joint in her mouth.

"Come on, be serious," Gabriel replied with a 'you must be joking' look on his face again. Anji took the cigarette out of her mouth and took another sip.

"At the very least you could write it from a historical point of view."

She made a good point but Gabriel wasn't about to admit that. "What you mean is: You have no interest in the subject so can't be arsed to research and write about it."

She had just made another good point, pretty much hitting the nail squarely on the head. She was talking in her forceful tone again, and this time it was not restrained by a cigarette. This was the tone that Gabriel always considered to be her 'nagging tone'.

"Okay, I'll think about it," Gabriel conceded, mainly just to shut her up.

"I think it could be a really interesting topic. If you do the article let me know, I'll help with the research." They sat in the garden and had a few more cups of tea, which soon turned into beers. Time wore on, the pair continued to drink, and the topic of the article didn't come up for the rest of the evening.

The following morning Gabriel was abruptly woken by the coarse sound of a crow cawing outside his window. He reluctantly rolled over and forced his eyes open, the blurry image of his room gradually coming into focus. He dragged himself into the bathroom to brush his teeth and have a wash, knocking on the door of the spare room on his way past. Gabriel covered his face in soap and rinsed it off with cold water in an attempt to shock himself into full consciousness.

Ten minutes later, as Gabriel was in the kitchen fighting his hangover, Anji emerged from the spare room and gently walked down stairs. She passed him in the kitchen, silently taking the cup of tea that he handed her and headed straight for the fresh air of the garden. Gabriel joined her, squinting as his eyes protested against the bright light. They both sat in a comfortable silence for a moment, enjoying the morning sun.

Anji was the first to break the quiet. "Thanks for the tea babe, it was just what I needed."

"No problem, Anj. Sleep well?" Gabriel replied, sinking further back into his chair.

"Like a log. But we did put quite a lot of booze away. What you doing today?" Gabriel knew what she was getting at.

"Think I'll have a look around for a new article, I might even take that occult one yet." Gabriel was actually thinking that he'd write the article when Hell froze over, but was too hung over to argue the point.

"If you're not busy this evening, I'm playing at gig night over at Chandlers in Chesterfield," Anji said, her thumb toying with the top of the mug handle.

"Sounds good, I'll see who else I can round up. What time do you start work this morning?" Gabriel asked, gesturing to Anji's watch.

"Ten. I'd better get moving soon."

After Anji had left, Gabriel turned on his computer and made the usual cup of tea while he waited for it to boot. He did his ritual pointless email check, talking to himself as he did it. "Spam, Spam, Spam, Bacon, Beans, Spam and. . . hold on, you're not spam."

He had received an email from an Edward Tomlinson. The mouse clicked twice and the message appeared on screen:

```
Dear Mr Jones,
    I understand from our mutual associate Mr Lowe that
you are reluctant to be commissioned to write a series of
articles  regarding  the  occult  in  rural  England.  I
consider this to be a great shame as I have read your
work and was looking forward to seeing what you would
have produced on this subject. I have been authorised by
my editor to offer you £200 'up front' and we agree to
cover all travelling and research expenses, above and
beyond the commission for the articles. If you reconsider
please contact me at this address.
```

Very odd indeed, thought Gabriel. *I usually have to beg them for work, not the other way around. Three words, Jones: gift, horse, mouth.*

Gabriel wheeled his computer chair across the room to the beaten-up chest of draws where his mobile phone was charging. His fingers fumbled with the wire and finally managed to detach it. He found James Lowe in the phone's memory and hit the dial button.

The phone began to ring. *Come on Jim, pick up the damn phone.* No answer. Gabriel slipped the mobile into his pocket, picked up his keys and left the house.

Walking helped Gabriel to think; it always had. Two hundred pounds was a lot of money to Gabriel. He really didn't want to do one article about the occult, let alone a series of them. That said, two hundred pounds extra was a difficult offer to refuse, especially when it was coming upfront. However, *something* about it didn't feel right; he'd never been offered money up front before, and he wasn't successful enough for it to be common practice. Hell, Edward Tomlinson hadn't even sought him out in the first place. If it was just a favour for Jim, two hundred pounds more would make it an expensive favour.

Gabriel found himself heading in the direction of the Hunter's Moon, cutting across the churchyard as he did so. The church was old, as most country churches are, built in the fourteenth century but kept in good repair. The grass in the graveyard was kept trimmed and the shrubs and trees were neatly pruned. On the west side of the graveyard grew a large yew tree, its branches stretching wide but not too low. Gabriel would often sit in its shade in the summer, making notes for whatever he happened to be writing at the time. Today, however, he was just passing through. He strolled down the gravel path, listening to the sound of the crow that had rested on a gravestone a few feet away. Gabriel couldn't help but wonder if it was the same bird that had so rudely awoken him that morning, an unnecessary reminder of how hung over he was.

The Crow seemed to be watching Gabriel as he passed. The light reflected off the sheen of the bird's oily black feathers as its head slowly turned following him. At that moment, Gabriel realized that he could hear no birdlife of any sort; the crow was silent now and so was every other bird in hearing distance. The writer glanced around the church yard, then back at the crow. It was the only bird he could see.

"You scared 'em all off or something?" he asked half under his breath. The crow didn't reply, but continued to stare. Gabriel matched the stare for a split second before a shiver ran down his spine. He suddenly felt very alone in the graveyard, and an irrational feeling of uneasiness was growing in the pit of his stomach. Gabriel quickened his pace away from the crow and the churchyard.

The pub was a comforting sight. Gabriel went inside quickly, the cool dim interior a welcome respite for his eyes.

"A bit early even for you, isn't it kid?" Elizabeth chirped, watching Gabriel as he let the door swing shut behind him.

"Yeah, give us a Coke, will yah?"

"Poor Gabe's hung over," She commented in a singsong voice. Gabriel raised an eyebrow.

"Anji came over last night. That normally means too much beer."

"How is the crazy ginger one?" Elizabeth asked cheerfully.

"She's not bad, she's got a gig at Chandlers tonight. I'm recruiting people. Want to come?"

"I'm not working tonight so sounds good, I'll drive if you like."

"Cool, I'll see if Jim wants to come as well. I need to talk to him at any rate."

"About the job?" Elizabeth asked, placing a cold glass of Coke on the bar, the ice cubes chinking together. "That's one-ninety by the way."

"Yeah, I wasn't gonna do it but they've just upped the money by a couple of hundred." Gabriel handed over his money and slid onto a bar stool.

"That's good. Why do you need to talk to Jim?"

"Because it doesn't feel right." He took a sip of his drink. "There's no reason for them to offer me the extra money, and I'm wondering what the catch is." Gabriel put his elbow on the bar and propped his head up with his hand.

"You're a pessimist," Elizabeth said in a dry tone.

"You mispronounced the word *realist*." Gabriel forced a half smile and took a hefty swig of Coke. "I'm gonna finish this then look into doing some research for the articles. It's probably gonna involve a lot of travelling, I can claim expenses for that, just like Jim Rockford."

"Who?" Liz asked with a look somewhere between humour and pity.

"Philistine."

Gabriel finished his drink and left the pub, re-tracing his steps to the churchyard. The atmosphere had changed; the birds were singing and the sun was beating down. Gabriel felt a little stupid that he'd let himself get a shiver over a god damn bird, especially as he had absolutely zero belief in anything that should give him a shiver in a churchyard. This time he paid the yew tree a visit, pulling a small notebook out of his pocket and sitting on the thin wooden bench beneath its branches. He started to scribble some ideas down, a difficult task due to his very limited knowledge of the subject. *Damn, this is what I need Anji for.* He wrote the word 'History' and underlined it twice, then put the end of the pen in his mouth. *Okay, that's probably a good jumping off point. So how do I start it?*

There was a crunch of gravel underfoot from Gabriel's left. He turned to see who it was.

"Good morning, Reverend."

"Good morning young Gabriel, how are you this glorious day?"

Gabriel wasn't really a religious man. He always thought of himself as agnostic when it came right down to it. He did, however, have a tremendous amount of respect for people with true faith. The Reverend Lincoln had arrived in Hoggersbrook as a student minister and was still there fifty-seven years later. He was of Afro-Caribbean decent and still spoke with a strong accent. The black of his robes and dark brown skin contrasted strikingly with the white of his eyes, adding to his already strong presence. He was a good orator, as all good ministers need to be, and also held a seat on the local council. On top of this, he knew a lot about history - especially local history. Gabriel was trying to weigh up the ethical constraints of asking a man of the cloth about occultism and devil worship.

"I'm not doing badly, thank you Reverend. I could use some advice but feel a little awkward asking you."

"I've been a minister a long time Gabriel, I would be surprised if you could ask me anything more indelicate than I've been asked in the past." He gave a wide smile. "Even if you are a heathen." The Reverend strolled over and sat beside Gabriel on the bench. "So, please ask your question."

"Basically, I'm writing some articles on the history of occultism in England. As a history enthusiast, how would you start researching?"

The reverend considered his answer for a moment.

"Outside the obvious answer of a library? I often find that a good place to look for the more unusual things is the lecture circuit. Why don't you try the local colleges and see what they have coming up?"

"A good idea Reverend, thank you."

"You're welcome my boy, good luck with it." The Reverend was about to stand when he read Gabriel's expression. "What is it my boy?"

"You said I was a heathen," he replied, looking quizzical.

"I was being light hearted. Secularist would have been more polite." Reverend Lincoln bowed his head apologetically.

"You know I didn't take offence Reverend, I just wondered how you knew."

The Reverend shuffled on the seat slightly.

"When you deal with faith and belief every day for fifty years, you develop a sixth sense for it. You can see belief in a man's eyes. Figuring out what he's believing in is another matter, but you can see if he believes in something. I look at your eyes and I do not see belief anymore. I don't think you'll ever believe in God again, but I look forward to the day when you start to believe in something. Even if you're only believing in yourself." He gave Gabriel a compassionate smile. "My love of God and my love of history have taught me many things, and one of them is always keep an open mind. Remember what Shakespeare said. There are more things in heaven and earth, Horatio, than are dreamt of in your philosophy. Remember that when you're doing your research."

"Hamlet, act one scene five." Quoting literature at each other had been a bit of a game that the two men had adopted years ago. Long before Gabriel could have been considered to be a man.

"Correct."

"But these days, faith is feeling more like the undiscovered country from whose bourn no traveller returns."

"Puzzles the will." Reverend Lincoln smiled again. "Remember what I said, keep an open mind, and never underestimate the faith of others. Faith is a powerful motivator. For example, we're sitting under a yew tree. This tree was originally considered to be sacred by the pagans. The church adopted the tree, amongst other things, to ease the populous' transition from paganism to Christianity. Your own faith is buried in there somewhere; it will surface when you need it. Good luck with the articles.''

He placed a reassuring hand on Gabriel's knee, stood up and walked in the direction of the church. ''If you want to talk you know where I am."

"Thank you, old friend," Gabriel replied, taking the pen out of his mouth.

Professor Tony Harrison walked out of his front door, a folder under his left arm and his car keys grasped in his right hand. He was in his mid-sixties and currently lecturing in the History department of Sheffield Hallam University. He wasn't a physically imposing man, only about five foot five, and had lost most of the use of his left hand to what he always said was childhood polio. However, when he spoke he commanded attention, his diction was precise and his oratory enthusing.

Tony unlocked his car, opened the door, put his keys in the ignition then took the folder from under his left arm and casually placed it on the passenger seat. As he started the engine, the compact disc player automatically started up to the London Symphony Orchestra playing Rossini's *The Thieving Magpie*. Tony shifted the automatic gear stick into drive and pulled out of his driveway.

A little over an hour later the professor arrived at his office in the Owen building of Sheffield Hallam University's city campus. It wasn't an overly large office; it had a full bookcase down one side and an old-fashioned coat stand in the corner. Natural light came from a small window at the far end near three filing cabinets. Tony's desk was covered in paper; his colleagues often joked that they couldn't work out how anyone could find anything in such a mess, let alone a man with only one properly functioning hand. However, Tony managed to pull it off. He could normally find any paperwork in a matter of seconds, even if it was buried in the paper monolith that was Professor Harrison's desk. He was a quirky man, who would sometimes come out with some of the most random rubbish anyone near him had ever heard. Behind this, however, was a remarkably sharp mind.

Tony took a seat in his studded leather chair which was certainly not university issue. He pulled his keyboard towards himself and logged onto the computer on his desk. A quick email check revealed a few messages requesting advice from his students, one regarding budgeting from his head of faculty.

And one regarding the current status of his lecture circuit covering the history of occultism in Britain.

Jim Lowe left his office, squinting as his eyes were assaulted by the late afternoon sun. He removed his mobile phone from the inside pocket of his suit jacket and started to walk to his car. It had been such a hectic day, he hadn't had chance to look at it. A couple of text messages and a missed call.

Jim checked the missed call first... Gabriel Jones. *Okay Gabe, have you changed your mind?* he wondered. Jim had been working at an advertising agency in Rotherham for several years. He was a likable fellow with a quick wit. Most people found him easy to get on with, which had made him a good choice for an advertising company. He was a large built man, about six foot two in height with short dark-brown hair. Jim hit the dial button to return Gabriel's call.

"Hello mate, I've got a missed call off you."

"Yeah, I got an email off your friend Edward, he's offering me an extra two hundred upfront. This bloke is for real, right?"

"Yeah, he's a good man, his editor will take his advice most of the time as well. He might have swung it himself. You taking the job?" The phone was starting to feel sweaty against his ear in the sun.

"At that money, I'd be an idiot not to."

"Sounds good, drinks are on you next time then.''

"Speaking of which, Anji's playing at Chandlers tonight. Liz and I are going along to watch, you coming?"

"Alcohol and Jazz. Sounds good. We decided who's driving yet?"

"Liz says she'll drive, see ya about half seven."

"Thanks mate, see you then." Jim grinned and snapped his phone shut.

Gabriel hung up the phone. He headed to his computer and fired up a search engine. To his amazement, he could find next to nothing useful about occultism in rural England. *The biggest repository of information in the history of mankind and I can't find a single useful thing? Typical.*

Gabriel spent a few more hours on his book before he had to get ready to meet Elizabeth.

The three friends arrived in Chandlers Cocktail bar quite early. It was what both Jim and Gabriel would describe as a 'poncy wine bar.' Or 'a place trying far too hard to be posh.' But they could both appreciate live music, and all three were having a good time. The bar was large and open plan, with hardwood floors and what most reasonable people would say was far too many blue neon lights around the place.

Anji came up on stage and the three cheered loudly. Jim made an aborted attempt at a wolf whistle that sounded more like the dying breath of a very small shrew. Once Anji had finished performing her songs, she joined them at their table. Her friends congratulated her on the show and had a few drinks. The last live act had just finished and the normal speaker-delivered variety had replaced it.

"So Gabe, how's the research going?" Anji asked, raising her voice to be heard over the music.

"It's not, so far. I can't find much on the internet, at least not in amongst the maelstrom of pap that's out there and I've not had chance to visit a library yet. The Reverend suggested that I check the lecture circuit."

Elizabeth's ears pricked up.

"I think one of my lecturers, Professor Harrison, might do something useful. I'll check for you tomorrow if you like."

"That'd be great, thanks. Is he any good?" Gabriel asked leaning forward and cocking his ear towards her.

"Very, he keeps things interesting. He can be a little odd though. I'll email him for you tomorrow."

"Cheers, I'll get the next round. I've got two-hundred quid coming my way so I can afford it."

At this point Jim spoke up. "Christ, I nearly forgot." He looked around the room shiftily then retrieved a fat looking envelope from his inside pocket. He slid it under the table to Gabriel. "It's the two-hundred in cash from Ed." Jim had to speak loudly to be heard over the music.

"Cheers mate, but next time can you try to look less like you're passing me drugs."

The quartet had a few more drinks before heading home.

Elizabeth's car came to steady halt outside Gabriel's house. He clambered out and steadied himself by placing a hand on the car's roof. "Cheers Liz, see ya soon, you lot," he said, heavily pushing the door shut and giving the car a quick pat with the flat of his hand.

Gabriel walked to his back door and paused before putting the key in the lock. He inhaled deeply and removed his hand from his pocket, clenching his fist at his side as if to grasp at the air. "Umm, it's a nice night, don't think I want to go to bed yet." He coaxed the key into the Yale lock, gave it a brisk turn then entered quickly and shut the door behind him. Gabriel opened the cupboard under his stairs and was met by the familiar musty smell of a room that needed a good airing.

After some fumbling around in the darkness he found his laptop computer. It was marginally better than its desktop counterpart sitting in the lounge. Gabriel didn't like laptop keyboards, so only used it when he wanted to write outside. He briefly walked into the living room to check that his desktop was still turned on. As long as the desktop was on Gabriel could get to his novel from the laptop. He didn't understand how; Jim had helped him set it up. It used something that had an 'I' and too many 'e's along with a nonsensical number in the name.

Gabriel picked up his laptop, an oil lamp off the shelf and Anji's lighter that she'd left in the kitchen. Hands full, he headed into the garden. The laptop clunked as Gabriel placed it on the table. He lit the lamp, placing it next to the computer, then returned to the kitchen for a beer while he waited for the machine to boot. Half an hour passed while Gabriel stared at the monitor thinking of other things. He looked disappointingly at the screen, the brightness of the virtual page glaring defiantly at the darkness around it, the cursor alternating between black and white, winking at him. The unemployed writer gave a heavy sigh. *The flashing cursor that says: Write something, you arse.* The night air was still and quiet, the sweet scent of jasmine lingered from the climber by the window. There wasn't any cloud cover and Gabriel took a sip of beer before looking up at the pricks of light that pierced the night sky.

He was enjoying the quiet but still couldn't shake the feeling that something was wrong with this article. Two-hundred pounds was the going rate for an article; two-hundred on top and upfront was odd, even for several articles. Gabriel exhaled, still looking up. "Is this the calm before the storm? Or am I just being an idiot as usual? Or both?" He exhaled again, this time with a half-laugh and put the thought out of his mind. Gabriel opened an internet search engine, abandoning his novel for a while. *What was your name? Tony Harrison?*

He did a search for 'Antony Harrison': too many results. He tried again, this time trying 'Antony Harrison Hallam.' *That's better.* He browsed the first couple of sites. Professor Harrison was indeed an authority on Occultism, Wicca, Demonology, and quite a few other things. Gabriel continued to read. If he was going to be taking advice from this bloke, then he wanted to make damn sure that the man knew what he was talking about, professor or no professor. Some of the most moronic people Gabriel had ever met had been academics.

As it turned, out Tony Harrison was well educated and well-travelled. He had been across most of Europe, much of Africa and both North and South America, all the time researching some form of occultism. *Okay Prof, looks like you know your stuff.*

Gabriel turned off the laptop and blew out the lamp. Taking another sip of beer, he stretched his legs out, and took a deep breath enjoying the warm night air. In the distance he heard a heavy rumble. Thunder. Maybe it was the calm before the storm after all...

He took another sip of beer, and the rumble came again, this time louder. "Well, Jonesy, looks like the nice weather has dried up, time for bed soon." Gabriel picked up his laptop and took it inside before returning to his seat. He sat down, this time resting his feet on the chair that Anji had occupied that morning. He took a gulp from his glass and closed his eyes. Gabriel listened to the approaching thunder and tried to arrange the next chapter of his novel in his head. He periodically took heavy swigs of the drink in front of him.

Then it came, the feeling of a raindrop hitting his nose... time for bed.

Chapter 2

Gabriel awoke not long after dawn broke. It was Friday morning and the rain had arrived at long last. He lay in bed for a few hours, listening to the tenacious pelts of water hitting his window and dozing in and out of consciousness. Gabriel loved the sound of rain; it had always relaxed him. When the rain subsided he climbed into the shower, got dressed and went downstairs. He entered the kitchen and picked up his phone from the worktop, flipping it open to check for missed calls and messages. One new message from Elizabeth:

```
"Prof Harrison is giving an open lecture on occultism
at 1pm today.  Meet me in the Howard at 12."
```

Gabriel checked his watch.

"Okay, I've got an hour and a half to get to Sheffield. Better get a move on." The man made himself look presentable, or at least his version of presentable. He threw on a pair of blue jeans, a clean t-shirt and jumper. He then made a half-hearted attempt to make his hair look like a style that belonged to someone who didn't live in an insane asylum and left the house.

The cooler air outside came as a shock. "Bloody hell, it's got cold," Gabriel cursed as he walked swiftly to his car. The car had hardly been used in the past week; most places he had needed to go had been in the village and with the sunny weather, he'd walked. Gabriel liked driving; his car was one of his most prized possessions and had been paid for with a large chunk of his inheritance. He started the engine and sedately drove through the village, past the church and the Hunter's Moon and into open country. As the buildings gave way to fields and hedgerows, Gabriel became a lot heavier with his right foot, enjoying the feel of speed and the sound of the engine. He knew the roads, he knew where the danger spots were and he knew when he could get away with breaking the speed limit. The whole journey took about forty-five minutes.

Gabriel had gone to university in Sheffield himself and knew where the hidden parking spaces were. The first of his old regular ones was free, a space on a quiet street of terraced houses near the Sheffield United football ground. The car pulled up neatly by the curb, scaring a crow out of the way. The space was still a good ten minutes' walk from the city centre but it beat paying for parking.

Gabriel looked at the rain. "You're gonna get wet, Gabe." He checked his mirror, opened the door and hastily made a mad dash for the boot, the oversized drops of rain penetrating his hair and landing directly on his scalp. A moment of fumbling with the boot catch and it was open. Gabriel grabbed the large golf umbrella that he kept there and frantically opened it out above his head. He slammed the boot shut, pressed the lock button on his keys and made a beeline for the city centre. Gabriel had long legs; people often commented that he walked like a 'man on a mission' or with a 'purposeful stride.' Gabriel just considered himself to walk quickly, nothing more.

Leaving the claustrophobic enclosure of the terraced houses, Gabriel looked out at the city skyline with a heavy sigh. He didn't like cities; he particularly didn't like Sheffield, he found it grey and cold and without soul. He didn't like the taste of the pollution in the air. He didn't like the 'chavs' who aimlessly wandered the streets in tracksuits and baseball caps. Or how they held conversations that seem to consist mainly of swearing and making gestures that made them look like they were trying to find something to head-butt. Gabriel had lived in Sheffield for three years; even then it had always felt alien to him and he had not been sorry to leave it behind. He could never understand how anyone could prefer city life to that of the country.

He quickened his pace, dodging around puddles and dawdling people, taking short cuts down alleyways at the sides of shops and giving silent greetings to places where he used to eat or shop. Another thing that always confused Gabriel about both cities and towns was the necessity to move out of people's way. No one ever seemed to move out of his way; like they were on some form of autopilot. It had always bewildered him that they didn't just continually bump into each other like anorexic sumo wrestlers. Gabriel smiled at that thought as he reached the Howard pub.

He pulled the cumbersome wooden door open with its large brass handle, shook his umbrella off and ducked inside. It wasn't a bad place as city pubs went; it was one of Gabriel's old haunts between lectures, so got sentimental 'Brownie Points' for that. The pub was a fairly spacious place, with a red felt pool table in one corner and a plethora of students scattered about the room, bunking off lectures and making the place look untidy. Gabriel often felt hypocritical having a distain for students; after all he used to be one. It didn't bother him enough to make him change his way of thinking though. He checked his watch and scanned the pub for any sign of Elizabeth; no sign of her. The rain had motivated him to walk faster than usual so he was a little early. Gabriel walked to the bar and ordered a lager and a Guinness. The pub was in much better repair than The Hunter's Moon; it had a shiny brass footrest running the length of a well varnished bar, and the carpet was deep red and kept well vacuumed. The brunette behind the bar took Gabriel's money with a smile and moved onto the next customer like an automaton. Gabriel picked up the drinks and started sauntering towards his old regular table. He slid around the back of it so he was facing the door, and as he did so Elizabeth walked in and noticed him immediately. Seeing the two drinks, she walked over.

"How's it going, our kid?" she asked, sitting down across from him.

"Not bad, Liz," Gabriel replied, sliding her drink over.

"Cheers dude," she chirped, bringing the glass to her lips and taking a deep gulp.

"So, where we got to go then?" he asked, taking a drink himself. Elizabeth put her own glass down.

"Over to the Adsett building. We'll drink these then head over and get a good seat."

Elizabeth and Gabriel walked through the double sets of doors into the Atrium of Sheffield Hallam City Campus. Gabriel always thought of the Atrium as the university at its best. The scent of expensive coffee hung in the air from the café on the top floor. It was bright, as you'd expect from an atrium, with pale cream floor tiles and tubular metal railing on the stairways and balconies, painted bright white. It looked productive; herds of students moving from room to room, others sat with folders and note books discussing work with one another. Of course Gabriel was fully aware that they weren't really discussing work, no more than the students they'd just left in the Howard were. They were in fact discussing anything other than work, they were just doing it dry. In some ways there was more honesty to the students wasting time in the pub; they may have been dossing, but they were doing it openly. However, the fact remained that the illusion of hard working students did add to the atmosphere. The duo made their way to the elevators, then across the atrium and to an outside walkway which took them into the Adsett building. After wearily climbing a few flights of stairs, they arrived at the back way into reception.

"Got us VIP passes. In other words... we don't have to pay," Elizabeth whispered to Gabriel as Bob the security guard came over. "Hello Bob, has Harrison seen you?"

Bob was an elderly gent with a long white beard. Gabriel remembered him from his own student days; he used to refer to him as 'Captain Bird's Eye.' Others called him Gandalf.

"Yes, Elizabeth, you and your friend can go right in," Bob smiled, pointing a wrinkly hand towards the door to the lecture theatre.

"Cheers, Bob," Elizabeth said, heading through the door with Gabriel in tow.

The lecture theatre was another relic Gabriel remembered from his own time at the university, especially the time that one of his friends had fallen asleep in a lecture. It was a large room with a high ceiling; dim defused lights could be seen around all four walls with equally dim mini-spotlights in the ceiling. The walls were painted a slightly darker shade than magnolia and a large projection screen stood proudly on the front wall with a podium to its right hand side. Elizabeth led Gabriel to a seat on the second row near the centre. He felt the blue fabric with his hand as he wearily sat down, the other rows of seats climbing successively higher behind them.

The room started to gradually fill. A scruffy-looking student in combats and a German army coat sat down in the empty chair on Gabriel's left, kicking his rucksack under the seat as he did so. Less than a minute later, Professor Harrison made a quiet entrance, leaving some papers on the podium then walking over to a side table followed by a young woman who Gabriel couldn't help but notice. She was very slender, about five foot six wearing a pencil skirt and suit jacket. She had dark brown coloured hair cut into a medium length bob. Gabriel watched as she strode confidently across the floor. Elizabeth gave him a light thump to the thigh.

"What?" Gabriel protested with an innocent look.

"Stop perving," Elizabeth said in a hushed tone, thumping him again.

"I wasn't."

"You were staring at her legs."

"Only a little bit," Gabriel smiled. "Who is she anyway?"

"His assistant," she replied.
"Lucky Professor."

Professor Tony Harrison returned to the podium and tapped the microphone; the dull thud resonated throughout the room as all other noise quickly subsided. Gabriel could see the scruffy-looking student out of the corner of his eye. The man pulled a Palm-top out of the inside pocket of his army coat. He tossed back the lid, pulled out a stylus and started to manically tap parts of the screen with it. As the professor started to talk, he frantically jotted down notes with the stylus. *Posh bastard,* Gabriel thought, retrieving his faithful tatty note pad and mini-biro from his own inside pocket as he began to listen.

Alan Hatchcroft walked the perimeter of his northern-most field, inspecting the barbed wire. The grass rustled under his heavy footsteps, covering the sound of his heavy breathing. Alan was getting on in years and was probably walking a little more briskly than a man with a heart condition should. But he was angry, damn angry. Six sheep had gone missing from his flock in as many weeks. He was used to losing the odd animal here and there, usually due to 'stupid walkers' leaving his damn gates open. But this was different, one a week. It didn't even make much sense - why steal sheep? You can't make much money from a single one, and a desperate hungry hobo would have trouble slaughtering and skinning one. Rabbits or pheasants would make more sense, but sheep?

Alan got back to the gate where he had started his circuit; the fence was fine. Of course, a three and a half foot barbed wire face would keep sheep in without a problem, but was only an obstacle rather than a barrier to a person. It was completely feasible that someone could climb over, bludgeon a sheep, throw it over the fence and hop back over themselves.

He paused for a second to catch his breath, staring into the dark unknown of the dense woodland that lined the northern border of the field. That damn fool copper had been no use, he'd promised to 'keep an eye out'; that was going to help loads. Alan got back in his Land Rover and vented some of his frustration by slamming the door.

In Sheffield the lecture was drawing to a close. Gabriel might not have believed in any of the subject matter that the Professor had spoken about, but he couldn't deny that Tony Harrison had made the topic interesting. Tony finished speaking and was rewarded with loud applause that reverberated around the room. He smiled and bowed his head slightly.

Liz leaned over and spoke firmly over the clapping.

"He said he'd meet with you if you wanted to pick his brain. We can nip over to his office in a few minutes if you like."

"Sounds good."

Elizabeth and Gabriel approached Tony Harrison's office door. She gave a quick knock, then immediately opened the door and boldly bustled into his office. Tony was sitting at his desk while his assistant was at the back of the room putting some paper work away.

"How are you, my girl?" Tony enquired with genuine kindness in his voice.

"I'm not bad, you old git," Elizabeth said with a wide grin. "Good lecture, by the way." This was how Elizabeth spoke to someone that she felt completely comfortable with.

"Introduce me to your friend, then," Tony said, his good hand gesturing in Gabriel's direction.

"Professor Tony Harrison, meet Gabriel Jones. Gabe, the other way around." The two men gave each other a firm hand shake.

"Pleased to meet you, Professor. I really enjoyed your lecture, and that's probably the first time I've ever said that to anyone without lying." Both men smiled.

"Please, both of you have a seat." They sat in the two vacant seats just off to the side of Tony's desk. Gabriel glanced at Tony's assistant. Tony didn't like to have his visitors sat across from him, it felt too formal. He'd never been a big fan of formality. "So, Elizabeth tells me that you're writing some articles on Occultism."

"Yes, I'm just trying to get some ideas to springboard off. I was thinking of tackling it from an historical point of view. But I'm not sure how interested the average person would be in that, so I also wanted to look at a few different approaches." The two men talked at length about different approaches Gabriel could take, and Tony filled Gabriel in some of the more interesting and sensational aspects of demonology. A female voice came from the back of the room.

"Why not look into how people's modern lives have been affected by it?" It was the Professor's assistant.

"Sorry to interrupt, but I couldn't help overhearing. You still get the odd place where a bunch of kids try dabbling in the dark arts." She tilted her head from side to side. "It has knock-on effects that can involve families and friends. Either when they get caught doing something they shouldn't, or when they get so into it that it effects their lifestyle."

"This is my assistant Joanna, by the way." Joanna smiled and gave an excited wave. Elizabeth smiled back and Gabriel responded with a small coy wave of his own. He considered what she said for a moment then fumbled in his pocked for his note pad.

"That's a very good idea, thanks," he said as he made a quick note. The professor looked up.

"If you want to take that stance then I'd recommend heading over to a small village named. . ." The professor paused for a moment while clicking his computer mouse and looking at the screen, ". . .Stonebank. Wonderful things, mailing lists. I get all sorts of interesting stuff sent to me. Just this morning I got a message about some young ne'er-do-wells out there performing some form of black magic ritual. Could be a non-story but possibly worth a look."

"I'll take a look, thanks." Gabriel wrote the word *Stonebank* and underlined it twice.

"Glad to help, my boy... however." Tony Harrison raised a cautioning finger. "One word of advice: never underestimate the belief of others, and keep an open mind."

"There are more things in heaven and earth, Horatio, than are dreamt of in your philosophy." The Reverend's Shakespearian quote echoed through Gabriel's mind, making the hairs on his arm stand up on end.

"I'll remember that professor, thank you for your time, and your advice." Gabriel stood and offered his hand again. Tony took it and shook it vigorously for the second time.

"Any time, my son. Good luck, and if you want to talk again don't hesitate to get in touch."

"Thank you Professor, hope to see you soon. See ya, Joanna."

"Bye," Joanna chirped from the back of the office.

The friends left the office and started to walk down the long corridor in the direction of the main reception.

"*See ya, Joanna*," Elizabeth mocked, while rolling her eyes.

Gabriel smiled. "I just think you don't like it when I notice other women," he said in a sly tone.

"Yeah, 'cause I fancy you so much."

"So you should," responded Gabriel, nodding his head and choosing to ignore the sarcasm in her voice. "I'm a catch of legendary proportions." The main doors came into view. "Come on, you need a lift or did you drive in this morning?" he asked, looking at the rain outside.

"I drove thanks kid, anyway I've still got some research to do."

"Okay, see you later then." Gabriel made a move to the door but was stopped short by Elizabeth.

"Hold on. What are you going to do now?" Elizabeth had her right eyebrow raised.

"I'm gonna check out that Stonebank link, I'm in work mode. Please note it, because you won't see it often." Gabriel winked and vanished through the large set of glass doors, putting his umbrella up.

"Ain't that the truth," Elizabeth whispered with a laugh.

Gabriel weaved through the crowd, heading back to his car. The ideas were now running through his head in a torrent of thought. For the first time, he was interested in the topic; for the first time, he actually wanted to write the articles. He still didn't believe in any of that crap, but that didn't mean others didn't, and it didn't mean that he wasn't starting to find it interesting. The cynical side of him, which was by far the greater part, was still thinking that anyone who believed in Devil Worship, Wicca, Demonology or the supernatural were gullible at best, and certifiable at worst. But he was also finding that interesting.

Human stupidity can be an interesting topic in itself. Gabriel stopped walking for a second, gritted his teeth and shook his head, listening to the sound of the rain hitting his umbrella. *Don't think I'll write that line in any of the articles.* He smiled and continued back to the place where he'd parked. Up the side streets, past the shops, down and from end to end of the graffiti-strewn underpasses, then finally between the terraced houses leading to the welcome site of his car.

Gabriel dug deep into his pocket to pull out his car keys, and squeezed the unlock button, the orange glow of the indicator lights blinked in response along with the familiar clunk of the door locks disengaging. Gabriel shook his umbrella, hurriedly swung the car door open and ducked into the driver's seat, tossing his now redundant umbrella on the back seat.

The windows were opaque with condensation. Gabriel started the engine and routinely flicked all the heater settings into demist mode. He relaxed in the seat and sighed. He was still on the outskirts of the city centre, but he was in his car and mentally he was on his way home. The condensation was still covering the windows. Gabriel awkwardly coaxed his mobile phone out of the tight hip pocket of his jeans. He found Anji's number in the memory and pressed his thumb against the green dial button. The phone rang a few times before she picked it up.

"Hiya sugar, what's up?" came the cheery voice.

"Feel like an adventure this weekend?"

"What sort of adventure?" Anji asked with a reluctant tone in her voice.

"The sort where you keep me company while I poke my nose into things that are none of my business."

"You're such a charmer."

"That's why you love me so much."

"No, I love you because you make a good cup of tea and always give me beer when I visit you." A small laugh came through the phone speaker. "So where're we going then?"

"A place called Stonebank."

"Fantastic." The voice on the phone paused for a second. "Where's that then?"

"Damned if I know." Gabriel let out a chuckle. "Not had chance to find out yet."

"So why are we going there?"

"Apparently, there are some kids playing at devil worship or black magic, and I want to have a gander at the community's reaction. Should only take a day or two at most before we move on to somewhere else, but it'll give me a start."

"Okay, but you're driving. When do you want to leave?"

"Can you be ready by six this evening?"

"Sure, where we gonna sleep?"

"We can look for a guesthouse. I'll chuck my two-man tent in the boot just in case."

"Okay, see you around six. Bye," she signed off in a singsong voice.

The windows had cleared and Gabriel could see the outside world again. He pulled out of his parking space and headed for home, leaving the monolithic concrete eyesores and heavy air behind him.

Gabriel was happy to get home, entering his kitchen and throwing his keys on the worktop as he always did. He walked into the living room and shrugged his coat off, then tossed it on the sofa before walking over and turning on his computer. He had two hours to find out where Stonebank was, pack for a few days and pick Anji up.

Gabriel was used to using online maps and it didn't take him long to plan out a route. He hit the print button and the printer next to him sprung to life, gobbling and momentarily regurgitating paper before correctly grasping it and feeding it through. A few dozen tugs of the paper later and the map and route had printed out. Gabriel looked at the clock. *Still got over an hour and a half.*

He did a little internet searching on Stonebank. It was an old farming village, not unlike Hoggersbrook. He could find no recorded links to occultism apart from the local story of a couple of teenagers getting arrested for cruelty to animals when they cut off a chicken's head, apparently as part of an attempted satanic ritual. There wasn't much information: just that they were two school kids in their mid-teens who were bored, so tried some Devil worship at a stone circle near their village. *These sites never have the full story.* Gabriel picked up the printout and went upstairs to pack.

A bloody tent? Has he seen the goddamn weather? If he doesn't find us a guesthouse then he can have the chuffing tent and I'll drive his car to somewhere with a proper bed. Anji had her head buried in her large mahogany wardrobe and was throwing various garments onto the bed, trying to decide which were most practical. Of course, it would have been easier if Gabriel had known a little about where they were going. She didn't mind really. If she was honest with herself, spur-of-the-moment mystery trips were more her style than they were Gabriel's; she just liked to be the one in control.

Anji stretched and pulled a large rucksack off the top of the wardrobe, standing on her tiptoes to get the necessary height. It slid off the top, bringing an avalanche of fluff and dust with it. She coughed as she wiped it clean with a duster from the dresser and unzipped it.

Gabriel's car pulled up outside Anji's house, mounting the drop curb to keep the narrow road passable. The rain had subsided and the air was now still and quiet. He got out and headed in the direction of Anji's front door, leaving his car unlocked. He lifted his hand to knock just as the door was opened from inside.

"Hiya, babe," Anji said, passing Gabriel two heavy rucksacks, causing his knees to bend involuntarily to take the unexpected strain.

"Bloody hell girl - what have you packed?"

"Just the essentials."

Chapter 3

What the hell was he supposed to do about disappearing sheep? Constable Lloyd Brighton took a deep gulp of tea from his thermos flask. He was half sitting, half leaning against a large grey rock in the middle of one of Alan Hatchcroft's sheep fields. It was a cold morning after the recent good weather, and Lloyd had buttoned his three quarter-length police coat up to his neck. The warmth of the tea was a welcome comfort in the cold mist of the morning air.

If it really was a person taking the old coot's sheep, then how was he supposed to trace it? They'd be too obvious selling one sheep a week at a cattle market, not to mention the lack of proper documentation. There was also the fact that a live sheep would be difficult to catch and a dead sheep would be messy to move. That wasn't making sense to Lloyd at all. He had promised to keep an eye out but Hatchcroft hadn't seemed too happy about that. What did he expect? A solemn vow to bring his mystery sheep thief to justice, then have him killed and his corpse mounted in a cage as a warning to other sheep thieves? Lloyd grinned at the thought. Despite living in a village all his life, he still found farmers to be 'whinging bastards' and too full of their own self-importance.

He was one of the few 'true' village police officers left in the country; most just brought police in from the nearest town these days. Lloyd didn't like that idea. A police constable should know his community; you can't get that by being drafted in from time to time. A village is a community in a far truer sense of the word than you'd find in a town. He considered that the local copper should be part of that community, not some bloke ordered in from some other place. The people he's working with should be his people, not some village folk that he's been sent to go and work with.

The room of the guesthouse was cold. It was a clean place but in dire need of redecorating; the wallpaper a floral pattern that looked like it had been popular with the over-sixties set in the early nineteen-eighties. The counterpanes on the twin beds were white with a spiral pattern in candlewick, covering pale blue blankets and white sheets. Gabriel awoke early, he got out of bed and quickly threw on some proper clothes to insulate him against the cold. Anji and he had arrived the previous evening and after a fair amount of driving in circles, had managed to find a place with a twin room for them both.

"Wake up you daft ginger, we've got work to do," Gabriel said, not even looking over to the other bed. Anji responded with nothing more than a protesting groan. She managed to force out a single syllable.

"Tea."

Gabriel left the room in search of a cup of tea that he decided he could use as much as Anji. They'd checked in the previous evening, and had been given free run of the kitchen for hot drinks and small snacks. The guest house was named Woodbury House, a small establishment with only four guest rooms run by a Mr and Mrs Bailey, a couple in their late fifties.

Gabriel found the kitchen, filled the kettle and switched it on before hunting for tea bags and sugar.

A few minutes later he arrived back at the room. Anji had gotten dressed and was laying on top of her bed. Gabriel walked over handed her a yellow mug, turning it so the handle faced her.

"Here you go, kidda." He occasionally picked up vocal traits from Elizabeth.

"Thanks, sugar." Anji took a long sip and sighed.

"So what's the plan?" She closed her eyes and cocked her head back, leaning it against the wall.

"We'll have breakfast, then start snooping. It's been a while since I had to get human reactions to something when it comes to writing."

"In fairness, Gabe, it's been a while since you did *anything* when it came to writing. At least as far as paid work goes." Anji flashed him a sarcastic grin.

"You have a point." Gabriel smiled back and opened a newspaper.

"Where'd you get that?"

"Off the coffee table in the lounge. It's a local rag, and it's yesterday's. Might give me some useful leads." Gabriel took out his notebook and pen, then stretched out on the bed with a smug look on his face.

"Don't know what you're looking so cocky about, you didn't even want to take this job two days ago."

Gabriel ignored her and started to read the paper, jotting down names.

A little while later Gabriel was sitting in the dining room, his coat on the back of the chair next to him and Anji sat opposite. Both of them were shovelling down a full English breakfast. They were alone in the room apart from the landlady nipping in and out. Mrs Bailey brought in two large mugs of tea and placed them on the table.

"So what brings you two to Stonebank then? As you can see we don't get many visitors."

Gabriel took a quick glance around the room. The dining room had the same antiquated look as the bedroom they'd woken up in. The question finally sunk in and he cursed himself for not having a ready prepared cover story. He glanced at Anji, who looked mildly startled. Her heart was speeding slightly. *Think fast, Gabe.* She thought whilst racking her own brain for a good reason.

Eventually, Gabriel said: "I'm a freelance writer. I'm doing an article on lesser-known tourist sites around Derbyshire. The county are trying to revitalise tourism to bring money into the smaller villages." *Feasible, and beneficial to her, good thinking.*

"Do you know any places of local interest?" he carried on. "You know - landmarks, churches, beauty spots. I'd even heard that some of these villages have ancient Druid sites and the like. In fact, I read something in yesterday's paper about a couple of kids being a bit daft at some devil worship or witchcraft site. Something like that, anyway."

Martha Bailey was unsure for a split second, then steadied her thoughts. "Yes, a couple of local school boys, not bad boys. I know their teacher, Mr Greens, he said basically what you said. They just got a bit daft. There's an old stone circle up in the woods, do you really think that tourists would be interested in it?"

"Definitely, as long as I can write about it in a way that grabs people's attention. Could you give me directions to it? Or better yet…" Gabriel paused and stretched over to his coat, pulling an Ordnance Survey map from the inside pocket. "Could you show me on my map?"

Martha hesitated for a moment.

"I can't see any harm in showing you." She gave Gabriel detailed directions showing him the best route to take using the map that he'd spread out on one of the vacant tables.

"Thank you, Mrs Bailey, you've been a great help."

Anji and Gabriel set out following the instructions that Martha had given them. It had got cold, very cold for the time of year. Their route was taking them down the village high street.

"I must say, Gabe, it was a good cover story you came up with. What made you think of it?"

"It wasn't hard. That place was deserted apart from us, they don't seem to be getting much custom, so not much money, and the one thing business people like is money. It made sense to come up with a cover story that would make her think that she might get some extra customers."

"But you do know that you're now going to Hell for lying to an old lady, right?" Anji gave him a playful elbow and they continued down the street.

"Okay, she said turn left after the war memorial, right?" Gabriel asked, reaching into his inside pocket for his map.

"Yeah, and if you get that map out I'm gonna hurt you." Anji had her 'cold' look.

"Don't you like my map?"

"It's the size of a small country, and takes about three million years to fold up properly. We're fine working on her directions for the moment. Look, there's the war memorial." The memorial was a parsimonious stone block with smooth faces. Mounted on the front was an elegant bronze plate with twenty-eight names engraved into it. Around the base were well-maintained flower beds and a small amount of grass.

As the duo approached it a crow flew overhead landing gracefully on the top.

"We head left here."

The directions led to a church yard, and from there along a footpath up a hill through a small forest. The sun was beginning to break through the clouds and with it, the day was warming. Anji shrugged off her coat and slung it over her shoulder as they climbed the last few metres of the hill, emerging from the forest and into a clearing with a stone circle. She listened to the sound of birds from the woods and enjoyed the breeze against her skin.

She turned and looked back. The path they had come up had wound round the side of the hill; the church and village could be seen below them. Anji switched her attention to the stones. They were not large; the biggest was at the centre and was only about a foot high. Peripheral to this were three consecutive circles, the first containing four stones, the second five and the third eight. The whole thing was about twenty feet in diameter. Gabriel pulled out his notebook and started writing a description of the circle. Anji walked over to examine the centre stone, the surface of which was covered in candle wax. Two colours, the first layer black, with a second layer of red on top of it.

Anji ambled around the other stones.

"These five stones in the second circle all have black wax on them as well. No chicken blood though. The rain must have washed it away." Anji turned to look at Gabriel, who had an expensive-looking digital camera pointed in her direction. "Why are you taking photos if you've already made notes?"

"Writing can cover things that photos can't, and vice versa. Also, the odd photo will be good for the article... might be better *sans* ginger though." Anji performed a comic bow and moved out of the shot. Gabriel circled round, taking shots from different angles, then one of each stone. Unusually meticulous for Gabriel, Anji thought in passing.

"It might turn out to be a nice day now the sun's come out," she commented, re-entering the circle and sitting herself squarely down on one of the inner stones. Gabriel walked over to join her.

"You might be right, we should have bought a picnic up here. Candle wax aside, it's not a bad spot." The friends sat looking down over the village. "I always enjoy looking back at where I've come from. Of course, it's a little more invigorating when you've walked a good distance. But the principle's the same."

"It's a nice looking village, not the type of place you'd expect to find Devil worship." She said the phrase 'Devil worship' in a comically deep voice then laughed. "What do you want to do next?"

Gabriel pondered for a moment, staring out over the vista of Stonebank.

"Well, let's make a start by sitting here and enjoying the view for a little while. Then we could head into the village. We should definitely talk to the local gossip in the pub."

Anji looked sceptical. "How do you know that there'll be a local gossip in there?"

"Because there's always a local gossip in a pub. He's normally the one most people try to avoid because he'll talk your ear off."

"Okay, then what?"

"I wouldn't mind talking to the Devil worship lads. But I can't see that being overly easy. Apart from the school, I wouldn't know where to find them, and I'm not about to start hanging round outside the school gates. With a bit of luck we might get a lead off the gossip. One of them might have a Saturday job or something, and we can collar him there."

As Gabriel spoke, a crow landed on one of the outer stones. The wind died down and the birds had suddenly fallen silent. There was the same eerie calm Gabriel had felt in the churchyard back in Hoggerbrook. Anji shivered, put her coat back on and edged slightly closer to Gabriel as if to absorb some of his body heat. They both started to look around the clearing; it was ghostly silent now, a complete absence of noise; the wind hadn't just calmed, it had vanished.

The crow suddenly let out a loud caw, piercing the silence. Suddenly it took flight, careering directly at them. Anji let out a scream and grasped Gabriel's arm. As the bird passed over the second circle of stones, its wings stopped flapping but its momentum carried it forward, thrusting it to the ground near the centre stone where it lay there motionless. In the same instance, the breeze came back and the birds could be heard again.

Anji still had hold of Gabriel's arm but had relaxed her grip. He walked over and gingerly prodded the bird with his foot. "Looks dead. Do birds have heart attacks?"

"Was it just me, or was that thing flying right at us?" Anji asked with a slight tremble in her voice. Gabriel was equally shaken but was doing a better job of hiding it.

"It was probably just taking off and would have flown over our heads. We are not in a Hitchcock film." He was trying to convince himself as much as Anji; the sceptic in him was already working hard to provide rational and feasible answers.

The pair headed back into the village. It was now approaching midday and the village centre was less deserted than it had been earlier. People were in and out of the few shops and post office as they went about their business. The sun was still beating down, but the village did not have the relaxed atmosphere Gabriel was used to. It felt oppressive somehow, like a shadow was looming over it.

"Okay, let's look for the pub," Gabriel said, angling his lips to blow on his own face in an attempt to cool himself off.

"Always thought you had a homing instinct for pubs."

"Nah, that's just beer."

After a small amount of searching they found a pub, The Red Gate Inn, a stone building with a thatched roof and small windows.

Above the door hung a swinging sign which was swaying back and forth slightly in the breeze. Gabriel opened the heavy wooden door and allowed Anji to enter first. He followed her in and took a quick glance around the room. The interior of the pub was not unlike the Hunter's Moon, but in slightly better repair; the walls were half wooden panels and half magnolia painted woodchip. Behind the bar were glass shelves and the customary array of inverted spirit bottles with optic measures attached to their necks. Gabriel also noticed the array of 'Real Ales' they had on tap. He watched as the man at the bar ordered a substantially strong brew. The establishment was reasonably full for the time of day; there was the man at the bar and also an assortment of locals in the seats.

As the strangers entered, nearly every head in the pub turned to look at them. It felt like a scene from an old western, when a cowboy walks into the local saloon, the piano player stops as everyone gives him a menacing stare. The moment passed and the patrons returned to their conversations. Anji walked to a seat as Gabriel headed for the bar. The barman was in his late fifties with dark grey hair and a sizable bald spot on the crown of his head. He was overweight in the extreme, his protruding stomach straining the buttons of his maroon shirt.

"What can I get you?" he asked as Gabriel approached the bar. His voice was sandy and gruff and he made little attempt to smile.

"A Guinness and a lager please, mate," Gabriel asked, pointing at the Guinness tap. *Don't think it's worth asking this one for information.* The barman took the money while he waited for the first half of the Guinness to settle. Anji sat at the table surveying the pub, trying to spot the 'local gossip'. The man to Gabriel's left looked a likely candidate to her. He had been standing alone and had glanced in Gabriel's direction at least five times. Gabriel came over and placed the drinks down the table. He pulled out a chair and sat across from her.

"Thanks, babe. I think I've spotted your gossip."

"Which one?"

"The one stood next to you," she said, discreetly pointing a finger in his direction. "He kept looking at you like he was looking for someone to talk to." Gabriel turned, swinging his gaze over the full length of the pub but only concentrating on the man at the bar.

"Okay, I've got an idea. Drink that quickly." He said nodding at Anji's glass. "We need a refill at the same time he does." Gabriel had a wicked smile on his face.

"You've got a plan. You've got that cocky look on your face."

"Oh yeah, this is gonna work."

Anji and Gabriel continued to drink and discuss where to go next with the research, all the time keeping an eye on the man at the bar. The incident with the crow was starting to feel like a distant memory as both of their minds started to rationalise what had happened, mentally filing under *freak occurrence*. The man at the bar swigged the last drop of his ale and motioned to the barman. Anji and Gabriel did the same, and Gabriel returned to the bar taking the empties with him and placing them down on the counter.

"I've never tried any of those real ales," Gabriel commented to the stranger at his side.

"Have you not? You should try one," the man said, pointing at the chalked price list on the small blackboard behind the bar.

"What would you recommend?" Gabriel asked, a fake portrayal of interest on his face.

"Black Castle is my favourite."

"I'll give it a try." Gabriel turned his attention to the barman. "A pint of lager and a pint of. . ." he glanced at the man for a second, ". . . Black Castle please." The barman dispensed the drinks and placed them on the bar as Gabriel handed over the money.

"My name's Len, by the way. Len Tait." He held out his hand.

"Gabriel Jones," Gabriel replied, shaking the man's hand. He took a sip of the ale in front of him. It tasted like yeast and Gabriel was starting to wish that he'd thought of a different icebreaker.

"What do you think?" Len asked, pointing at the pint glass. Gabriel paused for a moment and looked at the creamy head of the sickening brown liquid in front of him.

"It's not bad at all," he replied, hoping that Len hadn't noticed the wince that he had given when sipping the drink. Anji walked over and picked up her drink, then returned to the table. The small smile on her face paled in comparison to the cascade of laughter that she was internalising. She knew how much Gabriel disliked ale and she knew that he'd force himself to drink it if meant getting a lead. She sat back down, and continued to watch perversely as the two men talked.

After a while Gabriel turned his back to her. He placed his hand behind his back and started to beckon her. A beckon which said: '*Save me.*'

She let him stew for a few minutes longer and then went over. "Come on sugar, we'll be late for dinner," she said, linking his arm.

"Sorry Len, got to go, nice talking to you." The two men gave each other a farewell handshake.

Gabriel and Anji were taking a slow stroll around the village, looking for somewhere to eat.

"You can take that bloody smile off your face." Gabriel said, feeling slightly ill.

"I'm just happy, I can smile if I want." The smile turned into a wide grin.

"You're happy because I had to drink that vile pond water and then got talked at by the dullest man on earth."

"Many things make me happy. Now stop whingeing, and tell me what you found out." Gabriel glanced across the street at a little tea room. It was a small stone building with a large bay window and open door. A few white painted metal table and chair sets had been placed outside, shaded by a red and white retractable canopy.

"Let's get some food first, it might make me feel better."

The inside of the tea room was quaint; it was a small, dim room with the current price list written in chalk on a blackboard similar to the one in the pub. Gabriel glanced at it and was given an unwelcome reminder of what he had just had to drink. He took a deep breath, trying to fight off the sickening feeling in his stomach. The air smelt of spice and scones baking. Curiously, this did help to settle Gabriel's stomach and he was ready to put his constitution to the test and eat something. Anji ordered some ginger cake, cream scones and a pot of tea.

"I'll get these, Gabe, you paid in the pub," she said, handing over the money. "Come on, let's sit outside and get you some more fresh air."

The sickness was subsiding as Gabriel drained his cup dry and took a couple of nibbles of the ginger cake. Anji enthusiastically devoured one of the cream scones.

"So what did your new best friend tell you, then?" Anji asked, stretching her legs out.

"Quite a bit - I've got the names of the two lads, and know that one of them works part time in the local post office. I know what school they both go to, although it's probably the only one in the village. He also said that no one was really surprised by the whole thing because they're all so used to stories of black magic around here." Gabriel raised an eyebrow.

"Stories," Anji asked, mirroring his expression.

"Well for a start there's a ruined manor house a few miles from here. Apparently, a family used to live there who all died off somehow, he didn't know how. There was a fire that gutted most of the manor, but he didn't know what started it. And the family were rumoured to be linked to 'black magic or witchcraft or something', the big surprise was that he didn't know how. The man knew a lot of half-stories. But at least we've got plenty of things to look into now."

"Okay, I say that we make a start at the post office."

"Good idea," Gabriel said, standing up. "We passed it earlier, didn't we?"

"Yeah, I think it was that direction," Anji pointed down the high street.

The post office had a medium-sized waiting area with a long queue. Around the sides was a shelf with pens attached. Towards the back were two glass service windows, one manned by an elderly woman with grey hair and the other by a woman in her thirties. Gabriel caught the glimpse of a young lad of about fifteen taking a baseball cap out of a backpack and putting it on his head.

Looks like he's about to knock off. Good timing.

Gabriel motioned to Anji to follow him. They both left and waited outside. "I think he's just finishing work." Tom Jackson exited the post office. He was a thin kid with glasses and straggly black hair flattened by his baseball cap. "Tom?" The young lad turned as he heard Gabriel speak his name.

"How do you know my name?" he asked, looking a little anxious.

"Don't worry, it's nothing bad. I just want to pick your brains about this whole 'devil worship' thing."

Gabriel's lack of tact didn't make him any less anxious. Gabriel held up the palm of his hand and added as much calmness into his voice as he could muster.

"I know you're probably sick of talking about it, but I'm not with the police or anything and you can walk away any time you want, no hard feelings. However, if you give me twenty minutes of your time I'll give you twenty quid." Gabriel flashed him a quick grin which, along with the offer of money, seemed to put him at ease.

"My name's Gabriel, and this is Anji. I'm a writer."

Tom accompanied Anji and Gabriel back to the tea room. As they walked Gabriel chatted with Tom, explaining the articles to him. Anji went inside to get another pot of tea as Tom and Gabriel sat at one of the tables. Tom was starting to feel a lot more relaxed. He'd been feeling very foolish the past few days; fortunately the animal cruelty charges had been dropped once the police had found out that the chicken had already been dead when they decapitated it. At least this man didn't seem to be laughing at him, judging him, or talking down to him.

"What's the story then?" Gabriel asked. "Oh, and do you mind if I make notes?"

"Uh, sure," Tom replied, shifting his weight a little. Gabriel pulled out his notebook and mini-biro.

"It's silly really, I don't know why we did it. I don't think either of us ever really expected it to work. It was just a bit of a laugh. My mate Alex's mum keeps chickens on their farm." He paused and shifted slightly in his chair again. "Anyway, one of them died. A few days before that, Alex had been reading some stuff in the Library about some old family around here. There are all these legends and things about them being devil worshippers and how it got them their money and power and stuff." Tom was starting to feel embarrassed again. Gabriel could read it in his face.

"Yeah, probably got them their fair share of women as well," Gabriel laughed, trying to lighten the mood. "Tom, you don't have to feel embarrassed... I did far stupider stuff when I was your age. For that matter, I occasionally do stupider stuff now."

"I don't doubt that," Anji said, placing a chrome-plated tray on the table. The tray had a hot teapot, three cups and three generous slices of ginger cake. "Help yourself, gentleman," she said as she pulled up a chair of her own.

Tom was starting to feel a little less embarrassed. He took a small nibble out of the cake while Gabriel poured him a cup of tea.

"Anyway I interrupted you, please carry on."

"Well, we just thought that it'd be cool to have a go and see what happened. We found an internet site about devil worship that told you how to perform a ritual, what to say and all that stuff. So Alex got the dead chicken, and I nicked some candles from home that we used at Christmas." Something clicked in Gabriel's mind.

"What sort of candles?" He asked casually.

"Just normal ones, my mum used them in the centre piece thing at Christmas."

"Green ones or something?" Gabriel asked, probing further without overtly asking the question he wanted answering. Anji wondered why he was so interested in the candles.

"No, red ones." Tom felt a little confused, but Anji now knew what he was getting at.

"Anyway, we went up there one night, and had a go at the ritual. Alex cut off the chicken's head with his penknife - it's a good one - and we read the stuff that we'd got off the internet."

"How'd you get caught?"

"We got followed by a couple of lads that left school last year, they don't like us much. I could never work out why. They grassed us up to the police."

"A bit harsh," Gabriel commented. "How'd your parents take the news?"

"Not well, they used a lot of words like *ashamed*, *disappointed*, that sort of stuff. I'm grounded and I'm only allowed on the internet when they're in the room now."

"How about people round the village?"

"It's not been too bad. It's been more the look on people's faces and the fact that they've deliberately not mentioned it. You'd think in a village like this, it wouldn't be such a big deal."

"What do you mean?"

"Well, everyone always says that we had actual devil worship in the area, years ago like. Then there's Tabitha."

"Tabitha?"

"Yeah, she's a little bit like a witch I think. She runs a weird shop on Ford Lane." He gestured to a narrow street a few dozen feet down the road.

"Okay, thanks Tom. I think I've got everything I need." Gabriel fished a twenty pound note out of his wallet and passed it over the table to Tom. He took it without hesitation. Twenty pounds was a lot of money to him.

"Thanks." Tom stood up. "See you both later." With that, he turned and walked off down the street. Anji watched him walk away and didn't speak until she was sure that he was far enough away that he couldn't hear.

"Red candles," she said.

"Yeah, red candles." Gabriel gave a slight nod. They didn't need to clarify it to one another; they were both thinking the same thing. If the two school kids only had red candles, then someone else must have been up at the stone circle burning black ones.

"What next, then?"

"Want to go and have a look for this Tabitha person?"

"Sure."

The pair headed in the direction that Tom had gestured towards. The shop wasn't hard to find. It was a similar building to the tea room, but a little larger. An assortment of candles and small porcelain and wooded figurines could be seen through the bay window. The black wooden sign above the door had the word 'Tabitha's' painted ornately in gold.

A small brass bell rang above the door as Gabriel and Anji entered, the bare floorboards creaking under their weight. There was a pungent odour of joss sticks in the air which emanated from the two swirls of smoke rising from the shop's counter. Gabriel looked around the room at the assortment of scented candles, scarves, tarot cards, tie-dyed bags and other things that he considered to be oddities. *This is a hippie shop*, he thought. *This is Anji's territory.*

A figure appeared from the back of the shop, a woman in her late thirties with long, wavy blonde hair capped with a black and white stripy head scarf. She wore a cream and red flowery blouse with a long, red tasselled skirt.

"Good afternoon to you both. Can I help you or are you just browsing?" The woman had an overtly friendly voice.

Gabriel was about to hit her with the same cover story he'd used on Mrs Bailey that morning. However, for reasons he didn't even know, he decided that honesty was the best policy with this woman.

"We were wondering if we could ask you a few questions." Tabitha looked unsure. "My name's Gabriel, and this is my good friend Anji. I'm planning on doing some writing about occultism in rural areas. We were told that you might be able to give us some insight into local rumours or history."

The look of uncertainty morphed into one of concern. "You two better come round back and have a seat."

Gabriel and Anji followed Tabitha into the back room of the shop. "Can I get either of you a cup of tea?" They both accepted, and she poured them a cup of green tea each. Green tea was not what Gabriel had been hoping for. It didn't taste of much, but at least it was drinkable, unlike the ale he had forced down earlier. Tabitha motioned to a medium-sized wooden table where the three of them could sit. The room had a low ceiling with uneven walls covered in yellow paint. In one corner stood a small cooker with a whistle kettle on the hob; next to this was a work surface with a few mugs and an assortment of spice containers. There were shelves at one end of the room cluttered with an array of unusual objects including a crystal ball. On the walls hung a few pictures, and an excess of spiritual symbols from different cultures. *Still in Hippieville,* thought Gabriel as he took a sip of the tasteless greenish-brown liquid.

"Let me start by telling you what I know of present day 'occultism'. I'm afraid that I don't know much beyond my own experiences." She paused for a second, interlocked her fingers and placed her hands on the table in front of her. "There are people in this world who understand the power of nature and who can harness that power to some extent or another. In the past, this has gone by many names, but the most famous is witchcraft."

Gabriel managed not to smirk.

"Now, there is truth in the concept of black and white magic - light cannot exist without darkness and vice versa. This is a recognised concept in many cultures." Tabitha pointed at the 'Ying Yang' on the wall behind her, then relocked her fingers. "In the case of witchcraft, the difference between black and white is often more pronounced in terms of intent rather than actual practice. For example, the white magic user will ward against evil spirits and demons as a matter of course. Whereas a *black* magic user would use the same type of ritual to protect themselves against the evil spirit which they hope to summon and command."

Gabriel let out a small smirk that he hoped didn't look too obvious. Tabitha smiled and Gabriel suddenly felt incredibly rude. "Please don't feel bad. I am used to scepticism and have grown a very thick skin. One thing I would point out is that from 1541 until 1951 it was illegal to practice witchcraft in England. It's real enough for the law makers to believe in it. As far as modern day witchcraft goes, or Wicca as it has become, it is for the most part directed toward the white side. However, I would be incredibly surprised if there are no black sects or covens out there at all and that's only including actual Wiccans. There are non-Wiccans who partake in demonism."

"What about local history as far as witchcraft goes?" Gabriel was trying to look enthralled in an attempt to make up for his previous rudeness.

"This village is rife with it. With witchcraft that is. We had countless witch-burnings back in the sixteenth century around these parts. About one hundred years after that, the Devereaux family reportedly had some demonic link. It was said that they had made a pact with some demon for wealth and success; I don't know the story well but something went wrong and they all ended up dead. All that seems to remain of them is a shell of a manor house, and I'm telling you, that place is haunted to high heaven. Not a place I like to go myself and not a place I'd recommend anyone visits." Tabitha shrugged her shoulders.

"Do you know anything about the stone circle?" Anji interjected.

"Not a lot of its history, I'm afraid. It's predominantly an energy centre for white magic though. If I'm interpreting the stone layout properly, then the centre stone represents the centre of the village; either the geographical centre or the most senior town official. The three inner stones represent the village itself. The five in the middle circle represent the village border, with the final eight representing the outside world." Tabitha pointed the palms outwards as she finished her sentence. "There are old stories of another, darker, site underground somewhere, rumoured to have been used by the Devereaux family. I've never been able to find it though. That's about all I can tell you. Ethel Birchwood in the local library might know a little more about the Devereaux family - she's a bit of a history buff."

Gabriel took her hand and gave it a gentle shake. "Thank you very much, you've been a great help. I've got a lot to write about."

Tabitha placed her free hand on top of his and squeezed it. "It was a pleasure, and it was nice to meet both of you. Make sure that you look after yourselves and don't take the subject too lightly. If you want to talk again, you know where I am."

"Thanks, hope to see you soon." Gabriel started to head out of the shop. As Anji came over to say farewell, Tabitha grabbed her arm, leant in close to her ear and began to whisper. "Keep an eye on him. This can be a dangerous business for sceptics."

Anji looked her in the eye.

"I intend to. Thanks for your help, we'll probably be seeing you again." She gave Tabitha a genuinely warm smile and followed Gabriel out.

Gabriel had found a spot on a bench a short distance from the shop. It was next to a river that ran right over the road. Looking at it, Ford Lane's namesake suddenly became apparent. Anji joined him as he frantically made notes before he forgot any of the conversation that they'd had with Tabitha. She sat quietly until he finished.

"Okay, what next?"

"I think we've done enough work for one day - let's go for a walk and I'll make a start on the article this evening."

The pair took a circular walk around the countryside surrounding Stonebank, returning to the guest house in the early evening. Anji sat on her bed quietly reading a book, as Gabriel sat on his own bed with his laptop on his knee, planning out the start of his article. He occasionally referred back to his notepad.

He was fiddling with the drawing tool on the laptop in an attempt to make a mock-up of the stone layout at the circle.

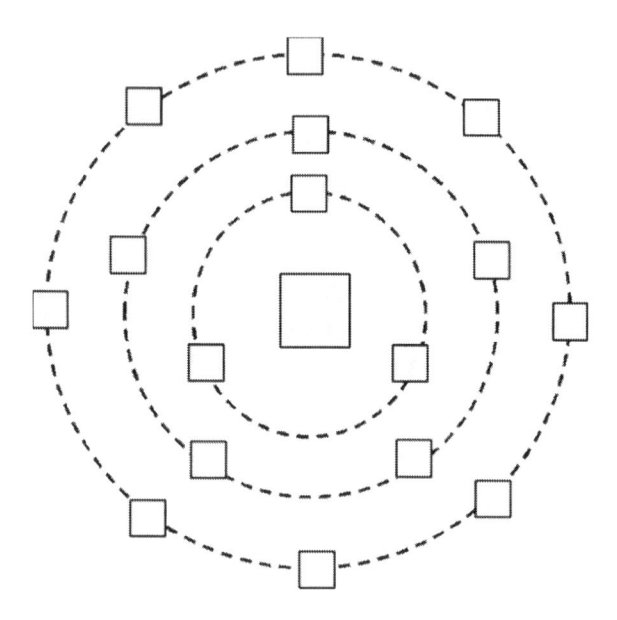

After a while he started to type properly, his fingers sliding over the keyboard with speed and precision. He paused for a second and pondered where he could go next with the article.

"Anji," Gabriel said to get his companion's attention. Anji turned her head from her book and looked at him.

"Yeah, babes."

"Feel like coming back next weekend as well? I'm getting a few ideas and I reckon that there are a few leads here that I could follow up when I start writing about the historical aspects."

Anji thought for a second. "We've got sod all work on in the garage at the moment, and they do owe me some time off. How about we stay on a few days?"

"Cool." Gabriel smiled.

"Tomorrow we're finding somewhere else to stay though."

Alan Hatchcroft had had enough. He was going to find out who it was. He wasn't about to have any more sheep stolen, not off his land. As far as he could work out from his headcount, they were getting taken on Sunday nights.

He zipped up his wax jacket and inserted a key into the heavy lock of his gun cabinet. The shotgun was heavy in his hands as he walked over to the secured drawer where he kept the ammunition. He opened the drawer and took a few handfuls of twelve gauge shells, stuffing them into the multiple pockets of his coat. He wasn't intending to shoot anyone, but was seriously thinking of firing a few shots off to scare them. In any event, he wanted to be prepared in case he was biting off more than he could chew.

He gave his wife Margret a kiss on the cheek and headed off into the night.

The moon cast a pale white glow over the stone circle. Gabriel could see the extinguished candles on the centre stone. The dead crow on the ground began to move; it grudgingly stood, then let out a loud shriek and flew over to a dark shape lying on the grass. Gabriel looked at the black bird and the shape with a curious feeling of uneasiness before he started to approach them, anxiety building up in the pit of his stomach. He knew that he didn't want to see what the shape was, but was slowly walking there regardless, watching the oily-looking crow as it pecked at the shape. As he got closer he could see the grass was stained with a black liquid, a liquid which was reflecting the glint of the moonlight. He moved closer still, and realised that the black liquid was only black in the moonlight.

Gabriel picked up the torch he found at his feet and cast its beam over the shape. The cursed bird continued to peck. The liquid shone deep crimson in the torchlight... *blood*.

He wanted to run but he had no control over his body. His hand moved the beam of the torch further up the body that he could now see was a woman. The crow stood, still pecking. Pecking where her face was. Gabriel couldn't breathe, couldn't move apart from the involuntary motion of his right hand shining the torch. The anxiety had long since given way to fear, and the fear was now surrendering to terror.

The red hair of the body's head was now glistening in the light as the spot moved over her face. Gabriel looked on in horror at Anji's face; he could see the blood streaming down her cheeks from the bottomless pits of her empty eye sockets as the crow continued to pull the flesh from the bone of her ocular cavities.

Gabriel woke up with a jolt, the sweat covering his body. He had never had nightmare that bad, not even close. He had never been so disturbed in his entire life. He took a deep breath and tried to mentally steady himself. It was no use; his heart was beating like a pneumatic drill, the image of his dead friend still waited behind his eyelids when he closed them. He wanted to look over to the other bed. He wanted the reassurance of seeing Anji there alive and well. Except the vivacity of the dream was too strong - he half expected to see a corpse if he looked over.

Gabriel sat cross-legged on the bed. He started to meditate, counting his breaths until his heartbeat began to slow and the rational part of his brain steadily re-engaged. He was finally able to look over at Anji's bed; his own breathing had slowed enough that he could now hear the slumbered respiration of his companion.

He quietly tiptoed over to her bed and looked at her face. A red curl spiralled down her right check and she had a slight smile on her lips as she slept. Gabriel returned to his bed, feeling reassured but still shaken.

He did not sleep any more that night.

Anji awoke a little after dawn, the light spilling through the inadequate curtains providing a dull, defused light. The door glided silently open and Gabriel walked in with a mug of tea in each hand. She gave an appreciative groan as he handed her one of the mugs. Gabriel stretched out on top of his own bed.

After a few moments Anji spoke.

"What's the plan then, babe?"

"Well, what do you reckon?" he asked before taking a drink.

"Stop being bloody indecisive," she said with a fake frown.

"How about we go take a look at that old manor house?"

Anji looked reluctant.

"What's wrong?"

"Tabitha said it was haunted," she said tightening her grip on her mug.

"Anj, my little ray of sunshine." There was a deliberately comic smack of condescension in his voice. "Ghosts don't actually exist."

"Says you."

"Says me and the second law of thermodynamics. Now don't be daft."

The Manor house was just a shell. The roof and first floor had long since collapsed and the sun streamed through the frameless holes once been occupied by windows. The gardens, however, had been kept in good repair; they were only a shadow of their former majesty but they were well looked after. English Heritage owned the premises and had made the building safe and kept the grass cut short and the hedges trimmed.

Gabriel's car pulled into a lay-by, a short distance from the start of the footpath they needed to find. They both got out and swung the car doors shut. Anji walked to the edge of the road and glanced up and down it as Gabriel retrieved a backpack from his car boot.

"There's the footpath sign." She pointed at a blue sign which directed people across a field.

"Cool, let's go." The pair scrambled over the stile and into a field of cows. The slightly shorter grass showed the path that arched across the field and ended at another stile in the far corner leading into a woodland path. The pair chatted as they crossed the field, stepping around the flat brown spots left by the cows. They reached the far corner and Gabriel hopped over the stile first, then took Anji's hand as she climbed over. It wasn't that she needed the help, or even that Gabriel thought she did. It was more that he had had this behaviour drilled into him as a child and Aunty Gladys' lessons died hard.

The woods were alive with the noise of wildlife. The leaves and branches of the trees made an unyielding rustle as they swayed in the gentle breeze. The brown dirt path that lay in front of them was marbled with the sunlight that penetrated the canopy of leaves above them. Patches of light shifted, morphing in time with the motion of the trees.

"You aren't really scared of ghosts are you?" Gabriel asked as he walked at Anji's side. She looked at him and took a moment to answer.

"I wouldn't say scared, exactly." She took another moment. "I'd just rather not tread where the dead walk." The way she phrased it struck a chord in Gabriel; it was a fairly poetic way of speaking, even for Anji.

"It'll just be an old ruin, might make some good photos though. I could really do with some background on this Devereaux family."

"We should check out the local library tomorrow. Tabitha gave us a name to follow up. Ethel something?" Anji screwed her face up slightly.

"Yeah, Ethel Birchwood, or Brightwood, something like that. I've got it in my notebook."

"Look at those!" Anji pointed at two large gateposts. Each was about three metres high and had fallen into disrepair. The left post had a well-established ivy plant growing up it. As Gabriel passed between the two posts, he was overcome with a strange feeling. The hairs on his arms and the back of his neck stood to attention as a coldness passed over his body. His senses felt heightened by the smallest amount. The sounds of the forest that had previously been a choir were now individually audible in their own right. Gabriel felt as if his brain was working that little bit harder to process everything he could see and hear. Along with this feeling came an incredibly uneasy sensation from the top of his stomach. Not exactly unpleasant, but not exactly comfortable either, it made him feel like there was someone or something watching him. He'd never felt it before. He'd heard people talk about feeling presences but this was the first time he'd ever come close to it himself, he'd just written it off as 'all in their minds'. The feeling had been a rush, but it was starting to subside. It was still there, but it felt like his body was compensating.

"Creepy," Gabriel muttered under his breath.

"Yeah, there's a dodgy atmosphere around here," Anji agreed, glancing from left to right, looking into the tangle of trees that flanked them on both sides.

The pair emerged from the woodland and into the grounds of the manor house. Gabriel inhaled as he saw the sun reflecting off the pale grey stone of the building's front. Despite being just a shell it still stood proud, as if in defiance of the trials of time and weather.

The warm sun was helping Gabriel to push the uneasy feeling to the back of his mind. It was still there, but had become a lot less potent. Anji stopped walking.

"That'll make a good photo, Gabe."

He looked at the front of the manor house where Anji was pointing.

"You've got a point there, sweetheart." Gabriel swung his backpack off his shoulder and searched inside for his camera. He crouched to get the right angle and took a couple of pictures. Anji took the camera off him and insisted on taking a few snaps herself.

"Come on Gabe, let's get one of us both in front of the house." The redhead set the timer running and placed the camera on an old stone fountain before grabbing Gabriel's arm and pulling him into the shot.

"Say cheese," she said with a giggle as she put her arm around his shoulder. The timer expired, taking a photo of Anji smiling and Gabriel looking unimpressed.

After Anji had done playing paparazzi, the two friends approached the manor house. As they got closer to the building the uncomfortable feeling started to return. It was still mild, but was definitely back with a vengeance. They walked into the shell of the building and through the old rooms taking photos as they went. Most of the rooms had plaques covered in text describing what the room had been used for in its heyday; some of them even had old photos. The uneasy feeling wasn't going anywhere; the cooing of the pigeons that nested in the alcoves echoed throughout the roofless rooms.

"Let's take a walk around the outside," Gabriel suggested, giving Anji's upper arm a quick squeeze as he darted through an empty doorway.

Gabriel and Anji walked the perimeter of the house. They turned at the first corner, taking them into the shade of the northern wall of the building. As they strolled down the edge of the wall, they came across the old goods entrance for the cellar. The stone steps led down to a dark opening that had been barred shut, presumably by English Heritage. Gabriel slowly walked down the steps. As he approached the rusty iron bars, the uneasy feeling erupted in his stomach. Every hair follicle on his body electrified as the cold feeling passed over him again. He took another step forward, peering through the bars into the impenetrable blackness that lay beyond. His heart began to quicken now. Gabriel took another step forward; the uneasy feeling was begging to give way to something that felt a hell of a lot like fear.

Pull yourself together Jones. It's an old wine cellar.

The rational, sceptical side of his brain was fighting a losing battle against his emotions. *Sod it.* He turned and quickly ascended the steps; the feeling subsided as he did so. "Let's head back and get something to eat in the pub," Gabriel said trying to keep a brave face.

"Okay, babe," Anji said, linking his arm. She could see that he was affected by the atmosphere of the manor. She could feel it as well; Anji had always been able to feel presences, or at least believed she could. She wasn't sure if Gabriel could feel it more strongly, or if it was just the shock because he'd never felt one before. *Tabitha was right, this place is haunted to high heaven,* she thought as they both headed towards the footpath.

The visit had pretty much been a waste of time apart from the photographs. The information boards had given little insight. There was a large wooden shed that was being used as a visitors' centre, but it didn't open on Sundays. Gabriel wasn't too bothered about that though. He wanted to get away from the place.

The twin gate posts came back into sight. Gabriel regarded the ivy-strewn one and noticed a reasonably large black coloured bird had landed atop it.

"A crow," Anji said, mildly reluctant to continue.

"Ah, the other one was a just a freak occurrence." Gabriel looked at the crow, and for a split second the image from his dream penetrated the conscious world. "Let's get rid of the bugger." He disentangled his arm form Anji's and walked quickly towards the bird, waving his arms and shouting 'bugger off' in a firm tone. The bird took flight and vanished into the woodland.

"My hero," Anji said in her sweetest sarcastic tone, and re-linked his arm. As Gabriel passed back across the threshold of the gateposts, the remainder of the uneasy feeling departed his mind and body.

Chapter 4

A dead body. It wasn't every day that Constable Lloyd Brighton got called out for a corpse. The call had come in that morning; a woman walking her dog had stumbled across the body of an elderly man grasping a shotgun.

As the local police constable, Lloyd had been first on the scene, but dead bodies were not his responsibility. He'd cordoned off the area, called the county police, and then kept an eye on things while he'd waited for them to arrive. The body was about fifty metres off a forest path in dense trees; it was sheer luck that it had been found so soon after death. Lloyd knew that the man hadn't been dead long because he'd spoken to him less than twenty-four hours previous.

The body was that of Alan Hatchcroft. He lay slumped beside a tree, his twelve gauge shotgun still in his hand, with two empty cartridges half a dozen feet away and his bottle of heart pills laying on the dry leaves near his feet. Lloyd leant on a tree and looked around the scene. It wasn't technically a crime scene yet, and it was completely feasible that Alan had been out hunting rabbits and had just succumbed to a heart attack. However, Lloyd's gut was saying that this wasn't the case.

The coroner was hovering over the body doing God knows what. His assistants darted about the area collecting various samples in small plastic bags and taking photos. Two men in suits stood in consultation and occasionally glanced at the coroner. Lloyd knew one of them by reputation, Detective Chief Inspector Donovan Brigham. DCIs normally only headed up major investigations; if a DCI was involved, then foul play must be suspected.

Brigham's reputation was a mixed bag. Lloyd had heard that he was good at his job, and he'd also heard that he was an arrogant and condescending arsehole. Lloyd figured that he'd reserve judgment. The Inspector's underling strolled over and addressed Lloyd in a dismissive tone.

"Okay mate, you can go."

The man was of a medium build with olive skin, brown eyes and a cropped brown hair. His jaw constantly moved, chewing on a stick of gum. *Sounds like arsehole is right,* Lloyd thought as he glanced the plain clothed officer up and down. Lloyd smiled. The man in front of him did technically outrank him, but was not directly in his chain of command.

"That's nice. Mind telling me who the hell you are?" Lloyd kept a neutral look on his face and a nondescript tone in his voice. However, there was a small amount of anger growing in the pit of his stomach.

"Sergeant Garry Dudley. CID."

Lloyd found it comical the way these people added CID to their names, as if baring their teeth would make everyone just fall in line.

"So I can take it that you wouldn't like any background on the area, the local populous, or the poor bastard who's lying dead over there?" He maintained his nondescript tone, despite being annoyed to the very fibre of his being. DCI Brigham was now striding swiftly towards the two men.

"Is there a problem, Sergeant?" Lloyd answered for him, but with another question.

"DCI Brigham?"

"Yes." Brigham gave a slight frown. The coroner looked up, not bothering to hide the fact that he was eavesdropping.

"Your subordinate informs me that I may go. Would you not like any information that I have before I leave?"

"We can handle it from here, thank you, Constable." Brigham's voice was polite but firm, almost aggressive. He was used to bullying people into staying out of his way. He was a commanding man of six feet four with a muscular build that he knew how to put into a subtly aggressive stance. He had short, almost black hair with a greyish-white fleck in his sideburns.

"Let me ask you two questions."

Brigham looked unsure. "Okay."

"Your team has been here for about two hours? Correct?"

"Yes."

"What's that bloke's name?" Lloyd pointed in the general direction of the coroner and a couple of the other police officers.

"The coroner?" Brigham raised an eyebrow.

"No, the less animated man over there. The poor dead bugger. Do you know his name yet?"

"No, constable." He replied rolling his eyes.

"You will soon, because you'll positively match the pill bottle to the body. A little after that, you will track down the doctor who prescribed the medication and he will tell you where the man lives and who his next of kin is. On the other hand, you could have just politely asked me. I could have told you that his name is Alan Hatchcroft, he's a local farmer who lives in the farm house about a quarter of a mile in that direction." Lloyd pointed to the south. "Also, that his next of kin is his wife, Margaret Hatchcroft." Lloyd paused, trying to calm himself slightly. "I understand that you have a job to do, but these are my people. I know them. If you want my help it's offered, if not, then that's your choice."

Lloyd turned and walked off in the direction of his car. He'd been off duty for the past fifteen minutes anyway. The dry leaves beneath his feet crunched in quick succession in time with his swift, heavy footsteps. He was annoyed, very annoyed. Surely to God, Brigham's sole goal should be to solve the case, assuming that there was one. This posturing served no one. Lloyd arrived back at his car. He wanted a drink; he planned to drive his car home then head down the pub.

Lloyd had calmed down a little. He was still annoyed, but the drive, followed by a swift walk, had exorcised a few of the demons. He swung open the door and walked into the Red Gate Inn, still dressed in his police uniform despite being off duty.

He glanced around the room to see who was in. The regulars were there; Len was at the bar having a chat to Neil, the landlord. Lloyd looked at two strangers sat at one of the tables. A man and woman in their mid to late twenties. The man was about six foot and of slight build. He had messy, blondish-brown hair, and was dressed in a t-shirt and jeans with a back pack on the seat at his side. The woman was about five foot six and quite slender. She was attractive, with red curly hair that dominated her looks. Lloyd pulled up a bar stool as far away from Len as possible and ordered a bitter.

"You look a little annoyed, lad," Neil commented to Lloyd. The stranger sat at one of the tables couldn't help but notice the barman's complete divergence in vocal mannerisms to which he'd been subjected the previous day.

"I'm bloody annoyed, Neil. Got a new case, can't talk about it yet, but we've got a bigwig DCI in. He's being a complete arsehole."

Neil put a cold pint of bitter in front of Lloyd.

"Cheer up lad, there's only one copper in this village as far as we're all concerned, and he's sitting in front of me right now." Neil's thick Yorkshire accent was now in full swing.

Lloyd noticed as one of the strangers left his seat and headed towards the bar. He pulled up a stool next to him, perching on the top while he waited to be served. Neil came over and reinstated his gruff tone.

"What can I get you?"

"Same again, please." The stranger gave Lloyd a glance.

"How's it going?" Lloyd asked in a reserved tone.

"Not bad, thanks. Been over to the old manor house this morning."

"How did you find it?"

"Bloody creepy, if I'm honest." The man gave a half smile.

"Yeah, it does have an atmosphere, doesn't it? What brings you to Stonebank?"

Lloyd took a sip of his pint. "I'm doing a bit of freelance journalist work. Writing an article about lesser-known tourist locations around Derbyshire."

Neil placed the two drinks on the bar and took the money for them.

"Well, it's a beautiful spot. How long you planning on being around for?"

"Actually my friend and I. . ." he pointed over at the redhead, ". . . are looking for somewhere else to stay. We're at Woodberry House at the moment. Could you recommend anywhere else?"

"Neil over there rents out a small house on the outskirts of the village. It's usually used by people who come here fishing - I think it's empty at the moment though."

Lloyd turned his attention to Neil.

"Neil!" He called across the bar. "Is that house of yours free at the moment?"

Donovan Brigham took one last look over the scene. Had the man just died of a heart attack? If so, why were there two empty shotgun shells on the ground and another in the gun? He was feeling a twinge of remorse over the way he'd spoken to the uniformed officer earlier; however, he felt justified. Donovan had been doing his job a long time, and in his experience, local law enforcement just tended to gum up the works. He knew he'd developed a bad reputation for being short with people and dismissive of local police.

He'd learnt the hard way in his first year as a DCI. Donovan had been heading up a murder investigation, his third case in his new role. It involved a real psycho who had already murdered two people. Brigham had tried to work with the local police as best he could; he was desperate that they should not only feel, but actually *be* involved in the investigation. It had worked in the past. That time, however, it was a case of 'too many cooks'. Too much second guessing caused needless delays - in the meantime, the murderer had struck again. This time his victim had been an eight year old girl.

Donovan changed after that. He'd never be responsible for another death if he could help it. If a few people got their pride hurt, then too bad. He had a job to do.

The coroner walked over as his team finished loading the sealed body into the back of their ambulance. He was a short and slight man in his early forties, with a full head of short grey hair and dark eyes.

"Okay, detective, I'll start the autopsy first thing in the morning. I can't confirm cause of death yet but I'm thinking heart attack is most likely at the moment. If I'm right we can all go home."

"You'll let me know the results as soon as you get them?" Donovan's voice was firm but polite. He'd worked with this coroner many times before. He trusted and respected his professionalism.

"Of course. Have a good evening, Inspector." Donovan silently nodded. The coroner returned to his car, slipped out of his protective overalls and stashed them in a sealable biohazard box that he kept in his boot. He slid behind the wheel and drove off.

A short while later he arrived at the Red Gate Inn. In his job, he had to play 'hunches' in the same way that the police had to. This time he was playing the hunch that he would find his friend in the pub. The coroner swung open the door, walked in, and immediately spotted his old friend at the bar.

"Thought I'd find you in here," he said as he walked towards Lloyd Brighton. Lloyd turned to acknowledge the familiar voice and gave a weak smile.

"How's it going, Tom?"

"Not bad, Brighton. Yourself?"

Thomas Agar had known Lloyd for a long time. He had grown up in Stonebank, but had left when he went to university. Lloyd was an old friend of his and right now, Tom knew he was pissed off.

"Bloody pissed off."

"I thought you might be. Let me buy you a drink." Tom gestured to Neil, who chalked up two more pints on his tab.

"Cheers."

"I'm guessing that you'll still be keeping an eye on this case on the sly," Tom remarked with a knowing look.

"You'd be guessing right." Lloyd returned the look.

"I'll keep you informed, though I still think it's a good chance that it's just a heart attack."

"What does your gut tell you?" Tom paused for a moment before replying.

"It tells me that there's more to it than that."

"So does mine." Tom turned his head as the two strangers walked past.

"Thanks again, mate," the man said as he passed Lloyd.

"What was that about?" Tom enquired with a genuine look of curiosity.

"Him?" Lloyd nodded in the stranger's direction as he left through the door. "He's writing some articles about tourism or something. He was looking for a place to stay. Neil sorted him out."

Anji gave the electronic window button a quick push and was rewarded with a sharp flow of air. Gabriel was driving and doing his best to follow the direction that Neil the landlord had given him.

"It was lucky, you running into that cop."

"Let's see what the place is like first," Gabriel replied, checking left and right before pulling out of a junction. "Then we'll decide if it was lucky or not."

"It's got to be better than where we're staying now."

"True. It should be around this next bend as well, I think."

Gabriel's car glided around the corner and the house came into full view. It was in a mild state of disrepair. The garden was a quite overgrown, and paint was peeling from the wooden sills of the single-glazed windows. The pebbledash had crumbled away in places, and weeds were growing through the cracks in the driveway where Gabriel parked his car.

The pair walked to the front door. Gabriel rummaged around in his pocket for the key; the key that Neil had given him in exchange for week's rent upfront. The lock was old but reluctantly turned.

The inside had an odour of must about it. Anji looked around the hallway, then moved on to the lounge and kitchen, her gaze skimming every surface. Despite the smell, the house was clean. Gabriel wondered through the house, opening windows as he went. Anji looked at the cooker; it was old but still serviceable.

"This isn't too bad." She called upstairs.

"Might have to nip back home at some point though, and pick up some extra clothes."

The two settled in. Gabriel made a quick run to a local shop for a few basic supplies and some beer, then spent a little more time working on the articles, occasionally passing the laptop over to Anji for proof reading. The pair worked and chatted into the evening.

The manor house stood tall, the moonlight bouncing off the pale grey stone and reflecting in the glass of its windows. The night air was warm and still. Gabriel breathed slowly as he walked through the immaculately kept gardens, strolling in the direction of the house. He looked up at the imposing building. *So that's what it looked like in its heyday,* he thought, continuing towards it.

"Gabriel." A singsong voice came from the open door to cellar. Gabriel walked down the steps.

"Anji, is that you? What are you doing down there?" Gabriel looked around but couldn't see her. He felt two warm arms gently wrap around his waist from behind and the feel of soft curly hair against his cheek. Anji's scent filled the air as she whispered softly in Gabriel's ear.

"I don't like it outside. I'd rather not tread where the dead walk."

The words echoed through his mind. She kissed his ear, then slowly kissed her way down to his neck. Every repressed romantic and sexual feeling Gabriel had for her broke free. He instinctively turned around and kissed her full lips, then moved to her neck, her ear and then back to her lips, running his fingers through her hair. Anji broke the kiss and held Gabriel close to her, resting her head on his shoulder.

"That was nice," she murmured. Gabriel's heart skipped a beat. Her voice sounded odd, distorted, almost mechanical. The scent in the air had gone and been replaced with a putrid musk.

She pulled away, and held his face directly in front of hers. A feeling of panic overwhelmed him as he once again stood staring at the blood running from the blackness of her empty eye sockets.

Gabriel sat upright in bed as he woke with a jolt.

Not again.

He exhaled deeply and tried to regain his grip on reality. He was unsteadied for two reasons. The first, that he'd just seen one of his closest friends without eyes. The second, he'd just been passionately kissing her in his mind. Gabriel exhaled again.

"You'd have thought that I'd cottoned on that it was a dream by the fact that the bloody manor wasn't a ruin," he said to himself, while trying to force a smile. Gabriel pulled the covers over himself and closed his eyes. The image was still there.

Looks like another sleepless night, Gabe.

The morning sun was warm. Gabriel had been to the local shop to get breakfast supplies that he'd failed to get the day before. He pulled onto the driveway and went inside just as Anji was walking downstairs in her pyjamas.

"Morning," he said abruptly, and headed for the kitchen without looking directly at her. Anji noticed the shortness of his words.

"You okay, babe?" she asked, cocking her head on one side slightly. Gabriel felt a little awkward. His dream had made him wonder if he actually had feelings for her; it wasn't the first time he'd thought about it and couldn't deny that she was an attractive woman.

He shook the feeling off and smiled.

"Sorry, just had a bad dream last night. Didn't get much sleep. Got us some supplies though." Gabriel held up his shopping bags. "I say we have breakfast and then decide what to do for the rest of the day."

Lloyd Brighton was enjoying the start of his day off work. He sat in the morning sun, eating a breakfast of bacon and scrambled eggs from his dark green plastic patio table. He swallowed a mouth full of egg and washed it down with a swig of strong coffee.

Lloyd's mobile phone rang. He checked the caller, then pressed the 'pick up' button.

"Hello Tom, how's it going?"

"Not bad Brighto'. I've got the preliminary finding and autopsy results back. Some odd stuff."

"Really."

"Yeah, I've got a briefing with DCI Brigham in a few minutes - if you want to nip over I'll fill you in after."

"See you in about an hour." Lloyd hung up the phone, left his breakfast on the table and headed inside to put some smarter clothes on.

Tom Agar tapped his fist against the office door of DCI Donovan Brigham.

"Come in," said the muffled voice beyond. Tom opened the door and walked in.

Donovan's office was a well-ordered room. Paperwork was kept filed away, there were few personal affects in view and his desk had a strange neatness to it. "Mr Agar, please have a seat." Donovan gestured to the chair on the far side of his desk. Tom sat down and looked at Donovan.

"What have you found?"

Lloyd's police car pulled into a vacant parking spot in the underground car park of the Derbyshire county police station. Lloyd got out and swiftly walked across the poorly lit concrete tomb, bypassing the elevator and heading directly towards the stairwell. Down. He was heading even further underground; he was heading to autopsy.

The corridor was painted in magnolia with a brown stripe along the centre. Lloyd could tell that he was underground. It was a feeling, nothing that he could explain in words, just a feeling at the back of his head. He opened a door and slipped inside one of the rooms.

The room was square with the same magnolia coloured walls as the corridor. There were metal cabinets mounted on the walls and a stainless-steel sink in one corner. At the far wall was a desk with a man sat at it. The man turned as Lloyd entered.

"Good morning, Brighto'."

"Morning Tom. How was your briefing?"

"Brief." Tom laughed. "Want to see the body?"

Lloyd paused for a second. "Okay. Is he over in the morgue?"

"No, still in autopsy." Tom gestured to the double doors at one side of the room. Lloyd wasn't usually the squeamish type. He had been around a few corpses in his time, but somehow a corpse that had had an autopsy performed on it was different. The fact that he'd known Alan didn't make it any easier.

"Come on, I'll show you." Lloyd followed Tom into the autopsy lab.

The threshold of the double doors seemed to lead to a whole different world. A world with blue and white tiles checkering the floor, and countless tiny white tiles on the walls. Illumination was provided by harsh florescent strip lights on the ceiling, and more powerful spot lights above the autopsy tables. The room smelt of antiseptic and had a heavy atmosphere. Tom also seemed to change as he entered the world. This was his domain; he was well regarded as one of the best pathologists in the country. If there was something to find, then he would find it. He was a wizard of the dead. He was a Necromancer.

The door to the large metal storage unit clucked as Tom opened it. The slab that he pulled out made a deep rumbling sound, yet appeared to glide effortlessly into view. The corpse was yet to be put back into a body bag and lay motionless on the metallic slab. Its skin was a greyish-blue colour, with the stitched-up edges of a 'Y' shaped incision on its chest sill bearing the slightest memory of pink.

Tom spoke. "Official cause of death was cardiac arrest. However, what induced the cardiac arrest is another matter." Lloyd was beginning to rationalise his feelings and the professional detachment was regaining its hold on his mind.

"How so?"

"All other crime scene evidence suggests that he was being chased." Tom held a magnifying glass over the body's left hand. "See these lesions on his hand?" Lloyd looked at several small grazes. Tom moved the magnifying glass to the corpse's other hand to show similar damage, then held it over its right cheek.

"As you can see, he has the same on his face." Tom looked at Lloyd. "We've analysed the residue around the cuts and found traces of sap and bark fragments in them. These were almost certainly caused as he was running through the forest. Take a look at these photos."

Tom led Lloyd to a table at the side of the room. Lloyd was happy to put a little distance between himself and the body and looked at the photos. They were of indentations in the ground at the crime scene; they were photos of footprints.

"Lucky we had the rain the other day, it softened the ground up. Judging by the size of his shoes, the weight of the man and the depth of the indentation, this man was running when he made this print."

Lloyd was beginning in to look impressed.

"Any prints from the assailant?" he asked, without looking up from the photographs. Tom didn't answer for a moment and when he did, his voice was devoid of its normal confidence.

"This is the bit you're not going to like." Lloyd's expression changed from impressed to one of mild confusion.

"There is no second set of prints apart from the ones that belong to the woman who found him and the ones from the officers at the scene. And if you don't like that, you're going to like this even less. As you saw, we found two empty shotgun shells at the scene."

"Yeah, I remember." He furrowed his brow.

"We also found one empty shell in the gun, along with one full one."

"So, Alan was defiantly shooting at something."

"Oh yes, and I have no explanation for what I'm about to tell you now." Tom took a deep breath. "We went over the area with a fine-toothed comb. Our team recovered all the shot, thirty-six balls of it. Twenty-four near the first two shells, and another twelve near the body."

"You're saying that the shot just bounced off whoever it hit?" said Lloyd, an incredulous look on his face.

"There's no other explanation."

"A bulletproof vest isn't too likely around there," Lloyd commented as a half-joke.

"No. Also, bulletproof vests are designed to slow and stop a projectile by absorbing its momentum in the same way that a sandbag does. At this range, most of the shot would have been lodged in the armour. Even stranger is the fact that the shot was concentrated in a relatively small area. If it had bounced off something then it would have been spread out. It's as if it just stopped dead, and dropped to the floor." Tom held his hands out at his side. "I'm stumped."

"How did Brigham take that news?"

"Surprisingly well, almost as if he was half expecting it." Tom was frowning. "Anyway, I suppose it's his headache now. I'll keep you posted."

"Thanks, Tom."

Gabriel and Anji sat in the living room of the rented house. Anji was reading while Gabriel looked through the photos that he'd taken of the stone circle.

"Anj."

"Yeah," she replied, only half listening to him while still engrossed in her book.

"Did you notice the lines of dead grass when we were up there?"

"Yeah."

Gabriel looked at her and wondered if she was paying any attention to him at all.

"The lines are made from tuna fish. I think the badger that lives in your hair might have put them there."

"Okay, babe."

Gabriel regarded her for a second. "Would you like a cup of tea?"

"Yes please, babe, my cup's down there."

"You heard that alright, then," Gabriel said slightly louder, with a smile on his face.

"Sorry sweetheart, I was miles away," she said, looking at him this time. Gabriel fumbled around the back of the laptop and pulled out the power cable. He passed the machine over to Anji.

"Look at those lines of dead grass. Did you notice them when we were up there?"

Anji squinted and thought back. "I think I might have. They never really registered though."

Gabriel took the laptop back and started to scroll through the images.

"It only seems to be the stones in the second ring. They all seem to have four lines of dead grass coming out of them. Give me a second." Gabriel opened the article that he'd started the day before and found the part where he'd drawn a plan of the stone circle. He selected the drawing tool, and started adding lines to the stones while referring back to the photos.

Anji noticed a look of excitement on his face. "You're about to have a 'Eureka' moment, aren't you?"

"I think I might be." Gabriel continued to battle with the drawing tools. "There!" he exclaimed triumphantly, turning the laptop to show Anji. Her eyes widened.

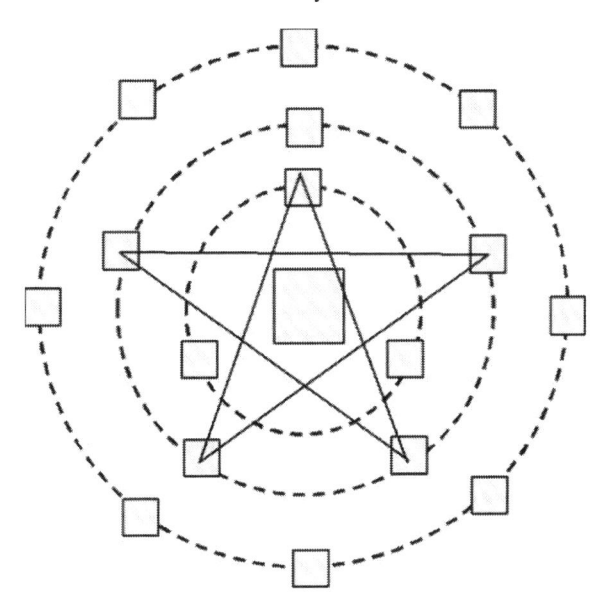

"A pentacle. You have had a 'Eureka' moment there, Gabe."

"I think I saw ones of these in a Johnny Depp film once," Gabriel said, looking proudly at his drawing.

"We need to talk to someone who knows about this stuff."

"True, I'll give Liz a ring and get the professor's number." He started fishing through his pockets for his phone.

"I wasn't thinking the professor. At least, not yet."

The small brass bell made a 'ding' as Anji walked into the shop with Gabriel close behind. Tabitha looked up.

"Welcome back." Tabitha held out her palms in greeting. "Come round the back, I'll put the kettle on." She led them to the back room again. "What can I do for you?"

Anji spoke. "Gabe was looking through the photos that he took at the stone circle when he noticed lines of dead grass. As far as we can tell the lines for a. . ." Tabitha cut her short.

"A pentacle, yes?"

This time, Gabriel spoke. "Yes. How did you know?"

"It might have something to do with the fact that I put it there." Tabitha gave a coy smile.

"Why?" Gabriel drew the word out slowly.

"The pentacle can be used as, and is predominantly, a protective symbol. As I said last time you were here, the stone circle represents the town and surrounding land. I performed a protection spell to help keep the town safe."

"Is this a normal thing?"

Tabitha's face looked grave for a second as she considered her next words.

"There is a darkness coming. I've read the signs. Something evil is brewing near Stonebank. I fear that some of its corruption has already reached the village. However, I'm doing everything I can to stop it going any further."

Gabriel looked sceptical as usual and strangely enough, so did Anji.

"For a while evil spirits will find it difficult to enter the village. And they should find it impossible to enter the edge of the pentacle at the circle."

For a second, Gabriel thought of the crow dying as if flew into the second circle. Then he realised how absurd the whole idea was.

"I can see from your expression that you don't believe me, that's okay. I don't expect you to. Not yet."

Anji looked quizzical. "What darkness?" she asked.

"I am unsure. At the moment it's just a feeling. I can sense something coming, something ancient and powerful."

Gabriel was becoming acutely aware of just how clichéd the whole thing was beginning to sound.

The pair exited the shop; they had made their excuses and left. Tabitha was getting a little over the top, even for Anji.

"I think she might be a little nuts, Anj." Gabriel reached into his inside pocket and retrieved his mobile phone.

"I think you could be right, sweetheart. Who are you calling?"

"Liz. I'm going to ask her to do a little research for me," Gabriel replied while placing the call. The phone rang three times then a familiar voice answered.

"Hello." Elizabeth rolled the word out.

"Ay-up, Liz. How's it going?"

"Not bad kidda, where you been hiding?"

"Village named Stonebank. Doing some research here for that article."

Anji started to stroll towards the seat near the ford as Gabriel followed.

"Blimey, you're actually doing some work."

"That's right." Gabriel sat down next to Anji.

"My Spidy senses tell me that you're after a favour." Gabriel cursed the powers that be, wondering how she always knew these things.

"Only a small one."

"Shoot."

"Just want you to do a little research for me. If I give you a name, could you check to see what history you can dig up?"

"Sure."

"Cheers Liz, the name is Devereaux. The family had a manor house here in Stonebank."

"Okay Gabe, I'll see what I can dig up."

"Cheers Liz, see ya later." Gabriel snapped his phone shut and looked at Anji. She responded with a condemning look.

"What's wrong?"

"You lazy bastard. Do your own research."

"I am doing, Liz is just helping out with the side that needs a net connection. Meanwhile we can go and have a chat with..." Gabriel paused, flicking trough his notes from their last meeting with Tabitha, "...Ethel Birchwood. The woman in the library."

Donovan Brigham sat across from his sergeant. They'd called in at the police canteen for a quick drink. The canteen wasn't exactly the Ritz; it had laminated chipboard tables which sported a fake marble effect. Donovan reclined slightly in his dark green plastic chair which creaked under his weight. The DCI sat daydreaming while staring at the polystyrene cup that contained what was left of his coffee.

He took a sip. It was cold.

"What do you think then, boss?" The sergeant's words snapped Donovan back to lucidity.

"I think it could be linked to the other one. Pity we don't have much evidence to support that, though." Donovan took another sip of his coffee; it was still cold. "Also, I'm not convinced that those two missing tourists aren't connected in some way."

The DCI tried to judge Sergeant Dudley's reaction to what he'd just said. He was wondering if it sounded as incongruous out loud as it had in his head. About a week before, another heart attack victim had been found in the woods about ten miles from Stonebank, close to one of its neighbouring villages. This had coincided with the disappearance of two tourists on a walking holiday in the same area. However, unlike Alan Hatchcroft, this heart attack victim was a thirty-four year old district nurse with a healthy heart. What they did have in common was the fact that both cases had strong evidence that they had been running from something.

"Anyway, Sergeant. Let's head back to Stonebank and see if we can determine what Mr Hatchcroft was running from."

Gabriel and Anji found Stonebank's library. Like most of the buildings in the village, it was old and built from stone. It had a slate roof with wooden framed windows. Gabriel held open the heavy oak front door and allowed Anji to enter first.

Inside were numerous dark brown wooden shelves, tightly packed. The large room smelt of wax polish and the must of old books. There were wood panelled walls which were mostly free of shelves but had a large number of paintings hanging from them. On one side of the room an elderly woman sat behind a mahogany desk.

Gabriel caught sight of a sheet of paper mounted on the wall. It looked like it had been typed up on an old-fashioned typewriter and boasted the title: 'in case of fire', all in lower case letters. The first line read 'In the event of fire a member of staff will shout FIRE very loudly...'

Gabriel cracked a smile but his thought was caught short as the elderly woman stood to greet them. She was a tiny old lady of about eighty years of age, with white frizzy hair and gold rimmed glasses. She wore a white and blue floral dress. The woman looked the two of them up and down for a second before speaking.

"Can I help you, dears?" Her voice was soft, kind, and a little sing-song. Gabriel replied in a humble tone.

"I hope so, we're looking for a... Mrs? Birchwood." He phrased the 'Mrs' part as a question out of politeness. Aunty Gladys's lessons were surfacing again.

"That's me dear, and yes, it is Mrs." She smiled as she spoke.

"I'm Gabriel, this is Anji." Gabriel took her hand and gave it a gentle shake. "We were told that you were an authority on the Devereaux family."

Ethel considered for a moment then gave an almost gleeful smile.

"I think 'authority' is a little flattering. I have an interest in the family, as I do much of our local history. As you probably already know, they used to own the manor house not far from here. Mottistone Manor as it's correctly named. The manor was originally built by Louis Devereaux in the late fifteen-hundreds, but was sold when his family returned to France. In the following years it was used as a private girls' school until Louis' great grandson Claude reclaimed it seventy five years later. Claude's family moved in, his wife Isabel, his daughter Christina and his son, Charles."

Ethel took a sip of coffee from a bright yellow mug on her desk.

"The painting on the far wall is of Claude Devereaux." She pointed at a large oil painting that hung below a brass picture light. Gabriel looked at the image. It depicted a man in his early fifties, with grey hair and steel blue eyes. It gave Gabriel an uneasy feeling, much the same as he got when he saw film footage of Adolf Hitler socialising with the high command, or Margaret Thatcher giving a speech. Cold and slightly inhuman, Claude Devereaux was a shiver just looking for a spine to run down. Gabriel didn't like it.

Ethel continued to talk. "An imposing man, isn't he?" Gabriel looked at her face; she didn't appear to share his sentiments. Her expression was that of admiration, as she looked up, almost through the painting.

"Unfortunately, the family was forced to leave the area in 1641. Superstition back in those days as it was. The Witchfinder General running riot in the southern counties, much of the hysteria travelled up here."

"What happened?" Gabriel asked in his politest tone.

"A hysterical local magistrate convinced the village that the Devereaux family had been responsible for the death of his wife and daughter." She shrugged. "One night a mob from the village stormed the gates of Mottistone and set the manor ablaze. Fortunately the family were visiting relatives in Hampshire at the time so they were spared." Ethel gave a sad smile. "They thought it best not to return."

She put her hands together. "That is about it. There is of course a substantial amount of background information if you'd like to help yourself to one of the free booklets here." Ethel gestured to her desk and Anji picked up one of the white A5 sized photocopied booklets. Gabriel took his eye off the painting.

"Thank you, Mrs Birchwood. You've been a great help."

Gabriel and Anji headed for the door. Anji waited until they were outside before speaking.

"Was she actually a great help?" she asked, a gentle breeze blowing a red curl across her cheek.

"That depends on what our Liz finds out. If it's the same stuff, then we've had a wasted visit." He pulled his notebook out and started to jot notes from memory again. "Either way, I've got a full article entitled 'Local Myth versus Fact'. I'll give her a quick call and fill her in on what we know."

DCI Brigham approached the front door of Alan Hatchcroft's widow pursing his lips for a second as he reluctantly walked down the path of the dead man's front garden.

This was the part of his job that he hated, dealing with the bereaved of the victims of the crimes. He wasn't sure why; was it simple hubris, did he just feel that his interpersonal skills were lacking and didn't like to be reminded of his shortcomings? Or was the problem that seeing the family's grief added to the pressure to solve the case? Either way, it had to be done and as much as he hated to admit it to himself, he was pleased to have Sergeant Dudley along with him.

The iron door-knocker produced a heavy thud as the DCI swung it three times. A moment later, the door glided silently open on its well-oiled hinges and a small, elderly woman came into view. Alan's widow must have been in her late seventies; the grey of her hair barely contrasted with her pale skin. The red rims of her eyes led to bloodshot veins ending at faded blue irises.

"Can I help you?" The voice was subdued and submissive. Dudley spoke first; he respected Brigham too much to say it out loud, but he knew he hated these situations.

"Hello, Mrs Hatchcroft. I'm Sergeant Garry Dudley, this is Chief Inspector Donovan Brigham, CID. We're terribly sorry to disturb you at this difficult time but I'm afraid we need to ask you some questions." Dudley's voice was soft, not a tone he let many people hear.

"That's okay, lovey. The young lady who came to see me yesterday said to expect you. Please come in." Margaret Hatchcroft stood back from the door and started to shuffle towards the living room of the cottage with the two police officers in tow. Brigham glanced around as he followed. The cottage had a faint odour of furniture polish and rose perfume. The room he entered had a low white ceiling with bare rafters, and a thick, dark brown carpet underfoot. The wall paper was white with a pale green fleur-de-lys pattern. Margaret sat down in an upright chair beside a small mahogany table supporting a chintzy lamp. Brigham and Dudley sat on the matching settee.

Brigham spoke, putting as much kindness into his voice as he could muster.

"Mrs Hatchcroft, when was the last time you saw your husband?" He deliberately neglected to add the word 'alive'.

"It was the night before he was found. We've had a lot of sheep go missing. Al was just going out to see if he could catch them in the act, put a bit of a scare into them." There was substantial emotion in her voice. Brigham gave her a moment to compose herself.

"Is that why he took his shotgun? To scare them?" His tone was devoid of any accusation.

"Partly I think, also partly just in case anything happened, you never know these days and you see such terrible things on the news."

"Mrs Hatchcroft, your husband was on medication for a heart condition. Correct?" His eyes widened slightly.

"Yes, lovey. He never went anywhere without his pills."

"Was it usual for him to over-exert himself, considering his condition?"

"Oh no, lovey." The sadness faded for a fraction of a moment. "He'd walk a little fast when he was angry, but apart from that he was always very careful. He'd had strict instructions from the doctor."

Margaret's eyes flicked to Sergeant Dudley who was making notes in a small, black, top folding notebook.

"Sergeant Dudley and I are strangers to the area; I'm afraid we aren't very knowledgeable about the location. Can you think of anything that your husband might have been running from?" It felt like a stupid question, but it had to be asked, he thought. Margaret considered for a moment.

"I'm sorry, Inspector, but I can't think of a thing. We had some youths on motorbikes charging through the woods a while back but we've not heard from them in months."

"One last question before we leave you. Did your husband have any enemies that you know of?" This wasn't a question that Brigham enjoyed asking.

"No lovey, Al might have rubbed people up the wrong way from time to time, but he was still a well-liked man."

"Thank you for your time, Mrs Hatchcroft." Both men stood.

The two CID officers were walking briskly back to their car. Garry turned to his superior.

"That was a bit of a waste of time for the most part, wasn't it sir?"

"I'm sorry to say that you're right, Dudley. But at least we now know why he was out there in the first place. To stop a sheep rustler. Looks like we're going to have to have a chat with Constable Brighton."

Elizabeth Moordomus' eyes were staring hard at her computer screen. She bit her lower lip as she scanned through the article on screen, bookmarked her current webpage then went back to the search engine page.

"The stuff I let myself volunteer for," she muttered, letting off a heavy sigh before taking a swig from the open can of diet cola resting on her desk. The young woman continued to read through the pages she'd found.

As a PhD student, Elizabeth was used to researching on the internet, but digging up information on the Devereaux family was proving more difficult than she expected. Most of the reputable places she'd look were coming up with nothing. However, there were quite a few of what she called 'kook' websites offering a wealth of information about how the family were involved in devil worship. A few of the more extreme of these 'kook sites' even suggested that the family were, in fact, demons.

Elizabeth had arranged her website bookmarks into two folders: 'Gabe's research' and 'Gabe's nutters.' Most pages so far were falling under the 'nutters' category. However, she continued the search trying to get some more reliable information.

"There you are!" she said eventually, with a mild triumph in her voice.

Gabriel was sat in the back garden of the rented house, enjoying the sun with his shirt off.

"Put your shirt back on Gabe, the sun's bouncing off you and making me go blind," Anji said with a giggle, one hand holding a glass of cold beer and the other one clasping a half-smoked joint. Gabriel took a sip from his own glass.

"If I wasn't so busy, then I'd have had time to get a tan weeks ago."

"You don't know what the word busy means."

"Of course I do, I'm a busy man. That telly doesn't watch itself you know." They both laughed as Gabriel's mobile started to ring. "The *Fraggle Rock* music. That'll be Liz." He ducked into the kitchen and returned with the phone to his ear.

"Liz, how's my favourite PhD student?"

"Knackered, after dong your research for you. What are you up to?"

Gabriel paused for a moment to consider if it was a good idea to admit that he was drinking beer in the sun while Liz had been researching for him.

"We're just following up a lead." Anji glared at him and mouthed the word 'liar' in his direction.

"I've found quite a lot of stuff... it's not all reliable but I'll send you everything I have. Can you still remember how to use your mobile as a modem?"

"Yeah, I wrote down the instructions that Jim gave me a while back."

"Sweet. I've emailed you a bunch of information that I've lifted from websites."

"Cheers, Liz."

"I've put it into two categories: Reliable and Non-reliable. I found loads about devil worship, cults and stuff but it was nearly all from hack sites."

"That's still good, though."

"Gabe, if I looked hard enough I could find you loads about Majestic-12, crop circles, and how Elvis assassinated JFK... wouldn't make it real information though."

"Okay, point taken. I owe you dinner. See ya later."

"Have fun, kid." Gabriel closed his phone as Anji started to speak.

"So what lead are we following up then?" He gave her a smile and walked into the house to fetch his laptop. About fifteen minutes later he'd accessed his email and was reading through the information that Elizabeth had sent him.

"Look another painting of Claude Devereaux." Gabriel tilted the screen so Anji could see it.

"He is a scary looking chap, isn't he? Anything useful?"

"Lots I think, it's just a matter of reading through it all. From what I've seen so far that magistrate wasn't the only one who thought that the Devereaux was up to something; it was a pretty much a consensus in the village back then. Of course, that's assuming this information is accurate, which it may well not be." He furrowed his brow.

"Can you use any of it for the article?"

"Oh yeah, lots of stuff. Just reading about Meetingstone Manor. Not my favourite place in the whole world, I must say."

"What's it say?"

"Well amongst other things it was supposed to have a secret tunnel that lead to an underground site where the family performed satanic rituals." Gabriel smirked at the absurdity of what he'd just said as he continued to read.

"We could go back tomorrow, get a few photos of that wine cellar," Anji suggested, before being met with a cold stare. "What?"

"That place was creepy." Gabriel spoke with a slight joke in his voice which failed to cover up his anxiety.

"Hold on, you're supposed to be the sceptical one round here. You're also supposed to be the 'man'. Or at least the Scully. You don't get to be scared by eerie old buildings."

"We'll sleep on it then. I also want to nip back home tomorrow to collect some more clothes and stuff. Otherwise we're going to spend our entire time washing."

"Okay, Gabe."

Elizabeth took Gabriel's hand and placed something in it, closing his fingers around the item. She then turned and silently walked into the blackness of the night. Gabriel opened his hand and examined the object in the moonlight. It was a brass pentacle on a leather necklace. He looked up and saw Meetingstone Manor. He heard the caw of a crow in the distance behind him as he started to walk towards the manor feeling the cool of the grass under his bare feet. The wine cellar entrance was illuminated with candle light; Anji and Jim stood either side of the doorway beckoning to Gabriel.

"How's the article coming along?" Jim asked as Gabriel approached. "You going to have a look for that tunnel? It's just down there."

Gabriel walked through the door way and down the stone corridor, glancing at the walls as he did so, looking for any sign of a hidden entrance. "It's on the left," Jim shouted after him.

"No, it's on the right," Anji contradicted. Gabriel paused and peered down the wide, candle lit corridor; it was long, very long, and seemed to go on into infinity. He continued to peer as he made his way down looking at the stone walls on either side of him.

"It's definitely left, Gabe," Jim shouted again.

"No, it's right," Anji argued.

The word 'right' had sounded odd, distorted as in his dream the previous night. The candles in his part of the corridor went out. Almost immediately afterwards, the set of candles ahead of Gabriel also extinguished, then the next set and the set after that continuing away from him. What had seemed an endlessly long tunnel was now just a black abyss with no light at the end.

Gabriel turned to look at Anji and Jim; the candles were still lit at the entrance but his friends were gone. In their place was blood, a lot of blood on the walls and the floor. Gabriel's vision blurred for a moment and he could feel panic setting in. He did his best to suppress the feeling and tried to focus on the light at the entrance. His vision started to clear; however something was different, someone was in the corridor with him.

There was a shape between Gabriel and the exit. The shape of a black cloaked figure, silhouetted against the candle light. It was moving towards him. Gabriel turned and ran, ran into the blackness of the unknown. His legs felt lethargic and his body heavy; he was running in slow motion. He turned, the figure was almost upon him. Gabriel felt something around his neck. He started to struggle, waving his arms, kicking his feet and shouting in blind panic.

"It's just a nightmare, babe," came the female voice. The figure faded as the walls of the conscious world started to rebuild around him. Gabriel felt Anji's hands on his shoulders. "Gabe, it's okay." He opened his eyes.

"Anj." The word was little more than a murmur. "Christ, that was scary."

"It must have been, babe. I could hear you from my room." Her voice was soft and caring. "Also, you've kicked the quilt half way across the room." A half-laugh encroached on her tone.

"What time is it?" he mumbled, looking for his watch.

"It's a little after four."

"I'm going to go and get a cup of tea. You go back to bed, sweetheart. Thanks for checking on me."

Chapter 5

The following morning, Gabriel pulled up at his house back in Hoggersbrook. He'd just dropped Anji off and planned on getting a few things before sending a couple of emails. He unlocked his back door and walked in, heaving a contented sigh. It was good to be home, if only for a while.

He walked into his bedroom and started to pack extra clothes. Gabriel rummaged through a drawer, retrieving a roll of black cloth. He unrolled it and paused for a second, regarding its contents. "Just in case," he said to himself, before rolling it back up and placing it on top of the bag he'd just packed. "Right… a couple of emails then a swift visit to the pub."

The door to the Hunter's Moon gave its familiar creak as Gabriel pushed it open. Eric Conway was in his usual seat, quietly chatting to Scott the barman.

Scott was a good barman, always remembering what the regulars drank, and he had an amiable personality. He was a tallish man in his mid-twenties with a stout figure, spiky black hair and large black tattoo on the inside of his left forearm.

"Morning, gents," Gabriel said as he pulled up a stool to Eric's left-hand side. Eric greeted him with a friendly nod.

"Guinness or Coke, Boss?" Scott asked.

"I'm driving," Gabriel replied with a laugh.

"Coke it is, then." Scott picked up a glass and started to fill it. "How's it going then, Boss? Liz said that you were working on some article about occultism or something." He placed the cold glass in front of Gabriel, beads of condensation starting to form on its side. "One-ninety, please." Gabriel handed him the correct change.

"Cheers."

"Thanks, Boss."

"Yeh, it's about occultism in rural England. I'm doing a bit of research in this village called Stonebank."

Eric's ears pricked up.

"Stonebank?" He turned to look at Gabriel.

"You know the place?"

"Not really. I'm just remembering something from a long time ago. There was a whole lot of folks going missing around that village. I must have been about your age when it was happening. Good lord, now think about it there was also a murder, a real nasty one; a man cut his own brother's heart out." Eric's expression took on a stern look as he took a sip of bitter.

This was sparking interest in Gabriel, a lot of interest. A cut out heart! It could tie in very well with what he was writing. Gabriel mentally chastised himself for being so callous. It might have been in the past, but a man had still died.

"How long ago was it, Mr Conway?"

Eric considered for a moment. "The summer of fifty-five. The year of mine and Mrs Conway's fifth anniversary." A smile ghosted across his face for a second. "So that'd be about fifty years ago, a nice round number for you, Mr Jones."

"That it is." Gabriel took a long gulp of coke.

The writer had finished his drink and was back in his car heading out of Hoggersbrook. His eyes were fixed on the road as he relayed Eric's story to Anji in the passenger seat.

"A cut out heart!" she exclaimed, wincing.

"Yeah, and he did it to his own brother!" Gabriel replied, turning the steering wheel as he drove back to Stonebank. "I'm going to check the library. They're bound to have some old newspapers in the archives."

"Okay, just make sure you drop me at the house first." Anji paused for a second as they drove past the church. "Look, they're having a fête... let's call in."

"I sort of want to get going on this whole 'missing heart' thing."

"Then drop me off, I'll walk back to the house later."

"Okay, you're the gaffer." Gabriel pulled up outside the church as Anji jumped out and almost skipped towards the churchyard. Gabriel shook his head and continued on to the library.

"Bloody hippie," he murmured to himself with a smile.

The library still smelt of wax polish, but now had a slight smell of must about it as well. Mrs Birchwood placed a cup of tea on the desk next to where Gabriel was skimming through the microfiche.

"Thanks." Gabriel looked up and gave a smile.

"Found what you're looking for, dearie?"

"I think so," he said, gesturing to the screen while taking a sip of tea. The headline read: *Victim's brother confesses.*

"Poor old Harry," Ethel sighed, a look of grave regret passing over her face.

"You knew him?" A twinge of shame hit Gabriel's heart.

"Yes, and his brother Howard… Howard Graves. A terrible business, they were always so close as well. Poor old Harry must have been so poorly in the head. Some of the silly stuff he said after he'd confessed." Ethel shook her head. "He kept babbling about cults and demons. The poor, poor man. He's still in an asylum to this day." Ethel began to walk away shaking her head.

"Mrs Birchwood, wait, please. This man is still alive?"

"Yes dear, like I said, he's still in the asylum, out towards Chesterfield I think. Shale something or other."

Gabriel examined the rest of the article in front of him looking for the name of the asylum. A few moments later, he found it. Shalebridge.

Gabriel headed back to the church to try and catch up with Anji. He parked down the road a little, and walked to the church entering the grounds via an old iron kissing gate. He cast his eyes over the fete; it was the normal array of tombolas, bric-a-brac and the odd person who obviously had a flea market stall in their spare time.

Anji wasn't hard to spot. 'You look for the hair,' Gabriel thought. A quick glance across the crowd and there she was, pottering over a bric-a-brac stall: 'red curls.'

"Hello, babe," Gabriel said, pleased to see her.

"I'm surprised you didn't just head back to the house," Anji replied, while prodding at what Gabriel assumed was a pin cushion.

"I thought I'd spend some time in the sun with my favourite redhead." He smiled as she looked up and linked his arm.

"I've seen something you'll like. Come on this way." Anji lead Gabriel to an enclosed wooden stall with the words 'Shooting Range' carved into a large wooden plaque. A man stood in the stall; he was in his late middle age with a white beard, matching cropped hair and a pair of black, thick rimmed glasses. In his right hand he held a BB gun.

"Fancy your chances, sir?" He gestured to a row of eight small metal figurines, each about four inches in height. "Knock down six and win another try. Seven and choose anything off the second row of prizes. Knock down all eight and choose anything from the first row." Gabriel looked over the prizes; both rows consisted of stuffed toys, the first prize row housing what Gabriel considered to be the stupidly oversized type.

"Come on, Gabe," Anji said, gleefully prodding Gabriel in the ribs. "You left me here for nearly an hour. Now win me a prize." Anji was well aware that hitting eight one-by-four inch targets at about four metre range wasn't a problem for Gabriel. At university he'd been heavily involved with the marksmanship club and became very accomplished with pistols, rifles and shotguns.

"How much?" Gabriel asked the bearded man.

"Only two quid, young sir."

"Okay," Gabriel said, fishing two pound coins out of his wallet. The bearded man took the money and passed Gabriel the BB gun. Gabriel aimed and hit each target in quick succession, knocking all eight down. The stall holder looked genuinely impressed.

"Well done you, sir. Feel free to choose a prize from the top shelf." He gestured again, this time at the prizes.

"I like the koala," Anji said, with an unusual amount of determination.

"The koala it is, then," the stall holder replied, seeming quite proud that someone had actually won something as he handed over an over-sized stuffed koala bear. He began to talk. "You must be that young couple Mrs Bailey mentioned. The ones who are writing the article about tourist spots."

"Well, I wouldn't class us a couple, but yes." Gabriel decided that he might as well stick to the same story as much as possible.

"Well, if you want any help, just let me know. I can usually be found at the tourist information centre in the village, or the visitors' centre at the Manor."

"Oh, you work in tourist information?"

"Well, we don't get many tourists. I'm also head of the parish council, seeing as I have the time. Ravenwood's my name, Charles Ravenwood." Charles gave Gabriel's hand and overly vigorous shake.

"If you're interested in local events, why not call in at our Midsummer Festival tomorrow evening? It's a local tradition dating back hundreds of years. It's actually a little pagan, but the good Reverend doesn't mind us holding it in the church hall." He pointed and waved at a young man wearing a dog collar. Gabriel started to answer.

"Well, I'm . . ." Anji interrupted.

"*We're* sure it'll be a lot of fun, Charles." Gabriel caught a beaming smile from Anji. "What time does it start?"

Charles looked overjoyed. "Half seven, three pounds at the door gets you a buffet and a very reasonably priced bar. I look forward to seeing you there, and I hope that you'll give this old coot the honour of a dance with you." Anji giggled, which also annoyed Gabriel.

"I'll look forward to it, Charles."

After leaving the fête Anji and Gabriel headed straight back to the rented house. As soon as they got in, Anji headed directly for the kitchen to put the kettle on. Gabriel bought up the subject of Howard and Harry and the murder.

"We're going where?" Anji asked.

"A nut-house called Shalebridge. But *we're* not going, I am."

"Why exactly don't you want me there?" Anji raised her left eyebrow.

"Because nut houses are depressing places and they're not the sort of experience you'd enjoy, or forget in a hurry." Gabriel's voice had no shadow of joviality about it; he was serious.

"Do you think I can't put up with it?"

"No, I think you shouldn't have to." Gabriel was expecting an argument; he could read Anji well and knew when she was about to get argumentative. He took a deep breath and considered for a moment.

"Listen, I know you don't like it when I get 'controlling.' And I know that's what you think I'm doing now. But I'm not. I've only visited an asylum once before. I hated it. It's not a memory I like having and it's not one I want you to have. Please just let me go alone on this."

"Okay, Gabe." She backed down, which was not a common occurrence.

"Right, I'll get a phone number and see if they'll let me in to interview this chap."

Gabriel pulled into one of many spaces in the largely empty visitor's car park of the asylum. He released his seatbelt while grabbing his notebook and biro from the passenger seat where he'd thrown them earlier.

Gabriel clambered out of his car and glanced over the building before him. Shalebridge Care Home, as it was now called, didn't give an outward impression of being overly high security. It had a large perimeter fence and gate that could be shut and locked easily, but the atmosphere outside wasn't exactly foreboding.

The sun was beating down and birdsong almost drowned out the sound of the nearby road. The building itself was four floors high and made of grey stone, with a tall slate roof and strong hints of gothic architecture. Gabriel followed the signs to the entrance and headed inside to sign in. The reception had much the same atmosphere as the outside, friendly and clean. The decor was modern, pine surfaces and fake brick that had never seen the inside of a kiln; brick that was as phoney as the image the asylum portrayed to the outside world.

Gabriel passed pleasantries with the stout woman behind the counter before receiving direction to Harry Graves' 'room' as they called it. He was even provided with a guide in the form of a medical orderly. Gabriel headed to the double doors that the receptionist had directed him to with the orderly in tow; the doors were quite heavy, but opened silently.

As Gabriel stepped out of the reception area, the atmosphere changed. That was what he hated about this type of place; the hidden depths are masked by a cheerful shell. The clinical, well-lit corridors felt somehow dark. The walls seemed to ooze with oppression. The air itself appeared very slightly opaque, dimming the corners of the walls. Gabriel looked around as he was involuntarily permeated by the atmosphere. He couldn't help but to mentally sum up the ambience with one word: Despair.

The orderly accompanying Gabriel to Harry's room -or cell, as Gabriel decided to think of it - inserted a ordinary-looking Yale key into the lock and opened the door for Gabriel. Not the big clunking lock one would expect in a Victorian asylum but it had much the same, if muted, effect.

Gabriel entered alone. He had been right: it wasn't a room, it was a cell. Not a padded one, but a cell none the less. The walls were grey and stained, and the bed had a metal frame with the thinnest mattress Gabriel had ever seen. The laminated chipboard bedside table was also grey, and empty save a single plastic beaker.

In the far corner of the room was a huddled shape that took a moment for Gabriel to recognise as a man. The man sat on the floor holding his knees against his chest, rocking slightly.

"Mr Graves?" Gabriel announced, with the slightest amount of anxiety spilling into his voice.

The shape stopped rocking. A head looked up and gave a wondering gaze from almost lifeless cold blue-grey eyes.

"Who are you?" came the dry voice.

"Mr Graves, my name is Gabriel Jones-"

Before he could continue, Harry cut him off.

"What do you want?"

Gabriel was suddenly hit by the stark realisation that there was no nice, polite or tactful way of answering that question. *Well, you mad bastard, I'd like to ask you about why you murdered your own brother, then mutilated his corpse by cutting the heart out.*

"To be honest, standing here I don't know how to say this. But I was going to ask you about your brother." The anxiety is his voice was a little more palpable now.

"Howard? I was sick, I understand that now." Harry was almost ranting; his words were quick and concise but spoken with no direction, as if he were addressing a whole room. "I want to go home. They were just dreams, they didn't mean anything, just dreams. I'm so very sorry. They were just dreams and didn't mean anything." Harry's eyes were wondering. "Are you my new doctor? I understand now, none of it meant anything. Even the crow was meaningless."

The word 'crow' sent a shiver down Gabriel's spine. Harry seemed to be strangely aware of this. His head shot directly towards Gabriel, his unnerving eyes locked in a blinkless stare.

"You've seen, haven't you?" snapped the insane man. "The house. The cellar. The man in black. The crow. My wife, my beautiful wife. The crow took her eyes, every night towards the end, every night apart from when I saw her in the cellar. She told me, she told me I had to take his heart, it was the only way to save her."

Harry was now ranting. "The crow. That bastard crow, it stalked me and followed me into my dreams. It's still stalking me... I hear it every day outside the window. Every day, and every night in my dreams. The doctors don't like me to see it." A look of concern came over his face. "You won't tell them will you? They don't like me to see it, they think I'm mad." Harry calmed all of a sudden. "I tried to tell them the truth for years. They wouldn't believe me. Christ, at times even I didn't believe me."

"What did you tell them?" Gabriel asked, with a slight stammer.

"The truth, the full story." He paused and exhaled. "I was a young man, happily married... I worked as a farm labourer. Life was good. Then one day the crow came; I didn't even notice it at first, crows weren't exactly uncommon in a farm field. But it was always there, I'd see it on the window sill in a morning and hear it cawing every night. One night it got into my dreams. I saw my poor wife dead, the crow had eaten her eyes. I started to dream of the manor and the black figure. Every night was the same, the crow the manor and the black figure, the blood. Then one night the figure dragged me down the tunnel under the house." His voice quickened. "The secret tunnel, the man in black, the voice told me that he needed my brother's heart, and that I had to be the one to take it. It told me that I had to take it before I could be its Avatar. It told me that it was the only way to save my wife and if I didn't the dreams would come true."

Gabriel looked a little shaken. "That was it? That's why you killed him?"

"No." Harry looked down and shook his head. "I tried to ignore it, but the dreams hounded me, in the end I could hear the voice even when I was awake. I would see my wife dead on the kitchen floor or in our bed or in the garden... I'd look away and look again, and she'd be gone. Perhaps I am mad."

Gabriel walked out of Shalebridge as fast as he could, jumped in his car and started frantically scribbling notes in the book that he'd neglected to use inside. He was finding it difficult to write; his nerves were making his hands shake. His scepticism hadn't even kicked in, what he'd just heard was far too close to his own dreams for comfort. He ran his hand over his forehead, through his hair and to the back of his neck.

"Sod it, I need to talk to someone normal." Gabriel flipped open his phone and called Jim, who picked up after two rings.

"Gabe, how's it going, mate?"

"You finished work yet?"

"Yeah, just left, walking to the car now."

Jim clocked the uneasiness in Gabriel's voice. "You feel like coming over for a quick drink?"

"Yeah, lob a couple of cans in the fridge as soon as you get in. I'll be there in about an hour."

"Cool, see you soon, mate." Jim closed his phone and slipped it into his inside pocket, then paused for a second and bit his lip.

Gabriel hadn't sounded right. In all the years he'd known him, he'd only ever sounded anything like that once, around the time that Gladys had passed. He headed home as quickly as possible and swung open his front door, heading directly to the fridge to check his beer stock. It was fine - about eight cans already in there. He took one out and poured the contents into a glass before heading out to the garden to wait for Gabriel. He didn't bother doing any tidying of the house. The two men had been friends long enough that 'house pride' was behind them.

Gabriel arrived, they shared a drink and talked over the past few days.

"Have you gone nuts?" Jim asked in a deadpan tone. Gabriel knew not to take this as a genuine lack of concern.

"Perhaps," he replied, with an equally deadpan expression.

"Gabe, you're just about the most sceptical person I know. And now, I think you're saying that you're having the same dreams as some mentalist in a nut house."

Jim didn't exactly disbelieve him, he just figured that logic was the best alternative. Certainly a better alternative than agreeing with his best friend that he was mimicking the dreams of an OAP who'd lived the best part of his life incarcerated in a mental hospital.

The two friends continued to talk. Gabriel off-loaded a considerable amount of anxiety and the conversation moved on. He gradually started to feel better; he gradually started to arrive at the conclusion that it was impossible for a crow to enter dreams or that a non-imaginary voice could exist in a person's head.

"So what you got planned for this evening then, mate?" Jim asked, leaning back on his garden chair.

"Some weird festival thing at that village I'm staying at. Anj said we'd go."

"It might be fun."

Gabriel turned his head to Jim.

"I've already met one nutter today, don't be my second one."

"Okay, it might be bearable. Want another beer?"

"No thanks, mate." He glanced at his glass. "Driving."

Anji and Gabriel strolled to the church hall, Anji linking his arm as she would do from time to time. The evening air was pleasant and still as the crickets sang invisibly from the darkness. Gabriel's experience at the mental hospital was still heavy in his thoughts, but he was pushing it to the back of his mind.

They arrived at the church hall, an old brick building with 1930s architecture. They were greeted by an elderly couple who deprived them of six pounds before letting them through the door.

The interior was much as Gabriel had expected; a barely polished wooden floor, a small stage at one end of the room where an even smaller band were playing quite lively folk music. Along one wall were tables decked with paper table cloths and an array of cheap buffet food. In a corner was a tiny bar that wasn't much more than a hatch.

"You get 'em in." Anji nodded at the bar. "I'll mingle." She spied Charles Ravenwood, who was delighted when he spotted her ambling towards him.

"Hello, young miss... I just realised that I never asked your name."

Anji grinned and held out her hand.

"I'm Anji, with a J." Charles took her hand and lightly shook it, bowing slightly.

"It's lovely to meet you again. Now, how about that dance."

"I never could say no to a gentlemen."

Charles led Anji onto the dance floor.

Gabriel was at the bar, which was manned by Neil from the Red Gate Inn. "You've been drafted in to help out then?" Gabriel asked, as he passed over money.

"Neil does the bar here every year," came a voice from Gabriel's left. He turned to see the policeman he'd met in the pub a few days earlier. "How you finding the house?"

"Good, thanks. And thanks for the recommendation, Constable."

Lloyd smiled and offered his hand. Gabriel gave it a firm shake. "My name's Lloyd."

"Gabriel," he replied. "How's it going?"

"Not bad, is the polite answer. Trust me, you don't want to hear the honest one." Lloyd discreetly pointed at Anji and Charles on the dance floor. "I see Old Man Ravenwood is taking your girl for a spin on the dance floor. He always did have an eye for the ladies."

"She ain't my girl." Gabriel corrected in a jovial manner. "We're just friends."

"Pity, you'd make a nice couple."

"So what's the deal with this midsummer festival thing then?"

Lloyd paused for a second; he had always considered himself to be a good judge of character. He wasn't sure what it was but he decided he liked this man.

"It's a Stonebank tradition, dates back to the sixteenth century, if memory serves. Charles is your man for local history though. I think most of us lot these days just use it as an excuse to get rat-arsed. Basically, we drink and dance, then take that straw man." Lloyd pointed at an effigy of a man made from straw, suspended behind the band on the stage. "Outside and set him on fire like good little pyromaniacs." He gave a shrug. "Then we drink some more. It's all good."

Gabriel regarded the straw man. There was something about it that he didn't like. But then he remembered that the same was true for clowns and garden gnomes. His attention strayed from the effigy as he started to scan the room. Anji and Charles had stopped dancing and were sitting at a table, chatting. Ethel Birchwood was at the buffet shovelling mini sausage rolls and pickled onions onto a paper plate. Mr and Mrs Bailey from the guest house were chatting in a group with other villagers which included the woman who'd served him at the tea shop. Even Tom Jackson from the post office was skulking in and out with a couple of other lads his age. Gabriel continued to survey the room.

"No Tabitha," he said out loud. Lloyd knew who he was talking about.

"No, she never comes. Odd - you'd think it'd be her scene."

"What do you make of her?"

"Tabitha? She's harmless. Off her rocker, but harmless." Lloyd studied Gabriel for a second. "Why do you ask?"

"No reason. I just had a talk to her the other day. An interesting character but like you say, off her rocker."

"Hope you're not talking about me," Anji commented, as she took her drink from Gabriel and returned to Charles.

"So you asked me about the deal with the festival. Now it's my turn." Lloyd smiled and looked at Gabriel.

"Go on, then."

"What are you two really doing here? It hasn't got a damn thing to do with tourism."

Gabriel began to quickly size the man up. He seemed sincere enough; he'd made a point of asking the question after Neil had moved out of ear shot. His gut said that Lloyd Brighton was trustworthy.

"Okay, you got me. I'm writing for a magazine, but not about tourist spots." Gabriel took a swig of beer. "I'm writing about occultism."

Lloyd was surprised.

"You believe in that stuff?"

"Hell no, it's a bunch of old wives' tales and bollocks. Turns out that writing about it pays well though."

"Well again, the man to talk to is probably Ravenwood. The occultism crap runs all through the local history here. Demonic land owners and the like. Even this festival."

As if on cue, Charles Ravenwood took to the stage and began to talk into a microphone.

"My friends, it's good to see you all here as it is every year. It's been another good year for the village..."

Apart from poor old Alan and his widow, Lloyd managed to not say out loud.

"...We've got a fine Festival King again this year." Charles gestured towards the straw effigy behind him. "Now, I say we take him out back and do what we've done for hundreds of years." The comment was received with cheers as the band took down the large straw man and began to carry him outside, followed by the entire of the room.

The back of the church hall was not well lit. Gabriel could make out what appeared to be cobble stones underfoot, and a field disappearing off into the night. He felt an arm link his as Anji appeared at his side. They both looked on as Charles began to move towards the effigy with a lit torch. He confidently lit the bottom part of the straw man, and looked almost gleeful as the crowd applauded and the flames crawled up and consumed the figure. Gabriel looked at Anji, her face illuminated by the pale orange light from the flames. He didn't like it, the whole thing felt wrong.

"Let's make a discreet exit. We've got beer back at the house after all," he whispered in her ear.

The crickets were still singing loudly as the pair strolled back to their rented house through the warm summer air.

"So, what were you and your new best friend talking about then?" Anji asked, prodding Gabriel in the ribs gently with a finger-tip.

"By 'new best friend' I'm guessing you mean the cop. He didn't buy the tourism story. He's a sharp 'un."

"So, what'd you tell him?"

"I figured the truth would do. Nothing major. Just the truth about the article. He seemed okay with it. Said I should try to quiz *your* new best friend." Gabriel prodded her back.

"Charles? Why?"

"He just said that he was the man to talk to about local history."

"Lucky for you that I got us both an invite to his house for tea tomorrow evening."

"Good girl. I knew there was a reason I dragged you along with me. Did you just use your feminine wiles, or did you feed him a line?"

"I told him that we were interested in local history and that I was very interested in witchcraft and the like. He didn't take much convincing."

"You are useful at times, kid."

The mood suddenly shifted.

"Gabe –''

Gabriel didn't like the tone in her voice. It was the tone she used when she was about to ask what she thought was an awkward question.

"Yeah?"

"You okay?" She squeezed his arm slightly. "You've been a bit, well, *odd* since you got back from the asylum. What did that man say? You've not even mentioned it." Gabriel was surprised that she'd left it this long to ask.

"Just a lot of crap about how sorry he was. It was a bit heavy." He decided that telling Anji the truth would be a bad idea but if he wasn't sure that she bought the lie, she seemed to at least accept it for the moment.

Gabriel returned to Shalebridge. This time it was the dead of night. The car park floodlights were out. "Must be a power cut," Gabriel said to Jim, who stood at his side. "Glad there's a full moon, at least we can see." The two friends headed to the front door, which wasn't locked. They headed into a candle-lit reception. Elizabeth was at the front desk, serving drinks.

"You two boozing again?" she asked.

"No, we're here to see the crazy man." Jim replied.

"Oh, go right on in then. You might have to wait though. The big black dude is in there with him already." Jim looked at the door to the ward.

"We'll go and check."

The electric lights in the wards were working, but the corridors were a lot dimmer than they had been during the day. The darkened corners had been replaced by true blackness, yet the sheen of the polished floor was as vibrant as ever. Jim seemed to know the way as well as the orderly had previously. Gabriel glanced down the corridors as they walked passed junctions; they were mainly empty and seemed to go on ever.

"Here we are," Jim said, pointing to the room signs. "Ninety-nine, one hundred, one hundred and one." He swung the door open. Harry was inside, rocking on the floor.

"Hello, Mr Jones, it's good to see you again. My wife would like to say hello. She's over there in the corner." Gabriel looked over the see the back of a woman's head. She had shoulder length red curls... he already knew what her face would look like. Panic was building in the pit of his stomach.

Jim started to walk over to greet her. Gabriel turned, headed for the open door and bolted through it. He didn't know the way out; he ran down endless corridors then stopped for a moment in a vain effort to get his bearings. He glanced to the end of the hall then looked back the way he had just come. A black cloaked figure was striding silently towards him. Gabriel turned and started to run again, running in a frantic effort to find his way out. Every time he looked back the figure was a little closer.

He darted around a corner and started to run down what seemed to be an endless corridor. He didn't notice at first, but the walls were suddenly made of stone. Gabriel was now in the cellars of Meetingstone Manor; he still had to get out though, and the figure was still following him. His legs were slowing their pace, every step felt like harder work to make than the last. It began to feel like he was running through treacle, he turned to see a black figure upon him. Consciousness started to return to his world.

"Damn. Another one," he said under his breath, rolling over and fumbling for his mobile on the bedside table. He flipped it open and checked the time. A little after four in the morning. After scrambling out of bed, Gabriel quietly wondered downstairs to the kitchen. As he got to the bottom of the stairs he realised that Anji was already up. He could hear her in the kitchen and see the crack of light around the closed door. He stopped being quiet and headed down the hall, saying "You're up early," as he opened the kitchen door.

"Yeah babe, couldn't sleep. Want a cuppa?" Anji had her back to him as she stood on her tip toes and reached into the already open cupboard.

"I'd love one."

"How'd you like it?"

"You know how I like it."

"Do I?" Anji turned to look at him. Or at least she would have if her eye sockets weren't empty.

"Bastard." This was Gabriel's first word of the day. He flicked himself on the forehead to check that he was actually awake this time.

Chapter 6

Detective Chief Inspector Donovan Brigham was sitting in his office; he hadn't slept well. He was stumped. The pathologist had found nothing that made sense about the farmer's death. The autopsy had been as fruitless as the district nurse's the previous week. Donovan's gut was telling him that they were linked and he wondered what would have happened if the nurse had also been carrying a double barrelled shotgun. The phone on his desk started to ring, Donovan picked it up almost immediately.

"DCI Brigham."

"Sir, they've found another one."

"Another heart attack, Dudley?"

"Yeah, and, well." A long pause followed. "You'd better get over here."

"Where's here?"

The latest police cordon was six miles south-east of Stonebank. DCI Brigham walked toward his Sergeant, who looked a little pale.

"Thank god you're here, sir. Here's the heart attack victim." Tom Agar was on the scene examining the body of a woman while his team combed the area.

"There she is. The other body is about fifty metres this way." Brigham followed Dudley in the direction he'd just indicated until they came upon the body of a man in his mid-thirties. He had short blond hair, hiking boots, a green puffer jacket and a deep incision in his chest where his heart used to be.

"Jesus Christ, Dudley, if the press get a hold of this they'll have a field day. When they turn up, keep 'em out of sight of this one and get him moved as soon as humanly possible." Brigham looked over to the coroner. "Tom!" he bellowed. "How long before we can get this poor bastard out of here?"

"My team still have a few things to do but it should only be about a quarter of an hour now."

"Good, make sure they know that they need to work quickly."

"They'll feel so appreciated," Tom said with a sarcastic smile. Brigham ignored the comment and turned his attention to the police car he'd just heard arrive at the edge of the scene. He looked as

Lloyd Brighton got out and slammed the door shut behind him. Brigham turned to Dudley.

"Please tell me that this is out of his jurisdiction." Dudley exhaled.

"I can say it, but it won't make it true." Lloyd was making his way towards them. He wasn't even sure what he was doing there. As far as he could tell, the deceased weren't locals; it just happened that they'd expired within the geographical borders of his little part of the world.

"Constable Brighton," Brigham said in greeting, emphasising the word 'constable'. "What brings you to my crime scene?"

Lloyd paused for a second in contemplation. "Well we seem to have a series of, shall we say, unexplained deaths."

"I'm not sure if three constitutes a series. But. . ."

"Four." Lloyd cut him off while raising an eyebrow. Brigham was a surprised, but kept his poker face.

"Last I checked, one farmer and two hikers makes three."

Lloyd tipped his hand. "Plus the district nurse." Brigham's poker face dropped ever so slightly. "Judging by the look of these two sods I'd say that there's a good chance that they're the missing persons."

Lloyd was about to look smug, then stopped. "Listen, I don't want to tread on your toes. But I've got my community to look after. As you can see, I've got enough moles to get information anyway so wouldn't it be better if I found out through official channels and we worked together?"

"No constable, I don't think that will be necessary."

"Sooner or later this will hit the press. When that happens a lot of people in my village will start getting worried. I have a responsibility to them, you must understand that. Plus, if we do get any more weird deaths around here you will need a local man." Lloyd broke off to judge Donovan's reaction. "Your gut must be telling you that none of this makes sense and also that it's not over."

Donovan's face became a little less stern. "Okay, constable, you've made your case. I'll keep you in the loop but just remember that you're working with me, I'm not working with you. I'm calling the shots."

"Fair enough. Now, what do we have here?"

Gabriel, walking into the kitchen of the rented house, squinted at the bright light from the window as he tried to contend with yet another poor night's sleep. Anji was busy sprinkling a moderate amount of dope into the tobacco of an open cigarette paper. She looked up.

"You look like hell, babe."

Gabriel gave a half-smile. "Thanks, Anj," he responded, giving a smallest of laughs.

"So what's the plan?" she asked, just before licking the adhesive part of the cigarette paper and dextrously rolling it.

"Well, we've got the invite to Charles' tonight. Are you up for another trip to that God-forsaken creepy house?"

"Thought you didn't want to go back there?"

"Needs must."

"Okay, you get your stuff. I'll make some sandwiches and a flask."

About an hour later they arrived at the manor house. It still felt eerie and Gabriel was still trying very hard to suppress what he was still telling himself was all in his mind.

"I want to have a look in the cellar." Gabriel said, remembering what Harry had told him as he was striding quickly towards the downward stairs. Anji had to jog slightly to keep up.

"Babe, it's got a big padlock on it," Anji said in her dry voice, deliberately pointing out the obvious. Gabriel paused his advance at the top of the steps and shrugged his back to the ground in front of him.

"I know," he replied dismissively, as he rummaged in his back pack and removed the roll of black cloth that he picked up on his visit home. Anji was confused, but kept quiet for the moment.

They descended the steps to the padlocked iron railings. Gabriel fought off his uneasy feeling and unrolled the cloth.

"Lock picks?" Anji exclaimed. "You know how to pick locks?" She was a little taken aback. "Where did you learn that?"

Gabriel was listening to the words, not really the tone. "I got a book off Amazon. Picking locks can be a useful skill when you're doing 'investigative journalism', you know."

"Yeah, a useful skill. But not many legitimate applications."

Anji's tone was beginning to catch up on Gabriel. He paused for a second and considered before speaking. "Coming from the lass who once said to me 'I've been ever so slightly stoned for all the time we've known each other', you can't whinge too much."

Anji gave a murmur of a laugh. "Fair point."

Gabriel selected a pick and the tension tool from the cloth and set to work. A moment later, the tumbler turned and the padlock sprang open. The uneasy feeling went into overdrive as Gabriel swung the gate open. He put the picks away, and pulled a high powered torch from his bag. All he could think of was the blood from the dream.

He tried to push the thought to the back of his mind as he gingerly walked into the darkness. Gabriel shone the torch from left to right; the corridor was about eight feet wide with an arched roof, grey stone with no hint of either wood or brick. Square and rectangle rooms jutted off periodically, but contained nothing but stone shelves alcoves and dust.

Anji looked at Gabriel inquisitively. "Okay Gabe, out with it. What're we looking for?"

Gabriel played dumb. "What do you mean?"

"You wouldn't have come down here without a bloody good reason."

"I'm not sure if I'd class it as a bloody good reason."

"Whatever, just spill it!"

"Harry seemed to think that there was a tunnel down here. Only in his dreams, but I'm not sure if he could tell the difference. Basically I'm playing a hunch."

"Gabe, this is a tunnel. We're walking down a tunnel right now."

"Probably 'tunnel' is the wrong word. Passage is probably more accurate. Yes, passage. Of the secret variety." Gabriel was doing everything he could to keep the mood light.

"You do know that Harry's a nut-job, right?"

"Like I said. Playin' a hunch."

Gabriel slowly walked down the tunnels that made up the cellars of Meetingstone Manor. His heart beat slightly faster, and an unyielding feeling of dread plagued him with every step. He shone the torch beam over the walls then stopped for a moment, looking at two narrow pillars about two metres apart, set into the stonework. They were the fourth set he'd passed but these were slightly different; they had a circular brass adornment about ten centimetres in diameter near the left pillar.

"What do you think?"

Anji looked confused. "About what?"

"The other pillars didn't have that." He aimed the torch beam at the brass adornment.

"Weird, it's got an odd symbol indented in it." Anji traced her fingers over the brass. Gabriel reached into his pocket and pulled his notebook out. He removed the pen and slid it into the indentation until it couldn't go any further. He put his thumbnail where the lip of the symbol and the pen met, then retracted the pen and examined it.

"About four centimetres deep."

"You sure it isn't just a posh-looking attachment to hold a lamp or something?" Anji asked, looking quizzical.

"Honestly? No. I've got no idea. Either way, I'm getting a photo." Gabriel pulled his camera from his backpack and turned the flash on.

"Don't forget you're meant to be writing an article. Still, you'd better get a few photos of the tunnels and stuff. Let's face it, this place has got atmosphere in spades."

"Fair point." Gabriel replied with a shrug. He took a few snaps of the indentation then paid a quick visit to the few stonewalled rooms they passed on their way down the tunnel.

Anji shut the gate and closed the padlock on their way out. They were both relived to be outside in the sun again.

"Let's get out of here."

Tom Agar threw his arms in the air.

"I have to say heart attack again on that one." The body of the female hiker was laid out, post autopsy, on the slab. Donovan Brigham glanced at her then towards Lloyd Brighton and finally looked back to Tom.

"No evidence of foul play at all?"

"None at all. There is blatantly foul play afoot. There just isn't any evidence of it with this poor woman." A large amount of frustration was slipping into Tom's voice; he didn't like it when he couldn't prove what he knew had to be there.

"And the man?"

"The man with the cut out heart? Yeah, we've got evidence of foul play there." The coroner's voice was raising and about to hit its zenith for this conversation. "His goddamn heart's been cut out." The frustration was now a little more obvious. Donovan gave him a sympathetic look, which was not something he did often. "I'm sorry. I'm a little worked up." Tom took a breath and brought his voice back down. "That one doesn't make sense either. Here's the really nasty part: the removal of the heart had to have taken place pre-mortem, so obviously that's what killed him. However, if you start cutting folks' hearts out then there's a lot of blood. The only problem is that my team didn't find any blood near the body. Neither did they find any evidence of anyone else being present at the scene, or even that the body had been moved post-mortem. So basically, the body had to have been moved but there's no evidence to prove that."

Donovan raised an eyebrow. "But the man was found on a forest floor with loose leaves all around him. There's no way . . ."

Tom cut him off. "That anyone could have dumped him there without leaving tracks? Damn right."

"So where does that leave us?"

"Nowhere. Nothing about this makes sense. Nothing at all."

Lloyd and Donovan walked swiftly down the corridor towards the lift, not speaking at first.

"What do you think?" Lloyd asked, breaking the silence.

"Honestly constable, I have no idea. I've never seen Tom stumped before and not to blow my own trumpet, but it's not often I get stumped either." The two men stopped walking for a second and looked at each other. "This makes no sense." Donovan almost regretted saying it; he didn't like to show any sign of weakness.

"Something's tugging at me about this," Lloyd said. "I'm remembering something my dad told me when I was a kid." *Give me a day and I'll get back to you.*

"Your dad? How's that going to help? What is it?"

"It's a gut thing. Give me a day."

Donovan considered for a second. Was he really going to give any credence to what sounded like a farcical hunch of a village plod? He decided that he didn't have a better option.

"Okay, constable."

Lloyd drove back to Stonebank and headed to the local library to see Ethel Birchwood. He remembered that last time he'd heard of a missing heart, there had been a local murder his father had once told him about. Lloyd's father had been dead for a good few years, so he went to the next best thing.

Lloyd swung the door open and entered the world of paper, wood and wax polish.

"Lloyd, how are you, my boy?" Ethel asked from behind her desk.

"I'm doing well thanks, Ethel." Lloyd gave her a warm smile.

"So dearie, what brings you here?"

"Work I'm afraid. I need to look up an old newspaper story, but I'm not sure about the date or even the year. I know it's not overly pleasant but I remember my dad once telling me about a local murder where the victim had his heart cut out."

Ethel gave a sudden surprised look and Lloyd cursed himself for being so blunt. "I'm sorry Ethel, I know it's not a very nice subject."

"Oh, it's not that dearie, it's just that you're the second person to ask about that this week."

"What? Who else?"

"Not a local. A tall man, quite thin with messy hair. Nice enough chap."

"Did he have a pretty redhead with him?"

"Not when he asked about the murder, but he had been in before with one, yes."

"Odd, can you show me what he looked at?

"Of course, dear."

Lloyd studied the story on the microfiche; it matched the current murder as far as he could tell, but it was only a newspaper report so it didn't have any of the finer forensic detail. Lloyd noted down the date on the article and started to skim back through previous issues, not really expecting to find anything.

His expectations were unfounded. The front page story less than a week before was about a spate of missing persons, five to be exact. Lloyd noted down their names.

The evening drew on. Gabriel and Anji were taking the half-mile stroll to Charles Ravenwood's.

"By the way, Anj, keep mum about the whole tunnel thing. It's probably nothing."

Anji still wasn't sure what to make of the fabled tunnel idea. "Okay, Gabe, but I'm starting to think that you should be in Shalebridge with that nut-job yourself." Her words caught a nerve with Gabriel but he managed to not let it show.

The duo turned a corner and their destination came into view. Charles owned a large house, two floors made up of what looked from the outside to be lots of rooms. They turned and made their way down the long driveway.

"This chap must have a bit of money," Gabriel said as they approached the front door.

Anji rang the doorbell. Charles answered within a moment and greeted them warmly.

"Come in, the wife's put a lovely spread on for us." Charles gave Gabriel's hand a vigorous shake, but was far more gentle when shaking Anji's. "Let me take your coats."

"Cheers," Gabriel said, as Charles took their coats and disappeared into a small room beneath the staircase to stash them.

"Please come and sit down; my wife will be in to say 'hello' in a moment." The three of them entered the sitting room and Gabriel started to take in his surroundings.

The house seemed even bigger on the inside than the out. It had unusually modern furnishings for a couple as old as the Ravenwoods – or so he thought until Mrs Ravenwood entered the room.

"Hello dear, these are our guests, Gabriel and Anji."

The woman before him was not what Gabriel had expected. She was a good thirty years Charles' junior, placing her in her mid to late thirties. She was slender yet shapely, a look that was accentuated by the knee-length low-cut black dress that she wore. She was of average height and had slightly longer than shoulder length blond hair. The woman extended a hand to Anji then to Gabriel, regarding him with cobalt blue eyes.

"Nice to meet you, Gabriel," she said in a well spoken English accent that Gabriel couldn't place.

"Likewise, Mrs Ravenwood." She still had a hold on his hand and placed her left hand on top of the shake.

"Please, call me Heather."

Gabriel smiled but felt a little uncomfortable.

"Shall we sit down for tea then?" came the welcome interruption form Charles.

The four sat enjoying a light tea. Gabriel continued to examine the room, partly out of interest and partly to help him keep his eyes from Heather's prominently-displayed cleavage. The dining room, much like the rest of the house, had modern furnishings and magnolia-painted walls with a selection of tasteful paintings hanging on them. A display cabinet occupied one corner of the room. Gabriel's eyes focused on the cabinet; it contained a few vases, a pair of antique flintlock pistols resting on a stand and, finally, a strange brass hexagonal object with a prominently raised symbol on top.

Charles clocked Gabriel's interest in the cabinet.

"I see my cabinet has caught your eye, young master Gabriel." He looked overjoyed. "Come, let me show you." Charles stood and gestured towards the cabinet. Gabriel joined him and the two men walked over to examine the contents.

"I'll get dessert," Heather said, almost unnoticed. Charles tugged on a chrome-covered chain at his waist, pulling a key from his trouser pocket. He slipped the key into the cabinet's lock and began to talk Gabriel through the different vases. Most had some tenuous and tedious link to the Devereaux family. After dispensing with the pottery, Charles gently picked up one of the pistols using both hands with a look of pride – almost exhilaration – on his face.

"Now, just look at this beauty. The pride of Claude Devereaux. One of two duelling pistols."

Charles turned to Gabriel holding the gun at eye level. Gabriel regarded the weapon with genuine admiration but couldn't help but feel that it looked somehow familiar. The pistol had an ebony stock with a pewter plated barrel, lock and trim, giving the whole weapon a dark appearance. Light almost seemed to slide off it.

Charles continued to talk, pointing with his index finger to a carving on the handle. "The indentation is the Devereaux family crest."

The crest was made up of a shield displaying the image of a chained man on his knees. The shield itself was flanked by two identical but mirrored figures; each figure was naked and had the horns and legs of a goat, not unlike the Greek god Pan. Gabriel couldn't help but think what a strange crest it was for an English, or indeed French, family. He'd drawn the fairly obvious conclusion that the name Devereaux was French.

Charles took the gun in his right hand, straightened his arm and pointed the weapon at the window. "Claude used this to defend the Manor the night it was stormed by villagers, you know? At least that's how one of the stories goes."

Gabriel's mind flickered back to his conversation with the librarian.

"Really? Mrs Birchwood seemed to think that he wasn't in residence that night." Gabriel fervently hoped that he hadn't just sounded incredibly rude.

"That's one story, my boy," Charles replied with enthusiasm, closing his left eye to look down the gun's barrel sill, aiming at the blackness outside the window.

"Really? There's another story? Sounds interesting, tourists love a bit of blood-soaked history. Could I trouble you to tell me?"

"No trouble at all, my boy." Charles sounded almost ecstatic.

"Mind if I make notes?"

"Not at all."

Gabriel pulled his ever-ready notepad from his back pocket.

"What did old Ethel tell you then, son?"

"Basically, that a local magistrate blamed the Devereaux family for the death of his wife and daughter. Then he riled up the village against them under the anti-witchcraft banner. She said that the villagers stormed the Manor but the family were in Hampshire at the time."

"Depending on who's telling the story, there was a little more to it than that." Charles winked. "This was way back in sixteen forty one," he said, waving a hand from side to side. "The magistrate – Nathaniel Knight was his name – was married with one daughter and an infant son. Both Harriet, his wife, and Mary, his daughter, were in the employ of the Devereaux family – Harriet being a cook and Mary a chamber maid. Rumour had it that that Claude had a bit of an eye for the young servant lasses, especially the more innocent ones, if you take my meaning. He'd made a few unwanted advances towards Mary."

Gabriel looked up from his notepad for a second. "Wasn't Claude married?"

Charles raised an eyebrow. "Yes he was, married to a very beautiful woman as well. However, there were rumours that both Claude and his wife were jointly involved in, shall we say, stealing the virtue of the young women." He phrased it in an old fashioned polite manner but the meaning was still clear. "People said that most of the lasses would submit to his advances in the end; money, power and status are strong aphrodisiacs, after all. However, Mary didn't succumb and not long after she disappeared. They had the whole village out searching but to no avail. Her mother, Harriet, found out about Claude's advances – gossip as it would have been –

and was convinced that he had something to do with her disappearance."

Anji kept quiet, but noticed how much Charles was enjoying telling the story and how delighted he was that Gabriel was interested enough to be making notes.

Gabriel looked up from his shorthand.

"What happened next?"

"Well the magistrate's wife, Harriet, confronted Claude with her suspicions and was dismissed on the spot. The story goes that that very night she contracted a withering illness, the doctors could not diagnose and four days later she was dead. However, not before she found out Mary's unfortunate fate."

Anji was intrigued by this point. "What was that?"

Charles was happy that his audience had doubled, but gave a slightly uncomfortable look. "Unfortunately, the poor girl's body was found in the woods near the house, and it was found mutilated. Whoever had killed her had cut out her heart."

The words made Gabriel's head swim for a second; he felt a crawling sensation at the base of his skull as his psyche was dragged back to Harry's cell.

"Nasty fate for anyone, let alone a young woman," Charles admitted on noticing Gabriel's discomfort. "Anyway, the Devereauxs' coach driver had been quite fond of Mary and turned up at Nathaniel's house in the dead of night, ranting about how Mary had been killed in some ritual. Rightly or wrongly, Nathaniel rallied up a mob. He was grief-stricken and public hysteria back then was high regarding witchcraft. It didn't take long for him to amass a small army who marched on Meetingstone manor. They stormed the house room by room, setting fires as they went. Claude armed himself with one of his two matched duelling pistols. Very long reload time but he was able to wound or kill more than a few of the villagers, before he took refuge along with the rest of his family in the library. They barricaded themselves in as the mob looted and torched the manor. How the family escaped is a mystery, but somehow they did, and gave the public impression that they'd been alternating between Hampshire and London at the time. Nathaniel had fallen to a shot from this pistol." Charles raised the firearm for a second. "The family never returned, so the fuss died down and Nathaniel's infant son was raised by the coach driver."

Heather re-entered the room, placed dessert on the table and everyone returned to their seats.

"Thank you, Charles. That was very interesting, and a good story."

"Happy to oblige, my boy."

Heather looked at Gabriel and posed a question. "Do you think it will be useful for your article, Gabriel?" Her soft voice matched her looks.

"Very. I'll have to stress that it's all a rumour, but people will gobble it up either way." Gabriel was only half lying; what he said was true for a tourist article, but was equally, if not more so, true for an article on occultism.

Charles finished his dessert and put the pistol back in the cabinet along with the vases, before locking the doors and returning the key to his pocket. He turned to his guests and smiled.

"I must leave you for a few minutes, call of nature. Would you top up the drinks, my dear?" he asked, looking at Heather.

"Good idea, my love," she answered. "Same again?" Anji and Gabriel gave polite affirmative responses as they were left alone in the dining room. Gabriel quickly pulled his mobile out of his pocket and slid it to Anji.

"Anj, quick, turn the bloody camera on for me, will you." Anji did so but grumbled under her breath about how 'the lazy sod should learn that stuff himself'.

Gabriel quickly but quietly strode over to the display cabinet, aimed his phone's camera and took several photos. He then hastily returned to his seat before Heather could return.

A short while later Gabriel and Anji were sauntering back to the rented house, Anji linking Gabriel's arm as usual, breathing in the warm night air.

"Interesting story he had, Gabe. What do you think?"

Gabriel considered for a moment. "Well, it was a damn sight more interesting than Ethel's version of events. Sex, murder and devil worship are always crowd pleasers." They arrived back at home. "Shall we get a beer and sit in the garden for a bit?" Gabriel asked as he unlocked the door.

"Ask a silly question. You get the beers, I've got a joint to roll."

The pair sat close to each other under a starry sky. The aroma of Anji's perfume, mixed with the scent of a nearby jasmine plant but with the occasional intrusion of smouldering marijuana filled the air.

Anji flicked the end of her joint at the ashtray on the table as she started to talk.

"So then, let's have a look at those photos you took." Gabriel dug through his inside pocket for a moment then pulled his phone out. He flipped it open and started to fumble with the buttons. Anji rolled her eyes and snatched the phone off him. "Good God man, you're like a simpleton with technology, aren't you," she said, the light from the screen illuminating her face with a pale glow.

"Yeah, and proud of it. Luddite to my dying breath." Anji ignored him; she was busy flicking through the photos.

"Here we are, babe. Two shots of that gun and two of…" She paused. "Gabe honey, why have you taken two photos of that random brass thing?"

"You mean the brass thing that had no apparent ornamental or practical application?" Gabriel asked smugly. "The same brass thing that Charles, after going on and on about those bleeding pots, didn't even mention."

Anji rolled her eyes again.

"Yep, and you're not impressing anyone," she chirped in a deliberately dismissive tone.

"Well, it's a key." Gabriel was still smug and being deliberately matter-of-fact.

"Okay, I'll bite. A key to what?"

"Nothing important really, just the secret passage under Meetingstone Manor," he smiled.

"Bollocks! How'd you know that?"

"You see the raised symbol? It's the same shape as the indentation in that creepy cellar. We'll compare the photos tomorrow and I'll show you."

Gabriel was back in the church hall and the celebration was still going on. Neil was still serving beer from his little hatch as Jim and Liz arrived.

"I see everyone's here," Jim commented, waving his hand in front of him. Gabriel regarded the room and clocked just about everyone he'd met in Stonebank; still no Tabatha though.

Liz looked at Gabriel to ask a question.

"Anji's playing tonight again, right?" A drum roll thundered across the room and Charles appeared on stage. He took the microphone and began to talk into it.

"My friends, it's good to see you all here as it is every year. It's been another good year for the village and we've got a fine Festival Queen again this year." Charles gestured behind himself and a curtain rose to reveal a young woman with red curls and duct tape over her mouth and eyes. She was wearing a white dress and was struggling to free her feet and hands, which were tied to the chair where she sat.

"Anji," Gabriel breathed, his mind flushing with terror. "We've got to get her out of here." He stepped forward but Jim and Liz grabbed his arms, holding him in place.

Charles continued to speak. "Now I say we take her out back and do what we've done for hundreds of years." The crowd cheered and Anji's struggling became panicked and frantic.

"Are you two bleeding nuts, they're gonna kill her!" Gabriel yelled from left to right.

"It's tradition," Jim said in a reassuring tone. "Come on, we'll take you out back to watch." Jim and Liz picked Gabriel up by the arms and followed the crowd.

They had placed Anji's chair atop a large pyre. Gabriel was struggling in vain; Jim and Liz seemed to have super-human strength. Charles thrust a lit torch into the heart of the pyre, and the flame spread outwards at astonishing speed.

"Anji!" Gabriel yelled at the top of his voice. The flames licked upwards, burning the bounds from Anji's hands. She ripped the duct tape from her mouth a moment before the flames engulfed her. The scream she gave chilled Gabriel to his core and followed him back to the conscious world.

Chapter 7

The covers to Gabriel's bed had fallen to the floor. He rose his hands to his forehead and let out a self-sympathetic groan. As he did so, he realised that his shoulders and arms ached from thrashing around in his sleep.

"When's this going to stop?" Gabriel asked himself, as his mind uncomfortably flashed to the thought of Harry's cell. He shook off the feeling and checked the clock, six in the morning. "May as well get up."

Anji didn't awaken for several more hours, so Gabriel took the opportunity to do some work on the article. He began a section covering the main parts of Charles' uprising story. He was trying to decide how much was truth and how much was just old wives' tales.

Parish records. The thought drifted through Gabriel's mind. A half-conscious Anji plodded into the living room and collapsed onto the sofa next to Gabriel, resting her head on his shoulder for a moment.

"Tea, babe?" he asked, already knowing the answer. The response he got was little more than an affirmative moan. He got up and returned with two hot mugs of tea, passing one to Anji. She took a deep sip and sank further into the sofa. A few moments passed before she spoke.

"What's today's plan, then?"

"I'm thinking that Charles' story needs a little more credibility. I'm thinking if the parish funeral records tally with what he told us, then the story moves from interesting fiction to 'bloody hell, that actually happened' territory."

"Not a bad idea for so early in the morning. I'll finish this cuppa, then get dressed."

The church yard was sunny with countless moss and lichen-covered gravestones. The church was not unlike that of many small Derbyshire villages; small, stone and old. 'Quaint', as the tourists would say. Anji and Gabriel made their way up a flagstone path to a large oak door. A breeze blew up and Gabriel heard a strange whisper in his ear.

Gabriel, came a voice. The writer looked around in astonishment. Was the voice there, or was it the wind in the trees? He chalked it up to his imagination and opened the heavy door for Anji.

The interior of the church smelt old and musty, a smell Gabriel quite liked in its place. It reminded him that he was just one of the many thousands of people who had trodden the stone floor through the ages. He looked up at the stone arches that stretched up to the roof of the nave, then around the stained-glass windows. He realised that with everything that had gone on, he really missed talking to Reverend Lincoln.

Gabriel looked down the regimented dark wooden pews that faced the pulpit and simple lectern. He was already reaching into his inside pocket for his wallet. He unzipped the coin compartment, fished out a couple of pound coins and deposited them in the brass collection box by the door.

"I've chucked a quid in for each of us," Gabriel assured Anji in a hushed tone, before making his way down the aisle in search of the vicar. A man not much older than Gabriel appeared from beyond a heavy wooden door by the pulpit.

"Hello. I'm Reverend Boyle. I believe I recognise you from the fête; you were talking to Charles I believe. Can I help you?" The man offered an open hand.

Gabriel gave it a firm shake as he sized the man up. He was about six feet and of slight build, with rimless glasses and short, dark blond hair. The white of his dog collar was emphasised by the blackness of the rest of his garb.

"I hope so, Reverend. I was hoping to take a look through your parish records, if that's okay."

"No problem at all, if you'd care to come with me I'll show you where they are. Would your friend care to join us?" the vicar asked, his head turning towards Anji who gave an awkward smile.

"Oh, no thanks. I'll just have a quick look around and wait in the churchyard if that's okay." She wasn't used to talking to men of the cloth and seemed almost embarrassed.

"That's quite alright, it's such a pleasant day to sit in the sun," the vicar responded. Gabriel noted that his voice had a strong southern accent that showed no signs of diminishment. This man wasn't a local and hadn't been in the area for any extended period of time.

The vicar led Gabriel down a flight of stairs into the church basement, making polite conversation as he walked. "What are you looking for, if you don't mind me asking? Baptism, marriage or burial?"

"Burial; well *burials* to be more precise." Gabriel was starting to feel a little uncomfortable with the subject matter.

"Oh, really? Not every day I get people checking on that. Are you researching your family tree or something?"

"Honestly no, I'm a journalist. I'm writing an article about the local area." Despite his lack of faith, Gabriel decided that withholding information wasn't as bad as outright lying to a servant of the Lord. "I heard a story about a rather interesting, if gruesome, uprising back in the sixteen-forties. I wanted to check if it was just an old wives' tale or if the records supported it." They continued to descend the stairs.

"Well, Mr? I didn't get your name."

"Jones. But please, call me Gabriel."

"Ah, a good name. A name after an archangel of our Lord. Anyway, where was I? That was it. I've not been in this community long. But there does seem to be a rather dark history about the place."

The vicar unlocked a heavy wooden door at the foot of the stairs and swung it open. "Here we are. I'll give you a hand." Reverend Boyle walked over to the old wooden filing drawers and started to search for the sixteen-forties. "Do you have an exact date?"

"Unfortunately not, just the year... sixteen-forty-one."

"Well it was a very small village back then, there can't have been that many deaths." It only took moments for the vicar to find the correct year. "I may not have been here long, Gabriel, but I flatter myself that I've done a good job getting to know these records. Here we are. What names are you looking for?"

Gabriel pulled his note book from his pocket.

"The Knight family - Nathaniel, Mary and. . ." he turned a page. ". . . Harriet." The Reverend started to look down the list of handwritten scrawl on old yellowed paper that radiated a strong musty smell. His eyes focused on the names but not the dates.

"Here we . . ." His words were cut short and his eyes widened slightly. "Oh dear. Not only did the Knight family all pass away at the same time, but. . ." He moved his finger down the page counting under his breath. "Sixteen other souls passed that very same week."

Gabriel looked over his shoulder; the records didn't show cause of death.

"I assume that this corroborates the story you were told."

"I'd have to say that it does. Thank you, Reverend." Charles' voice popped into Gabriel's head: *". . . able to wound or kill more than a few of the villagers."* He didn't agree with Charles' modest definition of 'more than a few.'

"I'll get out of your hair."

On some level, Gabriel had hoped that he'd find nothing. His experience with Harry was still preying on his mind; part of him wanted to just call it a day. Chalk the whole thing up to experience and forget about the article. On the other hand, he needed the money and he never could resist a mystery - and a mystery was what this was starting to feel like, though he was still only scratching the surface.

The Reverend showed Gabriel through the door and into the church yard; a crow startled away from the flagstone path. The two men bid each other farewell with a hand shake as the Reverend spoke.

"If there is anything else you need, please call back."

"Thank you Reverend, I will."

Gabriel took a stroll around the churchyard in search of Anji. He found her sunning herself on an old worn bench. He walked over and sat at her side.

"Find anything out, babe?" she asked with her eyes shut, as she cocked her head back to catch rays on her face.

"Well, turns out that Charles' version is looking a little more likely. There were a lot of poor buggers who died that week - or more to the point, that night."

"No wonder that manor feels so haunted. Though I knew most of the Knight family had died that year," Anji said matter-of-factly.

"How?" Gabriel looked a little confused, for a second hoping that Anji wasn't having odd dreams as well. Anji smiled.

"Use your eyes Gabe, you're normally so good at this." Gabriel look dead ahead of Anji; three weathered gravestones stood in front of her. Nathaniel, Mary and Harriet Knight.

"Well spotted." The graves didn't offer any more information than Gabriel had already got from the records, but Nathaniel's grave did bear an unusual symbol. It was difficult to make out detail after the years of weathering, but it seemed to be the shape of a shield with some sort of large tree inside it. The writer continued to stare for a moment, the slightest chill shooting down his spine. If he'd been wearing a hat he'd have removed it. The breeze rose for a moment.

Gabriel, the wind seemed to say again. This had to be in his head, he told himself as something crossed his mind that would offer a timely change of subject. "Knight was my mother's maiden name you know. I always think that I might use it as a pen name if I ever get a novel published. It has a better ring to it than Jones."

Anji giggled. "What next, then?"

"I say the pub for dinner, then back to the house. Time I did a little work on the article."

Constable Lloyd Brighton had returned to the county police station. He'd spent the morning in the records office, looking up reports from the fifty-year-old murder of Howard Graves. The coroner's report was unnervingly similar to what Tom Agar must have filed regarding the recent murder. However, it was the investigating officer's reports that really interested Lloyd. They were very detailed and cross-referenced to other reports. It seemed that Howard Graves' murder was just one part of a far larger picture; the officer at the time had linked both the murder and a spate of disappearances to an active satanic, or demonic, cult.

This is starting to read like a bad horror novel, Lloyd thought.

The report went on to mention two of the five missing persons. They were both found dead in the forest surrounding Stonebank; cause of death had been attributed to heart failure in both cases. The remaining three were missing to this day. There were certain individuals mentioned by name as having suspected cult involvement. Two stood out to Lloyd: Douglas Ravenwood, Charles' late father; and a woman he'd known all his life, Ethel Birchwood.

The officer had believed that the cult had a meeting place near Meetingstone Manor, but was never able to find it or any conclusive evidence against any of his suspects. Lloyd was toying with the idea of tracking the officer down and asking him what had happened first-hand. He started to search the records for the man's file. Jonathan Cobb had retired some ten years ago; the file still had an address listed, some village named Hoggersbrook. Lloyd noted it down, unsure if he'd actually use it or not.

He headed out of the records office and towards the lift. He'd told Brigham to give him a day, and he'd had that day. Time to report in. What was he going to say? Was he really going to tell a DCI that he thought that there may be some link to a fifty-year-old suspected cult? He couldn't expect a DCI of all people to believe that poppycock. When it came right down to it, Lloyd didn't really believe it himself, not in his head at least.

His gut, however, was all for the idea.

Lloyd reached Donovan Brigham's office and tapped on the frosted glass pane of the door.

"Come in," came a muffled voice. The constable entered the room, still unsure what he was going to say.

"Ah, constable, have seat," Donovan said gruffly, gesturing to the empty chair in front of the desk where he was seated. "So, what have you got for me?"

Lloyd hesitated, wondering how to phrase what he had to say, or even if he should say it at all.

Donovan frowned. "Come on, I can see you've got something to say." He made no effort to hide his impatience. "Spit it out, man."

Sod it, Lloyd thought. "There are possible cult links."

Donovan's impatient tone disappeared. "Cult, as in lots of stupid drugged-up kids blindly following some nut-job?" Lloyd couldn't pinpoint the man's new tone.

"No, more like a demonic or satanic cult."

"*What*?"

"Far-fetched I know - but it's that or a copycat, copying a fifty year old murder and let's face it, copycats aren't exactly common either outside television programmes." After hearing himself say it out loud, Lloyd realised just how ridiculous he sounded.

Donovan stood up and moved to the window, staring out of it. Lloyd was mentally scrambling to think of something more run-of-the-mill to say. Donovan spoke without turning around.

"Wouldn't be the first time." The voice was still gruff, but sincere.

"You've had this before?" Lloyd asked, unable to contain his surprise.

"No. Not me, but I've heard of more than one case in the past and as we've already said, nothing about this makes sense. Always keep an open mind, Constable Brighton, and never underestimate people's stupidity or their capacity for suggestion. That's what my boss told me back when I was a sergeant. On the other hand, he also used to warn me to never expect an open mind from anyone else." Brigham turned to face him. "So for the moment, any official reports are going to indicate that we are acting on the assumption that it is a copycat. The only other person we share this with is Sergeant Dudley. Capisce?"

Lloyd nodded.

"Right, fill me in then," the DCI instructed as he returned to his seat.

Lloyd spent the next twenty minutes or so recounting his investigation so far. Donovan leant back in his chair for a second. "So the question is, Constable: where do we go from here?" He shifted his weight and the chair tilted forward. "We can talk to your Mrs Birchwood, or we can go and quiz a retired police officer. And by 'we' I mean you. At least, for the minute."

Lloyd was a little surprised. "Why me?"

"Two reasons: firstly, as you pointed out the other day, these are your people. Secondly, although I don't disbelieve you, I'm not anxious to get openly involved until you have some proof."

Lloyd's riotous indignation boiled over; he stood up and leant forward slightly. He began to speak and his tone was less than polite.

"So basically, you think I might be right, but you're hedging your bets to protect yourself from looking stupid if I'm wrong?"

Donovan considered for a moment. Nothing the constable had said could really be classed as untrue; however, he didn't think that the constable fully appreciated the situation of a DCI. He also stood up, and leant forward, resting his palms on his desk. His voice deepened.

"What the bloody hell do you expect me to do? You come in here with a story about a demonic cult, with a link to a murder fifty bloody years ago." He leaned forward a little more. "Yes I think it adds up, and yes I think it's worth looking into. But my superiors will think I've lost it if I tell them this story without any evidence. What did you think would happen? I'd say 'Great job, Constable. Here, take Mulder and Scully and go round up that evil cult.'

The DCI paused and took a deep breath. "I'm sorry, Lloyd." His voice had lost all of its ferocity. "I know it's unfair and you're right to be pissed off." He ran his hand over his hair. "I'll give you as much unofficial back up as I can, but I need to keep this off the books until you have some solid evidence. If you are right and we do crack it then it's your feather, not mine." He looked Lloyd in the eyes. "That's the best I can do for you. Fair enough?"

Donovan sat back in his chair and after a brief moment Lloyd stood down.

"Fair enough. I'll see what I can dig up."

Lloyd started to mentally assess the best course of action; one name he hadn't mentioned to the DCI, the name of the stranger who'd suddenly turned up just after the whole business started. The same stranger who claimed to be writing about this occult stuff. The stranger who Lloyd honestly felt was a good man... but that wasn't going to stop him digging a little.

Gabriel sat in a tatty threadbare armchair in the living room, tapping away on his laptop. Anji walked in and put a cup of tea next to him.

"Thanks, Anj." He sounded, and was, genuinely sincere but his eyes didn't leave the screen.

"So, Gabe, what about the 'key'? You told me you'd explain."

Gabriel stopped typing and looked up.

"Come here I'll show you."

He started to browse his laptop for files, firstly loading a good quality image of the symbol from the cellar of Meetingstone Manor, then a less impressive grainy image of the brass object from Charles' cabinet. "Bloody crap phone cameras," he commented under his breath. Anji perched herself on the chair arm.

"Look at the shape of the indentation on the symbol." Gabriel switched images. "I know it's a bad picture but look at the relief on the brass thingy."

Anji studied the image. Gabriel put them side-by-side on the screen.

"Got to admit, babe, it looks like a good fit. But where's that leave us? It's not like you're going to break into his house."

Gabriel's mind flitted to his lock picks. For a moment he considered breaking in, then immediately wrote it off as a stupid idea.

"True, we could always ask him if we could borrow it."

Anji looked at him and raised an eyebrow. "Hi Charles, we think that there's a secret passage under Meetingstone Manor, can we borrow that brass thing. We think it's a key because we took a photo of it while you were out of the room."

Gabriel gave a half-forced smile. "I take your point. We'll file it under 'for future reference.' I really want to get a proper look at it though." He closed the laptop. "Come on, let's have a beer or two before bed."

The bedroom was pitch black. Gabriel could see nothing.

"Come with me," said a deep, husky, almost ethereal voice. He stared into the blackness, then turned, scanning the full three-hundred-and-sixty degrees around himself but could see nothing but night.

"Who, who are you?" he said with a stammer.

"You know who I am." The voice seemed somehow deeper and the room seemed a little lighter, allowing Gabriel to distinguish a black shape.

"I am the Vanguard, I am the Harbinger. I am the one who precedes. Now follow. It is long past time. The master will have his Avatar."

Gabriel felt his body being lifted by an unknown force; he was still upright but his feet weren't touching the floor. His body turned towards an outline of a doorway. The world became a blur as Gabriel seemed to be propelled through the opening, down the stairs and out into the streets. He seemed to move faster and faster, down roads, over fields and forests towards Meetingstone Manor.

Gabriel could see the house as his body started to slow, but kept on target. The cellar came into view. He came to a halt at the entrance. Anji stood at the doorway.

She looked at him with empty ocular cavities, dark red blood running down her cheeks. She spoke; her voice was natural but filled with panic.

"Are you going to let them do this to me, Gabe? Don't you love me?"

Gabriel could hardly speak. "Anj?"

Before he knew it the black figure was at his side. A cloaked arm reached out, grabbed him by the neck and thrust him into the cellar. He was flying again for a moment, then hit ground by the brass marking.

Charles walked in from a side room and inserted his brass object into the symbol. He turned it four times and a stone wall silently opened. Gabriel was lifted off the floor again, and this time his body was flung down the secret passage until he landed in a small, round room with a circular altar in the middle. There was a man on the altar with a sack on his head and his hands and feet bound to metal rings on the edges.

Gabriel felt something in his hand. He looked down to see a long dagger with a curved blade.

"Take his heart," came the deep, husky voice. Gabriel looked into the blackness of the tunnel he'd just travelled down.

"Take his heart, Gabriel, the master will have his Avatar."

Gabriel ignored the voice and pulled the sack off the man's head.

"Jim?" He was surprised to see his old friend and began to use the knife to cut James' bonds.

"Stop," came Anji's voice. "If he lives, then I die."

She stepped out from the shadows and walked towards Gabriel, her blue eyes intact and staring right at him. She moved in close, slipped her arm around him and held the back of his head in her right hand, running her fingers through his hair. She kissed him full on the lips, then held him close and whispered in his ear. "If you don't take his heart, then I lose my eyes followed by my life. Do it. Do what you know you have to do."

Gabriel pushed her away as a crow landed on Anji's shoulder.

"Do it now or I'm dead." She fell to her knees, a look of pure dread on her face. "Do it now," she pleaded. "Do it. Please. If you love me, you'll do it."

The crow took flight off Anji's shoulder. It spiralled around and then went straight for her face. Gabriel felt a spray of blood on his cheek as the bird set to work. The scream was even more blood curdling than the night before.

Gabriel slightly raised his head as he came back into an unexpectedly bright consciousness and uttered his first words of the day.

"Bloody bastard hell."

He collapsed his head back, expecting to feel the comfort of his pillow. Instead he found a hard cold surface hit the back of his head. The pain and surprise shocked the rest of his body and mind into full consciousness.

He wasn't in bed. He awkwardly stood up and looked around, a floor of stone slabs, a stone staircase and a set of rusty iron railings with a heavy padlock. He felt a mild escalation of his adrenalin levels, as he realised where he was; outside the wine cellar of Meetingstone Manor.

Chapter 8

Gabriel looked down at his feet and realised that he was fully clothed. *I must still be dreaming*. He climbed the stairs and looked out over the dew-laden grass warming in the morning sun. A shiver passed over him. *It's still bloody creepy here.*

He started to walk towards the gateposts. It was a good walk back to the house, and he wasn't exactly expecting to find his car parked around the corner. The obvious question was running through his mind again and again. How had he got there? He'd never sleepwalked to his knowledge, and he'd sure as hell never woken up in a different place to when he'd fallen asleep. What was he going to tell Anji and how long was it going to take him to walk home?

Before Gabriel got to the gateposts he noticed that the visitors' hut was open. He checked in his pockets, pulling out his notebook before disregarding it and putting it back. He continued to check and found his wallet. *Thank God,* he thought as he headed inside.

The door-mounted bell rang as Gabriel entered the visitors hut. It smelt mildly of paint and housed the random assortment of borderline-pointless exhibits that Gabriel expected. However, he was surprised to hear a familiar voice.

"Gabriel, my boy." Charles Ravenwood stood behind a counter.

Bugger, Gabriel nearly said out loud. He figured he'd slip in and out quietly and be on his way; he wasn't expecting to have to make polite conversation while feeling insanely disorientated and almost scared. Gabriel considered his appearance. *Full outside clothing including a coat and shoes, my hair always looks a mess anyway.*

"Charles! I forgot you worked here."

"Not sure I'd call it work, my boy, history is my passion." The two men shook hands. "What brings you here?"

"Oh, I just thought I'd have a bit of a walk. Speaking of which, do you sell any ordnance survey maps or ramblers' guide books?"

"Oh, fancy a few of our local footpaths do you? We've got quite a few over here." Charles led Gabriel to the 'shop' corner of the shed where a freestanding rotary book-holder stood. It held a couple of ordnance survey maps and an array of books about the local area, the manor and some dedicated to local footpaths. Gabriel made courteous conversation with Charles as he flicked through the footpath books.

"This one looks about right, Charles."

"That one's five-ninety-nine, my boy. A good book though."

"Give me a sec." Gabriel fished the correct change out of his wallet and handed it over before making a sharp exit.

The worried writer sat on the edge of an old stone fountain in the manor house grounds, studying a map in the book he'd just bought. He had found the manor and was trying to work out the quickest route back to the rented house on foot. *I reckon that's it,* Gabriel thought as he surveyed the manor grounds to get his bearings. He stood up and headed off in the direction of where he thought the footpath should start.

The atmosphere of the grounds hadn't changed; still creepy, still making the hairs on Gabriel's neck stand on end. Given his morning so far, he wasn't exactly in the right frame of mind to fight the feeling off. He couldn't help but think of all the people that died the night the manor was stormed; the night Claude Devereaux shot sixteen villagers, not counting Nathaniel Knight. Gabriel quickened his pace as he spied the green public footpath sign, anxious to get out of the grounds. He quickly mounted the stile and was on the footpath. The path wound into dense woodland; in Gabriel's current mood he thought it looked a little foreboding but decided that it beat the manor house grounds.

Gabriel had been walking for about half an hour; he'd left the manor house long behind him and was glad of it. The distance and time were helping and he was gradually starting to shake off a lot of the morning's strangeness. Gabriel peered into the dense woodland as he walked, looking at the shafts of sun that were breaking through the canopy.

Something caught his eye. A strange-looking stone structure nestled in the trees. Even after the peculiar start to the day, Gabriel's curiosity still got the better of him. He made his way off the path and towards the structure. As he approached, he realised that it covered a larger area than he'd expected. It was little more than a ruin and Gabriel couldn't identify the period. It had a few remaining stone archways and several ruined walls, only a few feet in height. A large circular altar stood near the centre of the ruin. The forest's birdsong had subsided; the ruin had much the same sinister atmosphere as the manor house.

Gabriel considered just turning around and heading back to the path, but his interest was piqued. He looked around at the archways and walls, then at the altar. Something stood out; both the archways and walls were overgrown, weeds at their bases and ivy growing up them. The altar was different, almost out of place. It was as old and weathered as the rest of the stonework, but strangely free of weeds, as if someone had been tending to it.

Gabriel approached the altar. The centre was slightly raised with a camber that sloped towards the edges, with the exception of what looked like four gutters heading outwards from the middle. For a second Gabriel's mind flashed to his dreams. The altar reminded him of the one he'd seen the night before, but he hadn't really focused on the details of the stonework due to his oldest friend being laid out on it.

There were some extremely worn letters skirting the circumference. Gabriel did his best to make them out but could only identify a few. He pulled his note book out and recorded the letters he could see, adding dashes for the illegible characters:

No--n ---iL----e-t, ---- mu--i ----s

Gabriel continued to explore the area. He discovered the remains of four more archways a few dozen yards from the main structure. Following them, he found they led to a large alcove cutting into an embankment. The alcove was about eight feet high by four foot wide, and about two foot deep.

The writer paused for a moment, a feeling of apprehension growing in the gut. He suppressed the feeling and approached the stone walls of the alcove; they were covered in ornate but worn engravings. Gabriel could make out what looked like some sort of crest, not unlike the Devereaux family crest that he had seen on the pistol at Charles', but it was too eroded to be sure.

"You might have to come back here with the camera, Jones," he said under his breath as he continued to study the engravings. "More letters." Gabriel still had his notebook in hand and jotted the string of letters beneath the first set.

--men --hi ----- --t, q--- m---i s----

"I'd say that's the same passage."

Gabriel walked back to the altar and perched on the edge as he tried to reconstruct as much of the passage as possible. Most of the words were still incomprehensible; however, he managed to reconstruct the first of them: 'Nomen'. *Well Jones, if you're Latin's not failing you then that could mean either 'power' or 'name'. Not much use by itself though.*

Gabriel was becoming acclimatised to the eeriness of the place. He was about to take a final walk around before leaving, when the light breeze in the air suddenly grew to a strong wind. The leaves of the trees began to sing out in chorus as the heavy breeze climaxed.

Gabriel, came the bodiless voice. Gabriel's heartbeat quickened slightly.

"It's your imagination, Jones. Pull yourself together." The wind rose again and the voice came again.

Gabriel. The wind died as suddenly as it had grown and the trees were silent again; the forest had become completely calm. The quiet was broken by the coarse caw of a crow. Gabriel turned to look in the direction of the sound. The black bird was perched atop one of the stone archways, looking directly at Gabriel and aggressively cawing every few seconds.

"Okay Jones, time to make a move." He turned and walked swiftly back towards the path, his strides bordering on a run. Gabriel looked back at the bird, just in time to realise that it had taken flight and was headed directly for him. He ducked quickly and the crow narrowly missed the top of his head by about an inch. He felt the hairs move from the air displacement the bird had caused. It landed on a nearby tree, and immediately took a second swoop. Gabriel rolled to his left, scarcely avoiding the crow but grazing his hand on a fallen branch as he did so.

"Okay, you bastard," he said, picking up the fallen branch and holding it like a baseball bat. "Try that again!" The bird had settled on another tree and was motionless, as if considering what to do. "Come on." The bird took flight into the forest and Gabriel's muscles relaxed. He lowered the branch and used it to support his weight for a moment.

Gabriel.

The voice came again, this time without the accompanying wind but the sound still seemed to be all around. The voice came yet again, this time from the direction of the ruin.

Avatar.

Gabriel spun around to look where it came from. He could see a black figure, a featureless silhouette against the pale stonework.

Avatar.

The figure started to move towards him. Gabriel's heart pounded in his chest as adrenalin coursed through his veins. He turned and started to run; he ran down the footpath, not looking back. He cleared a stile in a single vault and hit the ground running, the adrenalin pushing his body well beyond its normal limits. He hadn't run anything close to that speed since he was a boy, the forest around him almost becoming a blur.

Gabriel sped out of the edge of the forest and into the light. He was mildly disorientated but realised that he'd arrived at the stone circle. He turned, expecting that he'd outpaced the figure. He was wrong. The figure was striding quickly towards him. As it got closer, the feeling of Gabriel's heart pounding changed to one of extreme pain; it felt like his chest was being crushed and his heart was about to explode.

The figure continued to advance, and as it got closer the feeling intensified. Gabriel stumbled backwards into the stone circle, tripping over one of the rocks on the inner ring. As he fell backwards the pain in his chest vanished. He hit the ground, relieved that the pain had gone, but still acutely aware of his pursuer. He scrambled to his feet using the stone to help himself up.

The figure had gone.

Gabriel collapsed back onto the ground; he still had adrenalin in his system but his body was spent. He looked up at the sky and considered the enormity of what had happened. The most logical explanation was that he was hallucinating, but somehow logic was no longer ringing true.

There was one man he felt he really needed to talk to.

Gabriel returned to Hoggersbrook. He'd given Anji some cock-and-bull story about needing to check on some details with Eric Conway, and they'd both headed back. When she'd asked where he'd been all morning, he simply said that he'd woken up early and felt like a walk. He'd mentioned the ruin but left out the part about the homicidal crow and the black figure.

Gabriel wasn't sure if she bought the story or not. He was fully aware that he must have looked shaken, and had toyed with telling her the truth. He concluded that a lie was better for the moment; at least until he got his own head around what was going on.

Gabriel passed the yew tree in the church yard and headed for the church door. He hesitated for a second; despite regular visits to the church yard and vicarage, he hadn't actually been inside the church since Aunty Gladys' funeral.

The inside was cool and quiet. Gabriel dropped a few coins in the collection box and looked down the row of pews. He made his way to the front pew, sat next to the church's single occupant and began to speak.

"Shakespeare was right, old friend. There *are* more things in heaven and earth."

Reverend Lincoln turned to look at Gabriel, giving him a warm but concerned smile.

"We've not seen you in here in a long time, my boy." He placed a hand on Gabriel's shoulder. "What's wrong?"

Gabriel proceeded to tell the whole story. The Reverend listened intently. Gabriel could see no sign of disbelief on his face or in his mannerisms.

"You must think I'm as nuts as old Harry." He looked directly at the man he'd known all his life and swallowed.

"I'm scared, Reverend," he said with emotion. "I'm not sure what's more frightening. That these things actually happened, or that I'm losing my mind."

Reverend Lincoln looked at him for a second.

"Gabriel, I've known you your entire life, I've watched you grow from a crying baby to a strong, intelligent, kind, man. You've had more than your share of tragedy and heartache and I've never seen you waver. Believe me, I have never spoken truer words than when I tell you that you are not losing your mind."

Gabriel gave a sad smile. "Do you believe that demons exist?"

The reverend gently tapped the bible in front of him with the palm of his hand. "You should ask Mark, Matthew, Luke and John. All of them mention the dark servants of the Satan in one form or another. Demons exist, my boy. But you need one more informed than I to advise you. Perhaps the professor you mentioned?"

"That's a good start. Thank you, Reverend."

"By the way, the Reverend Boyle that you met?"

"Yes?"

"Did he mention what had happened to his predecessor?"

"No, he just said that he had taken over recently." Gabriel was mildly intrigued. "Why?"

"Nothing really, it just struck me as odd. He was a strong healthy man. God took him from us only a few months back when he had a heart attack. Anyway, it's not important. I'll let you get moving."

Gabriel felt a little better; he'd dropped his car off at home and was walking to the pub after texting an invite to Anji. He knew Liz would be working and he wanted her to set up a meeting with the professor. Plus, he really needed a drink; oh God, did he need a drink.

He swung the door open and strolled in, happy to be back with friends in familiar surrounds. He looked at the bar, Liz and Scott serving, Eric in his usual seat... it felt like a sanctuary. Then he was suddenly struck by a very out-of-place man.

"Lloyd?" Gabriel asked, a little confused. Constable Lloyd Brighton turned to see who was addressing him. "Gabriel? What are you doing here?"

Gabriel had his first genuine laugh of the day. "I live here, what's your excuse?" He heard his own words. "Well, I live in the village, not the pub," he began to correct. "Okay, I live in the pub a bit."

Lloyd laughed and decided that the tip of the iceberg couldn't hurt.

"Ah, I'm trying to find an ex-cop that lived here. Went to his address but turns out that our records are out of date. I've booked into a guest house for the night and I figured I'd ask around in the meantime. Let me get you a drink."

"You're in my village, I'm buying the drinks."

"You look like you need one, so I'm buying. You can get the next round. Fair enough?"

"Fair enough." Lloyd was about to ask what he wanted when Liz placed a pint of Guinness in front of him. "Cheers," Gabriel said looking at both of them, then looked back to Liz. "Oh Liz, very quick question. Can you set me up another meeting with your professor friend?"

She looked a little intrigued. "Sure, Gabe."

"Cheers." Gabriel turned back to Lloyd. "Sorry about that, urgent business. So what's the name of this cop?"

"Jonathan Cobb. He used to live down on Milroy's Place." Lloyd said before taking a sip of beer. Gabriel raised his eyebrows.

"Cobb the copper, yeah we all know him." He leant past Lloyd for a second and slightly raised his voice. "Oi, Mr Conway, where's Mr Cobb living these days?"

Eric turned on his stool.

"He moved to the market place. Froghopper Cottage, I think."

"Thanks, boss." Gabriel gave him the thumbs up.

"Funny you should ask, though," Eric added. Both Gabriel and Lloyd looked at him.

"He was the copper who arrested that nutter who cut his own brother's heart out."

Gabriel's brain shifted gear. Why was Lloyd, the local Stonebank plod, looking for Jonathan Cobb years after he'd retired? It was a strange coincidence that Lloyd was looking for the cop who arrested the man he'd spoken to only a few days previously. Gabriel didn't believe in coincidences and was wondering what had prompted Lloyd's search. His intuition was telling him that Howard Graves was no longer the last corpse to be found with a missing heart in Stonebank.

Lloyd's brain had also shifted up a gear. What was Gabriel's game? Did he have useful information, or was he just stumbling around looking of any signs of the occult to write about? He obviously knew Jonathan Cobb and could be useful to help him break the ice. Not to mention that he'd already proven useful by getting Cobb's address.

Two questions remained. Could Gabriel be trusted, and would he be a help or a hindrance? Lloyd looked at Gabriel, and noticed that Gabriel was looking back at him. Both men continued to consider for a moment before Gabriel spoke.

"We're sizing each other up aren't we? You're wondering why I've been asking questions about a fifty-year-old murder, and you know that I'm wondering why you're looking for the man that arrested Harry Graves."

Gabriel considered for another moment; he looked back at the insanity of the day and the events leading up to it. He lowered his voice. "I'll lay my cards on the table. I'd bet good money that you've had at least one recent murder victim with a missing heart. I'd also bet good money that this goes a little further than one victim, and that you're stumped for leads." Gabriel studied Lloyd's face. He could read that his assumptions were accurate and was thinking that having a police officer on side was a boon right now. "I know Cobb, I can help you break the ice, he'll feel more comfortable with me there."

Lloyd considered the implied proposal. "Why do you want to be there?"

"I'm nosy." Gabriel gave a shrewd smile. "Also, I'm writing about the Howard Graves murder and Cobb might give me a few more details with a police officer there." Gabriel didn't mention that he also wanted to ask him about strange black cloaked figures.

Lloyd continued to consider the proposal. Then he downed the rest of his pint and placed the empty glass down on the bar.

"Deal. I'll pick you up at ten in the morning. Where should I come and get you from?"

"I'll hang out in the church yard. Now let's have another drink." As Gabriel turned to order the drinks, he caught sight of Anji.

"Guinness and two lagers please."

Anji joined them, they filled her in on their plans and had a few more drinks before the pub's turning out time.

Lloyd stumbled off in the direction of his guest house and Anji and Gabriel headed back to Gabriel's house, Anji linking his arm as usual. She squeezed it for a second, and the warm air suddenly dropped to a chill. Gabriel looked around; the village wasn't well lit, dark streets sparsely punctuated with ageing street lamps. He could see nothing, but could feel something watching him.

Gabriel, came the now familiar voice. Anji shivered. Gabriel was sure that she didn't hear it but on some level she seemed to feel it. They quickened their step and returned home.

There was a mutually shared air of relief as Gabriel swung the door shut. Anji collapsed onto the settee in the living room, as Gabriel fetched two beers from the fridge and collapsed next to her. Anji took a sip then rested her head on his shoulder.

"Gabe?" she asked quietly.

"Yeah, Anj?"

"You gonna tell me?"

"Tell you what?" Gabriel knew what she was getting at, but played dumb.

"Tell me what's wrong. I'm worried about you." Gabriel wasn't sure what to tell her; he'd felt strange enough telling Reverend Lincoln.

"I know you're not okay, it's written all over your face."

"Okay. . ."

Anji shifted her head off his shoulder, and Gabriel proceeded to fill her in with an abridged version of events, mentioning the dreams but not mentioning her presence or loss of eyes. He was fully aware that the story sounded crazy but also aware that if one person would believe it, it would be Anji.

"One thing I'm really not sure about though, Anji." Gabriel struggled to say what came next. "What if I've lost it? What if I went sleep walking, ended up at Meetingstone, and the rest is all in my head?"

Anji considered for a second, then Gabriel continued to speak. "Me being nuts is the most logical explanation, you know."

Anji put her arms around Gabriel, pecked him on the cheek, and returned her head to his shoulder. "You daft bugger. You should know by now that I don't do logic."

Gabriel realised how much he enjoyed the feeling of her lips on his cheek and the warmth of her arms around him. *Damn it, Jones, this is not the time to start falling for one of your best friends.* Gabriel listened to his own counsel and tried to push any feelings to the back of his mind.

"You gonna drop the story?"

"I'm seriously thinking about it. I just want to have a chat to the copper and the professor before I make a final decision. Also, I want the copper's personal evaluation of Harry and I want to probe the professor to see if any of this stuff has happened before."

The moon beamed down, bathing the stone of the ruins in its pale white light. The tall black figure stood behind the large circular altar. Gabriel looked around the ruins; he could make out a number of other black robed figures. They stood motionless with their hoods up. As Gabriel looked back at the large figure, he noticed a grotesque crow sitting on its shoulder. The figure spoke in its usual husky, intangible tone.

"Welcome, Avatar. Have you come to prepare yourself for the master?" The smaller figure spoke in unison.

"Master." Gabriel thought the voices were human - for want of a better word - as he approached the altar and realised that there was a body on it, a body that had somehow escaped his attention until now. A body which lay lifeless, a body with a crimson cavern in the centre of its chest.

Gabriel looked into Jim's lifeless eyes, then realised that both his hands were full. His right held a bloodied curved blade. He was too scared to look at his left hand but continued to anyway. Gabriel felt like he could hardly breathe; panic was setting in, and he raised his hand in front of his face and the human heart came into view.

For the love of God please let me be in my own bed. Gabriel opened his eyes, trying to distance himself from the dream. The room came into focus and he felt a massive relief as he realised that he was, in fact, in his own bed.

Chapter 9

The morning air was crisp; the green grass of the churchyard almost glowed in the morning sun as the dew slowly evaporated.

Gabriel sat on a bench with his legs stretched out, flicking through his notebook as he tried to think of a good reason - other than the money - to keep writing the article. He'd known what Anji had meant when she'd asked if he was going to drop the story. She'd meant he'd be stupid not to.

Gabriel's mobile chimed. He pulled it out of his pocket and read the text he'd just received. It was from Liz, saying that she'd set up a meeting with Professor Harrison for six o'clock. He pocketed his phone and continued to flick through his notepad, looking over the notes he'd made after his conversation with Harry Graves at the Asylum several days earlier.

One note was unsettling him more than anything else. '*Must take heart to be Avatar.*'

Gabriel's thoughts were interrupted by the muted rumble of a slow-moving car. He looked out of the churchyard gate to see the white of a police car pull up. He flipped the notebook shut and pocketed it while making his way to the car. Gabriel raised his hand to his forehead and gave a little good morning salute with only two fingers outstretched. He pulled open the passenger side door and jumped in.

Lloyd's driving was controlled and steady. It wasn't far to Jonathan Cobb's house and Gabriel wanted to get as much information out of Lloyd as possible before they got there.

"So, what are you going to ask him then?"

Lloyd gave Gabriel a look. "What?" Gabriel returned a look that he hoped portrayed innocence. "I'm going to be there when you ask him anyway, what harm can it do to tell me beforehand?"

Lloyd considered for a second. "Okay, basically this bloke investigated a bunch of disappearances back in the fifties. The cases ended up, as you know, with a dead body with no heart. He reckons there was some link to a cult who thought they were worshipping the devil or a demon or something similar."

"What do you think?" Gabriel asked in a cautious tone.

"I think it's not actually that unfeasible that a bunch of nut jobs would believe that the Devil actually exists. Hell, you get that in church every Sunday. . ." he gave a small laugh, ". . . but actually worshipping him and killing someone. I'm not sure to be honest."

The car pulled up outside Cobb's house and the two men got out. Lloyd spoke as he approached the front door. "If you can ease us in and then I could take over, that would be good."

"No problem," Gabriel replied, before raising his hand to knock on the panelled wooden door. As his knuckles made contact with the hardwood, he realised the door wasn't properly closed. The force from the impact made it silently swing open on well-oiled hinges.

Feeling slightly uncomfortable, Gabriel knocked again on the now open door and called loudly into the house. "Hello. Mr Cobb, are you in?" No answer. Gabriel raised his voice slightly. "Mr Cobb?" A shiver passed over his body. He looked at Lloyd.

"Something feels wrong."

"Agreed."

Both men walked gingerly inside. Lloyd tried calling this time. "Mr Cobb, I'm Constable Brighton. I was hoping we could have a chat." Lloyd shifted into police mode. "Gabe, don't touch anything and watch where you step." Gabriel could feel tension growing. Something felt wrong, very wrong. He checked the living room, but no sign of life.

"Nothing in here." He shouted back to Lloyd. "You checked the kitchen yet?"

"Just about to." Gabriel heard the kitchen door swing open.

"*Jesus Christ!*" Lloyd's voice was a mix of alarm and disbelief. Gabriel rushed to see what was wrong.

"You might not want to. . ." Lloyd was too late in his warning as Gabriel reached the door way.

"Bloody hell!"

The floor was covered in blood. The lifeless body of Jonathan Cobb sat limply on a kitchen chair, his hands and feet tied to it to keep him in place. Gabriel only looked for a split second, but the image burnt itself into his mind.

Cobb's clothes were soaked in blood; his shirt had been ripped open and his heart cut out.

Gabriel stumbled for the front door, nausea building in the pit of his stomach; his head was swimming and his entire body was sweating. He got to the front door and sat on the step taking deep breaths. Lloyd exited behind him and headed straight for his car, pulling the radio's microphone and reporting the murder. He walked back over to Gabriel and sat down next to him.

"Sorry, mate. *Really* wasn't expecting to find something like that. You okay?"

Gabriel's world was coming back into clarity a little. The nausea had gone and he had stopped sweating, though it had soaked the back of his hair and much of his clothes.

"I think so. Just a bit of a shock." He looked out across the sun-filled grass triangle of Hoggersbrook's old market place. No stall had been pitched in over a hundred years but the flower beds and grass were kept in good condition he thought, trying to distance himself from what was inside the house behind him. He looked at Lloyd. "This can't have been random."

Lloyd exhaled. "I know. The question is, did they know we were coming to speak with him, or is it some sick revenge for the nutter arrested fifty years ago?"

"So what happens now?"

"I'm out of my depth. I've got to talk to the bloke I'm working with from CID. He's probably on his way right now. He can be a bit of an arsehole - I can't tell him that I was here alone but I'll try to keep him off your back. If not, do you have a number I can get you on?"

Gabriel almost smiled at the situation he'd got himself into. "Sure." He pulled out his phone and read the number out. "Lloyd?"

"Yeah."

"You never did tell me last night. Have you found any other murders like this one?"

Lloyd felt that Gabriel had earned an honest answer. "Yes mate, at least one," he replied in a sombre tone.

"Do you think you've got an active cult on your hands?"

"I'm not sure. It's looking more and more likely though. Now quick, make a discreet exit before CID get here."

Tom Agar arrived with his forensic team who promptly cordoned off the area. This generated some morbid interest from local residents. A crime scene wasn't exactly a common thing in the area, and a murder scene was almost unheard of in Hoggersbrook. Tom walked over to Lloyd and squeezed his arm.

"You okay old boy? Not exactly a nice thing to find."

"Just a little shaken up. I'll be fine in half an hour or so. We expecting the DCI?"

"Speak of the Devil." Tom nodded over Lloyd's shoulder at the black car pulling up by the curb. DCI Donovan Brigham and Sergeant Garry Dudley got out and headed for the front door of Jonathan Cobb's house.

The DCI spoke first.

"Doctor Agar, Constable Lloyd, what are your initial findings?"

Tom spoke up. "Adult male, approximately eighty-five years old, cause of death most likely shock before his assailant finished removing his heart."

Brigham looked at Lloyd. "The report said that you found the body. I have familiarised Sergeant Dudley with our arrangement and I have full faith in Doctor Agar's professional discretion."

"Bottom line. The address in our records was out of date, he didn't live there anymore. I couldn't get a forwarding address so I asked around in the local pub."

"You asked around in the local pub?" The DCI's tone was slow and deliberate, he emphasised each word in turn as if to say, *you idiot.* This was not lost on Lloyd.

"I had no lead on where he lived. What would you have done? Thought: 'I had better not ask in the pub in case...'" he paused and lowered his somewhat irate voice,

"... someone hears and tells a cult of nut-jobs to cut his heart out.' Well?"

"My apologies, Constable, you have a point. Please carry on."

"Well, I ran into a bloke who I have a passing acquaintance with, who knew Cobb. Seeing as this was a pretty much 'under the radar' job I couldn't see any harm in accepting some help from him. We drove over here this morning and found the poor bastard."

Donovan looked perplexed. "This 'acquaintance' of yours, I take it that he is trustworthy?"

"I trust him. I can get hold of him if we need him."

"Good," the DCI grunted. "What's your next step?"

"My next step?" Lloyd was becoming acutely aware of the amount of 'donkey work' he was doing.

"Dudley and I can take over if you like, but I thought you'd prefer to do this yourself. As you said, these are your people."

Lloyd gave a grunt that mirrored Donovan's.

"Well, I've only got two leads left, a nut-job in a mental hospital or a kind woman I've known all my life. To be honest I think I'd rather face the nut-job. Let's see what Tom's team turn up first."

Gabriel was heading back to Sheffield, with Anji in the passenger seat of his car. Any thought he'd had of finishing the article had died along with Jonathan Cobb. The image of his corpse was still very much vivid in Gabriel's mind. He had come clean with Anji about the full story of his dreams; she'd taken it fairly well, and she didn't seem upset or freaked by it. He decided that he'd have to give the professor the full truth and as Anji had insisted on coming along he didn't see as he had any choice about telling her first. They found a spot not far from where Gabriel had parked a few days before, and walked to the city campus of Hallam University.

Gabriel gingerly rapped his knuckles on the circular glass window of Professor Tony Harrison's office door.

"Come in," came a friendly, if muffled, voice. Gabriel swung open the door and entered with Anji in tow. The Professor offered his hand and guided his guests to the two vacant seats by his desk.

"So then, my boy, what can I help you with? I trust the articles are going well."

"The articles were going fine. However..." Gabriel gave a very long pause before breaking off his sentence. "Professor, I know you're well-travelled, and you sure as hell know your stuff, but you told me something last time I was here. You told me to never underestimate the beliefs of others and to keep an open mind. You're well versed in the subject so I have to ask. After all, the superstition and poppycock you must have waded through, how open is your mind? Do you believe that any of this supernatural stuff actually exists?"

The professor leant back in his chair, his crippled hand across his waist. He began to speak in a sincere, concerned tone.

"Mr Jones, I've travelled the world, I've seen just about every form of fakery and baseless superstition that there is. I've also witnessed exorcisms that make Hollywood films seem tame; people all but rise from the grave, apparitions, spirits, wraiths, possible lycanthropes. Even, believe it or not, a possible vampire once. Nearly every known religion believes in both demons and possession. So the short answer is yes, I believe in the supernatural, very strongly."

"In that case, let me fill you in on the past few days of my life. To be honest, I'm not convinced that I've not gone insane." Gabriel gave the professor a very detailed account of recent events, but did not mention Anji's presence in the dreams. "Basically, professor, I'm going to drop the articles. I want out. How the hell do I get out of this? I want these dreams gone. And I sure as hell don't want to be chased by any more black figures."

The professor had gone a little pale. "I'm sorry, Mr Jones, but it's not that simple. You can't just walk away. For some reason, you've been targeted. I've read of demons using dreams many times before; it's when your psyche is the most vulnerable to manipulation. Again, I'm sorry, I wish I could give you better news but all I can do is tell you everything I know that could possibly help you."

The professor's voice sounded genuinely grave. "You mentioned a black figure both from your dreams and an encounter in a forest. The most probable explanation is that he is an emissary of whatever demon this cult are worshipping. Very rare, but according to legend several demons use them. They have different names in different cultures, old German folklore refers to them as Schatten, meaning shadow, but the most common name for one is a Harbinger." The word sent a shiver down Gabriel's spine as he recalled the figure referring to itself as a Harbinger in a dream. "They reportedly have the ability to 'drain the life-force' from a person, which might explain the feeling in your heart when you encountered him."

Gabriel didn't like the sound of any of what Anthony was telling him. "Professor, how do I get out of this?"

The professor put a comforting hand on Gabriel's shoulder. "I'm sorry to say that it's not going to be easy. If the demon's not yet crossed over into our realm, then it's just a matter of stopping the demon's worshippers. Once the sacrifices stop, its power will gradually weaken and its hold over you will dissipate as it does. That's the best case scenario."

"And the alternative?" Gabriel asked. If he was honest with himself he was starting to doubt the Professor; even after finding Cobb's body he still had a twinge of doubt about whether or not the black figure, or 'Harbinger', had been one crazy hallucination.

"The alternative is that the demon has already possessed someone and if that is the case things are substantially more difficult. The only way to get rid of it will be to exorcise it, and for that we need to firstly know which demon it is."

"*Which demon*? How many are there?"

"Thousands according to Christian dogma, but that's just the church's take on things."

Anji had remained quiet so far but now spoke up.

"Thousands? How are we supposed to know which one it is?" Her blue eyes flashed as she spoke. She didn't share Gabriel's nagging doubt and despite the bizarreness of the situation, she was thinking practically.

"Well, if you can get a name then it's quite simple, relatively speaking. If not, then your best bet is to pick up on any symbols or phrases that you see." The professor grabbed a yellow post-it note off his desk, then slid a pen out of his top pocket and scribbled something on the square of paper before handing it to Gabriel. "Here, this is my personal mobile number. The second you find anything you call me, so I can start researching our next step."

Gabriel didn't see had he had much choice. "One last thing. What does 'Avatar' mean in this context? I'm assuming it means 'instrument of the demon' or something very similar."

"Very close yes, I believe it means that the demon is trying to prepare your mind for a long term possession. Unprepared hosts, even willing ones, tend to burn out within a few months in most cases." Anthony was sorry that Gabriel had asked. "As I said, first find out if the bastard is here yet, if it is, find out its name or something that we can identify it from. Then we can take it from there."

Gabriel stood up and shook the professor's hand. "Thank you professor, I'll be in touch." He started to make his way to the door then stopped for a second. "Professor, I have to ask. After hearing the full story, how strong would you say the possibility is that I've just lost my mind?"

"Honestly? Unlikely. There's too much authentic detail in your story for it to be anything but real. If it was just an unbalanced psyche then it wouldn't tally with demonological lore."

Gabriel felt slightly better but at the same time absolutely terrified.

Constable Lloyd Brighton and DCI Donovan Brigham exited the lift at the basement level of Police HQ, swiftly followed by Sergeant Dudley. They made their way down the magnolia-coloured corridor to Autopsy. Dudley started to speak.

"Boss, what do you think about all this?"

"I think we've got a bunch of nutters on the loose, Dudley. Isn't that obvious?" Donovan snapped back. He immediately regretted his tone but not enough to apologise for it. He did, however, make a deliberate effort to soften his voice.

"The cult idea is starting to look less and less farcical. It is sure as hell one massively unrealistic coincidence that he was killed just before Brighton would have seen him. Not to mention his connection to the murder fifty years ago."

Lloyd was genuinely surprised with just how readily Donovan was willing to accept that a cult was responsible. However, as much as he hated to admit it, a cult did make more logical sense than a random serial killer. No one knew his reasons for meeting Cobb so killing the ex-cop to keep him quiet wasn't really an option, not to mention the fact that a random serial killer would have no reason to keep him quiet. The murderer from fifty years ago was safely locked up in an asylum. Not to mention the fact that he was a pensioner, so the idea that he'd struck again was off the cards.

Lloyd swung the doors to Autopsy's annex open and the three men walked inside.

Tom Agar snapped off his latex gloves. "Hello gentlemen," he said, throwing the bundled-up gloves into a stainless steel pedal-bin. "This one is just as nasty, though I have to admit more straightforward than the last one. Though only a little." He turned and started to wash his hands. "Would you like to see the body?" Tom pointed over his shoulder with his thumb.

Lloyd's mind flashed back to the image in Cobb's kitchen. "I'm okay, thanks, Tom. Seen enough of that poor bastard already."

Donovan was starting to get impatient and moved the conversation on. "What do you have for us, doctor?"

"Cause of death: most likely shock. The deceased had aggravated grazing and friction burns from the rope that secured his wrists and ankles, suggesting that he had been alive when-" Tom winced for a second. "Alive when the bastard started to cut the man's heart out."

Lloyd wasn't used to seeing Tom affected like this. "You okay, Tom?" he asked, not really caring if Donovan disagreed with his deviation from the job at hand.

"Yes thanks, Brighto, this is just a bit of a nasty one. And he was one of our own; it was a long time ago but I remember Cobb, he was a good bloke. Didn't deserve to end up like this." Tom slipped back into 'doctor mode'. "Unlike the last case, the deceased was killed at the scene. The amount of blood confirms that. The incision was made with an eight to nine inch curved blade. The heart was removed but was not present at the crime scene."

"Not really surprising," Donovan muttered.

"Now comes the bit that you're not going to like. My team could find no trace of the murderer. Whoever did this must have been so close that he would have been sprayed with blood. On their way out, they should, at the very least, have left footprints. But there was no trace of anything."

Donovan didn't look surprised, he looked annoyed. He started to speak in a scolding tone. "Doctor Agar, are you telling me that your team are unable to find any leads again?"

Tom responded in a colder, less emotional and altogether more forceful tone than Donovan had been able to muster. "No, Detective Inspector, I'm not saying that my team 'are unable to find any leads.' I'm saying that there are no leads for them to find."

Donovan quickly assessed the situation. He decided that a tactical withdrawal was probably the best option against Tom Agar. "My apologies, Doctor. I shouldn't have taken my frustration out on you." He glanced at Dudley and Lloyd. "Come on gentlemen, let's leave the good doctor to his work."

The three men headed back down the corridor towards the lifts. Donovan glanced at Lloyd. "So then, Constable. By my reckoning we have three leads left. The chap in the nut house, your old lady in the library or the son of that Ravenwood chap."

Gabriel and Anji had arrived back at Gabriel's house. They had spent the journey back from Sheffield rehashing what the professor had said and linking it to the past few days. Gabriel opened the back door then stocked the fridge up with beer, before both collapsed onto the settee.

Anji gave him a long stare. "So what do we do now then, Gabe?"

Gabriel let out a lengthy sigh. "I'm heading back to Stonebank, doesn't look like I have much choice. I'll keep up the same cover story and do some poking around."

Anji was expecting what came next, but decided to force the issue to make sure. "Cool, shall we stay here tonight, then head off first thing?"

Gabriel gave a sombre smile. "Anj, as much as I love having you around, it's time that I started doing this by myself. If I am losing it, then it won't make a difference. If the professor is right then things are dangerous. No point in putting both of our heads in the noose. Plus, you've got a job that you're neglecting. I shouldn't have let you stay with me this long."

Almost before the words were out of his mouth, Gabriel realised that his last sentence hadn't been of the best phrasing that he'd ever done.

Anji's blue eyes flashed at him as her voice raised. "Let me stay with you? Jones, I wasn't aware that I needed your permission. As for my job, I called them three days ago and told them that I was taking all my holiday time. I did that because I was worried about you, you egotistical bastard."

Gabriel unconsciously raised his voice in response. "I didn't mean that the way it sounded. In the past two days I've woken up in the middle of nowhere, been chased by a strange black figure, found a body with a heart cut out and been told that a demon wants to possess me. Sorry if I'm worried that something bad might happen to you."

"Worried about me?" Anji yelled. "I'm not the one having mental dreams or being chased by big black geezers. Don't you think I should be allowed to worry about you?"

"Anji, I'm shit scared," said Gabriel, the hint of emotion in his voice matching the slight welling in his eyes. "No other words for it. But the one thing right now scaring me more than anything that could happen to me, is something bad happening to you."

Anji looked at Gabriel's face, and the anger melted in an instant. She threw her arms around his waist and held him close. Gabriel mirrored the action, pressing his face against her red curls. "Anj, it would kill me if anything happened to you. Please babe, stay here, stay for me."

Anji gave him one last squeeze before pulling away, then put a hand on each side of his head and looked him dead in the eyes.

"Promise me that you will call at least three times a day and send for me if you need me at all. Promise me that you will look after yourself."

Gabriel smiled. "I promise. Now, let's lob a DVD on, have a drink and try to take our minds off things for a night."

Gabriel looked around the courtroom. He regarded the wooden panelling, then shifted his attention to the people sat around him. They were wearing nineteen-fifties style clothes. A barrister spoke.

"The defendant will rise."

The judge began to pass sentence. Gabriel noticed a young Jonathan Cobb sat near the front of the court.

"Harrison Graves, you have been found guilty of the charge of murder. After listening to all the evidence and expert witnesses, it is my belief that you are in fact not responsible for your actions, yet you are a danger to both yourself and others. It is therefore the judgement of this court that you be taken from this place to an institution for the criminally insane until such time that it is deemed that you are cured and fit to re-enter society."

Gabriel hadn't realised that the man in the dock was a young Harry Graves, who had a look of blind panic in his eyes.

"No, no, please. I don't want to go."

"Mr Graves," the judge's voice boomed. "You murdered your own brother. Now you must pay the price. You were supposed to be the Avatar but you were found unworthy at the final hurdle. You will now go to the asylum."

"But I don't want to go among mad people."

"Take him away." The judge glanced at two robed figures who dragged Harry out of the courtroom kicking and screaming. The Judge straightened some papers on his desk, ignoring Harry until he was out of earshot.

"Next up is Gabriel Jones."

Gabriel felt a sting of panic shoot to his heart as a black cloaked figure grabbed him from each side then dragged him to the front of the court. The walls of the court melted to reveal the moonlit ruins in the forest near Meetingstone Manor. A large black figure stood where the judge had been seated. It spoke in its deep husky voice.

"Avatar, are you now prepared to do what needs to be done?"

"No chance," Gabriel said defiantly.

"You responded to your title. Good, you are accepting the path. You will do what is necessary when the time comes."

"Never."

"Then do it now."

The Harbinger moved to one side in a sweeping motion to reveal the circular altar with Jim already tied to it. Anji knelt next to it, restrained by the cloaked figure of a man. "His heart for her eyes. You can't fight this Avatar, you know that."

The crow landed on the Harbinger's shoulder. Gabriel looked down to see the curved dagger. "You have no choice, Avatar. Obey, take his heart."

Gabriel frantically looked around, desperate to find some way to set Anji and Jim free. The bird took flight. Anji screamed again and again as the bird pecked at her left eye socket, then returned to its perch. She lay doubled over, whimpering, her hands over the left side of her face, deep red blood steaming between her fingers and a look of sheer terror and disbelief in her remaining eye.

"Take his heart or we take her other eye."

Gabriel fell to his knees, overwhelmed with the feeling of helplessness.

"Pathetic," the Harbinger commented. The bird took flight a second time; Anji started to scream again. Gabriel looked up to see the large black figure advancing on him. His chest felt clamped, the same way it had in the forest a pain started to groan in his chest, at first just a twinge but quickly becoming unbearable. Anji was still screaming. She called his name.

Gabriel's bed-sheets were soaked with sweat. He awoke struggling, scared, but instantly relieved that the pain had gone from his chest. He stumbled out of bed and pulled some clean clothes out of a set of drawers, before heading to the bathroom to take a shower.

The warm water felt good. Gabriel rubbed shampoo into his hair while attempting to distance himself from his dream and considering what he should do next. The dream, unpleasant though it was, had given him an idea. Assuming that the whole cult concept was true, he realised that he had an almost undeniable link to it - or at least the one from fifty years ago.

Chapter 10

Gabriel swung his car into one of the empty spaces in the car-park of Shalebridge Care Home. He made a beeline for Reception, which felt just as fake as the last time he had visited. Again he went through the double doors and down the oppressive corridors. This time, he was not led to Harry's room but to the communal dayroom.

Harry sat in a comfy chair, looking out of a window at a mob of starlings fighting over kitchen scraps. The dayroom had a low ceiling with polystyrene tiles, discoloured in several places. This area of the hospital was a modern extension to the old gothic building, but had much the same depressing atmosphere.

Gabriel pulled up a chair next to Harry. "Mr Graves, we met the other day. My name's Gabriel Jones."

Gabriel was momentarily taken aback as he looked at Harry's face. His eyes seemed sharper, their movement more alert. Harry extended a hand which Gabriel shook, trying not to look too confused.

"I seem to recall meeting you in my 'room'. You're the man who asked about..." He cut himself short and glanced around the room before leaning in close and lowering his voice. "You asked about my brother. You've seen the crow!" Harry looked Gabriel in the eyes. "Dear God, you've seen the figure as well, haven't you."

Gabriel's eyes widened. "Yes. Did you see it too?"

Harry looked away for a moment, focusing again on the birds in the garden. Gabriel was about to repeat his question when Harry's head shot back around and looked him square in the eyes.

"Yes, young man. I saw it. It made me go down the tunnel, the tunnel under the house, it made me take my brother's heart. When I realised what I'd done I tried to kill it..." Harry's voice was only a whisper but his words were concise. "I remember it like it was yesterday. I raised the dagger in my hand but somehow couldn't strike. It mocked me, called me 'unworthy' then vanished like a ghost."

"Mr Graves, do you know any way to stop this? To stop these dreams?" Gabriel's question was clearly a plea.

Harry's eyes shifted around the room before fixing on Gabriel for the second time. He began to speak more quickly.

"Yes. Yes. There is a way." Gabriel felt a twinge of hope in his chest. "You must use the knife on yourself. Don't become a murderer." The hope fell flat on its face, giving way to despair. "It's the only way."

Gabriel tried not to let the notion sink in but it was no use. He changed the subject and slipped into journalist mode.

"Mr Graves, did anyone else know about this figure at the time?"

"Oh, you think I'm going to tell you about the others after all these years? Harry's too clever for that." The old man smiled slightly as Gabriel edged forward on his chair.

"Why not?"

"They said, the others said, if I told anyone then the figure would come back. I'm not telling you." Harry started to become agitated. "I'm not telling you!" he repeated.

Gabriel was starting to feel slightly panicked, but was also desperate to know anything that could help him.

"Please, Mr Graves. It could help-"

Harry cut him short and yelled at the top of his voice.

"I'M NOT TELLING YOU!"

An orderly immediately started to make his way over. Gabriel made a swift exit; he was still trying to shake Harry's suggestion of suicide. He wasn't considering it, but the notion was strangely eating away at him.

Lloyd Brighton pulled into the car park of Shalebridge Care Home. His stomach was in knots; interviewing the criminally insane was not a common occurrence for a village copper, but after the week Lloyd had had he was surprised how much the thought of visiting Harry Graves seemed to be bothering him.

Pull yourself together, Brighto, Lloyd thought to himself as he reversed into one of the many empty parking spaces. The officer got out of the car, squinting in the midday sun for any indication of which direction he should go. He saw a sign marked 'Reception' and headed in the direction indicated. He began to curse how hot his dark police uniform felt on such a sunny day, so much so that he nearly missed a familiar face heading in the opposite direction.

"Gabe?"

The writer looked up, flustered. "Lloyd? What are you doing here?" Gabriel was still shaken by the fact that a crazy man had just suggested that he kill himself.

"I'm here on police business." The constable's tone was a little short. "But I was about to ask you the same thing."

Lloyd felt slightly harsh, phrasing his response as he had, given the fact he'd subjected Gabriel to a mutilated corpse so recently. However, he was genuinely suspicious as to what his new acquaintance was doing visiting one of his leads, and why the man seemed so preoccupied.

"Oh, just following up a source for my article. Nothing important. Got to get moving. Probably see you back in Stonebank." Gabriel kept moving. Lloyd couldn't help but notice how bumbled the words sounded. So bumbled that he was starting to re-evaluate his previous trust in the man. After all, it had been based on nothing more than a god damn gut feeling.

Lloyd reminded himself that he didn't live in a Seventies American police film, and that gut feelings could be wrong. He decided not to press the issue for the moment. He wanted to get the Shalebridge visit out of the way before he did anything else.

Gabriel got back in his car; the sun had made the interior stifling. He hit all four electric window buttons in quick succession, trying to get as much airflow in the vehicle as possible. He closed his eyes for a second. *Use the knife on yourself.* The words echoed in his mind, giving him goose bumps despite the heat.

"Not bloody likely," he said under his breath, as he turned the key in the ignition. Gabriel headed out of the asylum's main gate as he tried to recall exactly which clothes he'd packed. He needed dark clothes with plenty of pocket space, preferably black. He decided to call in at home before heading to Stonebank. He wanted one extra item. First, though, he called in at the local arts and craft shop. He knew Margaret the owner; everyone did in the village. Everyone knew everyone.

She'd looked a little confused when he'd asked her for a generous quantity of modelling clay, but was too polite to pry. She simply took the money and popped the packs of clay in a blue and white plastic carrier bag. After this, Gabriel headed home.

He walked swiftly from the car to the back door, almost running. He entered the house, headed directly upstairs to the wardrobe in his bedroom and rifled through the few items of clothing. He glanced at his suit, a few shirts and some of his better pullovers, then abruptly pulled out a three-quarter-length black duster coat. It had seen better days; it was a bit frayed on the cuffs but had kept its colour surprisingly well.

Gabriel left the coat's hanger on the bed and placed the coat on one side. He dug through a chest of drawers and pulled out a black, loose fitting shirt and a dark pair of jeans. He tossed both item on top of the duster.

"That'll do," he said to no-one, scooped the three garments up and headed back to his car.

Gabriel arrived back at the rented house; it felt lonely without Anji but he had bigger problems than solitude.

He dumped the extra clothes he'd brought on the living room settee, along with the plastic carrier bag he'd got from the art shop. Gabriel walked into the kitchen and made himself a ham sandwich. He ate it while washing out the margarine tub he'd just used. The writer dried the tub and its lid, then made his way to the carrier bag in the living room.

He retrieved the modelling clay, six blocks in all. He unwrapped each block in turn, warming them a little in his hands until they were malleable enough to mould into the inside of the margarine tub. Then Gabriel threw on the black set of clothes and slipped the tub of clay into the inside pocket of his duster. He picked up a few sheets of kitchen towel and one more item, then locked up the house and headed to his next destination.

Gabriel's car pulled up at the side of the curb. He got out and closed the door as quietly as possible. The night was dark and silent, there was a full moon but intermittent clouds seemed to make the whole world black.

He causally walked to the edge of Charles Ravenwood's drive and looked up it. The house was almost devoid of illumination, no sign of life apart from the dull porch light. The driveway had two rows of small electric lanterns leading all the way to the garage. Gabriel disappeared between the driveway's gateposts then made an immediate right, keeping in the cover of the trees at the foot of Charles' garden. In his dark outfit, he was all but invisible in the shadows.

He waited a few moments for the moon to disappear behind a cloud, watching as its silver light faded from the ground he had to cover. Gabriel started to creep as quickly but quietly as possible over the long lawn, regarding the front door as he moved silently over the grass. He looked at the porch light and decided against that entrance. The back door would be better.

The writer-come-housebreaker moved surprisingly stealthily around the side of the house and located the back door. He knelt by the lock. First he unhooked a small battery-powered torch from his keys, cringing as they jingled slightly. Gabriel twisted the torch's top slightly to turn it on, before pulling the roll of cloth from his inside pocket. He selected a pick and the tension tool before placing the cloth on the ground. Putting the torch in his mouth, Gabriel prepared to set to work on the lock. He paused for a moment, considering the line he was about to cross.

Jones, you're about to become a house breaker, his internal monologue said. *Not got much choice though…*

He slid the pick and tension tool into the lock and a few moments later the door was unlocked. The writer put the picks away, pulled his right sleeve down over his hand, gently pushed the door handle down and slowly opened the back door to Charles Ravenwood's home.

Gabriel's small torch shone around Charles' dining room and then fixed on the locked cabinet. His heart was thumping in his chest and he could almost hear the blood in his ears.

Gabriel moved silently towards the cabinet and opened it in much the same way he had the back door. He then retrieved the tub of modelling clay from his coat pocket, removed the lid and placed it on the floor. Next, Gabriel pulled a sheet of kitchen towel from another pocket and used it to pick up the brass implement he had taken a photo of, when he and Anji had visited for dinner.

He pushed the raised side of it firmly into the clay for a moment, then gently removed it. He examined it closely, checking for any residue of the clay before returning it to the cabinet.

Gabriel relocked the cabinet, picked up his equipment and left the house. He stealthily made his way back across the lawn and back to his car, where he collapsed into the driver's seat for a moment and relaxed a little as the adrenalin levels in his body began to subside.

His shaking hands fumbled with the key for a moment before finally managing to insert it into the ignition. The writer started the engine and drove off, leaving Charles's house behind him.

Jim was sound asleep. He'd built up enough flexi-time for a full day off work and had made a point of turning his alarm-clock off. His wife was visiting family and he was looking forward to a nice day doing, as he put it, 'sod all.'

His slumber was broken very abruptly when his mobile rang on full volume. His arm pawed at his bedside table trying to find the phone in his semiconscious state. He barely managed to focus on the small front screen before flipping it open and oafishly putting it to his left ear, as his right ear never left the pillow.

"Gabe," Jim murmured. "It's seven in the morning."

"Mate, I need a favour before you leave for work."

"I'm not going to work. I've got a day off." He closed his eyes, wishing he was still asleep.

"Excellent, I'll be at your place in ten minutes. Get the kettle on and see you soon."

The phone went dead. Jim rolled over and sat up.

"Bloody typical."

Gabriel knocked at the door and walked in.

"Jim, you there mate?" Gabe projected his voice.

"Kitchen," came Jim's one-word reply.

"You've finally found where that room is? Well done," Gabriel retorted, with the slightly serendipitous realisation that he was still in high enough spirits to take the mickey out of his oldest friend.

"Funny," he said in a deadpan tone as Gabriel entered the kitchen. Jim passed him a bacon sandwich. "Brown sauce's over there mate, next to your cuppa."

"Fantastic." Gabriel lifted up the bread and squirted a generous amount of brown sauce over the fat-soaked bacon, before joining Jim at the kitchen table. Jim took a bite out of his own sandwich and started to talk with his mouth full.

"Okay Gabe, what do you need doing, you useless bastard?"

"Odd request. You know that friend of yours that makes film props and replicas and stuff?" Gabriel took a sip of tea before starting on the second half of his sandwich.

"Darcy? Yeah, he's still around."

"Do you think he'd be able to make me something from this cast?" Jim looked on in confusion as Gabe produced a margarine tub shaped lump with a deep indentation in it.

"What is it?"

"It's that modelling clay we used to use at school in art. The stuff you can put in the oven to harden it." Gabriel deliberately tried to evade the meaning of the question, but was pretty sure it was a futile attempt.

"I'll rephrase. What do you want casting from it?" Jim levelled a 'don't talk crap' look at his friend who knew he'd just have to come clean.

"Long story. You sure you want to hear it?"

Gabriel filled Jim in on the events he'd missed since their last meeting.

"So do you think your mate Darcy will be able to help? And yes, I know I sound nuts."

"A little, yes, but I'll give him a call. You make us a second cup of tea while I get properly dressed and give Darcy a bell."

Jim almost sprinted upstairs and listened for Gabriel boiling the kettle. As soon as he was confident that the noise from the kettle would drown him out, he called Anji, who immediately picked up.

"Hello flower, how are you?" came the singsong, but unusually deflated, voice.

"Anj. Gabe's here, he's acting a little odd, he's on about waking up in the middle of nowhere and some weird black figure and that professor that Liz was on about last week." Jim's voice was speeding up and his words were running into each other.

Anji cut him off.

"Listen, flower, I know it sounds crazy, but most of it definitely happened. Okay, the most mental stuff like the black figure I didn't see, but the Prof seemed to think it was all feasible."

"Are you sure he's not off his goddamn rocker? Because the story I just heard is bloody mental. Gabe is the most sceptical person I've ever met but he's just recounted a story that-"

Anji cut him off again. "Jim, I know. I know it sounds mental, and part of me is struggling to believe it, even the bits I was there for." She paused. "For the minute, give him the benefit of the doubt. You're his best friend. Hell, you're like his goddamn brother. Right now he needs that."

"Okay, Anj."

"One last thing, flower, get as much information as possible on what he's doing now and what he's going to do next. He might need us soon, whether he thinks he does or not."

"Okay, Anj. I'll keep you posted. Take care." Jim folded his phone shut, put some smarter clothes on and headed down stairs. "Gabe, chuck that tea in the travel mugs and grab that cast thing. We're heading out."

Gabriel had asked Darcy to cast him the 'key' in as strong a material as possible but as quickly as possible. It hadn't taken long and he now possessed a hardened plastic replica of the original, or at least the part that counted.

The writer had headed directly for the manor house. He'd located the closest place to park, much closer than the time he and Anji had first visited. It turned out that the manor had its own English Heritage car park. Gabriel pulled off the smooth road and onto the lumpy mud pit that English Heritage called their car park. He immediately slowed the car to a crawl to lessen the trauma on his suspension.

"A bit of tarmac would break the bank?" Gabriel asked himself as he slid out of his car. The only other vehicle visible was a muddy Land Rover with an 'I love History' sticker in the back window. "I'm guessing Charles is about then."

Gabriel had put his lock picks to good use once again and was now gingerly walking down the passageway of the old wine cellar. He'd neglected to bring his high-powered flashlight and was having to rely on his key ring torch again. The atmosphere of the old house was no less potent than usual; Gabriel could hear the slight echo from every step he made. Even after everything he'd been through he still had to consciously suppress his anxiety. He knew he'd done the right thing, but he was really regretting telling Anji to stay in Hoggersbrook. Some moral support would have made him feel a lot better.

He put the thought out of his mind and concentrated on finding the lock for his replica key. It didn't take long to locate it. Gabriel pulled the replica out of his pocket. He'd dropped the full black motif in favour of blue jeans and a T-Shirt, but had kept the duster for the pocket space. Gabe hesitated for a moment. He realised that what came next was worryingly important.

"Okay, Jones, if nothing happens here then it's time to check yourself into Shalebridge." Acknowledging the idea out loud did not make Gabriel feel any better; the sceptic in him was still very much alive. His hands were shaking as he placed the relief of the plastic replica into the brass receptacle. First he tried turning the key clockwise. No luck. His heart began to sink a little more as his internal monologue chipped in with its five pence worth.

Clockwise didn't work, Jones. Fifty per cent chance that you're nuts now. He held his breath for a second and tried anti-clockwise. Gabriel was amazed how easily it turned, and how quietly an entire section of stonework sunk back into the wall and slid to its right. He exhaled whilst being hit with a torrent of emotion; relief that there was now a very good chance that he wasn't out of his mind, but also a considerable amount of fear that everything up to and including the black figure could well be real.

Gabriel cursed himself for not bringing a decent torch with him but it was too late for that now. He headed into the newly found opening, feeling the adrenalin in his veins and his heart beating like a jigger pick. Every instinct he had was saying 'turn and run' but he knew that ultimately, he no longer had a choice, had nowhere far enough he could run to.

The tunnel was only about a metre wide with a low arched roof, curving slightly to the left with a downwards gradient. Gabriel continued to follow it, his heart still pounding in his chest. After about a hundred yards the tunnel opened up into an unusual circular room. Gabe stood at the opening; there were stone steps to his right and left, both leading upwards. He paused for a moment and opted to take the left set of stairs.

He found they lead to a viewing gallery that looked down on a central room with a circular altar, almost identical to the one that he'd seen at the ruins a few days before. The writer started by investigating the viewing area. The entire room was made of stone, but there was little else of note until he was about half way round the room. The outer wall had a large carving on it. Gabriel stood back from it and shone the torch at the wall.

"The Devereaux crest," he said under his breath. "At least I know who built this place."

He followed the upper floor round to find that it led back round to the set of stairs he'd decided not to take. Gabriel walked back down and into the central chamber and shone his barely adequate torch at the central altar. The first thing he noticed was the inscription around the edge. It looked identical to the one from the woods, and being underground, had been spared the years of damage from the elements.

Gabriel pulled out his notebook and mini biro and filled in the missing spaces:

Nomen mihi Legio est, quia multi sumus

Tap, tap, tap, came the sound of footsteps echoing down the corridor.

"Bastard," Gabriel whispered through clenched teeth as he put his notebook away with the inscription still untranslated. He frantically looked around the room, but already knew there were no hiding places and that the tunnel was the only way in or out.

Tap. Tap. Tap. The sound was almost upon him; less echo, less distortion... there were more than one set of footsteps.

Gabriel froze for a moment as panic started to set in. *Get a grip, Jones!* Gabriel darted towards the tunnel then up the left-hand side stairs to the viewing gallery, moving as quietly as he could without compromising speed. His situation hadn't improved much but at least he could try to find a shadowy corner to hide in.

The footsteps continued to approach. Tap. Tap. Tap. Almost in time with the thump of Gabriel's adrenalin-fuelled heartbeat. He'd taken a good look around when he first arrived; he knew that most of the walls were curved and there were only two corners.

The writer took an immediate right at the top of the stairs and pushed himself into the corner where the walls met. He pulled his duster across his chest and put his hands in his pockets in an effort to minimise how visible he'd be. The footsteps had reached the foot of the stairs and sounded as though they were splitting up. Some were unquestionably climbing the stairs.

Gabriel manipulated the keys in his pocket, bunching them into his hand but allowing one to poke between his fingers to make a dull blade. If he had to fight he wanted to take any advantage he could. Two figures reached the top of the steps and took up position, looking down on the altar. They were clad in black robes and one carried a storm lamp; neither had spotted Gabriel but the lamp was doing an irritatingly good job of chasing the shadows away.

He weighed up the benefit of staying put and hoping to go unnoticed, versus trying to sneak out. If there was no one at the bottom of the stairs then all he had to do was creep past the two figures in front of him. However if there was, then all they'd have to do is yell for help and he'd be trapped on the stairs.

His contemplating was broken when a voice started talking from the central chamber.

"Oh ancient one, we beseech you, appear to us. We offer the heart of an enemy and place it on your altar."

Gabriel cringed at the thought. It didn't take much to work out that the heart almost certainly belonged to Jonathan Cobb. Up to this point, Gabriel had thought that he'd started to believe in the supernatural, believed all the wild things that the professor had said, believed that the black figure truly was a phantom. This was the moment when he realised it had all been false belief. This was the moment when the terrifying surrender to true belief took hold. This was the moment Gabriel truly believed and truly knew fear.

A bright, pale-blue light burst from the central chamber and into the stone viewing gallery, and any hope Gabriel had of hiding in the shadows evaporated. A loud voice echoed through the chamber.

"Ah, little mortal, you have brought me my Avatar."

Gabriel couldn't see what was happening but the two figures in the gallery seemed to give each other a confused look. There was a pause before the human voice from the centre chamber answered in a quivering tone.

"With regret, no, my lord. We are working on nothing else but he is not yet ready to accept you."

"Then pray tell, little man, why is my avatar present?"

The word 'avatar' sent every kind of chill through Gabriel's entire body. He decided that the risk of staying outweighed any risk of running into someone at the bottom of the stairs. He abandoned his corner, but stuck close to the wall and made his way down the stone steps as the human voice replied.

"I do not understand, my lord." The ethereal voice ignored the human one and addressed the man it knew was present.

"Gabriel Jones, I know you are here, you are my avatar and I can feel your presence. Step forward and accept my gift."

Gabriel stopped trying to sneak; fear had gotten the best of him, and the muscles in his legs tensed as he started to run down the remaining stairs then flew up the empty tunnel.

"Minions, he is ready. Do not let him escape, bring him to me. Harbinger, assist them."

The inhuman voice echoed down the stone corridor behind Gabriel. He ran out of the secret door, down the passage and out into the grounds. Night had fallen but there was a full moon bathing the grass in a soft silver light. Gabriel ran for his car, across the lawn and down a very small set of decorative steps. He jumped rather than climbed down them but landed poorly, toppling to the ground.

He pulled himself to his feet and was about to continue for his car, when the writer turned to get his bearings and realised that one rather large black figure had gained ground on him somehow. Gabriel didn't even think; he swung a punch at the cloaked man. The blow knocked the man's hood off to reveal his face, but did little more than hurt Gabriel's hand.

The writer looked at the man's face. He recognised him; it was one of the men who'd carried the straw man at the festival. He was well out of Gabriel's weight class and barely seemed to notice the first punch. The writer was no scrapper and not overly strong; he swung a second punch which the man shrugged off. The burly thug then swung his own punch, knocking Gabriel to the ground. It felt like he been hit by a battering ram. He looked up as the man advanced on him with a sadistic smile.

"You're coming with me posh boy," he said in a thick Derbyshire accent.

Gabriel couldn't see a way out; the thug was clearly stronger and faster than him and he could hear more footsteps approaching at speed. He braced himself for the inevitable. The large man continued to advance but was suddenly staggered by a heavy fist blindsiding him. A second hit knocked him to the floor.

Gabriel looked up, still a little disorientated. "Jim! Bloody good timing, mate." The writer felt his arms being grabbed and put behind two unexpected shoulders as he was helped up. "Anji? Professor? How did you know where I was?"

Jim walked up to the recovering cloaked man and landed one final blow as the oaf started to scramble up. T
The man fell back to the floor with a dull thud and Jim turned to Gabriel.

"The redhead's gut. Let's leg it," he said, gesturing first to Anji, then to the small army of black figures appearing from the cellar.

"Sounds good," Gabriel replied with a half-smile.

Then the pain came. Gabriel, Anji, Jim and the Professor all fell to the floor, clutching their chests in a vain effort to stop the agony. Gabriel knew the feeling, it was the same as he'd felt when he'd been chased by the Harbinger. His vision started to blur, but he could make out that one black figure was substantially larger than the rest and was striding towards him.

"Avatar," The black figure hissed. "My master requires you."

The professor blurted out something in a language that Gabriel didn't recognise, and a moment later the pain subsided. All four humans scrambled to their feet, and the professor dusted himself off and started to walk slowly but purposefully towards the large black figure.

"Demon, I am a Cleric and former Knight of the Halcyon Order. I command you to leave this place."

Both the professor and the Harbinger stopped walking. The Harbinger hissed: "You are a relic of times well gone. Give up the Avatar and I may let you live, mortal. Refuse and you all die, then I will take him anyway." The professor assessed the situation; the human black figures were holding back, letting the Harbinger control the situation. He returned his gaze to the large black figure and let out a sarcastic laugh.

"Don't presume to threaten me, 'imp.' I stood against far worse than you for two centuries."

The black figure stood its ground but remained silent as the professor spoke.

"I've faced the Morning Star and lived, do you think some demon's lapdog can intimidate me? Leave and take this scum with you, or when I am done, I swear you will regret the day you crawled out of the pit."

"This is not over, Cleric." The figure dissolved into smoke and disappeared into the air. The human figures didn't retreat, but didn't advance either.

"Are you lot okay?" the professor asked, without taking his eye off where the cloaked figure was. His three companions were shaking off disorientation and just about back on their feet, their relief outweighing their confusion.

Jim looked around. "I think so, Prof."

"Then make haste, back to the car. Mr Lowe, if you could retrieve Gabriel's vehicle that would be a help."

"Not a problem Prof."

They quickly made their way back to the car park where Jim retrieved Gabriel's car keys from his coat pocket.

"Follow me, Mr Lowe," the professor enunciated and almost seemed to be enjoying himself.

"Prof?" Jim paused for a moment.

"Yes."

"The name's Jim," Jim pointed out with a wince.

"Duly noted, James. And an excellent time to point that out." The professor shot him a wink along with the sanguine sarcasm.

The professor drove his car in the direction of the rented house under careful direction from Anji, with Jim in pursuit. Gabriel was still a little dazed but was quickly regaining his faculties.

Once the team got to the house, Anji and Jim made a joint effort on the tea while the professor and Gabriel spoke.

"Right, Gabriel. Fill me in on anything new," the professor said in an encouraging tone. Gabriel recounted the latest incident then stopped and looked unsure.

"Professor, there was something I didn't tell you before." He spoke in a whispered tone then paused and looked at the doorway before continuing. "I didn't tell you about everything in my dream. Anji's there a lot, it's really horrible; she keeps appearing without eyes and they keep wanting me to kill her." He paused again and swallowed, fighting back the emotion that was starting to build. "Harry Graves had exactly the same thing with his wife."

The professor gave a sympathetic look.

"I'm sorry Gabriel, it knows she's a weak spot. It knows it can use her to manipulate you. I understand why you didn't want to tell me in front of her."

Anji and Jim walked in with four cups of tea, silently handing them to Gabe and the Professor.

"I think the first thing we need to do is shield your mind if possible. See if we can stop the dreams. When you were in the tunnel, did you find anything that could tell us any more about the demon?"

Gabriel's still slightly dazed eye lit up for a second. "Yep, I noted down some Latin. Hold on." Gabriel nipped into the hallway to grab his notebook from his coat pocket. In his absence, Anji shot the professor a quizzical look.

"Professor, not that I'm anything less than grateful, but how did you stop that Harbinger chappie from sapping us, and what was that 'cleric of the whatsit order' lark?"

The Professor waved a dismissive hand.

"Ah, it was just a bit of a protection ward that I picked up from a voodoo witchdoctor with some historical embellishment."

Before Anji could press the matter, Gabriel returned flicking through his notebook.

"Excellent, the Grail diary," Jim said, raising his mug and trying to lighten to mood, as much for his own benefit as anyone else's.

"Damn right," Gabriel replied, while flicking through to the right page. Jim looked at Anji and the professor's null reaction to his film reference.

"Philistines," he said under his breath.

"Found it!" Gabriel said, as he smoothed two pages out and began to read slowly. "Nomen mihi Legio est, quia multi sumus." His face turned grave, a look he saw mirrored when he looked at the professor. "You don't have to be a scholar to recognise that quote."

"Clearly you do." Anji interjected in a dry tone. "Or you at least need to be able to read Latin."

"That can't be good, Professor." Gabriel said, looking no less grave. Jim remained silent but Anji continued.

"Boys, what's the translation?" she asked, looking at them both.

The professor spoke up. "It's from the Christian Bible, the gospels of Mark, Luke and Matthew to be precise. It also tells us the name of the demon."

Anji started to get slightly agitated. "But what's the translation?"

This time Gabriel answered. "My name is Legion for we are many." The professor nodded then began to elaborate.

"It's a very powerful demon and very well known in Christian dogma. The bible has been retranslated and adapted for political reasons so many times it's difficult to get an accurate description. The most widely held belief is that Legion was many demons possessing a single person, but that's actually incredibly unlikely. The far more likely version is that Legion was a demon who absorbed the power of weaker demons, and along with it many of their traits."

The professor looked at the three rather stunned people in the room. "The first priority is still to stop it crossing over. If we can do that, its power will dissipate no matter how strong it is. I need to contact some people. Stick together and see what you can do. I'll be in touch. There's a woman in the village, her name is Tabitha." He clocked the look of recognition from Anji and Gabe. "You've met her?"

"Yes, quite a character, or so I thought at the time," Gabriel replied.

"Good, get hold of her first thing in the morning." The professor grabbed his coat. "Tell her I sent you, she knows me. Tell her that the house needs demon proofing. She'll sort the rest."

"Will do," Gabriel replied.

"Keep digging for information but don't act on anything that might put you in danger. As I said, stick together, look after each other, and I'll be in touch ASAP." With that, the professor left and the three returned to the living room.

Jim looked at Gabriel and Anji. "Well, looks like I'm in your gang now. What's our first move?"

"We can be pretty sure that Charles is involved." Gabriel said leaning back in his chair, before tossing his replica key in the air and catching it again. He looked at Jim. "Darcy did a fine job by the way."

Anji started to look confused. "Babe, why do you suddenly seem so cocky?"

"I've just realised. You all saw it. I'm not crazy. This thing is coming, I can't run from it and fear is only really useful if running is an option. So, I'm embracing the fight."

Anji smiled. "I'm embracing it with you then."

"Me an' all, mate."

"Thank you both so much, but no." Gabe looked at Anji. "I meant what I said, I want you out of this." He moved his gaze to Jim. "Both of you."

"Not happening, mate," Jim protested in a firm but friendly tone.

"You're bloody right it's not happening. You lasted about twenty-four hours without me there to keep an eye on you. Plus the prof said we should stick together."

Gabriel tried to respond.

"Bu. . ." He was cut short.

"No arguments, I am my own woman and Jim is his own man. We're sticking with you. You can waste time arguing the point or we can put a plan together."

Jim added his two pence worth. "Know when you are beaten, Jonesy."

Gabriel sighed and smiled at the same time.

"Okay, and thank you. It means more than I can put into words. And I'm a writer so I can put quite a lot into words."

Jim flashed him a smile. "Yeah, but you're probably failing here because you're not a very *good* writer."

"Cheers old friend, now let's talk plans. First let's do as the prof says and see Tabitha. Once she's done her thing I vote we stakeout and follow Charles. Jim, you'll need to be the front man seeing as he doesn't know you."

"Always did like the Rockford Files," Jim said, as Anji looked at her watch.

"Sounds good, seeing as it's now nearly six in the morning I'm guessing we're not going to bed."

Chapter 11

Anji swung open the door to Tabitha's shop, causing the usual tinkle of the door's bell. Tabitha looked up from the counter as the three friends entered. She fixed her gaze on Gabriel.

"Oh, my poor man. You have been through the wars haven't you, I've not seen such a dark aura in years."

"I've been better. This may sound a bit odd, but do you know a Professor Harrison?"

"Oh yes, dear, I know him well."

"He suggested that I ask you to 'demon proof' the house we're currently renting." Even after everything Gabriel had been though, he appreciated that Tabitha hadn't been there and felt odd asking in spite of her own eccentricities.

"It'll be a pleasure, give me five to get my stuff together and I'll be with you. Gabriel, if you wouldn't mind driving with me to show me the way," she asked, disappearing through the curtain to the back.

"No problem," Gabriel shouted after her as he handed his car keys to Anji.

"See you back at the house, babe. Come on, flower," she said, tapping Jim on the arm. A few moments later, Tabitha returned with a worn wooden box which she held by a brass cupboard door handle that had obviously just been screwed on the top. Gabriel immediately reached for the handle and took it off her.

"Why, thank you. Nice to see that chivalry is not completely dead." Tabitha flipped the 'open' sign on the door to 'closed' and pulled it shut behind them before locking it. "My car's just over here."

The car suited her perfectly, a pale blue VW Beetle from the eighties. Tabitha opened what on any other car would be the bonnet, and Gabriel carefully placed the box inside the luggage compartment. "Thank you, Gabriel. Let's get a wriggle on, I can tell by the look on your face you're dying to ask me something."

They both got in the car. Tabitha turned the key in the ignition and started to gently pull the choke, coaxing the engine into life. The car trundled up the road as Gabriel started to speak.

"Okay, if you turn left. . ."

Tabitha giggled slightly. "Oh Gabriel, I know where we're going. I just wanted to talk to you by yourself for a while. But come on, get your questions off your chest first. You'll probably have more by the time we're done."

"Okay, how do you know the Professor? It seems very coincidental to say the least."

"We have mutual associates for one thing; for another... well, for another we go back a long way. I honestly would like to tell you more but I can't right now, I'm sorry. The one thing I can tell you is that he's a good, a very good man and you can trust him. Things will become clearer soon but it's not my place to say. Right, my turn. If you need a house demon-proofing then something big is happening. Fill me in."

"Well, erm... er..." Gabriel clearly wasn't sure what to say.

"Gabriel, I'm currently driving to perform demon-proofing on a house because you were sent to me by a professor of demonology and the occult. Please for the love of the goddess tell me that you don't think it's going to sound silly." Tabitha smiled slightly.

"You have a point." Gabriel filled Tabitha in on everything. She listened patiently as she drove the slow, rickety car down the poorly maintained country roads.

"Well, the good news is that once I'm done you should be able to sleep in the house without the bad dreams. Hopefully the bags under your eyes will be gone by tomorrow."

Gabriel laughed. "God, I hope so."

They arrived at the rented house where Gabriel carried the wooden box in the house and placed it down on the kitchen table. Tabitha flipped the catches and opened the lid releasing an earthy aroma. She went around the house hanging small bags and speaking in a language neither Gabriel, Anji nor Jim recognised. She broke the chanting and switched back to English for a moment, as she retrieved a thick black marker pen from the box.

"Neil might not like what I'm going to do here," she said as she moved through the house drawing a symbol above every door, window and air-grate. The whole process took a little over an hour. "Okay, all done. That should do it. I'd better get back to the shop. Look after each other and trust the professor." All three saw her to the door. "One last thing, if anything happens, and you can't get back here, try to get to the church."

"Holy ground?" Gabriel asked, fully aware of how clichéd it sounded.

"Yes, but the church yard won't be enough. You need the walls. Your other option would be the stone circle." With that, Tabitha turned and headed out the door and to her car.

"Okay," Gabriel said to his companions. "Let's get started. Do we have enough stuff to make sandwiches?"

"No chance," Anji replied.

"Pub for food then, check out Charles?" Gabriel asked.

Jim spoke up next.

"Not that I'm disagreeing, but. You have a dangerous, demon cult on your tail, we got attacked by some malevolent force dressed in black. We've just had a hippie 'demon proof' this place, but even with all that you still want to go to the pub?"

Gabriel looked at him and shrugged. "We need to eat."

"Sold."

Jim held the door open for Gabriel and Anji as the three entered the Red Gate pub. They had a quick glance around; pretty empty as usual, with Neil behind the bar and Len Tait propping it up from the public's side.

Gabriel walked up to the bar.

"Hello Neil, A Guinness and two lagers please. Also," he added, squinting at the menu chalked on a small blackboard, "three burgers and chips please."

"Coming right up." Neil's tone was substantially more inviting that it had been the first time they'd visited the pub. The three grabbed a seat near a window and began to formulate a plan.

"So," Jim said in a low tone. "The plan is to follow this Charles chap."

"Only good lead we have," Gabriel pointed out.

"And for my money, you can drop the word 'good'," Anji clarified. "So, gents?" What do you make of the. . ." She was cut short when Neil arrived with their food.

"Thank you very much, Neil," Gabriel said. Neil grunted something in an almost jovial tone and returned to the bar. Gabriel started to add generous amounts of salt and vinegar to his chips. "What do we make of the professor?"

"I'm not sure, it's very odd. He's clearly not telling us anything close to what he knows, same goes for Tabitha for that matter. Can either of you remember exactly what he said at the manor house?"

"Sorry, mate. That's all a bit of a blur."

"Same here, babe, but he did fob me off when I asked him about it."

"He and Tabitha have some sort of connection," said Gabriel. "I couldn't get much out of her in the car though. There's something going on with him, and Tabitha for that matter. He does seem to be genuinely concerned though, and I think we all have to admit that whatever it was he did with the 'Harbinger' pretty much..." Gabriel suddenly became aware of how loud his voice was becoming. "Saved our lives," he continued in a lower voice.

"True," Anji agreed. "But next time he's here, let's not let him go until we get some answers."

"Okay, let's eat up and go all Sam Spade."

Anji, Gabe and Jim were parked up across the road from Charles' house with a clear view down the driveway. Jim sat up front with Anji and Gabe took the back seat, trying to keep a low profile.

"Are you sure we can't be seen?" Anji asked.

"Tinted windscreen and front side windows. Privacy tint on the rear windows. It's unlikely. He'll have a hard time seeing Jim, let alone us." Jim was smiling. "Why do you have that mental grin on your face?"

"Nothing, I was just wondering why you need a privacy tint on your car's back windows." Gabe let out a half-laugh.

"Get your mind out of the gutter, they were tinted before I bought the car." Gabriel looked up and noticed Charles' wife Heather walking down the driveway.

"Can't we follow her instead?" Jim asked rhetorically with a laugh. "By the way, didn't you say that Charles was getting on a bit?"

"Yeah, in his sixties, I'd say."

"Big house, stunning busty wife half his age. If it wasn't for all the ritual murder, I'd be thinking of joining this cult."

"Heads up, it's Charles," Anji noted. Charles' Land Rover pulled into the driveway. He pulled up close to the front door and jumped out, surprisingly spritely for a man of his age. He walked around to the back of the vehicle and pulled a cooler box out of the boot. Anji winced.

"Please tell me that's not got in it what I think it's got in it."

"It could be anything," Gabe replied, trying to convince himself as much as Anji. "Jim, drive us back to the house please, mate."

"What?" Anji exclaimed.

"If that's what we think it is, then we can get the police involved. It won't stop the cult but taking Charles out of the equation would slow them down, I would have thought."

"So, why are we going back to the house?" Jim asked as he started the engine.

"Because I've not had a good sleep in days and I want one before I break in there again."

"So," Anji began to enquire, "your plan is to break into Charles' house, find a human heart in a cooler box, then ring the police to tell them what you found during your illegal break-in."

"I'll call Lloyd. I think I can trust him."

Lloyd Brighton watched as Gabriel's car left the vicinity of Charles Ravenwood's house. All he could see was a stranger driving and two silhouettes in the back, one of whom had a lot of curly hair. He wondered why Gabriel had been watching Charles' house, and was still wondering what he'd been doing at Shalebridge Care Home.

He'd tried to speak to Harry Graves but Gabriel's visit had left him incoherent. Lloyd didn't want to start questioning Ethel Birchwood; he'd known her too long and had a lot of genuine respect and affection for her. The village policeman had decided to make Charles Ravenwood his next port of call. Yet again, he'd found Gabriel there before him, or at least someone who he was ninety-nine percent sure was Gabriel.

He was starting to really doubt his initial assessment of the writer. He was starting to think he'd been wrong, and Lloyd hated being wrong. He began to toy with the idea of following Gabriel and keeping an eye on him; he considered walking up to Charles' front door and questioning him.

Instead, he decided to do his own stakeout. He'd already borrowed an unmarked car from the county depot; the usual squad car was more than conspicuous. Lloyd adjusted the driver's seat, reclining it a little, then pulled out a book from the bag he'd left on the passenger seat. He began to read, occasionally glancing up at the road or at Charles' house. Hours passed with very little change, then night fell and Lloyd had to abandon his book due to poor light.

The lights in Charles' house began to come on one by one; hours later they went out one by one. Lloyd angled his watch to catch the illumination from the street lamps. *Half one, time to head home.*

He reached for the key in the ignition and was about to turn it when a dark figure caught his eye. The figure was tallish, dressed in black and almost invisible in the shadows. He saw it creep between Charles's gateposts, but lost it in the dark of the lawn.

He exited his car as quietly as possible and headed in the direction of the shadow. The police constable moved through the gateposts and onto the lawn, trying to keep low in an effort spot the figure against the night sky. *Damn it. Lost him.* Lloyd continued to search; he'd initially refrained from using his torch in an effort to keep his own presence unknown. He abandoned that idea and was now busy shining his bright torch through the shrubs at the foot of the garden in a vain effort to flush out the intruder.

The silence of the night was suddenly broken by a loud scream coming from the house. Lloyd turned and immediately bolted for the front door. Unsurprisingly, it was locked. The constable ran round the side of the house in search of the back door which he eventually found. He burst through and headed for the sound of raised voices emanating from Charles's living room.

Charles and Heather were stood there, with a table separating them from the intruder. Charles had his shotgun levelled at the trespasser who Lloyd recognised immediately.

"Gabriel?" Even after his recent suspicions, it had been a surprise.

"Lloyd, I can explain," Gabriel said with his hands in the air.

"Can you?" Heather asked. "You broke into our home carrying a knife, and now you can explain?"

"Knife?" Lloyd asked as he noticed the knife on the dining table. It was unusually ornate with an intricately carved bone handle and decorated curved blade about eight inches long. *". . . The incision was made with an eight to nine inch curved blade. . ."* came the memory of what Tom Agar had said in the autopsy lab.

"Lloyd, I've never seen that knife before," Gabriel protested, managing not to add the phrase 'outside my dreams.' "I don't know what they're talking about."

"Poppycock!" Charles bellowed. "You broke in here, with that knife. If I'd been unarmed I hate to think what might have happened. Constable, are you going to indulge this armed intruder's professions of innocence, or are you going to do your duty and arrest him?"

Lloyd did his duty. He reached for his radio and called for backup, which promptly arrived. They bagged the knife and took

Gabriel directly to the county police station; the station in the village was more for small-time crime such as drunk drivers.

Two officers stayed behind to search Gabriel's car while Lloyd followed in his borrowed car. Something didn't feel right to him. He may have been starting to suspect Gabriel of something, but it wasn't house breaking or murder. Then again, the facts spoke for themselves and he hadn't liked the look of that knife.

The squad car's driver didn't stick to the speed limit and it didn't take long to reach the county police station. Gabriel was finger printed, processed and put in a holding cell.

Chapter 12

Gabriel hadn't slept. Even if he wasn't scared of the dreams, he didn't want to sleep on, or indeed sit on the wafer-thin, plastic coated mattress that passed for a bed.

Gabriel looked around the tiny white-walled cell he'd been placed in. It was devoid of windows and its only discerning feature was the imposing iron door. He'd made his phone call and let Anji know where he was.

Thoughts had been running through Gabriel's mind all night, none of them good. Even if he could prove that the knife was nothing to do with him, he was still looking at a charge of breaking and entering. If the cult had found some way to pin the knife on him, then he may be looking at standing trial for multiple counts of murder and end up in a place far worse than Shalebridge Care Home.

Gabriel's train of thought was broken when the iron door was opened abruptly by a uniformed officer.

The officer didn't make eye contact. "This way please." He escorted Gabriel to an interrogation room. The writer mentally noted that the room wasn't like the ones he'd seen on television. For one thing, there was no two-way mirror, just a Formica-topped table with a plastic chair on either side. The officer cuffed Gabriel to one of the chairs and left the room. Moments later two men entered; one was Lloyd Brighton and the other was a heavy-set man in a suit whom Gabriel didn't know.

"Mr Jones," The heavy-set man started. "I am Detective Chief Inspector Brigham. As you know you have been arrested for breaking and entering and can expect to be charged soon. It is also my duty to inform you that you will most likely soon be charged with multiple counts of murder as well."

"What?" Gabriel asked.

"We found your prints on the knife, Gabriel," Lloyd explained.

"Yes, and our lab has confirmed that it is the weapon used in a string of - until now - unsolved murders."

"Lloyd, you know something odd is going on here." Gabriel sounded panicked. "I've had dinner at Charles' house, I've touched cups and glasses. Anyone can transfer a finger print with something as simple as Sellotape, for Christ's sake."

"True, but that's not our only evidence," Brigham added.

"Not your only evidence?" Gabriel asked. Lloyd was curious as to what he'd been kept out of the loop on, and Gabriel's mind was racing ten to the dozen.

"After you were arrested, we had two officers search your car. They found a cooler box that contained a lot of ice, along with another item." Brigham's voice was gradually becoming aggressive. "Would you like to tell me what the other item was or shall I tell you?"

"What?" Panic was setting in fully and Gabriel's head was starting to swim a little.

"What was in the box, Mr Jones?" Donovan pressed.

"The bastards have set me up." The walls felt like they were literally closing in on him.

"Oh, so you do know what's in there then?"

"I saw Charles carrying the box into his house. That's what I went in there looking for."

"Bollocks, Jones. What was in the box?" His eyes flashed with what looked like genuine anger.

"I never saw inside it." Gabriel's heart was thumping and he could feel droplets of perspiration running down his inner arms.

"It was a heart Jones, a human heart. The heart you put there. The heart you then drove around with in your car, you sick freak. Where are the others?" Gabriel was dumbstruck and Donovan pulled back a little. "Constable, let's give 'Mr' Jones a moment alone to think."

The two officers left the room. Lloyd had to admit that the evidence was damning, but something was tugging at him from the inside. He couldn't stop thinking how badly Gabriel had taken seeing Cobb's body; the blood had drained from his face that day, and that wasn't something you could fake.

Gabriel listened as the door shut. "DCI Brigham, there's a man insisting on speaking with you," was the last thing Gabriel heard another officer say before the door closed.

Gabriel simply didn't know what to do. He had a cult wanting to possess him, the damn cult who were doing an excellent job of framing him for murder. He had no idea how the heart had got in his car. He could only assume that one of Charles' flunkies had planted it there while Lloyd was inside the house. He was looking at possession, insanity, incarceration or some mad combination. Gabriel was quickly coming to the conclusion that no matter what happened, his life was over. He could see no way out, no hope.

The door opened again and two men entered for the second time.

"Mr Jones," came the now slightly softer tone of Donovan's voice. "I have agreed to release you into the custody of Professor Harrison." Gabriel spun his head around in disbelief.

"Prof?"

"Hello, my boy. I'll explain on the way home." He put a reassuring hand on the frightened man's shoulder. "Officer," the professor said as the uniformed officer re-entered the room. "Please un-cuff Mr Jones."

The professor and Gabriel headed down the corridor with Donovan and Lloyd looking on. Lloyd was more than curious. The stranger had taken Donovan into a side room. He hadn't spoken to him like a subordinate, but it was close. Certainly no less than an equal. They'd had a brief, private discussion, then Donovan just handed Gabriel over. With, as far as Lloyd could tell, no contact with or clearance from anyone further up the hierarchy. He looked at Donovan.

"What just happ..."

"Need to know Constable, suffice to say that this is bigger than you." He began to walk away then stopped and turned his head. "Or me, for that matter." He continued to walk.

Gabriel sat in the passenger seat of Professor Tony Harrison's car.

"I have to start by saying I'm grateful, there really are no words that express just how grateful I am. However I have to ask, how did you just do that?"

"I need you to trust me for just a little longer, Gabriel. I'll explain it all once we get to our destination."

"Are Anji and Jim safe?"

"Yes, Anji called me, I told them to stay in the house. Tabitha will drop them some supplies off so they can stay under its protection."

"Thank you." Gabriel glanced at the professor. He noticed he was wearing a ring with a strange emblem on it. A shield with a leafless tree in the middle.

"I've seen that before."

"What before, my boy?"

"The emblem on your ring. It was on a grave in Stonebank."

"Yes, Nathaniel Knight's grave, I should expect. As I said my boy, just a little longer."

The professor drove the car hard and turned up the wide driveway of a stately home. The house came into view; it was large, not quite as large and certainly not as grand as Meetingstone Manor would have been in its day, but imposing none the less. Tony slowed the car to a snail's pace as it crawled up the loose gravel driveway. The house was stone, four floors high with wooden bay-windows and a sprinkling of ivy. The car stopped.

"Come along Gabriel, there are some people you need to meet." The two men got out of the car and headed to the large wooden front door, which the professor opened without unlocking. They both stepped inside.

Gabriel was taken aback by what he saw. Two large mahogany staircases, curving up and converging on the same landing. Old paintings on the stone walls, some landscapes and some portraits, two suits of medieval armour and a large seal in the middle of the tiled floor. His eyes rested on the floor for a moment; the terracotta tiles were clean and polished to shine.

The large seal had a gold trim with an obsidian centre; within the centre lay the outline of a gold shield surrounding a large golden tree with no leaves. The gold on black was striking. A diminutive blonde in black trousers and blouse quickly walked from a side door, nodded and smiled at the professor and trotted off up the stairs. On a normal day Gabriel would have taken more notice of her but this was not a normal day.

The professor looked at Gabriel.

"Welcome to the HQ of the Halcyon Order." He nodded towards to the seal on the floor. "That is the seal of the Halcyon Order, the black-gold shield and golden oak. Come, the council are waiting for us."

The professor led Gabriel up the stairs and through a set of double doors, then down a long wood-panelled corridor and into a large stone meeting room with a set of heavy wooden doors. The room was rectangular with a bay-window at one end and several black banners hanging down the walls, all sporting the same seal as the floor in the entrance hall.

Four men sat around a long oak table. All were roughly the professor's age and were wearing black and gold robes, each man wore a ring bearing the black shield and gold oak. The professor gestured to an empty chair and then joined the other four men at the far end of the table.

The man in the centre spoke.

"Mr Jones, I know you have many questions. I will answer what I can, then we will leave you to have a chat with Tony over there."

Gabriel remained silent. "I am Father Artemis, head of the council." Artemis' robes were slightly different; the gold trim was more ornate and the sleeves seemed baggier. He had a white goatee and white hair tied back in a small ponytail. His features were stern and sallow. Gabriel didn't like the vibe he gave off as he continued his introductions. "Cleric Harrison, you know; these are clerics Jonah, Ford, and Samson. We are the Council of the Halcyon Order and custodians of its legacy."

"The Halcyon Order?" Gabriel asked.

"Yes, we have gone by and do go by a variety of names. The Halcyon Order, The Grand Order of Halcyon, and in the past The Knights of Halcyon, The Knights of the Halcyon Order and simply the Halcyon Knights. The Order goes back to before the crusades and has links going back even further." Artemis cleared his throat and Gabriel interrupted for a second.

"How come the word 'Knights' got dropped?"

"The simple answer is that we no longer have any knights amongst our order. In our current form, we have agents in just about every town and village in the country and agent networks in every city. We are a political, economic and to a lesser extent, covert force. We fulfil many roles. We deal in money and intelligence. However, our main role is to help keep the darkness at bay, so to speak."

"In what way?" Gabriel was a little taken aback, but decided that he'd reached the point where he'd just go with the flow.

Artemis continued. "The world most people see, and the world that actually exists beneath the surface, are two very different things. We work with others to control the truth and protect people from what they'd rather not know is real." Artemis read Gabriel's expression. "I understand why you think that is an arrogant, if not oppressive, approach but let me ask you. You have scratched the veneer of the perceived world, a veneer that we helped put and keep in place for over a millennia. Are you more or less happy with life since you started to learn the truth?"

"You have a point in this case but..."

Artemis cut him short. "Please Mr Jones, I respect and understand your scepticism. I only ask that you give us chance to put our point of view across. I'm hoping we can help you, and possibly in the long run we may be able to help each other."

"Fair enough," Gabriel conceded.

"Do you have any questions?" Artemis asked sincerely.

"A few, if it's okay?"

"Ask away, my young friend."

"How did your professor get me out of police custody?"

"As I said before, we wield a large amount of political and economic sway. We made certain assurances that you were innocent and agreed that we would put our resources into apprehending the actual culprit. You should find that you get no more trouble from the police in this matter."

"Thank you, very much." Gabriel gave a genuine smile and felt at least some of his troubles lifting.

"Glad we could help, dear boy. I sense that you have more questions though." He waited for Gabriel to continue.

"In Stonebank, there was a grave, the grave of Nathaniel Knight. He had your seal engraved on his tombstone."

"Ah, that's an easy one. He was a knight of our order. All of our combat-ready field agents back then, all of our knights, took the surname 'Knight' to facilitate contact and identification with other members."

"What happened? Why don't you have knights anymore?" Gabriel asked, hoping it wasn't an indiscreet question.

"A fair question. In years gone by, we had considerably more power than we have now. The knights were our most respected and feared members. They undertook our most important missions. If an acolyte, or even a cleric, couldn't successfully mediate or solve a situation peacefully then we'd send in a knight. If mediation and non-violence wasn't working, then a knight's silver sword often would. They were wise, just, noble but deadly. I said before that we work with other agencies; that's true and has been for centuries. However, not all of the agencies are strictly human. We have treaties with, and work with, many non-human agencies."

The professor interjected: "Do you remember when I said I'd come across a possible Vampire? I was being selective with the truth."

"Indeed, the majority of the vampire clans work with us for mutual benefit."

"Vampire clans?" Gabriel's eye widened a little.

"I'm sorry, Mr Jones, I know this is a lot to take in. To get back to the point. Several factions that we had agreements with felt that the knights gave us too much power. We never had more than twelve at any one time, but they were still a force to be reckoned with. These factions made a deal with a very powerful and evil demon, even more powerful that Legion. The demon helped them hunt down and murder every last knight. Only Cleric Harrison survived, but even he was too badly wounded to be able to keep up his former duties."

"Okay, last question. I don't want to sound ungrateful, but why are you showing so much interest in me?"

"We believe you to be special, Mr Jones. As does Legion. You were targeted for a reason by the cult. There is a prophecy that says: "The seed of the vanquisher of Legion will rise to power, either as a knight of the light or a puppet of the Many as One. The 'Many as One' being Legion." The cult has been pushing you down a path; Legion would not have been able to possess a sceptic, you've been..."

Gabriel finished his sentence for him. "Manipulated from the start?"

"Yes, how did you know?"

"Things seemed a little too simple, leads linked together a little too easily, a little too convenient. Was Lloyd Brighton in on it?"

"We don't believe so."

"Good, I liked him. How about 'the seed of the vanquisher of Legion', why do you think that's me?"

"As far as we can tell, Nathaniel Knight had a son who was raised by a coach driver. You are the descendant of that son."

"Nathaniel Knight? But from what I've been told, Claude Devereaux killed him."

"That's more or less true, Legion killed him while possessing Claude's body, but Nathaniel was able to somehow exorcise Legion with his dying breath, or so the records show.

"Time is a factor, so I'm going to put my cards on the table. As the Halcyon Order, we have a duty to stop Legion; he's far too powerful to be allowed to get a foot hold in this world. We intend to work with you and help you. However, as we do that we'd like you to consider joining us. Frankly, Mr Jones, we'd like you to consider letting us train you as a knight. We have prepared quarters for you here for the evening and have granted you the honouree rank of Acolyte; that will give you access to all non-restricted areas of our headquarters."

Gabriel wasn't sure how to respond.

"Have a chat to Tony. We'll leave you to it for a while."

The professor stood up. "Come on Gabriel, we'll have a chat in the library. It's a nice quiet place." The professor led Gabriel back out of the door and down the panelled corridor. "In here." He opened both of the double doors and entered. He waited a moment for Gabriel to enter then closed them behind them.

Gabriel looked around the room; the word 'impressed' didn't come close. It had large hardwood bookshelves reaching up to a high ceiling with moveable ladders to reach the top. There was a roaring open fire, several work desks with bankers' style brass lamps with green glass shades. The whole room smelt of old books and wax polish. There were two Chesterfield red leather armchairs by the fire.

The two men sat down; the chair was one of the most comfortable Gabriel had ever sat in. It seemed to mould to his body.

The professor looked at him for a moment.

"I'd bet good money that you could use a drink after the day you've been having."

Gabriel smiled. "You'd win that bet."

"Give me a moment, I'll see if I can find a helpful acolyte to send to the bar," the professor said as he stood up. "What would you like?"

"Guinness, if you've got it." Gabriel was surprised. "You have a bar?"

The professor popped his head out of the door. "Joanna, would you mind nipping to the bar for me and our guest?"

"Of course not, sir," came a cheery female voice. "Thank you. Could you get us a Guinness and a mild, please."

"I'll be right back, sir."

The professor sat back down. "That's service for you, and yes, we have a very nice bar. Many of the acolytes live here for days at a time. Relaxation is very important; we've got a gym down in the basement."

"I'll stick to the bar, I think," Gabriel said, relaxing into the chair a little more.

"Don't blame you." The professor smiled. "Come on, then, I'm guessing you've got stuff you'd rather ask me than Father Artemis."

Gabriel nodded. "He said you were a knight once?"

"Yes, I was, long ago, until the day that darkness took us all. I nearly lost my life. I was saved by a very good friend at the cost of his life and the full use of my left arm. It was a dark time, a lot of good men and women died."

Gabriel felt bad for bringing it up. "I'm sorry, professor," he said with a look of regret.

"That's quite alright, my boy, it was a long time ago. There's just no nice way of telling the story."

"Why do you need me? Why am I the only one who can be a knight?"

"It's complicated. You're not the only one who can be a knight, however becoming a Knight of the Halcyon Order is something that only a handful of people in every generation have the ability to do. There's quite a bit of mysticism involved. The only people who can see the true potential candidate are existing knights, and I lost more than the use of my arm if I'm honest. If we can train you, then you can help recruit and train others." The professor paused. "We used to be about a lot more than controlling truth. We used to be about helping the innocent and vulnerable. I have to confess, I'd like to go back to that."

The acolyte Tony had spoken to quietly walked in and placed the drinks on coasters on a nearby table.

"Thank you," Gabriel said as she walked out. "So what's the plan?" he asked before taking a long sip from his cold glass.

"Remarkably little has changed. It looks like pinning the murders on you was an attempt to break your spirit while deflecting any suspicion. They'll know we're involved now though so we have to move as quickly as possible. My guess is that they'll take enough hearts to generate enough mystical energy to bring Legion on to this plane, and let him possess anybody for the time being."

"What does he need me for? That's one of the things I don't understand."

"When a demon possesses a mortal, it puts immense strain on the body in most cases, especially a powerful demon like Legion, this quickly burns the body out forcing the demon to find new lodgings. A lot of the physical and mental traits that make you a good candidate for a knight also make you an excellent candidate for possession. Once you are properly prepared, i.e. you fully believe in the supernatural, he could walk round in your body for a thousand years. We know Charles is involved but we lack evidence, as within reason we have to work within the law. We can compel the police to arrest him but they'll still need evidence to charge him."

"Any ideas prof?"

"I'm going to send Tabitha - she's one of our field acolytes by the way - a bit of extra manpower. They'll get Anji and Jim home safe, then keep an eye on Charles until he makes a move. If you're agreeable I'd like to do some basic training with you."

"What sort of training?" Gabriel asked tentatively. "Artemis has asked that I give you basic acolyte training; however, I'd like to give you some knight training. It'd only be a flavour of proper training as full knight training takes about three years. But it'd be useful stuff and will pass the time until we have something to act upon."

Gabriel considered for a moment. "If I say yes, that's not a yes to staying on after we've sorted this Legion thing out. Assuming we manage to."

"Fair enough," the cleric agreed. "Here's a mobile phone." He fished a rather expensive-looking mobile out of his inside pocket. "You'll find that you won't be able to get a signal on your own phone here and I'm guessing you'll want to get hold of Anji and Jim. In the meantime, let me show you to your room. Feel free to make use of all the facilities."

The professor lead Gabriel down yet another maze of corridors to a small yet comfortable room featuring much the same decor as the rest of the mansion, a small television and a very comfortable bed.

"Here you are, my boy, and don't worry about the dreams. This place is like Fort Knox as far as supernatural incursions are concerned. Get a good night's sleep and we'll do some training tomorrow."

Chapter 13

Gabriel woke from a good night's sleep, the first he'd had in a long time. He'd kept the window open and could hear the birds singing outside the room. He stretched his legs out under the covers and for a moment, just enjoyed the feeling of being blissfully comfortable. He had to admit that although it had been a strange experience arriving at the Halcyon Order he did, for the first time in days, feel safe. He lay on his back staring up at the arched ceiling, then came a knock on the door.

"Come in," he murmured. The door opened to reveal the same acolyte who'd brought them the drinks the day before. She was very pretty, with dark shoulder length hair and sparkly blue eyes. Gabriel had to admit that there were worse things to look at first thing in a morning.

"Good morning, Mr Jones," she chirped cheerfully. "Cleric Harrison asked if you'd meet him in the entrance hall in half an hour."

Gabriel sat up in bed squinting slightly.

"Sure, yeah, thanks." He was a little incoherent still. "Is there anywhere I can get a shower?"

"Of course, the men's shower block is at the end of the hall on the right. You should find a robe and fresh towels in your cupboard."

"Thank you."

"No problem, Mr Jones. See you later." She shut the door. Gabriel was sure he recognised the acolyte from somewhere but couldn't think where.

He got out of bed and headed for the showers before making a beeline for the entrance hall. The professor was already waiting at the foot of the stairs and smiled when he saw Gabriel.

"Good morning, my boy. Did you sleep well?"

"Yes I did, thanks. Very well," Gabriel replied as he bounced down the staircase.

"Good, let's see if we can tire you out. If you're still agreeable to training."

"Yeah, but like I said, no promises for anything more."

"Let's go then. I never did like gyms, I've arranged for one of our assembly halls to be cleared. Joanna should be waiting for us there now."

"The pretty, but painfully cheery brunette?"

"That's her." The professor led Gabriel to the makeshift training room.

Like the rest of the large house the room was stone, but this one did not have the panelled walls that much of the place did. The room had been completely cleared save for three chairs and a table. Joanna was milling about the centre of the room, dressed in tight fitting black sweat clothes. She turned around when the men entered.

"Hello again," Gabriel said with a smile. Then it dawned on him. "Ah, now I know where I know you from. You were the Prof's assistant at the university."

The Professor responded for her. "That's right, she's been training up as a field acolyte, so she has some basic combat training. Also, as my assistant, she has higher clearance than most of the acolytes so we can speak freely in front of her."

"What are we starting with then, gentlemen?" Joanna asked while limbering up. "Hand to hand?"

"Not today," the professor informed her as he walked over to the table. "This morning, let's teach Mr Jones a little sword play." He picked up a wooden training sword off the table with his good hand and threw it to Joanna. The training blade arched through the air, and the acolyte caught it by the handle in a single smooth control motion. "Think fast Gabriel." He threw a second training sword in Gabriel's direction. Gabriel also, much to his own astonishment managed to catch the sword by the handle, though his catch was far jerkier and less impressive looking then Joanna's had been. "A very good start there," the professor praised.

"Am I likely to need to use a sword at any point?" Gabriel asked sceptically.

"No, but I want you to start thinking about yourself as a warrior, not an average person, not vulnerable. You need to start seeing yourself as a force to be reckoned with. Swordplay sharpens the mind and the body. Now let's start with basic defence. When we train, we train with slow strokes to start with. Joanna, vertical attack. Gabriel, defend yourself."

The acolyte raised the sword above her head and began to bring it down towards Gabriel. He raised his wooden blade horizontally in an attempt to block the strike. "Not bad, hold it just a little higher and angle it so the opponent's sword glances off." Gabriel did as the professor suggested. "Good."

Joanna immediately attacked again, this time from the side. "Move the sword vertically to meet my strike," she said. "Parry the blow."

"Excellent!" the professor congratulated. "You're a natural." Joanna took over the majority of the lesson with Tony adding the odd bit of advice, but mainly watching. They went over the basics several times, taking it in turns to attack and defend. Gabriel was noticeably sweating; he was far from in condition. Exercise had always been pushed down his 'to do' list by more important things, such as eating pizza and drinking beer. Joanna, on the other hand, *was* in condition and looked as fresh as the proverbial daisy.

The Professor took pity on the red sweaty man. "Okay, you two. Let's take a break. Joanna, nip and get us some cold drinks please."

"Not bad at all for a novice." She smiled at Gabe. "Where'd you learn the basics?"

The writer gave a slight grin at what he thought was an odd question. "From you, right now."

"Oh," was her only response, which she gave with a slight look of confusion. "I'll grab the drinks." She disappeared through the door.

"Did I say the wrong thing?" Gabriel asked the professor.

"No, Gabriel, she's just a little confused. Jo just taught you some basic defence, but those weren't the 'basics' she was referring to. She was talking about how to stand, how to grip the sword. The fact that you were able to catch a blade out of the air. Did you even notice that after the first three for four attacks she stopped striking you at training speed, and started to hit as fast as she would in any expert sparring match?"

"I have to confess, I didn't."

"I told you a half-truth before. What I said was true about my reasons for teaching you the sword, but I also wanted to see how quickly you picked it up. Knights tend to pass on a sort of genetic memory to their descendants. We don't know if it's a result of biology or mysticism, but it does happen. I wanted to see if you truly are the prophesised saviour. If you were, then Nathaniel's genetic memory would have been present."

"I'm assuming from this that you think it is present?"

"Oh yes, more than that, I've never seen such a strong innate ability." He walked over to the table again and flicked open the catches of a long black box. "I'd like you to meet an old friend." He reached inside the box and retrieved a shining blade.

"A longsword!" Gabriel's eyes widened. "I've got to say, Prof, it is a thing of beauty."

Gabriel was almost transfixed by the blade. It was about four feet long but quite slender. The hilt was a dark metal, almost black. The handle's grip was finished in black leather with a silver trim. The pommel was silver and had been fashioned into the shape of a dragon's head. The blade had an intricate ivy motif etched along its entire length; the metal reflected so much light that it almost glowed. The professor looked on it in pride.

"This is Sirius. The smith who made it named it that after the brightest star in the night sky."

"Why is it so shiny?"

"It's silver, or rather a steel core with a silver coating. A lot of non-humans have a hard time with silver. The blade is blessed to cause extra grief to the undead, and enchanted by a few of the more mystical religions. Here." He offered it to Gabriel. "Hold it, but be careful, it's razor sharp." Gabriel took the sword, it was lighter than he'd expected. "Most of the knights have had unique swords, but Sirius is the finest sword to ever be seen by the order."

Gabriel slowly moved the blade through the air, looking on in wonder as it caught the light. The grip felt comfortable in his hand and the whole thing felt perfectly balanced. Something about it just felt *right*.

"Very impressive, Professor." The door creaked open and Joanna returned with a tray of drinks. Gabriel handed Sirius back.

"Right, we'll have these, then continue."

The writer looked at his drink. It was lemonade, with several ice cubes and a slice of lime. The glass felt cool in his hand. He took a long swig; the drink was more than refreshing.

"That hit the spot," he said, placing the emptied glass on the table.

"Excellent, let's continue, shall we." The professor was back in teacher mode. "Gabriel, this time I want to concentrate on your attacking."

"Sounds good, Prof." He joined Joanna, who had already returned to the makeshift sparring area.

"Okay, please begin."

Gabriel performed a vertical attack the same way he'd seen Joanna do it; she blocked it in much the same way he'd done earlier.

"One thing I'm not sure about?" he began to ask, as Joanna performed a leg attack.

"Yes. Go on," the professor encouraged as Gabriel deflected the strike.

"You say you work with non-human organisations. Vampires and the like." He made a thrust. In a graceful chain of movements Joanna parried, pirouetted and used the momentum to counter attack to the neck. Gabriel quickly but awkwardly parried the blow; the force of her strike staggered him slightly.

"Yes we do, and she nearly had you there." The professor smiled. "Don't forget, angle your sword slightly. It helps the blows to glance off."

"Noted."

"You were asking about non-human organisations?"

"Yes, can't that cause, shall we say, a 'conflict of interest' at times? You must get situations where you have disagreements between human and non-human." He was amazed how quickly he'd simply accepted the concept of 'non-humans.' Gabriel attacked again. Joanna countered the move and performed a sweeping attack.

"We do, but the Order is neutral in terms of 'species', shall we say." Gabriel jumped back to dodge the attack and lunged forward to counter.

"Can't that be difficult at times?"

"I thought it would as well when I first became an acolyte. I think we all do."

"Agreed," Joanna added, as she circled Gabriel like a cat stalking its prey. The professor watched as he continued his reply.

"It doesn't take long to realise that not all the darkness is non-human, some monsters are men, and some men are monsters."

"And some women," Joanna added as she thrust at Gabriel. He attempted to copy her parry-pirouette-counter attack move. He didn't do a bad job, though it lacked Joanna's grace.

"How was that?" he asked, rather proud of himself. The professor began to interject.

"Joanna, earlier on he referred to you as, what was it? 'Painfully cheerful.' That was it."

Joanna smiled at Gabriel with a wicked look in her eye.

"I was joking."

She started to perform a vertical attack to Gabriel's head. He raised his own sword to block; she then quickly revealed the attack to be a feint and with lightning speed, used the flat of the wooden blade to sweep Gabriel's legs from under him, sending him crashing on to his back onto the floor mats.

"Fair enough, but don't make that joke again." She let out a small laugh and helped him to his feet.

"Two lessons there, my boy. One: don't become over-confident. Two: even after all the things I've seen over the years, hell still hath no fury."

Lloyd Brighton was driving quickly. This was one of the rare times he bothered to use his siren and lights. A call had come in: poor Ethel Birchwood had found two dead bodies, bodies that yet again had missing hearts.

His squad car arrived at the scene. She'd found them in Tabitha's shop, God knows what had happened. Lloyd jumped out of his car and ran to the ambulance, where Ethel sat with a blanket over her shoulders.

"Ethel, dear God, are you okay?" He shook his head for a moment. "What a stupid question, of course you aren't." He sat down next to her and put his arm around her shoulder. "I'm so sorry you had to see something like that."

Ethel didn't say anything. She kept blankly looking forward, though she was taking the whole ordeal better than Gabriel had when they'd found Cobb's body.

One of the paramedics came over. "Hello sir, we've kept an eye on things. We understand that CID and forensics are on their way."

"Speak of the devil," Lloyd commented, as he spotted Brigham's car and Tom's van arriving. Dudley and Donovan exited their vehicle and headed in Lloyd's direction. Tom got out and started to organise his staff.

"Constable," Brigham shouted. "What is the situation here?"

Lloyd gave Ethel's shoulder a final squeeze, then stood up and started to walk towards the DCI. *The situation is that you need to learn people skills,* the constable almost said out loud. He nodded his head towards the shop and made sure he was a good distance away from Ethel before speaking in a low tone.

"I've not been inside myself yet, but Mrs Birchwood over there has found two new bodies. Apparently, both have missing hearts." He looked over at the small old lady draped in a blanket. "If you want to question her, please be as gentle as possible."

Donovan was not unaware that he could have a brisk manner with people and he respected Lloyd's protective instinct. "Sergeant Dudley, would you please question Mrs Birchwood, and do so as delicately as possible. Constable Brighton and I will examine the crime scene."

Lloyd looked at Donovan, almost apologetically.

"Thank you, Inspector."

The DCI gave a grunt and started to move towards the door of Tabitha's shop with Lloyd in tow. "I'm assuming I don't have to tell you to be careful what you touch and where you tread, Constable."

"You assume right." Brigham pushed open the door with his elbow and began to slowly enter, scanning the floor with his eyes and taking slow and very deliberate footprints. He stopped walking when he reached the blood; there was a lot of it over the walls, ceiling, merchandise and floor. Lloyd couldn't help but stare are the carpet-less floor; the blood had soaked into the floorboards. The wood went from greyish brown, to dark brown where the blood had soaked in, to red where it had saturated the wood and couldn't soak in anymore.

"That's new, Constable," Brigham said with a grave look.

Lloyd looked up.

"Bloody hell!"

There were two bodies hanging upside down from the ceiling. Both had their hearts cut out, but this was far more gruesome than any of the other murders had been. Both men had been strung up by one leg; the other leg had been removed at the knee. Both arms were removed and both men's intestines had been ripped out, a cross incision had been made over the eye sockets and the eyeballs had been removed. On the floor below, the limbs had been arranged in the shape of a shield and the intestines arranged in the shape of a tree with the eyes at the centre.

Brigham looked away. He'd seen a lot of morose things in his career, but this had it all beat.

Lloyd was trying not to throw up. He currently had one priority. "Tabitha," he shouted (he didn't know why, as the chances of her being alive and well at the crime scene were zero). Oddly enough, there was no sign of a struggle in the front of the shop.

Lloyd was trying to professionally distance himself from the horrific scene. He couldn't bring himself to get any closer to the hanging men. "I'll check the back door," he managed to say, retreating to the outside world for a moment and heading around the exterior to the rear of the property.

The back door was unlocked. Lloyd hesitantly entered, taking him directly into Tabatha's kitchen. He looked around the room but nothing was out of place.

Brigham was still on the shop floor. "What's it like back there, Lloyd?" he shouted.

"Looks normal, no sign of a struggle, but Tabitha wouldn't have gone out and left the shop open and the back door unlocked. I think we have to assume we have a missing person and probable kidnapping," Lloyd shouted back.

"Agreed, I'll radio it in." Brigham headed for the door and left the shop, glad of the excuse to get away from the mess. He had to report the possible kidnapping and he was also under orders to report any more of the missing heart murders to his superiors immediately. He assumed it was connected to the same organization that arranged for Gabriel Jones' release.

Tom was geared up and entered the shop as soon as he saw the DCI leave. He saw the same blood the two police officers has seen, then the arranged entrails and limbs then the mutilated corpses.

"Dear God," he said under his breath. Tom had also seen some bad things in his time, but this was up there amongst the worse. "The poor bastards." He felt angry, angry that anyone could do this to another person and angry that his team had to see it. Most of them were still young, in the job because they loved science and they wanted to help people. They didn't deserve to take this image home with them tonight. "It's what they signed up for," he consoled himself under his breath.

"Okay, team," he shouted back through the open door. "This is a really bad one. Standard procedure with a few extra photographs. Brace yourselves though, and if anyone starts to feel faint just get out as quickly as possible for some air."

Lloyd had returned to the front side of the shop and was walking over to where Donovan had just finished radioing in.

"Ah, Constable. Find anything?"

Lloyd shook his head. "Unfortunately not," he said in a sombre voice.

"Do you recognise the deceased?"

"No, they're definitely not locals. When we're done here I'll check the local guest houses."

"Thank you, Constable. For what it's worth, I'm sorry this had to happen here. You're a good man, you care about the people you serve, that's becoming a rare thing these days."

Lloyd struggled to hide his surprise. "Thank you," he said, almost stumbling over the words as he realised that Donovan had picked up on his reaction.

"It's okay, Mr Brighton. I know I'm not the most personable chap you could meet, and I'm aware of my reputation. To be honest, it often helps me do my job. But I wanted you to know that though I may have been abrasive in the past, I do respect you."

"Thank you. And I'm sorry if I've been less than respectful to you." Lloyd paused for a second, considering if whether to ask the next question or not. "Can I ask you, why did we release Gabriel Jones? I know you said it was 'need to know', but just between us…"

The DCI also considered for a few seconds.

"It was unusual to say the least. The man he left with ask for a private word. I then received a phone call, on an official line directly from the Home Secretary. He assured me that Jones was not involved and that all evidence was planted." The DCI shrugged. "You spent time with him, what do you think?"

"Honestly, it didn't fit for me, despite the, albeit damning, evidence. He was really knocked for six when he saw Cobb's body. He went white. No way could he have done what we saw in there." He nodded at the shop.

"I've had a couple of people keeping tabs on Ravenwood, but he's not done anything suspicious."

The Professor was driving like a madman, with Gabriel in the passenger seat and Joanna in the back. Despite the constant fear of death Gabriel had to admit that fast though it was, the amount of car control the Professor was showing was phenomenal. Not long after the training session Tony had suddenly bundled Gabriel and Joanna off with him but had given no explanation. Gabriel was concerned.

"Prof, where are we going?" Gabriel asked.

"Stonebank. We have information from the police that there's been a murder in Tabitha's shop."

"Tabitha's dead?"

"No! Two unidentified males. Most likely the two acolytes I sent in as back up. Tabitha's missing."

Gabriel now understood the professor's haste.

"Bloody hell."

Tony's car finally arrived at the crime scene. All three passengers jumped out of the vehicle as if their life depended on it. Sergeant Dudley quickly moved to intercept the civilians.

"I'm sorry, people. This is a crime scene." His words were polite but his tone wasn't. The Professor dismissively flashed a pass without bothering to make eye contact.

"Home Office clearance. These two are with me." He was heading directly for Donovan and Lloyd. Gabriel couldn't help but notice the change in the professor's voice. He'd always sounded like a kind old uncle. At the moment he sounded like a sergeant major.

Donovan looked up. "Hello, Professor Harrison. I'd be lying if I said I was surprised to see you."

"Good evening Detective Chief Inspector. Mr Jones you know; this is Ms Joanna King, my assistant. I understand you have been given instructions to cooperate fully with me?"

Donovan did not like relinquishing control but had very little choice.

"That is correct, sir. The current situation is that we have two male, mutilated corpses with evidence that suggests a ritualistic motive."

"What about the proprietor of the shop?" the professor asked, successfully masking his personal anxiety.

"We're not sure, we've put out a missing persons call on her."

"May I examine the scene?"

"Of course, though it's a little rough. This way."

The professor turned to Gabriel. "My boy, this may be very hard, but it's important that you see what they're capable of."

Gabriel considered for a moment. He still had the image of Cobb's body behind his eyelids from time to time.

"Okay professor. Lead the way."

The professor gently raised a palm to Joanna, telling her to stay put.

Tony opened the shop door. The tinkle of the little bell seemed somehow mocking in the current situation. Gabriel looked around for a second before seeing the horrific sight. He wanted to bolt for the door, he wanted to be anywhere on the planet but there. The only thing that slightly steadied him was the Professor's presence. The cleric looked grave; it was worse than he'd expected.

"Some monsters are men, and some men are monsters." He looked that the dead acolytes he'd sent to help Tabitha. He'd never been good at losing people, especially the ones he'd put in harm's way. He bowed his head and closed his eyes for a second. "I'm sorry." He whispered. "They will pay. I swear it. They will pay."

He opened his eyes and examined the bastardised Halcyon Order seal the cult had made out of the body parts and entrails.

"Come on, my boy. Let's get out of here. We've seen what we needed to."

Joanna was milling about outside. She looked on as Tom Agar packed away and gave Brigham his preliminary report.

"It's not pretty, I'm afraid. I'll have the full autopsy report in a few hours but the evidence suggests that the mutilation was carried out while they were still alive and conscious, so the official cause of death will probably be shock. Not that it matters with the state those poor bastards are in."

"Thank you, Doctor. We'll let you finish up." The acolyte noticed Tony and Gabriel leave the shop; even the professor looked shocked. The professor beckoned her over.

"Come on, let's take a seat for a moment. They took a seat by the ford where Gabriel and Anji had sat a few days previously. The tranquillity was doing little to calm Gabriel's nerves, but anything was better than nothing.

"Prof?" Gabriel started to ask. "What was the deal with the Halcyon symbol on the floor?"

Joanna looked at her superior, unsure what Gabriel was talking about.

"That was a declaration of war." He paused for a moment. "Gabriel, you are not an average man on the street." The professor looked him directly in the eye. "You are not vulnerable, you are a fighter and you are a warrior. You have the blood of a Knight of the Halcyon Order, you may not want that for yourself but right now we need you to believe it. If Legion gets a proper foothold in the modern world, nothing will be able to stop him. I'm not being dramatic here. The world literally needs you. The Order needs you, and right now, more than anything else, Tabitha needs you, as they're almost certainly going to sacrifice her. They know what you have the potential to be. They fear you. Right now, we need you to act the part. Are you with me my boy?"

Gabriel gave a firm nod.

"If they've taken Tabitha, then they're most likely going to be either in the tunnel under the manor or the site in the woods."

"From what you've told me the woods is far more likely for a big sacrifice."

"Let's go then." The professor's talk had done a lot of good. Gabriel still wasn't sure if he'd be any use but he liked Tabitha, and she'd helped him. He'd be damned if he'd let them cut her heart out without doing everything he could to stop it.

He made a beeline for Lloyd. "Lloyd, I think I know where Tabitha is. I think she's in mortal danger and I think we need every man we can get. You in?"

"Damn right," Lloyd replied with a firm nod, not unlike the one Gabriel had given a few moments earlier.

"I have orders to 'offer every assistance' so it looks like I'm in as well," Donovan added.

"Thank you. I'm guessing by now you've cottoned on to the fact that there's something big happening."

"Yes, calls from the Home Secretary tend to give me that impression. I'll call in the two men I put on Ravenwood. Where are we going?" the DCI asked, looking at Lloyd and Gabriel. Gabriel looked at Lloyd. "We need to get to the ruin in the woods between the manor house and the stone circle. Any idea on the best place to park up a car?"

"We should go via the stone circle," Joanna interjected.

"She's right," the professor added. "We may need that as a fall-back point."

"Okay, in that case the church car park is the best place," Lloyd said, pointing his fingertips in the air slightly. The DCI pulled the radio mouthpiece out of his car.

"I'll call in the two chaps I put on Ravenwood," he said, before pushing the talk button and speaking into the microphone.

"Manfredi, do you read me? Over." Dead air.

"Johnson, do you read me? Over." More dead air.

"Odd, Manfredi and Johnson are not the types to leave the radio. Let's move. I'll try again *en route*."

The professor stopped them for a moment. "This is going to sound a little odd. If anything out of the ordinary happens, then make a run for the stone circle or the church, whichever is closest."

Donovan was about to ask for further explanation, but the professor cut him off before he could open his mouth. "I'm sorry I can't say more, but trust me, if you need to run, you'll know about it."

The DCI spoke again, this time not giving Tony time to cut him off. "I'll send for backup."

"I'd prefer that you didn't."

The DCI didn't argue. He had a strong gut feeling that the professor could make a call and overrule any request he could make.

"I need you to trust me, Detective Chief Inspector." Tony looked him directly in the eyes.

"Okay, Professor, let's go… we're quickly losing the light."

"Agreed," the professor replied, clapping him on the arm for a moment.

It wasn't far to the church but the journey on foot was another matter. Both cars pulled swiftly into the church car park and quickly lost their passengers.

The professor popped loose his car's boot and opened it with his one good hand. He retrieved two heavy-duty torches and handed one each to Gabriel and Joanna. Lloyd did the same for himself and the DCI. The torch felt heavy in Gabriel's hand; for a moment his mind flashed back to his sword training.

Joanna looked over at Lloyd. "Lead the way, Constable."

The small team headed to the footpath which Gabriel and Anji had taken the first morning they'd been in Stonebank. Gabriel wished he'd given Anji a call; despite a very eventful and distracting couple of days, he was missing her a lot and couldn't shake the feeling that something bad was about to happen. Something really bad.

It didn't take them long to reach the circle. The sky was approaching dusk and the entire place felt eerily still.

"Remember!" the professor warned. "If anything happens, get back here and get inside the circle."

The DCI was having second thoughts. This 'get back to the stone circle' talk felt odd, to say the least. Unfortunately, stopping whoever was responsible for the murders was paramount, and the Home Office had made it clear that he should cooperate with the professor in every respect. However, nothing had come through the correct chain of command. He had never trusted orders that skipped his immediate superior, let alone ones that came directly from the Home Secretary and skipped the entire British police force. He'd tried to contact his local officers again but had had no luck. This also worried him but it was all a bit late now. He decided to play it out and see what happened.

Lloyd continued to lead the way, this time down the path that Gabriel had run along when he'd fled the Harbinger – not a pleasant memory for him by any stretch of the imagination. Lloyd retrieved his torch from his pocket and switched it on. Donovan, Gabriel and Joanna followed suit. It wasn't quite dark yet but the tree canopy was blocking out what light there was. The group were making good progress, even in the low light.

"Shhh," the professor whispered, while gesturing to everyone to stop. "Listen."

Gabriel squinted in concentration. "I can hear something. Sounds a bit like chanting or something."

"Looks like the ruin in the woods was a good choice," Tony remarked. "Keep as quiet as possible and try to stay out of sight. Use cover and shadow to your advantage." The professor had now fully taken charge. His tone was commanding but not rude. It was a tone that said: 'I know what I'm doing and it's in your best interest to trust me.' Even Donovan didn't question it.

The group began to converge on the source of the noise, each of them flicking their torches off. The grey walls of the ruin could now be seen clearly in the dark, its dry stone bathed in an orange-yellow light emanating from a dozen or so flaming torches. As the team moved closer they could see black robed figures, but the walls were still blocking much of their view.

The group moved closer still, doing everything possible to keep out of sight. The chanting seemed to be increasing in speed and ferocity. They approached further and the altar came into view.

"Bloody hell," Gabriel whispered to himself. The black figures were surrounding the altar; there were a lot of them, far more than had been under the manor house.

The chanting suddenly stopped and all the figures bar five knelt down, unblocking much of the view. Gabriel immediately recognised Tabitha. Naked apart from a gag across her mouth, she was chained to the altar with a black robed figure standing over her. He was too far away to see her eyes properly, but he knew they contained a look of sheer terror.

There were two other people present. Both men, also naked but chained to the walls at the side. Both were flanked by two robed figures.

"Those are my men. Manfredi and Johnson," the DCI said, with a grave look of concern. The figure standing over Tabitha pulled down his hood and started to chant a language only the professor recognised as Aramaic.

"Ravenwood, no surprise there." Gabriel looked at the professor. "Prof, we've got to stop them!" Gabriel's hushed voice did nothing to hide its urgency.

"I know," the professor agreed, cursing himself for not coming armed. "Our best bet is to rush them and..."

He stopped talking the moment he saw Manfredi and Johnson die. The black figures plunged curved knifes into each of their chest cavities. Donovan looked on helplessly as his men's hearts were removed and their bodies convulsed. Charles raised his hands to reveal two other hearts, and began to speak.

"My lord, I offer you these hearts of your enemy that they may bolster your strength and bring you forth."

He tossed the two hearts into a large flaming bowl. The figures from the side approached and did the same with the organs of the doomed police officers, leaving their lifeless bodies hanging limply from their chains.

The anger inside Donovan erupted.

"Bastards!" he said in a low tone, and for a moment started to advance. Then came a brilliant smoky blue-white light rising up from the flaming bowl; fluxing, pulsating and swirling in the air, almost forming a shape.

Charles continued to speak. "My lord, I offer you myself as a vessel. With this final sacrifice of the Halcyon Order, I empower you to step forth." Ravenwood raised his own sacrificial blade above his head then plunged it into Tabitha's chest.

Gabriel was stunned; the world seemed to be moving in slow motion and sound was almost muffled. For a moment his mind retreated into itself. In that moment, the professor, the stone altar, the horrific sight – everything simply didn't exist. The smoky light circled above the altar then flew into Tabitha's body, then out through her eyes and then directly into Charles' chest, permeating his flesh.

"Okay, I'm going for them," the DCI said, and began to advance again.

"No," the professor urged, pulling him back. "We must withdraw."

Donovan was about to protest when he saw Tony's eyes. They gave a look, the like of which he'd never seen before. A look that existed deep in the soul where agony and rage met. The professor had known Tabitha for over ten years; they'd been friends for most of that time, good friends. Every fibre of his being wanted nothing more than to charge in and exact immediate revenge on Charles Ravenwood. But that wouldn't help, he knew what was coming next and he couldn't allow his heart to rule his head.

He looked at the altar. Charles' body spoke.

"I hear you, broken knight." He was projecting his voice. *"Nomen mihi Legio est, quia multi sumus."*

"Legion!" Gabriel warned.

"We need to go. We need to go now," the professor urged.

"Okay," the DCI conceded.

"Let's go," Lloyd said, turning to see a familiar face behind him. *"Ethel?"*

Ethel Birchwood, along with four other people, were standing behind them. Lloyd was so startled to see her, he didn't even notice that she was wearing a black robe. He would have done if he'd had more time.

The old lady quickly thrust an eight-inch curved blade into Lloyd's gut. The pain was excruciating. Before anyone could stop her, she swiftly pulled it out and sliced it across Lloyd's throat. The blood ran down his neck, into the fibres of his white police shirt and up into his mouth. Even in his shocked state he could taste the coppery blood as the life faded from his eyes. The woman he'd known all his life, the woman he'd thought he was comforting a few hours earlier, had become his murderer.

Gabriel, Joanna and Donovan were processing what they'd just seen. Even Donovan's long years of service hadn't prepared him for something like this. Then the moment was gone, and survival instinct kicked in.

Legion continued to speak.

"Kill the girl and the other one, but I want the Avatar and the broken knight."

The robed figures blocking their escape were advancing. Gabriel looked over his shoulder towards the altar. "We've got lots of 'em coming from behind," he commented.

Tony checked the rear as well. There were countless robed figures closing in. Their only chance was through the few cultists who were blocking their path back to the cars.

"Charge!" cried the professor. All four of the non-cult members rushed the black figures, knocking them to the ground. "Run for the circle," he added as he steadied himself.

The group bolted down the path, the figures in pursuit. They reached a stile and began to climb it one by one, giving the black cultists time to catch up. Donovan's foot landed on a rock as he climbed off on the far side. He lost his footing in the dark and tumbled to the floor.

The closest of the cult members was over the stile in moments, and began to lunge downwards towards Donovan with his knife. Brigham braced himself for the pain, only to see Gabriel unceremoniously barge into the figure, knocking him into the foliage. The writer helped Donovan to his feet and they continued to run from their pursuers.

Finally, they got to the circle and almost collapsed to the ground in the centre ring. The cultists arrived in dribs and drabs; all with knives, all with hoods up but none would enter the circle.

The professor spoke to Gabriel, puffing slightly as he recovered his breath. "When talking to a demon the important thing is to not show fear or weakness. They like to act as if they already know everything, but lack of knowledge is actually their biggest weakness. They will know a lot and it may surprise you but it'll be ignorant of many other factors. It will try to trick you into giving it information. Watch what you say, try not to give anything away and act cocky as hell."

After a few moments Charles' body arrived. It gave the impression of being more youthful, not so much in appearance but more in movement. It looked at Gabriel.

"So then, Avatar, we meet at last. I wasn't expecting to have to address you in the body of another." Legion piloted his vessel around the outer edge of the circle. The black robed figures remained still and silent in the moonlight.

"Yeah, well. That's life."

"Amusing, you will make – and, for that matter, have made – an excellent puppet. Or didn't you realise that you'd been manipulated all along?"

Gabriel was still playing it as nonchalantly as he could. He was doing an excellent job of hiding his anxiety.

"The boy who offered up his story," he said. "The absurdity of the animal cruelty police charge. The landlady at Woodberry House. The crows everywhere. You weren't exactly subtle, now were you? As for the dreams, your previous victim warned me about them, even if they did cost him his sanity. I'm guessing you didn't figure on him."

Gabriel winked. In another time and place he'd have been proud of himself.

Legion laughed.

"Harry Graves was also part of the charade mortal. The charade that started fifty years ago, before you were even born. He may not have been overly willing to help, but that's not important, is it Harry?"

One of the black figures pulled his hood down.

"Harry!" Gabriel said. "I really did feel sorry for you and really did think you were trying to help me."

Harry looked down. "I truly am sorry. I wasn't part of this fifty years ago. They set me up and had me committed. They did send me the crow and the dreams, some of it was true. They said if I helped them convince you and joined the cult, they'd get me out." He looked up and gave Gabriel a sombre apologetic look. "I needed to get out of there, I'm so sorry. When you live in Hell, sometimes you have to make a deal with the devil."

He looked back down and Legion began to speak again. "What of you, Cleric? Are you not going to confess your part in this? Your part, and that of your has-been Order." The demon's words were dripping with contempt.

Gabriel looked at the professor, who didn't seem shaken by Legion's words.

"Go on then, demon. Tell him, tell your 'avatar' what part the Halcyon Order played."

"I want to hear it from your mouth, Cleric. I want to hear the broken knight confess."

Gabriel's mind was churning over the past week or so, momentarily displaced from its dire situation. The professor had been the one who had sent him to Stonebank. Tabitha could have warned him of the danger but didn't, and the professor had been incredibly forthcoming with information but encouraged him to keep prodding the cult.

A twinge of betrayal turned in Gabriel's gut, but he wanted to give the professor a chance to explain. Also, the back-and-forth between the professor and the demon was showing Gabriel something. It was showing him that the professor was right. Legion was pretty sure that the Order had been manipulating him in much the same way the cult had. However, it had no true idea as to the specifics.

Tony was almost toying with the demon now. "Well, pit-fiend, you may want to hear me 'confess' but I can tell you now, you'll be waiting the best part of some time."

Legion dismissed the Cleric with a sneer and turned to Gabriel.

"What of you, Avatar? Are you ready to give yourself to me? Are you ready to be my instrument?"

Gabriel was amazed by how the demon so completely possessed Ravenwood. It wasn't how it looked in films, with the face having an expressionless aspect. If anything, the expressions were exaggerated, almost showman-like.

"Hate to disappoint you, but no." Gabriel remembered the professor's advice to be cocky. "However, I am curious as to why these inbreeds follow you. Do you have a large supply of Jaffa Cakes, or something?"

"They possess something you lack, mortal. They possess faith. They see this world that your kind have spread over like a cancer. They see the chaos your weapons and armies have wrought. They despair at the dichotomy of people fighting wars or committing mass murder in the name of peaceful religions. They see the rich nations devouring the world's resources and exploiting the poor nations. They know you cannot be trusted to continue down this path. They know the human race was born to kneel. They know you are better off realising that you are sheep. They know that I will rise up and bring order to the chaos of this little world."

Gabriel put his hands in his pockets raised an eyebrow. "So you *don't* have Jaffa Cakes, then? Damn."

The professor wasn't sure about Gabriel's attempts at humour, but he had to admit that the cocky vibe was coming through loud and clear, especially considering the trauma of the day.

Charles' head turned and Legion looked at the professor. "I was wondering, broken knight, did you like the little message my followers left for you? Not the classical declaration of war, I will grant you, but oh so much more memorable."

Gabriel could see the anger building up in the professor. "He's baiting you, Prof," he said quietly.

Tony knew Gabriel was right but it didn't stop the anger.

"Let me introduce you to two of my faithful," continued Legion. Two of the figures around the periphery stepped forward and pulled down their hoods. Neil the landlord and Len Tait, the pub gossip. "They were so helpful in that trifling matter."

The professor made a mental note of their faces, but cloaked down and controlled his anger. It was time to end this standoff. It hadn't happened how he'd wanted it to. He'd wanted to save Tabitha, and he should have expected the sneak attack and never have lost Lloyd.

None of that could be helped now though. The only silver lining was that it had given him chance to observe Gabriel, and Gabriel was starting to show rapid progress. The council would be happy about that, if nothing else.

"Do you intend to talk us to death, demon? We are in stalemate. You can't come in and we won't come out. You can starve us out, but the Order will send overwhelming backup long before that happens and you'll be forced to abandon this little siege."

"This is no siege, Cleric, I just wanted a chance to talk to you and my avatar. In the end he will come willingly or I will kill him. I promise you that. And when that happens, your order will pay for what that knight did all those years ago. I will take this world under my protection but I will be clearing out the deadwood first. Starting with that relic that you belong to."

He looked at Gabriel. "I will be seeing you soon, Avatar." With that, he turned and strolled off into the forest, the black robed figures following suit.

The surviving four members of the team gave the demon time to get some distance away, then made a quick dash through the woodland to the church and their cars.

"We should get back to the Order," Gabriel said, almost taking charge.

The professor didn't comment other than to agree. "Yes, Detective, you should come with us, we can debrief you." He paused. "I'm sorry, I didn't have chance to say before. Lloyd seemed like a good man."

Gabriel walked over as well.

"He was a good man, a damn good man."

Chapter 14

Gabriel rolled over in bed and checked the watch he'd left on his nightstand. Half one in the morning. Sleep was impossible. Everything was running through his mind like a torrent.

The concept of him being a knight, the sword training, the professor manipulating him. The murder scene, and most of all the look on Lloyd's face when he died. That, he wasn't taking too well. He honestly felt like he was toughening up. Back in the circle, facing Legion, he'd almost started to believe the character he was playing. However, when his mind went back to Lloyd, he felt like the same old out-of-work writer he'd been for years.

Lloyd was a good man and didn't deserve to die. The thought hadn't been far from his head all night, with the thought of poor Tabitha not far behind.

Gabriel gave up on sleep, put on some clothes and went for a walk through the dimly lit corridors. The atmosphere in the headquarters at night felt strange. Not creepy or eerie, but at the same time not welcoming. The corridors oddly reminded him of a place he'd stayed in on a school residential trip when he was eight or nine. They looked absolutely nothing alike, but the feeling was the same.

Lloyd was a good man and didn't deserve to die.

The thought echoed again. He tried to suppress it. His mind wondered past one thought and onto another. Did he want to be a Knight of the Halcyon Order? As a boy he'd wanted to be a knight, he'd loved the old Tony Curtis film *The Black Shield of Falworth.* Cheesy as hell, and Tony Curtis made no effort to hide his Bronx accent, but as a kid he'd loved it. It occurred to him that this part of his own situation wasn't dissimilar from the film. A country boy, taken into a castle to fulfil his birth right of being a knight. At this point, it also occurred to him that it was also similar to part of the plot of *Star Wars*, the difference being that neither Mark Hamill nor Tony Curtis had a demon that wanted to possess them, though that might go a long way to explain the downward trajectory of Hamill's career.

Gabriel consciously pushed the film musing from his head. *Christ, Jones, even your thought process procrastinates,* he thought to himself. *Did* he want to train as a knight? The headquarters were pleasant, the name was cool and he didn't have a steady job. On the downside, the council were creepy, the job would be dangerous and he still hadn't had time to speak to the professor about being played like a puppet.

Lloyd was a good man and didn't deserve to die. The thought shot through his head again. He did his best to shrug it off; it felt disrespectful, but his conscience was twinging. He wondered if he'd never got involved, would Lloyd still be alive? The answer was probably yes. But he had to put it out of his mind for the moment, he had to focus.

Gabriel opened a set of double doors and entered one of the acolyte common rooms. He'd expected to find it empty, but to his surprise he saw Joanna sat in the glow of a single table lamp. She looked up.

"Can't sleep either?" she asked, then took a swig from the bottle of beer in her hand, emptying the last drops. She then looked confused for a second. "What am I meant to call you? Sir, Mr Jones?"

"Gabriel will do, or Gabe, a lot of people call me Gabe."

"Okay Gabe, there's beer over there in the fridge. Get two." She'd obviously had a few already. She deserved it, they both did. It suddenly dawned on him that he hadn't heard her say a word since Lloyd was killed. It then dawned on him that the professor had deliberately kept her out of Tabitha's shop. He'd assumed she was a stone cold, highly trained operative. He was now thinking that she was simply a very competent, yet inexperienced, acolyte who'd had a very rough day. They had lot more in common than he'd realised.

He walked over to the fridge and opened the door. The light jumped out, illuminating part of the room for a moment. Gabriel grabbed two beers and popped the caps off with a nearby bottle opener. He used the light from the fridge to see before closing the door and walking back over to where Joanna was sitting. He placed the beers on the coasters to protect the table, and sat down across from her.

Her blue eyes sparkled as they reflected the lamp light. She really was a very attractive young woman and Gabriel couldn't help but remember how graceful she'd looked when they'd been training. He chased the train of thought from his head. He felt oddly disloyal to Anji for even thinking about Joanna in a romantic way. *Did I blink and miss something, Jones?* he asked himself. He had to admit he was confused about his feelings for Anji, and even if he wasn't, Joanna was half drunk after what was probably the most traumatic day of her life. She needed a friend, and for that matter, so did he.

"Cheers," Gabriel said, raising his bottle.

"Cheers," she repeated moving her own to meet his.

"So, how'd you end up here?" he asked, taking his first swig. The beer was good; it was cold and crisp and tasted expensive.

"Long story. My parents were arses. Abusive druggies. Bastards. I got taken into care, I bounced around from one foster home to another for years, got kicked out of a couple of schools. Some kind people would say I never had a chance, but that's not true. A few of the foster parents I got put with were really good people, I had the chance to turn it around back then and I just didn't. I ran with the wrong crowd and took to house breaking; one time I picked what I thought was the wrong place at the time. Turns out it was the right place, it was a residential home, a big one. I staked it out. Just an old crippled university professor, good alarm system though. I'd gotten good at getting past alarms and this one screamed money." She took a very long swig of beer.

"One night, I picked the lock, disabled the alarm and was about to start helping myself to his stuff. Before I knew it he was behind me. I attacked him, or tried to at least. I couldn't land a blow, even with only one hand he deflected every punch and kick I threw at him. He may have looked like an old cripple but my god that man knew how to fight, and he moved like lightning. He pinned me to the floor. I was thinking I'd be arrested at best and raped at worst. But he helped me to my feet. I still remember what he said." She deepened her voice. "You have talent, girl. To break through my security is not an easy thing. If you've grown tired of how you live, then stay. I can show you a different way, a life of honesty and purpose."

She took another swig and switched back to her regular, though now a little slurred, voice. "You'd probably seen by now he likes to make speeches."

Gabe smiled. "Yeah, he does them well though."

"Damn right. After I'd run off and calmed down, I started to think about what he'd said. I went back a few days later and rang the doorbell. He gave me a life, he's the closest thing I've ever had to a real father." She let out a sorrowful laugh as she exhaled. "A real dad. He's a good man, a really good man. I know what Legion said to you and I'm not saying it's not true, but please hear him out. If you don't trust the order, that's one thing but he wouldn't have done anything without good reason."

Gabriel finished his beer and headed to the fridge again.

"Fair enough," he said, as he retrieved two more bottles.

"I don't tell everyone my life story, in truth I'm quite private, but you need to know what sort of man Tony is."

"You call him Tony?" Gabriel placed the two beers on the table.

"Yes, but don't tell anyone. It's against protocol. In front of others, it's Cleric Harrison or Professor Harrison. But I've been under his wing a long time now. Like I said, he's the closest thing I have to a dad."

"What about the order?" Gabriel was suddenly aware that he was essentially about to take advantage of her drunken state to get information.

"They took me on with the intention of making me a security expert. They made Tony responsible for me, they trained me in security, self-defence. . ."

"Swordplay," Gabriel added.

"Oh yes, also infiltration, and covert tactics."

"How did they break the whole 'supernatural' part to you?" Gabriel asked with a quizzical look.

"They didn't, for a long time. Initiates are trained at facilities across the country but are given the impression that they're being trained for a government agency. Some of the initiates that show a lot promise but are deemed a security risk are often passed on to MI5 or 6. They only tell you the truth once you've completed basic training and they trust you to some degree. At which point you become a junior acolyte and are generally allowed to choose your specialisation. I want to work in the field." She took a large slow mouthful of the newly cold beer.

"How many end up acolytes?" Gabriel asked while she was still drinking.

"Very few. The basic training's not easy and you have to pass psych tests as well. Like I said, a lot of the very good candidates who they decide can't be trusted end up at Military Intelligence. The ones who don't do so well are often passed to police training or military service if they want it. To this day I don't believe I passed the psych exam, I think my crippled guardian angel had a hand in it. The order is usually very careful; they haven't remained a secret organization for over a millennium by being sloppy. They - " She laughed slightly. "We, have become masters at controlling the illusion of truth that the world sees."

"What about the DCI?" Gabriel had been wondering about that for a while.

"In the first instance, he'll be debriefed and given a gagging order to sign under the Official Secrets Act. Then he'll be watched to make sure he sticks to it. I won't lie to you, Gabe. If the council want to recruit you, lying wouldn't be right. We act for the greater good. We do the right thing where we can. Even after all these years, we still try to protect the innocent and all that. But." She paused for a drink. "If we need to get our hands dirty, we do." She looked at the condensation rolling down the bottle in her hand. "I'm glad I'm not the one who has to make the decisions. I like things simple, I like things black and white but the world is seldom black and white. Certainly not the world we live in."

"Shades of grey." Gabriel held his bottle up in the direction of her own.

"Shades of grey," she repeated, and clinked her bottle against his.

"Do you ever regret joining? Do you ever regret ringing that doorbell?"

"Not for a second. It's not a perfect life." She gave a weak, half-laugh again. "What is? But it's a good life, and I get up in the morning knowing that I'm part of something big. Something that is doing some good in its own way." She looked at her watch. "It's late, we should hit the sack."

Tony Harrison strode the corridors of the Halcyon Order's HQ as he headed to the morning council conclave, his official robes flowing behind him in the breeze of his brisk pace.

He'd never liked conclave. If he was honest, he didn't much like the other council members, not least Artemis. But he felt he had a duty to sit on the council, it was the one place he could still make a real difference. Those reasons notwithstanding, he missed being in the field. He always felt that he'd done more good, back in the day, with one swing of his sword than he could do in a week of deliberation with what he'd taken to secretly thinking of as the 'old wives' club'. What's more, he'd rather face a pack of angry werewolves than that bloody council.

God, I miss the old days, he thought as he reached the council chambers. Two acolytes opened one of the double doors each as the cleric approached. He entered and took up his seat amongst the other four members.

Artemis began to speak the mantra of the council.

"We are The Council of the Grand Order of Halcyon. The stalwart defenders of the light. We hold the line against the darkness. We are the watchers in the night. We bring order to chaos, peace to discord and calm to strife. From now, until the end of days." He paused while the council nodded. "Cleric Harrison, would you please start us off regarding the potential."

The professor looked at the other four council members.

"You have all read my report, I take it?"

Grunting agreement came from all four men.

"He is showing positive signs of becoming a real candidate. Once this Legion matter is cleared up, we should fill him in on the full implications of his choice."

Artemis raised a hand, gesturing that Tony should stop talking for a moment.

"What course of action do you suggest with Legion, cleric?"

"I think our safest option, and this is not a matter I take lightly, is death of the host. If we can find the right weapon for a demon of this magnitude that is." In truth, it was a matter that Tony took as lightly as breathing. Ravenwood had murdered Tabitha along with several others. Killing him would simply be an execution.

"We have been discussing that at length and we feel that the potential should be the one to make the kill."

Tony didn't like this. "You have discussed it at great length?"

"Yes, cleric."

"While I was not present?"

Artemis gave a smug smile and looked at the other council members.

"We meant no offence, Cleric Harrison. It was simply that you were on assignment and not available at the time."

Tony often got the impression that as the only former knight on the council, he was regarded as somewhat of a blunt instrument. Just there as a gesture to his service to the Order. The strange thing was, that to hear Artemis speak, he seemed to almost revere the knights – but for some reason, he appeared to almost go out of his way to show Tony that he held him in little regard. Maybe Artemis felt that Tony should have died with a sword in his hand, maybe he felt he had disgraced the knights that fell.

Tony knew that only another knight could understand what happened that night. To be almost dead but to be saved by the sacrifice of a friend. To awake to find yourself a shadow of your former strength, and to know that you could never get back what you had.

Even as acolytes, the rest of the council had seen little field action. They'd raised through the ranks as trainers, assistants, liaisons to other agencies; any work that had kept them out of harm's way. Tony knew they'd never truly seen the face of the enemy; they were the Order's answer to Etonian politicians. They may not have respected him, but he had zero respect for them. The difference was that he had the manners to not show it as blatantly without provocation. He often wondered what would happen if he walked into conclave one day, and just slammed Sirius on the table as he sat down.

His train of thought returned to the moment.

"Yes, I was on assignment at the time, Father Artemis. However, I am curious as to how the honoured council were able to arrive at such a decision before Legion had even taken a host."

The council knew what he was implying; he was implying that they'd given Tabitha up for dead and assumed that the cult would use her heart to bring Legion across. Artemis gave a politician's smile.

"Just one of a multitude of scenarios of course, Cleric Harrison. You understand, I'm sure."

"Of course, Father. Now you wish Gabriel to make the kill?" Tony asked, looking each member in the eye.

Cleric Jonah addressed the inquiry.

"Yes Professor, we feel that it will aid his transition to knight candidacy."

"You want him blooded?" Tony asked with a frown.

"Those are not the words I would use, but yes," Jonah replied.

"This is not a good road to send him down, but I bow to the majority," the Professor said sombrely. *Coward, Harrison,* his own internal monologue chastised him.

"Excellent, we have already assigned your assistant the job of finding a suitable weapon and given her a small research team."

"In future I would prefer it if all orders to my assistant went through me. As is protocol." It was a small victory, but a point worth making.

"Apologies, cleric. In future, I will ensure that happens," Artemis was obliged to say.

"My thanks, Father. I will meet with her now."

Joanne's head hurt, she felt hot and her eyes felt dry. She hadn't been drunk in a long time. As a result, she hadn't been hungover in a long time.

She had a small team of lower-ranked acolytes under her command and had been given unrestricted access to the library. Not a position she was used to or felt comfortable in at the best of times. She knew the assignment was important. She knew she had to find a way of killing Legion's host that would also take the demon with it, or at least send it back to whatever hell it came from. She was terrified that she'd fail.

"You'll do fine, my girl," came the paternal voice from behind her. She had no idea how the professor knew what she was thinking. She'd heard that some knights could read thoughts, but she knew beyond a shadow of a doubt that Tony had lost his knight abilities long ago. It had never entered her head that while she looked on Tony as her surrogate father, he often looked on her as his surrogate daughter. He knew her well, and he knew she'd be worried.

"Cleric Harrison." She straightened up, hoping he wouldn't pick up that she was hungover. "I've assigned Acolytes Stebbins and Newton to book research. Watson is performing net research while Sheldon and Rosenberg are liaising with our multiagency and international links." She hoped that sounded good.

"Excellent work, acolyte," the professor said loudly before leaning in and speaking softly. "Good job kiddo, keep it up. And don't worry, we all had a bad day yesterday. You weren't the only one who hit the bottle hard."

He winked at her and walked off in search of Gabriel.

Gabriel's hangover wasn't too bad. Apart from the fact he'd drunk less than Joanna, his system was used to it. If his liver had a mobile phone it'd have the paramedics on speed-dial.

The bewildered writer had just left his room and was heading in the direction of the common room. He was quickly realising that he had no clue where he could find the professor in this labyrinth of a building. Luck was with him, and he ran into the professor in one of the many hallways.

"Prof, good timing."

The Professor ushered Gabriel in the opposite direction. "Come on, my boy. We can talk in my office."

The two men walked down the corridors, saying nothing to each other until they reached their destination.

The Professor's office was impressive by any standards. Behind two large oak doors lay a wooden panelled room with large inbuilt bookshelves on one side, and an integrated lit display-case containing an assortment of curiosities along the other wall. The carpet was a thick, dark red shag pile. At the far end sat a large desk with a green banker's lamp on it. The professor had mounted Sirius on the wall behind the desk; even in the low light the sword's blade glistened and the ivy engraving almost seemed to come alive.

"No less impressive second time, is she?" the professor asked.

"No Prof, she isn't." Gabriel wasn't being polite; it was an impressive sword. He turned to look at the professor when he caught sight of what he thought was another person in the room.

His head jolted back to look again. It wasn't a person, but a display dummy with a somewhat archaic outfit over it. The outfit looked Georgian. It was entirely black; black boots, trousers, shirt and waistcoat topped with a long cape-like overcoat and black gloves. It reminded Gabriel of the sort of thing Dick Turpin would wear.

"The garb of a Halcyon Knight, my boy. Mine, to be precise."

Gabriel looked surprised. "You didn't wear armour?"

"Oh no, for a start it would been a bit conspicuous, not to mention that armour would have slowed me down. The Knights of the Order relied on speed and agility, and armour would have made things awkward."

"Didn't you look a bit 'conspicuous' walking round like something out of a Brontë novel?"

"Oddly enough, no. But that's a conversation for another time. And don't worry, if you do decide to join us we'll find you something a bit more modern. Now please, have a seat."

Gabriel sat at the visitor's side of the desk. The professor grabbed his own chair with his good arm and pulled it round the side so the desk wasn't between them.

"I have a confession to make, my boy. Legion was right, the Order has been manipulating you. Not to the same extent that the cultists have been, I can't pretend that is a good excuse but there it is. I'd like to be able to say that I'm sorry for my part, but that would be a lie and I feel that at this point the least you deserve is the truth. I'm sorry that it was necessary, and if I could have seen another way I'd have done everything I could to make sure the Order took that course. However, there was no other way. You are the one from the prophecy and you are the only hope for the Order. Doing what we did wasn't a choice we made, it was the only course open to us."

"Why didn't you step in earlier? Why wait 'til I was arrested?" Gabriel was beyond feeling anger at this point. He wasn't sure if he was just accepting his role or if he lacked the mental impetus to care. He was, however, curious if nothing else.

"You had a closed mind. You needed to see things for yourself; even after your encounter with the Harbinger, part of you still assumed it was a hallucination. Belief can't be forced on a person, it was a realisation you had to arrive at on your own. If it's any consolation, the cult would still have got to you in some way. We just made sure that we got in there to achieve at least a small amount of control."

Something suddenly occurred to Gabriel. "Was Liz in on it?" He was really hoping the answer was no.

"No, her being in my class was simple serendipity that made things easier. We contacted Jim's editor and offered him money to throw the articles your way via Jim. Don't forget you're fulfilling prophecy; things tend to fall into place by themselves, or seem to at least."

"What's our next move with Legion?" Gabriel still wasn't convinced about the prophecy lark. He had heard what he wanted to know so he decided it was time to move on.

"The safest way is to kill the host. However, it's not that simple. Demon hosts are very hard to kill; the demon tends to be able to regenerate their bodies very quickly, allowing them to heal from what should be mortal wounds in a matter of moments. Even a particularly damaging attack such as decapitation would only kill the host, while the demon jumps to a new body. Once they're in our domain they can possess people at will."

"So what do we do?"

"Well, every demon has a weakness, a weapon that if used on the host will also either kill the demon or send it back beyond the veil. The trick is to find it. Even a demon as powerful as Legion will have one. Nathaniel Knight must have found it, but he didn't live to tell anyone unfortunately."

Tony's pocket began to vibrate. He pulled out his phone and looked at the screen. Joanna was calling. "Excuse me, my boy." He pressed the 'pick up' button. "Hello, my dear. Do you have anything for me?"

Gabriel waited while the professor listened to Joanna.

"Thank you my dear, keep looking, see if you can find something specific."

"Problem?" Gabriel asked.

"Unfortunately, yes. Joanna's team has found some useful information but it's not a specific weapon."

"In what way?"

"She's emailing it to me now." The professor stood up and walked behind his desk to his computer. He tapped in his password with his good hand and checked his email. He began to read out loud from the screen. "The Many as One may only be vanquished with a weapon of sentiment to two hosts."

The professor checked that Gabriel was still in his seat, then continued. He looked at the screen and this time pretended to read from it. "The weapon must be wielded by the Many as One's Avatar."

He felt dirty. It was one thing to manipulate Gabriel for the greater good, manipulate him to save the Order. However, he'd just lied to him in order to follow the council's orders. They wanted him blooded so Tony was making sure that it happened. It still left the issue of finding an actual weapon.

"Calling it a tall order doesn't come close. I've got no idea where to start looking, if I'm honest. Joanna's team are on it but I think we can expect it to take a while. I will need to meet with the council and discuss an interim strategy."

Gabriel raised his hand in a slow, polite manner, gesturing to the professor to stop talking.

"If I'm understanding that, it means that we need a weapon that holds some sentimental value to two of Legion's hosts, past and present."

"Yes, or two of his past hosts, but finding something like that –" Tony paused. "Will be hard to say the least. We'll have to start by confirming as many of Legion's past hosts as possible, then . . ."

Gabriel raised his hand again.

"Prof, I've got an idea. Charles showed Anji and I a set of duelling pistols. They belonged to Claude Devereaux back in the old days. They're expensive looking and a unique set. Claude would have been proud of them and Charles sure as hell was."

The Professor was amazed. "Gabriel my boy, that's brilliant."

"I'll go and get them if you can organise shot, powder and someone who knows how to load them."

"Not a problem, I'll organise some shooting lessons for you as well. The Order doesn't use guns but I'll find someone."

"No need. Swords are one thing, but guns, guns are something else. Can I borrow your car though? Last I know, the police were searching through mine in Stonebank."

The professor threw his car keys which Gabriel caught in one hand. The prudent thing would have been to send someone with him, but knights tend to work alone, and he wanted Gabriel thinking like a knight. He was happy with the progress so far; saving the DCI, taking charge in the car park and now taking the initiative again.

He smiled for a second, the council were expecting a mindless foot soldier that they could order around. None of them had ever met a knight, and strangely enough hadn't bothered to read the tenets of the order to find out just how much power the Knight Commander would have.

As the only knight, Gabriel would be Knight Commander.

Gabriel was nearing Stonebank. The professor's car was a smooth ride. It was an automatic transition; manual transition couldn't have an option with his disability. Gabriel wasn't used to it, but found himself really enjoying the drive once he was.

The Order had had his stuff picked up from the shared house the day before so he'd been able to don his full black motif and duster, not to mention his lock picks. Gabriel pulled up behind his own car near Charles' house and headed for the driveway. He was expecting the house to be empty, but he thought it was best to stick to the shadows just in case.

Gabriel prowled across the lawn the same way he had twice before. He looked at the house for a moment. No sign of life. Gabriel continued to creep up to the back door. He unrolled his picks and set to work with one of them and the tension tool. A moment later he was inside.

The house seemed deserted; this time there'd be no Heather and Charles screaming at him. *Lloyd was a good man and didn't deserve to die.* He couldn't shake the thought.

Gabriel moved through the house with his key ring torch. He crept to the living room and slowly moved over to the display cabinet to find it unlocked. *Odd,* his internal monologue commented. He opened the glass door and shone his torch over the shelves.

One of the pistols was missing!

Gabriel grabbed the remaining gun and left as quickly as possible. He made his way across the lawn and back to the car, then back to the Order's HQ.

The Professor was pacing around the top of the stairs at the HQ. He was starting to worry. Should he have sent someone with Gabriel – what if he'd come across more cultists, or even Legion?

The front door opened and Gabriel entered. Tony's worries vanished. The writer strode across the seal on the floor, still dressed in full black with his black duster fluttering slightly behind him. The professor watched for a moment and then shouted down the stairs.

"Well, my boy. If you do join us I'd say you've found the modern knight outfit."

Gabriel thought for a moment and realised there were some striking similarities between what he was wearing and what he'd seen in Tony's office.

"Did you get them?"

Gabriel pulled the lone pistol out of his pocket. "Only the one, I'm afraid. The other one was AWOL."

"Let's hope you don't need more than one shot then. Come on, we can load it in my office."

The two men walked into Tony's office for the second time.

"Did you find someone who can load it?" Gabriel asked.

"No need. I know how."

"A man of many talents," Gabriel complimented, as he passed the flintlock to the professor.

Tony took a small piece of oily cloth from a tray on his desk and dropped it in the barrel. He gave it a quick tap with a small ramrod that he also took from the tray. Then he added some gunpowder from a powdered pouch. Next, he wrapped the shot in a second piece of cloth, dropped it in the barrel and tapped it down with the ramrod. Finally, he added a new flint to the cock.

He passed the pistol back to Gabriel before picking up a small paper sachet off his desk.

"This is primer. It's finely ground gunpowder. When you are ready to fire, pull the hammer back then add a little to the flash plate here." He pointed to the area near the cock. "The rest is just point and shoot."

The phone the professor had given Gabriel vibrated in his pocket.

"That must be Anji," he said, pleased to hear from her. He pulled the phone out of his pocket, anxious to see what she had to say. The text was from Anji's number.

Avatar, we have your pretty friend. If you wish her to remain pretty, then come to Meetingstone Manor immediately.

Terror gripped Gabriel's mind.

"They've got Anji." His voice was filled with panic. "They want me to go to the manor house."

He looked the professor in the eyes and raised his voice. "Why didn't you protect her? Why didn't you make sure she was safe? If this is more of your manipulation, I swear to God that this demon cult will be the least of your problems." His eyes were a mix of fear and anger.

"Gabriel, I put four acolytes on her. I'm sorry, I should have put more." The professor felt genuine regret but a small part of him did like the ferocity Gabriel was showing. He would need that in the hours or days to come.

The writer composed himself.

"I'm sorry. You did what you could. I have to go after her, though."

"Of course you do. Surrender is not an option though," the professor warned. Gabriel turned to him; his entire body had slipped into a fighting stance without him realising.

"It bloody well is an option, if it's the only way to save her." The anger was back in his eyes.

"The only way to save her is to send Legion back to the pit. If you let him possess you, the first thing he'll do in your body is kill her and force your helpless mind to watch through your own eyes. He'll do that because it'll give him pleasure. That's the sort of twisted thing we're dealing with and that's the thing that wants to rule the world."

Tony now had some passion in his own eyes and was speaking in a very sharp, heavily enunciated tone. "Put that pistol shot in Charles' head, send Legion back to the pit, save the woman you are clearly in love with, ride off into the sunset and preferably come back here and join the Order. That, my boy, is a sound battle plan." The professor felt he'd made his point.

Gabriel looked at him and gave the slightest of nods.

"Damn right. Let's go."

"Let's go, indeed," the professor agreed. Both men headed for the door. "Where did you park my car?"

"Out front."

"Good." Tony wiped his mobile out of his inside pocket as he walked. He selected a name from the contacts list and held the phone to his ear. "Jo, we've got a situation. We need you out front and ready to leave ASAP."

"On my way," came the reply.

The professor's car pulled up a little way down the road from the manor house's car park. Gabriel, Tony and Joanna exited the vehicle and made their way towards the manor house. It was dark. Night had fallen, but moonlight was peeking through a gap in the clouds.

"Okay my boy, we'll hang back. Remember how to deal with him – be cocky, keep him off balance, and take the shot as soon as you get a good opportunity. Best of luck." The professor clapped him on the arm.

Gabriel was about to head into the grounds when Joanna threw her arms around him. She held him close for a second then kissed him on the cheek. She looked at him with her blue eyes.

"Go save her. Don't get killed."

Gabriel smiled for a moment. "Thanks."

He made his way through the car park and into the grounds with the professor and Joanna following at some distance. The clouds were now obscuring any moonlight, but he could see a very wide ring of flaming torches staked in the sprawling lawns.

The writer paused for a moment, retrieving the pistol and primer from his pockets. He ripped open the sachet of primer and teased the contents out onto the flash plate of the pistol. Gabriel folded his arms so that the gun was concealed in the folds of his duster, then continued towards the torches.

There were several figures in the circle; Charles' possessed body in the middle, with two robed figures holding an unconscious Anji behind him. There were other robed figures beyond the torches. Gabriel had no idea how many. They ghosted into the dark of the night.

The writer crossed the threshold of the circle. He hadn't realised just how big it was.

"Okay, I'm here, fiend. Let her go."

He rested the pistol on the top of his inside pocket so the primer didn't spill out of the plate, then extended his hands out to appear unarmed.

"Avatar," came the sound from Charles's vocal chords. "If only it were that simple." It smiled. "You see, I've come to realise that since you have been infected by that sanctimonious Order and that broken knight, you will never willingly be my Avatar. And unfortunately, the rules are that you must be willing. So I've decided that I want you dead. You see, I have no intention of letting them train you up to be the saviour foretold in that irrelevant prophecy. Also, as the descendent of Nathaniel Knight, I have a personal score to settle with you. After that, I will kill your little redheaded friend over there. But don't worry, she won't die for a while yet. She'll wish she was dead, but she won't be." It smiled again. "Now I've been thinking about the most poetic way of killing you."

One of the black figures entered the circle and handed the demon a pistol. "You may not recognise this but it's what my last host used to kill your ancestor as I left his body. Now, I intend to use it to send you to meet him. The demon in Charles' body brought the pistol to bare on Gabriel. Gabriel looked at him, assessing the situation for a moment. He stood his ground and folded his arms, discretely grabbing his own pistol from inside his coat. He looked directly into the usurped eyes of Charles Ravenwood.

"Go ahead demon, take your best shot. Unless you want to talk this over like men." The demon smiled at the mortal's stupidity, it steadied Charles' hand and aimed slowly.

"Men? You insult me," Charles' finger pulled the trigger and fired the single shot. The round missed its target by about a meter. Gabriel advanced aiming the matching flintlock at the demon.

"Sorry, Charles."

He squeezed the trigger and the shot flew directly at the centre of Charles's forehead. A miniscule of a second before the ball broke the skin, a bright blue light shot out of the body's chest; Gabriel was sure he could see a shadow of realisation in Charles' eyes as the shot smashed its way through the front of his skull. The bright blue light circled the abandoned body as it collapsed to the ground. It pulsated twice, then shot directly at Anji's unconscious form. Her blue eyes opened, and looked at Gabriel. His world collapsed. When Anji spoke, she spoke with hate in her voice.

"Hello, 'babe'. Nice try."

Legion spat the words out, mocking Gabriel and hurting him to his core. In that moment, he knew that he loved her and he knew that he'd never told her.

Chapter 15

Tony and Joanna ran in. Gabriel was beaten, they knew it. If they didn't get him out, then the thing in Anji's body would kill him.

"Take him, Cleric," the demon said. "I'm looking through this vessel's memories. Leaving him alive while I'm in here is far more fun than killing him. I doubt he'll be of any use to you now, broken knight." Anji's body laughed.

Tony wished Gabriel was unconscious, wished he couldn't hear Anji's voice. He should have insisted that Anji be taken into the HQ, stuff security. An innocent woman was now possessed and the hope for the Order's salvation may have died with that possession.

The two members of the Halcyon Order grabbed the former writer under each arm. Joanna noticed the spent flintlock on the grass. She picked it up and discreetly stashed it in Gabriel's pocket. They helped him back to the car and headed back to HQ.

"Bastard," said Gabriel. "Bastard."

The professor looked at Joanna for a moment before putting his eyes back on the road.

"Call ahead, get someone from the medical wing to prepare a sedative. He'll need a few hours' sleep before facing the council. And don't tell anyone that you picked that pistol up. As far as anyone back at HQ knows, it was left at the scene. Also, hit the research, find as many examples as you can of hosts surviving possession by powerful demons. It's unlikely that we'll be able to exorcise something as powerful as Legion with traditional methods. If at all."

"Will do, Tony."

"Good girl."

The following morning, Tony entered the council chamber. The other members we already seated, and the atmosphere could be cut with a knife. The members had received Tony's preliminary report; there was a feeling that Gabriel was a lost cause for the moment as far as knight candidacy went.

The Professor took his seat and Artemis began to speak.

"Gentlemen, for reasons of haste, I think it best that we get straight on with business. As I see it, the bottom line is this. Our potential candidate may not be a viable option for some time at least. Legion is manifest in our world, has declared war on us, is planning to take over the world and has taken an innocent body as host."

"Don't count Gabriel out yet," the professor said. "He's gone through a hell of a lot the past week. Most men would have broken days ago. I have my assistant looking into unorthodox exorcism methods, so I may have some news on that."

"We will need to act within the next few days. Once he gets acclimatised to the host, Legion's full powers will manifest," Cleric Samson warned. "We should give it forty-eight hours. If we haven't found anything then we should use the pistol again, point blank range. Don't give him time to leave the host."

Artemis, Ford and Jonah nodded. The Professor looked enraged.

"What? We failed to protect this woman, we put her in danger. Also, if we kill her then we lose any chance of getting Gabriel to join us. We need Gabriel."

"Agreed," Artemis said, folding his hands together. "We need to do it in a way that shows we had no choice. Spin it the right way, and the potential will simply believe that the ultimate blame lies with the demon. If anything, that would inspire him to join us. Loss can be a powerful motivator."

"Loss?" Tony didn't like what he was hearing. "Loss? You aren't talking about loss. You're talking about anger and revenge. If he steps on the path with those motivations, then we are dabbling in very dangerous waters."

"Nonsense." Artemis dismissed Tony's concerns. "In fact, someone with those motivations would find it that much easier to make the hard decisions. Decisions that a knight must make from time to time."

"It is not nonsense sir, it is a fact. Hard decisions are meant to be hard. May I respectfully remind you that out of the five of us, I am the only one who has actually been a knight and am the only one who has undergone the training or the ritual of accolade."

"And may I remind you, cleric, that I am the head of this council." Tony listened to the father's self-preening words and momentarily considered decapitation. It would be a good way of shutting him up. Had he been armed, it may have been more than a thought.

"This is moot point. We no longer have the pistol."

"What?" Artemis looked furious.

"We were outnumbered ten to one, and were facing a demon older than recorded history. The realities of the field don't always make life in the council chamber easy." Tony was walking the line of insubordination and decided to change track. "Anyway, I have a better idea that may kill two birds with one stone."

Artemis raised an eyebrow. "We're listening, professor." He still looked angry.

"The girl means a lot to Gabriel. I suggest we explain the ritual of accolade to him. If he's successful, then Legion will be dead and we'll have a very powerful new knight."

"And if he's not successful then we've handed Legion a perfect host. One that he'll be able to walk around in for millennia."

"And if that happens, then we send an infiltration team to find the pistol and use it," Cleric Harrison retorted.

"Do you really think it's wise, to send a man without the most basic knight training into a mental battle with one of the oldest and most powerful demons known to man?" Cleric Ford asked.

"The battle of the ritual isn't about training, it's about self-belief, strength of will and cunning."

Artemis was tired of this deliberation.

"I'm sorry, cleric, it's not going to happen. Forget about it. We'll start the potential on formal training. Have the pistol retrieved then have the host terminated."

Before the Professor could argue, there was a knock at the door. Tony was surprised; they were never disturbed during conclave.

"Ah, the potential is here. I have asked that he join us."

The double doors opened and Gabriel walked in, dressed in his usual jeans and t-shirt.

"Hello, dear boy. Please join us. We were just discussing this frightful business."

"I prefer to stand, thanks. I just stopped by to say thanks for all you've done and to say goodbye."

"Why do you wish to leave us, dear boy?" Artemis had a kind look on his face. Ever the politician, thought Tony.

"Honestly?" Gabriel decided it was time for some bluntness. "You've been manipulating me and you're still manipulating me."

"Still manipulating you?" Artemis asked. Tony wondered where Gabe was going with this.

"Why did I have to be the one to pull the trigger on the pistol?" He looked at Tony. "The weapon must be wielded by the many as one's Avatar," he quoted. "You looked at the screen and pretended to read it. Before you looked, you checked that I couldn't see and judging by the direction of your eyes, you were looking at the same sentence you'd just read. Not a sentence after it. On top of that is the fact that it simply didn't make any sense. We can assume that Nathaniel must have found a similar weapon to us, and he was able to use it without being the 'Avatar.' I'm guessing you lot wanted me blooded. I didn't argue at the time because I wanted to save Anji. I still want to save her, so I'm leaving."

He turned to walk out then stopped for a moment and turned back. "Professor, I know you were doing what you thought was right. I know you were following orders. You've put your own life at risk for me more than once now. Thank you."

Artemis kept up the smile and soft tone. "Gabriel, dear boy, what do you intend to do? You can't stop Legion alone."

"I'm going to give him what he wants. He didn't think I'd ever be a willing host. He was wrong. I'm going to give myself up if he agrees to let Anji go."

Tony's eyes widened. "He won't do that, Gabriel. You know he won't. What I told you wasn't a lie, he'll take your body and kill her with it."

"Maybe. But it's my only option. Once he's inside me. Do what you have to do kill him."

"There's another way," The professor started to talk.

Artemis cut him off. "Mr Jones. You should not be hasty, give it a few days. Let us come up with a plan."

Gabriel let out a small laugh of contempt. "With all due respect… if you lot had been more open earlier about this, Anji would be at home living her life right now." Gabriel glared at the council. "You can go to hell. I'm doing what I have to."

Artemis' politician smile melted into a scowl.

"I don't think so, Mr Jones." He pressed a button under the table and two armed acolytes stepped in. "Acolytes, take Mr Jones into protective custody."

The two large men advanced on Gabriel. He knew he stood no chance against them but refused to go quietly. He swung a punch at one, mentally adapting his small amount of sword training for hand-to-hand. The punch landed and staggered the much larger man for a moment. He swung at the second acolyte, but the punch was blocked. The first man came up behind him, grabbing his arms to restrain him.

"Take him away," Artemis commanded.

Tony looked at the Father. "Self-sacrifice, compassion, determination and willing to fight a lost cause. That is what makes a knight. Not the anger and revenge that you seek." With that, he stood up and walked out.

Artemis waited until he was out of ear shot. "Cleric Samson."

"Yes, Father," the cleric replied dutifully.

"You know Cleric Harrison's pet acolyte?"

"I believe her name is Joanna, Father."

"Yes, have her room searched."

Samson was uncomfortable with this order, as were the other two men present. The Order did not spy on its own.

Artemis sensed the apprehension in the room. "I know it's not our way, and I know it's not protocol. However, these are unusual times and I need you to trust me."

Gabriel paced around the small cell that he'd been thrown into. He had to admit it was preferable to the one the police had put him in. It had a proper bed with real sheets, and he was expecting the food to be better. None of this changed the fact that he had to get out.

The thought of that thing walking around in Anji's body made his skin crawl. He couldn't help wonder what the professor made of the situation. He seemed sympathetic, but he also seemed to follow orders. Not quite blindly, but indiscriminately, which Gabriel thought was somehow worse.

If he was too stupid to know the orders were wrong, that was one thing, but the Professor seemed to *know* they were wrong. Gabriel could see it on his face. Did Artemis really inspire this level of loyalty or was it loyalty to something else? Either way, the former writer decided that he had to find some way out.

Joanna looked the two acolytes square in the face, her eyes flashing a look of righteous indignation.

"You want to search my room?"

The two acolytes, Michael and Jeff, didn't want to. But they had orders. It was awkward, they both knew her. Not well, but they did know her. Jeff had played pool with her a few times and had even thought about asking her out, if he'd ever found the courage. He figured this altercation would put the dampers on any chance he had.

"Not want to, Acolyte King. Have to. We have orders."

"Whose orders?" She felt like crying. The Order had been her home for so long, the only time in her life that she had had any stability. She had given her life to the Order and trusted it. She felt more betrayed than she ever had.

"Cleric Samson's."

She was speechless. She knew they had no choice, but at that moment she hated them both regardless. She walked off.

The two men reluctantly entered her room and began to search it. They went through shelves, drawers, under her bed, her mattress. The most uncomfortable Jeff had ever felt was checking her underwear drawer. He cursed Samson for not having the basic common sense to give this job to a pair of women.

"This is odd," Michael said, as he pulled a flintlock pistol from behind some books. "We should tell the Cleric."

Joanna stomped down the corridor in the direction of the professor's office. She knew they'd find the pistol, but not sure how they'd react. This was a situation she couldn't talk, bribe or flirt her way out of. She was in trouble.

Two HQ security acolytes were making their way towards her. She felt her heartbeat speed up. Were they coming for her? Should she turn around? They were a few steps away; her heart felt like it had almost stopped but they walked on by.

She decided it was time to leave. She could try and contact the professor later. She'd disappeared plenty of times before; it wouldn't be hard to do it again, though the thought of going back to life on the streets was not one that she relished.

Regardless, she took a left turn and headed for the entrance hall, trying to hurry without looking like she was hurrying. She reached the landing and made her way down the curved staircase. There were a few acolytes criss-crossing about, but no sign of any security. The door was in sight. She continued down the stairs, resisting the urge to run. She was crossing the seal on the floor when she heard a loud but familiar voice.

"Stop that acolyte."

"Tony?" she questioned under her breath, hardly able to believe her ears. She turned to see Cleric Harrison at the top of the stairs.

Her heart sank into her stomach. How could he? She was nearly out. He'd been the one who had told her to keep the gun a secret. Was he really going to sell her out to protect himself? She could come clean and say what had happened but they'd never believe an acolyte over a cleric.

There was always the possibility that he had some secret plan that he hadn't had chance to tell her. That made sense, but the thought was fighting a losing battle to the evidence of her eyes. Tony had always ultimately done what the council said.

Joanna thought about making a last desperate dash for the door, but two of the passing acolytes blocked her path. Four security acolytes swiftly descended the stairs, two of them roughly grabbing her arms, and led her towards the holding area while the other two walked in front.

Joanna lay flat on her back on the holding cell's bed. She was trying to convince herself that Tony was hatching a plan and would be by any moment to get her out. Trying to convince herself that he wasn't just one more person in her life that had ultimately disappointed her.

What if he had sold her out? What would the Order do to her? She'd never heard of any member being a traitor before, but then again she wouldn't have. The Halcyon Order dealt in secrets; it was something they had become extremely proficient at.

Joanna looked at the lock. It was electronic. If she had her tool kit, she could have it open in the blink of an eye. She began to wish that she'd at least tried to fight the acolytes off. At least tried to escape when she had the chance.

Two questions kept running through her head over and over.

Will I ever get out of here? And if so, will I be alive?

She wondered again if Tony had just been playing a part. Her life before the Order had forced her to get used to expecting the worst.

Gabriel sat on the floor in the next cell over. The door was almost soundproof, but he'd heard murmurs through it. They'd put someone in the next cell.

His bored mind started to run though scenario after scenario of who it could be, most of which included some fantasy of how they might help him escape. He was bored, really bored. He wished he had a laptop with him. It would force him to write. He laughed at the idea.

As if writing is ever going to be a realistic option again for you Jones, he said to himself. He wished he at least had a baseball like Steve McQueen. "Cooler. Indeterminate amount of time," he said in a German accent, and gave a small defeated laugh.

Cleric Harrison sat in conclave yet again. It was becoming far too often for his taste. Father Artemis was already in full flow.

"One of our own has been found to be working against the common good. A search of her quarters revealed that she had possession of Legion's Bane."

The Professor couldn't help but be amused at Artemis' presumptuousness; he'd named the pistol. Tony was starting to get the impression that Artemis' main goal was to write himself into the history of the Order.

"The weapon was clearly in her possession. I recommend termination of the acolyte, but a ruling of that magnitude requires a majority verdict. Does anyone have any objection to an open vote?"

Tony knew the reason for this. It was a loyalty test. Artemis suspected that he had been complicit in withholding the pistol, and wanted to see how dedicated he was to the Order.

None of the council raised any objection. "Excellent. Cleric Ford, how do you vote?"

"I feel that termination is too strong a sanction without at least the attempt at rehabilitation. I vote nay."

"Cleric Jonah?"

"I bow to your wise council, Father. We must set an example for the safety of all. I vote yea." No surprise there, thought Tony. He always was a lapdog.

"Cleric Samson?"

"I believe that the ultimate sanction should be reserved for the most heinous of crimes. I must, in good conscience, vote nay."

"The deciding vote lies with you, Cleric Harrison. What is your choice?"

The professor wondered if the deciding vote landing on him was the product chance or if the situation hand been engineered.

"I took the acolyte into the Order. I helped to train her and I have a great deal of personal affection for her. However, the security of the Order must always come first. With the deepest of regrets, I must vote yea."

He closed his eyes. The pain on his face moved even Artemis.

"A difficult decision, and not one the chair takes lightly, but security must be paramount. Termination is scheduled for eight in the morning." Artemis did look genuinely sombre, almost regretful. "Moving on. Now that we have recovered Legion's Bane I have formulated a plan of attack."

The other members of the council looked shocked.

"Attack?" challenged the professor. "Might I remind you, Father, that the Halcyon Order is no longer a combat-ready institution? We can perform covert combat missions in extreme circumstances, but our acolytes' martial training focuses on defence. We have not equipped them with the skills for an overt combat mission, certainly not one with a demon as the target. Even in Legion's current state he would have presented a substantial threat to a fully trained knight."

The other clerics remind silent.

"I assure you, Cleric Harrison, this is not a decision I have arrived at lightly. Legion has declared war on us, he will come for us soon. I for one do not trust our allies to honour the treaties under these circumstances. The acolytes risk their lives now or die for certain once Legion is at full power." There was a certain cold logic to Artemis' reasoning. "The plan of attack is simple yet elegant. Intelligence tell us that Legion has retreated to Ravenwood's house, protected by a large number of cultists. We assault the house with a large force of acolytes, we send our members with the most combat training in front with the least trained in the back to create the illusion of a much stronger force."

Tony didn't like it. "You propose a frontal assault?"

"Only as a ruse. While Legion and the cult are distracted, a small contingent of our best infiltrators will covertly circumvent their lines, enter the house and terminate the host with Legion's Bane."

"There will be a lot of casualties. You are sending a lot of your children to their death, Father."

"I know, but there is no choice. The mission is scheduled for twenty-one hundred hours tomorrow."

Joanna had a bad feeling. They'd brought her food along with whoever was in the next cell, but part of her had expected a rescue by now. She was resigning herself to the idea that Tony had caved and used her as scapegoat.

She looked at the impenetrable door; she was fighting back tears and complete despair. The tough girl from the street had become soft, she thought. Too many good meals, too many nights in a soft bed, too much trust in a man she'd loved like a father. She felt angry with herself for getting soft. Ten years ago she'd have shrugged something like this off as just another bump on the road. Of course, ten years ago she'd had nothing to lose but a life of drugs, squalor and crime. Was going back to that really an option? She contemplated for a moment.

Then came a click from the door, the surprise of the sound breaking the silence made her jump. *Tony,* she silently hoped. The door opened to reveal the two gruff security acolytes who had thrown her in the cell in the first place. Her heart sank yet again.

"Come with us please, Acolyte King," the slightly larger of the two knuckle-draggers said. "Father Artemis wants a word with you."

Fear gripped her but she had no choice but to go with them. She left the cell as instructed but they gestured that she should stop. The larger man opened the neighbouring cell.

"Step outside please. Farther Artemis wants a word with you."

Joanna was slightly surprised to see Gabriel step out. "Prisoners, you will walk in front of us and follow all instructions." He looked at them both as if expecting a response. "Proceed out of the detention area and follow the corridor left to the council chamber."

Joanna and Gabriel did as they were instructed. They left the room and turned left. The two security acolytes followed them with side-handed batons drawn.

The larger of the two men never saw the blow coming. The sliver dragonhead pommel came down with tremendous force on the back of his head, knocking him out cold in a single strike. The other man spun around, raising his baton in a vain attempt to attack the closest thing to a knight that the Order still had. He tried to strike but Tony easily parried the blow with Sirius, still in its scabbard.

Gabriel and Joanna turned. Joanna's heart jumped out of her stomach and sang. Gabriel looked at Tony; he was armed with his silver sword and was wearing his antiquated knight's garb. He saw what Tony had meant when he said that a knight relies on speed and agility. The former knight was a blur of black cloth as he deflected every attempted blow and finally knocked the second man out cold.

Tony looked at the two people in front of him.

"Sorry it took me so long. I had to play along until I knew Artemis' plan. We need to get out of here." He raised his eyebrows. "We need to get out of here now."

Joanna leapt for him, throwing her arms around him and resting her head on his shoulder. "I'm sorry Tony, I thought you'd sold me out. I lost faith in you. I'm so sorry." She couldn't fight the tears this time.

Tony hugged her back. "It's okay, kiddo. If you hadn't, I'd have been offended that you didn't think my acting was good enough," he joked before breaking the hug and looking her in her tear-filled eyes. "My dear. You've had a bad life. You've been let down time and time again. I can't blame you for giving up on me. And I'm truly sorry that it took me so long to come for you. As long as I'm alive, I will always be here for you. Now let's go. We have a world to save." He tweaked her chin and smiled. "Come on."

The three fugitives from the Halcyon Order headed towards the professor's car. Gabriel and Tony jumped in front and Joanna in the back.

"Where are we going, Prof?" Gabriel asked.

"I have some things I need to discuss with you. We need several hours where we're safe. I suggest we go to your place, my boy. After that, I swear I'll help you do whatever you think is right."

"Sounds good."

Gabriel directed Tony as he drove. Joanna had been quiet since they'd left the headquarters, but broke her silence.

"I've been wondering, and I'll grant you that it's an odd time to ask, but when you were facing off with Legion you seemed to know that he'd miss when he fired. How?"

Gabriel turned his head as best he could to look at her. "Anji and I were invited to Charles's house for dinner the other day. He showed me one of the pistols, and closed his left eye when he pretended to aim it. The only people who do that are right-handed people who are left eye dominant. If they keep both eyes open, their aim is off. When Legion aimed at me in Charles body, he kept both eyes open. He had no chance of hitting me at that range."

The professor chuckled. "You are a knight, my boy, you truly are."

The party arrived at Gabriel's house. He no longer had his keys or lock picks, so Joanna dealt with the lock. The professor opened the boot of his car and passed two bags to Gabriel. They felt quite heavy.

"What's in here?" the former writer asked.

"Some of your stuff, some of Joanna's stuff. I had to get it in a hurry before getting you out. Now, I know you are resigned to trading yourself over for Anji. Will you let me teach you some skills in the next few hours? If you still want to give yourself over, then I'll support you as I said I would." Tony paused for a brief second. "I want to offer you a different option, though."

"Okay, Prof. Let's go inside."

Joanna paced a lot. She watched a bit of television, had a few hours' sleep, paced some more and kept an eye out in case the Order found them. Then paced some more.

Gabriel and Tony had been upstairs for what felt like an eternity. To say that she was curious as to what the professor and Gabriel were talking about didn't come close. She'd hear the murmurs of them talking at great length, then long periods of absolute silence.

She frequently looked out of the front window; she was half expecting the Order to turn up. They had no way of knowing where Gabriel lived, but that didn't usually stop them from finding things out. She chased the fear from her mind with the logic of the fact that they had far bigger problems with Legion on the loose.

She heard footsteps coming down the stairs. *At last,* she thought. The Professor was speaking as they entered the room.

"Get the stuff you were wearing the other night when you retrieved the pistol. Put it on. It's very important that you look the part." Gabriel rummaged through one of the bags of oddments the professor had retrieved, and disappeared upstairs for a few moments.

Joanna looked at the professor. "Did you convince him?" she asked, hoping the professor might tip his hand.

"I think so. He may not be one hundred percent committed at the moment, but I think he'll come through."

Gabriel re-entered the room dressed in full black with his black duster on, and his hands in his pockets, feeling a bit awkward.

"Okay," the professor said, drawing Sirius from its scabbard. The sword made a pleasing high pitched sound as he unsheathed it. "Mr Jones, if it pleases you. Take a knee. Let's do this right."

Gabriel considered protesting, but reconsidered and did as the professor asked.

Tony stepped towards him. "By the power vested in me by the Council, Father and Knights of the Grand Order of Halcyon, I find thee worthy of accolade. Let your deeds carry our name, your valour give hope to the innocent and your fury strike fear into the heart of the darkness. I confer on thee the title of Knight in Training." Tony rested the flat on his sword on each of Gabriel's shoulders. "Arise, Gabriel Jones, Knight in Training."

Gabriel stood up as the professor re-sheathed his sword and began to rummage in one of the bags. He produced two long black boxes much like the one Gabriel had seen when Tony had given him some sword training. He flipped open the catches of one and lifted a plain sword from inside. The professor partly unsheathed it to look at the blade, then took the whole thing out of the box.

"You're giving me that sword?" Gabriel asked.

The professor looked at him. "No my boy." He undid the belt that was holding Sirius. "I'm giving you *this* sword." He passed the magnificent silver sword over to the new Knight in Training.

Gabriel's eyes widened. "Seriously?"

"As I said. It's very important to look the part. Sirius will help a lot with that."

Gabriel fastened the belt around his waist. The professor and Joanna looked at him.

"What do you think, my dear?" he asked.

Joanna nodded. "I think he looks like a knight."

"Then let's go. Time is not on our side. We've got to get to Anji and Legion before Artemis starts his assault."

Chapter 16

The Professor, Joanna and Gabriel were almost at Charles' house. They were cutting it close; the Order's acolytes would be there at any time.

Gabriel's stomach was in knots. He was running through the past week or so in his head. This was the first time he'd really taken stock of just how much had happened and how much had changed. How much he had changed!

The professor parked the car. "Okay, this is it. Point of no return. Are you both ready?"

"Yep," said Joanna.

"As I'll ever be," Gabriel said with a half-smile.

"Good. Time to go then."

They got out of the car and headed for Charles' driveway. This time, Gabriel wasn't going in stealthily. Even if he'd wanted to, he would have found it difficult.

Legion was standing on the front lawn, surrounded by countless cultists in a ring of torches. The ring was a little smaller than the one at the manor house. Gabriel strode over to the circle. He moved swiftly but with no outer appearance of hurry. The professor and Joanna followed, each carrying a sheathed sword.

The demon turned Anji's eyes to look at them.

"Ah, Avatar," came her soft, yet unnerving, voice. "Did you wish me to end your life for you?"

Gabriel ignored the question and stood in front of Anji's body and, in the twilight of the garden, looked into her blue eyes.

"Anji. I'm sorry I got you into this, I'm sorry I didn't protect you. I promise you, things will be okay."

Anji's vocal chords were compelled to laugh. "What makes you think she can hear you, Avatar?"

Gabriel narrowed his eyes. "Silence fiend, I am not addressing you. I am addressing the one who's body you have usurped." His words were calm, but with very clear enunciation.

Legion laughed again, this time louder.

"You amuse me, mortal. Do you even know who you face?"

Gabriel leant in closer to Anji and spoke two simple words.

"Do *you*?"

The demon was unsure about the homo sapiens in front of him. No lesser being had ever spoken to him in this fashion. He felt ill at ease.

"I propose a trade," said Gabriel. "That body for mine. With the agreement that you allow her and my friends here to go free and unharmed."

Joanna was confused. *This can't be the plan. If Gabriel gives up his body willingly, then Legion would have a permanent host.* As for the demon honouring his side of the bargain, the professor had made it very clear that it would not happen.

"I sense that you are ready for me now, Avatar. But I'm enjoying the anguish I see in your eyes when I manipulate this body."

Gabriel drew Sirius, the lights of the flaming torches bouncing off the polished silver of the blade. Tony and Joanna unsheathed the spare swords Tony had brought, and threw the scabbards to the ground.

"The alternative is, demon, that we slaughter every last one of your followers. Everything that moves and fails to hide or run will be dead."

The demon's expression on Anji's face was one of disinterest. "Why would I care about these insects?" it said, gesturing to the robed figures around.

"Because even when you reach full power, you will still require lackeys. Killing them won't stop you but it'll slow down your plans. In the meantime, what do you think the Halcyon Order will be doing?" The demon remained silent. "You have ten seconds to make a decision."

Anji's head turned to look at the cultists, then back to the human with the ornate silver sword.

"Deal," came the one-word response.

The bright blue light shot out of Anji's body directly into Gabriel's. Anji crumpled to the ground, and Gabriel dropped to his knees before crawling over to Anji's recovering body. Tony and Joanna ran over with their swords readied before the cultists had time to react. The monster was establishing a foothold; Joanna looked on as Gabriel lost consciousness.

She looked up. Every cultist drew a curved blade; there were too many to count. She had no way of seeing how many were hiding in the darkness, nor did the professor. Joanna readied her sword.

Robed figures advanced on all sides; they were surrounded. There was no hope of survival, there were simply too many of them. She was contemplating how they'd attack and trying to work out the best course of action to kill as many of them as possible. She'd never killed anyone before, but this was kill or be killed; in fact, almost certainly kill and be killed.

Tony looked at her, he felt sorry, sorry that he'd got her involved and sorry that he'd brought her along. She should have been tucked up in a warm bed back at HQ, not about to die in a place she should never even have been.

The cultists continued to advance. Joanna glanced at him. She didn't understand why Gabriel was on the ground. When Legion had entered Charles and Anji, his control had been immediate. She was glad though. If the demon was in the fight, either her or the professor would have had to disable or kill the host – not a thought she relished. Gabriel was a good man in her book.

The cultists were still advancing. She looked out into the blackness of the night, trying to steady her thoughts; her hands were sweating, the sword's grip felt moist in her hand. The figures advancing were people, they had mums and dads, children. Hell – some probably weren't much more than children. But they wanted her dead. They'd murdered Tabitha, they'd murdered Lloyd, they'd murdered the acolytes, the policemen and God knew who else.

'Some monsters are men.' The professor's words echoed through her soul. She came to terms with what had to come next; either through genuine rationalisation or through survival instinct, it didn't matter.

More and more figures were approaching. She'd be dead within the next few minutes, and death from stabbing would be an incredibly painful way to go. She resigned herself to her fate. *Protect Gabriel.* She hoped to hell that he hadn't just given up to save Anji, but if she was honest, that was the most likely interpretation of events.

The first line of cultists were now on top of them, with countless more in the shadows. The acolyte looked at the professor.

Well, I never thought I'd go out like this. If she was going to die, at least she was going down fighting at the side of the only person she'd ever truly called family.

Both Tony and Joanna prepared for the first attack, their swords held in a defensive posture that would allow for a quick counter-attack. To Joanna, the plan seemed to have become to stay alive as long as possible and take as many of them with her as she could before she fell.

More cultists emerged from the shadows, shoulder to shoulder. Even with Tony at her side she stood no chance. They would both be dead in moments.

An unexpected sound bounced through the night air – footsteps, lots of them, coming from the driveway. At first a few, then more.

She turned to look. Acolytes of the Halcyon Order, lots of acolytes.

"Bloody good timing," she said, as she deflected the first attack from a cultist and drove her blade into his throat. "One down."

The figures scrambled to avoid being flanked.

The moon cast a pale white glow over the stone circle. Gabriel could see the extinguished candles on the centre stone. The dead crow on the ground began to move; it grudgingly stood, then let out a loud shriek and flew over to a dark shape lying on the grass.

Gabriel looked at the black bird and the shape with a curious feeling of uneasiness before he started to approach them, anxiety building up in the pit of his stomach. He knew that he didn't want to see what the shape was, but was slowly walking there regardless, watching the oily looking crow as it pecked at the shape. As he got closer he could see the grass was stained with a black liquid, a liquid that was reflecting the glint of the moonlight. He moved closer still and realised that the black liquid was only black in the moonlight.

Gabriel picked up the torch that he found at his feet and cast its beam over the shape. The cursed bird continued to peck. The liquid shone deep crimson in the torchlight; it was blood.

"Isn't this a little familiar?" he asked.

"Is it?" came the distorted voice.

Gabriel turned to look at Anji, her face, as expected, horribly mutilated and missing its eyes.

"Perhaps this is different," came Joanna's voice.

As he turned, the darkness faded and Tabitha's shop built itself about him. Joanna and the professor were hanging upside down from the roof, with no arms, one leg and cut out eyes. The sight was horrific. Gabriel turned away and saw a man he recognised form a painting as Claude Devereaux.

"This is what my followers will do to them," he said. "This is the price you pay for presuming to make a deal with me."

Devereaux smiled. His eyes turned yellow and his skin began to turn orange, then red. His clothes disintegrated and his whole skin became leathery and hard. The man's legs morphed in to those of a goat, and horns erupted from his forehead.

The creature licked his lips with a forked tongue and continued to speak. "This is how your pathetic kind see me in my natural form." Legion laughed. "Your body will live for thousands of years. Your mind will be trapped in here with me all that time. I look forward to many happy hour,s torturing you."

The demon struck out with a clawed hand, throwing Gabriel across the flood and causing what felt like extreme physical pain.

The acolytes' attack had confused the cultists, but they were fighting on. The professor handled his sword with the skill of a true master. Any cultist who got within striking distance was dead in the blink of an eye.

Tony kept checking the darkness around him. He knew the infiltration squad were coming with the pistol. He was guessing that Artemis had predicted his strategy and would have given orders to eliminate Legion's host, whoever it was. He wasn't about to allow that to happen. If they came, he hoped they'd listen to reason.

Gabriel stumbled through the streets of Hoggersbrook. The fingers on his left hand were broken and he was wearing rags.

It felt likes days, even weeks, had passed but it had been perpetual night. The street was strewn with the bodies of people he'd once called friends. This was Legion's latest torment, the latest of many both physical and mental.

Gabriel turned, the demon was behind him.

"I've been thinking, Gabriel. I feel at this stage I should be using your first name." His red lips smiled to show yellow pointy teeth.

Gabriel couldn't move. The demon wasn't permitting him that much control over his body.

"I've been thinking about those fingers of yours, the ones I broke. I really shouldn't leave you with a useless hand like that, now should I?"

The smile widened and one of the cultist's curved blades appeared in his leathery hand.

"Hold out your arm." Gabriel's arm shot out involuntarily. "This might sting a little bit." The monster began hacking at his wrist; the pain was white hot, beyond agonising. A conscious person would have passed out, but Gabriel was far from conscious. Tendons were severed, the crunch of breaking bones was audible.

The beast continued to hack, a look of zeal in his cruel yellow eyes. With the fourth blow, the hand came off. Gabriel collapsed to the floor, blood pouring from the stump at the end of his arm.

"Oh dear, that needs cauterising," the demon said gleefully, then grinned as the stump burst into flame.

The professor was still on lookout while fighting off robed cultists. The pile of bodies around him was becoming considerable.

Aside from the infiltration squad, he was also looking for Neil and Len Tait. Their involvement in the death of his acolytes had not been forgotten. If he saw either of the men, their death would not be swift.

The cultists seemed to be losing the will to fight. Faith is one thing, but large losses will still rout any force. One by one they surrendered, and the acolytes brought them to the professor with instructions that they lay on the ground. The fight was over. Joanna looked at Tony, happy to be alive.

"We did it." She smiled with relief.

"Yes, we did," he agreed, leaning on the pommel of his sword.

"Now for the demon," came a gruff voice. The infiltration team approached; Tony knew the acolyte who was leading it. A competent man, but stalwart in his devotion to duty.

The pain of the stump on his left wrist was finally starting to subside. Legion had locked Gabriel in a small room, not big enough to stand up or lay down in. He had no idea how long he'd been there. It felt like an eternity.

Legion had been bouncing him from one mental or physical torture to the next; what felt like weeks passing had long since turned into months. Legion has assumed full control over what passed for reality inside Gabriel's mind. Finally, the walls of the cell expanded and the demon stood before Gabriel with his cloven hooves.

"I've got a new game to play, little mortal."

A chessboard appeared, fully set up with a chair either side. "You presumed to make a deal with me. Now I will make a deal with you. We'll play chess. I've not had your little redhead friend Anji killed yet. If you win, I'll let you decide if I kill her, or your oldest friend Jim. He won't be hard to find. I can pull that out of your memory same way I did his name. If I win, I'll flay them both and make you watch."

Legion gave another grotesque smile as Gabriel stumbled to the table and silently collapsed into one of the chairs. "White goes first," teased the monster.

Gabriel reached out with his one remaining but shaky hand, and made his first move.

Tony looked the head of the infiltration squad in the eye. "Stand down, Acolyte Stanton. You are not fully aware of the situation."

Stanton looked stern. "I'm sorry, cleric, but my orders from Father Artemis are quite comprehensive. I am to use Legion's Bane on whoever the demon possesses." Stanton looked awkward. "I am also under instructions to take you into custody if you were found to be involved."

Joanna stepped forward. "To coin a phrase – you and which army?"

Stanton looked at the other acolytes.

"This one."

Gabriel was struggling to concentrate. The pain from where his left hand used to be was back with a vengeance. Somehow, he seemed to be winning the match.

"Check," he said, moving a rook.

The demon gave a sickening grin. "Is it?"

Gabriel looked at the board. His rook had become a pawn.

"Acolyte Stanton. Regardless of your orders, I am the only cleric present and I am informing you that you are not in possession of the full facts."

Stanton looked at Gabriel on the ground. Anji started to stir and opened her eyes.

"What's going on?" she murmured.

Gabriel tried a second time to get the demon in check.

"Check," he said in a defeated tone, as he took Legion's black queen and placed the demon in check with his white knight.

"Oh Avatar, you really should pay more attention. As the cleric can tell you, knights are such fragile things." The demon moved his newly fabricated queen and took Gabriel's knight.

Anji looked around and pushed her red curls away from her face. As she became aware of her surroundings, she noticed Gabe on the ground next to her.

"Gabe! Babe, wake up."

Stanton pulled the flintlock out and began to add primer.

Gabriel was beat. He never stood a chance; the game had been just one more method of torture. Legion smiled his sickly smile and he moved his bishop into position and put Gabriel in checkmate.

"Checkmate, little mortal."

Gabriel looked up with a defeated expression. He glared at the beast for a moment before the look of defeat melted into a snide smile.

"Is it? Fiend," he said in a contemptuously defiant tone.

Legion's yellow eyes looked down at the board, a look of confusion on his red, leathery face.

"What?" The board had changed. Only the black king was left, blocked in by a bishop and a pawn.

Gabriel stood up. His ragged clothes were gone, replaced by the full black that the professor had been keen to make the new garb of a Halcyon Knight. He reached forward with his left hand and place Legion in checkmate with a white knight.

"Checkmate, you moronic imp." Gabriel's voice was mildly aggressive and full of disdain.

The demon started to back away, unsure what was happening. He looked left and right as if trying to control the environment, but nothing happened.

"Trying to weave your little tricks?" Gabriel took a step closer. "Trying to torture the mortal?" He took another step. "Newsflash, red boy, this is my mindscape. In here, I'm not mortal." The human looked the demon directly in his yellow eyes. "In here, I am God."

Chains shot from the blackness and clamped around the demon's wrists. "I've been biding my time. Learning how to control things. Learning to do what you've been doing. The difference is, this is my mind. I'm in charge, you can do nothing unless I allow it now."

He took another step forward. "And I'm not going to allow it. You see, the 'broken knight' as you call him taught me a thing or two. Do you know why the Knights of the Halcyon Order were such a powerful force and so hard to kill in the end?"

Legion said nothing.

"It was because they ended their training with something called the Ritual of Accolade. They tricked a demon, a stupid one like yourself, into possessing them. They then trapped it in their own mind and killed it. But a bit of it... well, a bit of it they keep, keep it as their little slave. The little bit they kept gave them extreme strength, agility, heightened senses, healing ability and extended their life. Did you know that the 'broken knight,' even after losing his demon over a hundred years ago, is still over five hundred years old?"

Legion still remained silent but his yellow eyes showed panic.

Tony still stood between Gabriel and the acolytes. "Stanton. If you aim that pistol, with regret, I will kill you where you stand," the Professor warned, as the acolyte continued to tap in primer.

Gabriel leaned in close to the demon. "Here's the ironic thing. If your little cult had never pulled me into this – never manipulated me into believing – never lifted the veil. You would never have been able to try and possess me, you would never have been trapped in here and I would never have been able to kill you."

"I have my orders, Cleric." Samson's voice was respectful yet firm. He finished tapping in the primer and began to bring the pistol to bear.

The demon smiled again. "You think you've trapped me in here, mortal?" it hissed. "Fool." The demon's body started to glow.

"No, I just needed to trick you into trying to leave." Gabriel thrust his hand into the demon's dematerialising body, and clenched his fist.

The professor lifted his sword and held the point under Samson's chin.

"Don't make me do it, boy," he warned. "This man's life is worth more than ours. Whatever the Father thinks, he is the one who will save the Order."

Joanna started to move closer to Gabriel; she put a hand on Anji's arm and looked at Samson.

With no warning at all, a flash shot from Gabriel's unconscious body. The flash immediately concentrated into an orb of blue light above where Gabriel was lying. The orb pulsated and shifted shape violently, a small stream of light being dawn back into its abandoned host.

Then came the scream, a deafening fanfare that shot out across the night. The orb continued to change in shape, then colour, then size. The scream died to an echo, the orb faded.

Then a demon, older than time itself, died.

"There is no more reason for us to fight," the professor instructed, looking into Samson's confused eyes.

"My orders stand, sir."

"The demon is dead, Acolyte."

"It could be a ruse. Please lay down your sword or I will be forced to order the other acolytes to attack you."

"I'm not convinced they'd follow that order," said Gabriel, as he clambered to his feet. "Now would you be so good as to put that pistol on the floor."

He picked up Sirius from where he had dropped it and turned to face Samson. "The demon is dead. You can thank Cleric Harrison for that." He looked at Tony. "You were right, my friend. Time did run a lot slower. It feels like I was in there for months."

Samson was still holding the gun. Gabriel took a step towards him. "Acolyte, I am now something you have never seen. I am something the Order has not seen in over a hundred years. I am a Knight of the Halcyon Order. Do you really want to risk trying to kill me? Or do you want to start following the orders that make sense?"

Samson looked at the gun. He slowly dropped the hammer and placed it on the ground.

"My apologies, sir. And to you, cleric."

"No apology needed, my boy," the professor said magnanimously. "You were doing what you thought was right." He shifted his view to Gabriel. "You've undergone the Ritual of Accolade. Now let's make this fully official. Take a knee again. Acolytes Samson and King, please bear witness."

Gabriel knelt at the professor's feet.

"By the power vested in me by the Council, Father and Knights of the Grand Order of Halcyon, I find thee worthy of accolade. Let your deeds carry our name, your valour give hope to the innocent and your fury strike fear into the heart of the darkness. I confer on thee the title of Knight."

The Cleric rested the flat on his sword on each of Gabriel's shoulders once again. "Arise, Sir Gabriel Jones of Hoggersbrook, Knight of the Grand Order of Halcyon."

Gabriel stood up and saw Anji watching him, a look of confusion and amazement on her face. He ran over to her, threw his arms around her and held her close to him.

"I thought I'd lost you," he said, the emotion nearly bringing tears to his eyes.

"I knew I wouldn't lose you," she said, hugging him back. "Even trapped in there, looking out, I could see and hear you. I knew you'd come for me."

Joanna decided to give them as much privacy as possible for a moment, and walked over to the professor and Samson. The professor looked around at the bodies, wounded and captured cultists.

"Looks like clean-up. Did you bring medical backup, Samson?"

"Yes, Cleric."

"Then get them active. Get our people to the infirmary and get the prisoners taken into custody. The council can decide what to do with them."

He saw Len and Neil. The images of his acolytes' mutilated bodies flashed in his mind. "Leave those two here with me."

The acolytes set to work, helping their brothers and sisters to the medical evacuation vehicles or carrying them on stretchers.

Tony turned to Gabriel. "Gabriel, take Anji and Joanna if you would. I'll meet you shortly back at the car."

Gabriel did as he was asked. It wasn't long before the sight was clear and all that remained was a lot of corpses, the cleric and the two cultists. Gabriel was walking towards the car, his arm around Anji, but he could hear what was being said behind him.

"We have unfinished business." The cleric glared at the two cultists. "Pick up your weapons. I'll give you more chance then you gave my people."

Gabriel heard the swoosh of steel cutting the air, followed by hacking sounds and the most blood-curdling screams he'd ever heard. He didn't look back. He knew what was happening. He knew the former knight was demonstrating the most literal meaning of the phrase 'an eye or an eye'. He was fulfilling a vow he'd made over the bodies of his murdered acolytes; he was making their murderers pay.

A few moments later Tony joined his companions at his car. No one passed comment. They headed home.

Gabriel opened the front door of the HQ.

"This is it," he said to Anji. She looked at the seal, then around at the panelled walls and the suits of armour.

"You sure as hell weren't joking, Gabe."

Gabriel looked at her and placed his hands gently on her shoulders. "Will you stay here a few days with me? I have things I need to sort out here but I want you close. I have a lot to tell you. A lot to ask you."

Anji smiled. "I'm a little overwhelmed babe, but of course I will."

Gabriel smiled back. And caught the attention of a passing acolyte.

"Acolyte, would you please take our guest to some temporary quarters?"

"Of course," the acolyte said dutifully, and started to escort the redhead to a guest room.

The professor looked at Gabriel.

"Ready my boy?"

"Damn ready!"

The knight strode down the corridors of the Halcyon Order's headquarters with the only living former knight and Acolyte King at his side. He reached the council chamber and opened both doors before the guards had time to react.

The councillors turned, startled. Artemis began to speak, his voice growing to an enraged bellow.

"What is the meaning of this intrusion? And why, Cleric Harrison, have I been informed that you have allowed a civilian access to this enclave?"

Tony remained quiet and let Gabriel answer.

"The 'civilian' is here at *my* order."

"What right do you think you have to be giving orders here? And why is there a condemned acolyte in the council chamber? Guards, take this former acolyte back to her holding cell."

The two door guards stepped forward. Gabriel turned to face them.

"Lay a hand on her and you will lose that hand."

The guards looked at Gabriel's face and stopped dead in their tracks. Tony also looked at Gabriel's face. This persona was not an act, as he'd used with Legion. What he'd gone through the past weeks, what he'd endured from Legion in his own mind, had taken its toll. A small part of him had become much darker… Tony could see it in his eyes. Had either of the acolytes given him cause, he would have followed through on his threat.

The knight turned back to Father Artemis. "To answer your question, 'Father,' I have the right of the Knight Commander of the Halcyon Order."

Artemis' voice lost its bluster and switched to condescension.

"My dear boy, Cleric Harrison may have told you that you are a knight, and even the Knight Commander, but that does not make it so."

Tony stepped forward. "Actually, it does. One knight can confer another, one council member can confer a knight. And by the tenets of our order, the knight with the most years' service is automatically Knight Commander. Also, I believe that you were unaware that the Knight Commander is generally advised by, but still technically outranks, the council."

"That is preposterous," Artemis began to protest.

"Actually, Father," Cleric Ford began, "Cleric Harrison is quite correct."

Artemis was dumbfounded and Gabriel took a step towards him.

"Father Artemis, you condemned a dedicated acolyte to death and risked the lives of dozens more in a fools' gambit. As Knight Commander, I find you unfit for the title and position of Father. You will be taken into custody while the council decides on a just fate for you."

Artemis' silence continued; he looked confused and overwhelmed.

"Guards, take him to the detention area and lock him up."

The two security acolytes stepped in and took Artemis away without question. He didn't struggle or even say anything.

Gabriel looked at the council members. "The council is dismissed."

The three men stood up and filed out, also without question, shutting the door behind them. Gabriel sat in one of the spare seats. "Well, Prof, that worked."

"Yes, it did. Now we a few changes. But first, how are you? How is the demon shade?"

"Quiet. It's not spoken to me yet."

"It will, you will need to tame it fully. That will be an easy job compared to what you went through." The professor sat down next to Gabriel. "Remember what I said, try not to look on the shade of the demon as the demon you killed. It's different, it will still have violent thoughts and hate you at first, but it is different. As you spend time with it inside you will tame it, you will learn to use more and more of it to your advantage. Odd though it may sound, it will become your friend." The professor put his hand on Gabriel's shoulder. "I once told you about the friend who saved my life."

"Yes, I remember."

"That friend was Azeel, my demon shade. I was mortally injured, so badly hurt that he couldn't save me without expending all the power he had, so that's what he did. He used every bit of his essence to repair what he could of my body. It cost him his life, but saved mine." Tony looked mournful. "You'll understand better after a month or two."

Gabriel got the impression that Tony wanted the subject changing. "What's our next move?"

"Training for you, if you're still in agreement, and we need to acquire facilities to train up new acolytes and new knights."

"I'm still up for it, Prof. You saved Anji, and you saved me. You've shown me that the world needs the Halcyon Order."

"We'll need a big facility. We'll have to house recruits, trainers and support staff. Fortunately, money is practically no object. If there's one thing we didn't lose, it's our ability to invest."

"I've got an idea," Gabriel smiled. "However, I should give you this back." He unfastened his belt and offered the ornate silver sword to the professor. "Thanks for the loan."

"It wasn't a loan, my boy. Sirius should be carried by a knight. It's why she was made in the first place. She served me well for over a century. It's time she served another."

Epilogue

A full year had passed since the events at Stonebank. Anji pulled up at the newly restored and furnished Meetingstone Manor. The village had become a ghost town. Most of the residents had been part of the cult and were either dead, or still in custody; the remainder were rehoused after being given a cover story by the MoD.

She got out of her car and headed for the front door. She spotted Gabriel walking towards her; they hadn't seen each other in days. He worried about her; she was still having night terrors and didn't like it when he wasn't there with her. He ran to her and kissed her full on the lips.

"Here it is," he said with a beaming smile. "The fully restored Meetingstone Manor, the first Knight training facility in years and a new academy for the Acolytes in training… and the garage needs a foreman. Are you still up for the job?"

"Oh, I think so." They put their arms around each other's waists and walked inside. The Manor had lost its eerie atmosphere; the ghosts had been put to rest. The atmosphere now was excitement. Nothing this big had happened to the Order in over a century. The manor had taken a lot of restoring and the village had been taken over by the Order. Shops, houses, everything. The entire staff and student body would live in the village or the manor. Gabriel and Tony had built something spectacular. "Have you thought up a name for this place yet?

"Oh yes, the building keeps its name of course; but the academy on the other hand, I've named."

"And?"

"The Lloyd Brighton Academy."

Gabriel's phone vibrated in his pocket. He looked at Anji. "That'll be Tony," he said, as he tapped the pickup button and held the phone to his ear. He listened for a moment and Anji levelled her blue eyes at him.

"Duty calls?" she asked.

"Duty calls," he replied. "Go and get settled in. Joanna's round here somewhere. I'll be back in a few hours. Tony wants to discuss future knight recruitment." He kissed her again and gave her a long hug.

"Okay, babe. See you later."

Gabriel started to head to his office when the shade addressed him from inside his own head.

The demon shade sat cross-legged in a chesterfield armchair inside Gabriel's mind. It didn't have the red-horned beast appearance of its former and full self. At least, not at the moment. It looked like a thin, middle aged man in an expensive suit.

Gabriel's inner-self walked over and sat in the chair opposite.

"How's it going, Liege?" (which was what he had taken to calling the shade.)

It ignored the pleasantry.

"So, Knight, I've been wanting to ask you something for a considerable amount of time." Its voice was well spoken. "As we are starting to 'bond' I feel it's appropriate now."

There was a mild hint of contempt with undertones of sarcasm. Gabriel ignored the subtext. Harmonising with the shade of Legion was a slow process but it felt like he was making weekly, and at times daily, progress. His psyche reclined a little in the mental construct of the chair.

"Go on then. Ask away."

"The night you enslaved me. The night you bound me to this plane. Bound me inside your mind. That night, your mentor slaughtered two men who never stood a chance against him in combat. Personally, I don't mind a little wanton slaughter, but how did that make you feel about him?"

This was the shade's game. It tried to encourage violent thoughts and cause Gabriel to become conflicted.

"He killed two men who were his prisoners." Gabriel levelled a gaze at Liege. He mentally projected an image of the two dead acolytes in Tabitha's shop.

"Never forget what they did. Not all monsters are supernatural, Liege. Some monsters are men, and some men are monsters."

The End

Thank you for reading Halcyon Rebirth.

If you enjoyed this book please leave an honest review on Amazon.

Gabriel Jones' exploits continue in The Haunting of a Lord. Available on Amazon

You can also follow the author on twitter @halcyonorder

More information can be found at www.thehalcyonorder.com

Printed in Great Britain
by Amazon